Wiltse, David
The hangman's knot

24.95
8/02

THE
HANGMAN'S
KNOT

also by david wiltse

Novels

The Wedding Guest
The Serpent
The Fifth Angel
Home Again
Prayer for the Dead
Close to the Bone
Bone Deep
The Edge of Sleep
Into the Fire
Blown Away
Heartland

Plays

Suggs
Doubles
A Grand Romance
A Dance Lesson
Crazy Horse and Three Stars
Hatchetman
Temporary Help
Triangles for Two

a novel

THE HANGMAN'S KNOT

david wiltse

st. martin's press ☙ new york

www.stmartins.com

Library of Congress Cataloging-in-Publication Data

Wiltse, David.
    The hangman's knot : a novel / David Wiltse.—1st ed.
    p. cm.
    ISBN 0-312-28371-7
      1. Secret service—Fiction. 2. Conspiracies—Fiction.
    3. Lynching—Fiction. 4. Nebraska—Fiction. I. Title.

PS3573.I478 H36 2002
813'.54—dc21

                         2002017776

First Edition: July 2001

10 9 8 7 6 5 4 3 2 1

THE
HANGMAN'S
KNOT

The rope was thick hemp, designed for heavy-duty hauling, with loose fibrous strands sticking out like wires. It was a cruel rope, fierce on the skin, and Lawton cried when he saw it. He had fought wildly, desperately, when they first grabbed him, and it took six men to press him now into the earth—but he cried like a child when he saw the rope.

"Cut some," someone said, and a dozen onlookers produced pocketknives. A man knelt in front of Lawton, holding the rope where he could see it as he sawed off a short length with one of the knives.

"Sweet Jesus," Lawton muttered. "Oh my Jesus." It was all the prayer he could muster.

"What's he say?" someone demanded.

"I don't know. What does it matter?"

"Oh Jesus," Lawton repeated. One man sat with his buttock on Lawton's head pressing his mouth against the grass so his words were muffled and indecipherable.

"Did he confess?"

"Does he have to?"

There were a dozen voices, all competing, all offering commentary and advice, but Lawton could hear none of them until the man on his head rose. They turned his face so his lips were free. He spat dirt and grass.

"You confess?" one of the men demanded.

"I pray to Jesus," Lawton said.

"Well, that's a good idea 'bout now."

"You confess? Just confess, admit you did it."

"I ain't," Lawton sputtered.

"Lying son of a bitch."

"It don't matter," said another. The man sat back down, his ass cheek settling over Lawton's head like a brooding hen.

Lawton struggled, doing all he could do, twisting his body until he was exhausted when he felt the rope go around his wrists. The men atop him pressed down harder and they lifted and twisted his arms and tied them together behind his back with a section of the callous cord. Another section was lashed quickly around his ankles. That one wouldn't matter at all. Lawton knew he wasn't going to be able to run anywhere.

They yanked him to his feet and held his arms, as if fearful that he might still hop to safety. A studious-looking man with glasses held the longer section of the rope and knotted it slowly, with concentration. Behind him, the Ford tractor they used for mowing rumbled toward Lawton.

Oh, God, they goin' drag me, he thought. They goin' tie me to the tractor and drag me like a dead beef. He had thought that they were only going to whip him with the rope, a prospect terrible enough, as the hemp would lacerate his skin like razors, but dragging would be worse.

"Please don' do this," he said. "Please."

They made him hop like a toad, hands in his armpits, and lifted him onto the top of the mower attached to the rear of the tractor. Two of the men ascended with him and held him steady as the tractor began to move again. He was facing backward, so he saw only the crowd of men following him. So many of them! They regarded him with scorn; some spat, many cursed, and a few laughed. The man knotting the rope was in the center, still looping the hemp around itself, as if it were the most important thing he could think of.

The tractor jerked to a stop and Lawton nearly fell face-forward into the crowd, but the men beside him caught him and held him upright. He heard the noise of the hydraulic lift, felt it rattle beneath him as he rose slowly upward. He could see well over the heads of the crowd now. In the distance, the face of his sister peered out of the kitchen window, sweet little girl's face. Her mouth was open, but he could not hear her above the noise of the men and the tractor. He wanted to tell her to get back inside: Don't let them see you. Don't get messed up in this.

Sister, he mouthed silently. This be all righ'. Don' worry. This be all righ'. He moved his lips exaggeratedly so she could read them. Some of the men in the crowd thought he was begging them for mercy and they laughed.

The man with the rope had finished his knot. He stepped forward and tossed it high in the air. Lawton saw the glasses slip on the man's nose from the effort of his throw, then turned as best he could and saw the end of the rope sail over the limb of the tree next to the tractor and fall toward the ground. The knot the man had been making was a hangman's noose. Lawton realized for the first time that they were not going to whip him, were not going to drag him. They were going to kill him.

"Sweet Jesus," he cried, and tried to pray, as he had been trying to do all along. No prayer came to him. He could not think of what to say; he was too frightened to remember the magic words.

Face contorted with fear, he looked to the crowd for some sign that it was a joke. He knew many of them. One was a minister, not of Lawton's church, of course. One man brought the mail. One had given a quarter to Lawton once, for no particular reason, and another was always asking Lawton to dance. He recognized a doctor, and a man who worked in the courthouse, and a man whom Lawton had helped with baling hay. That man caught his eye, then looked away, ashamed. But he stayed in the crowd. Lawton saw the boys on the periphery regarding him with fear and awe.

"Them boys . . ." he started to say. Someone slipped the noose around his neck, and Lawton felt his sphincter release his body's waste.

"Confess now," someone said in his ear. The voice was kindly, even as Lawton felt the man's hands adjust the knot. "You'll feel better for it."

"I confess!" Lawton yelled. "I done it!"

There was a pause, and for a heartbeat Lawton thought he had won his freedom. They had not expected him to say it and were momentarily derailed in their passion for his death. A car came racing toward them from town, a wild plume of dust rising in its wake. It skidded into the parking lot and slid to a stop. Lawton's heart rose, certain this was his rescue, although he didn't know what form it might take.

"Well, we knew that," someone said finally, breaking the silence.

"Shit, let's just do it," said another.

No one else seemed to notice the newcomer scrambling from his car and rushing toward them with something in his hand.

"Wait!" said Lawton. "He here!"

The man came to a halt at the edge of the crowd, panting. Lawton kept his eye on him, certain he was his savior.

"Wait," Lawton said again, but no one understood his meaning; they heard it only as a wail of fear.

The newcomer raised the object in his hand and held it to his eye. From where he stood, teetering on the edge of oblivion, Lawton realized that the instrument of his salvation was only a camera.

Someone slapped the high fender of the tractor as if it were a horse, and the machine lumbered forward. The men beside him released his arms and Lawton swung free of the tractor. The merciless rope tore into his skin and tightened and tightened with every swing and every twitch of his body. Lawton slipped from this life and into history.

CHAPTER ONE

Heat. Heat like the floor of a furnace, like a dragon's breath, heat like the cracked door of Hades. It closed over the Great Plains like a steaming quilt, all-encompassing, suffocating. Heat was the matrix, the element in which their universe was suspended, heat unwavering and unrelieved. Heat suffused their bodies and blood, infected their limbs, cramped and twisted their muscles. Everyone suffered; the old and the careless died. There were rumors of genetic sports, mutants, evil births of two-headed calves and wingless chicks. Heat baked into the ground and burned into the corn, the wheat, the soy and the canola, the grass and the alfalfa, scorching the roots, stunting the shoots, withering the leaves. Even the earth itself burst open, the soil cracking with a thousand tiny mouths screaming silently for relief.

Cattle and hogs huddled against the fences, gasping, seeking what shade they could find, heads hanging as if stunned by the weight of the sun, but lesser animals thrived. Serpents and insects, energized by the encompassing heat, arose in great numbers. Snakes were reported to be bolder than usual, slithering their way into gardens and homes in pursuit of rodents lying inert in stifling holes and cellar walls. Garter snakes were broomed from kitchens, king snakes hacked in two on sidewalks, box and snapping turtles smashed while crossing highways in search of new ponds. Glass lizards slithered to safety from porch and garage, leaving their shattered tails behind as hostage to their retreat. One Falls City widow, a known hysteric, swore she found a rattlesnake entwined around her dining table centerpiece, hungrily eyeing her torpid, overfed cat, and no number of the summoned firemen could convince her otherwise.

"Hot as the hinges of hell, hot as Tophet," said the locals, perversely proud of their suffering. Hot as Billy-be-damned, as Billy Tree's grandfather used to say, adding another dollop of guilt to the young boy's steadily accretive load.

"It's not your 'dry' heat," said Acting Sheriff Lapolla with audible contempt for the famously comfortable desert heat of the Southwest. This was Nebraska heat, prairie heat, aswim in humidity, so the denizens felt every degree, every calorie of temperature, and then some. One hundred degrees felt like one fifty. "Like sitting in an oven, wrapped in a wet horse blanket."

Billy Tree made no attempt to improve on the description. After the first few days of the hot spell, he had become similied-out. If they were made to endure this torture, the people of the prairie wanted it known that it was torment of record-breaking, biblical stature, but after awhile the imagination lagged and words no longer sufficed. Even the popular and stoical "Hot enough for you?" with which they had started had fallen out of fashion.

They drove north out of Falls City, past the hamlet of Barada, the sheriff's car slicing through mirage after mirage of illusory, shimmering waves that rose from the road and any barren patch of ground. Lakes and ponds and false horizons seemed to levitate above the rounded tops of car and pickups and the tin roofs of outbuildings. Only the green planted fields were free of dancing heat.

Lapolla slowed the car as they turned onto a gravel road and the tires sent a hailstorm of tiny rocks against the undercarriage. Since acceding to the role of acting sheriff following the death of his predecessor, Lapolla had stayed in the office as much as possible, feeling the perquisites of rank were better enjoyed as a sedentary official; but the air conditioning had begun to falter in the past few days and he had taken to the road again. The cool air of the Dodge was reliable, the fan could be manipulated with a snap, and, if need be, he could direct all the vents toward himself. Not that Lapolla was a selfish man, but he did not cope well with hot weather, or wet—two of Nebraska's primary options.

The dog wavered out of a ditch and onto the road, appearing from the adjoining field of milo like a wraith conjured from steam and dust. It sidestepped once on its long, spindly legs, its large frame leaning in the direction of the men as if into a heavy wind before righting itself. From a distance, it looked more like something from the African savanna than the Nebraska plains, all jaw, chest and shaggy coat carried on limbs too delicate for such a burden. Lapolla hit the horn, but the dog remained on the gravel, slowly swinging its massive head to face the oncoming car. He honked again, holding the button down, but the dog stayed squarely in their path, its neck moving back and forth like a fighting bull exhausted by the picador's piercing insults.

"It can't move," said Billy as Lapolla slowed too gradually to avoid the animal.

The acting sheriff continued to blare the horn, as if the force of sound alone might clear the roadway. The animal took a wobbly half step toward the oncoming car, squaring its muscled shoulders to meet a charge.

"It can't *move*." Billy yanked the steering wheel and the car slued into a skid, sliding sideways toward the dog. A shower of pebbles rained before and beneath them, cascading off the bottom of the car like a drumroll.

The auto struck the dog at the rear door on the passenger's side, a heavy, hollow, stomach-jarring thud, followed by silence as the car finally came to a stop. Lapolla cursed under his breath, and then aloud, turning to Billy, his eyes filled with self-recrimination and justification.

"It didn't *move*," he said. "It wasn't my fault; it just didn't *move*."

"It couldn't."

"Couldn't? It got out there, didn't it? What'd it do, fly?"

"It's all right, Bert. It's not your fault."

"That's what I'm saying. Damned thing didn't move."

Billy looked out his window before opening the door. The dog was still on the roadway, only a few yards from where it had been hit, lying on its side, its ribs rising and falling with every breath and its eyes open, looking at the men. Billy opened his door a crack, watching the animal carefully.

Lapolla stepped out of the car on the driver's side and started around the front of the vehicle.

"Stay there," Billy said.

"What? *What?*"

"Just stay put, Bert," said Billy, trying to hide the exasperation in his voice. The acting sheriff was habitually slow to respond, and Billy was not the most patient of men to begin with. Dealing with his nominal superior, although he liked him, was frequently an exercise in tact and hypocrisy, taxing his reserves of diplomacy.

Billy eased his door open wider and placed one foot on the gravel road. The heat of the day rushed into the car like a solid wall. A few feet away, the dog continued to watch the men. Its tongue lolled from its open mouth, moving back and forth with each panting breath.

"It's still alive," Lapolla said. He carelessly put a hand on the hood of the car and immediately withdrew it with a yelp, waving it to fan away the burn.

"Stay away," said Billy.

Unheedingly, Lapolla moved forward.

"Poor little son of a bitch," Lapolla said.

"No . . ."

"I think we can save him," Lapolla said. He moved within a foot of the dog's head and squatted to comfort the stricken animal. Billy put his foot on Lapolla's shoulder and shoved him away from the dog. The acting sheriff sprawled on his back, sputtering indignantly. Billy dragged the man's legs away from the dog with his boot.

"You just will not be told, will you, Bert?"

Lapolla scrambled to his feet, brushing at his backside as if it were hurt as much as his dignity.

"The dog's rabid," said Billy. He passed his boot cautiously in front of the animal's muzzle, keeping it well away from the teeth. The dog snapped listlessly and flecks of froth dribbled from its jaws.

"Jesus. Why didn't you say so?"

"Kicking you was quicker."

"And more fun," Lapolla added under his breath.

"You're always good fun, Bert. It's why I like working with you."

Lapolla walked to the dog's hindquarters, now giving it a respectful distance. "What do we do with it? Looks like both legs are broken."

"And the pelvis, I'd say."

"What do we do?"

Billy felt the first drop of sweat running from his armpit down his side. He had been out of the car less than a minute.

"You shoot it."

Lapolla looked stricken.

"Shoot it?"

"You can call the vet, have him come out here, risk having him get bitten when he gives it an anesthetic. Or you get bitten helping him—because you're doing that, not me. I'm not going to get any closer to a rabid dog than I am right now. The vet hauls the dog back to his office and nicely puts it to sleep there; then you and the doc go get the ten shots in the stomach because of your bites. Meanwhile, the dog lies here on the road with half its bones broken for a good hour before the vet gets here, assuming we can contact him right away. Does that sound more humane to you, Bert? Because this dog is going to die either way."

"I meant why do *I* have to shoot it?"

Billy tapped his empty holster. "I don't carry a gun. You do."

"There's a shotgun in the car."

"I don't carry a gun because I don't *shoot* a gun. As I made perfectly clear to you when you asked me to take this job. I'm here to advise you, Bert. And my advice is shoot the dog before it suffers any further."

As if to emphasize Billy's point, the dog scratched at the ground with its front paws in a vain attempt to move its body. A faint keening could be heard, something less than a growl forcing its way past the restricted throat. Billy turned his head away to avoid seeing the animal's agony, and drops of sweat from his brow hit the gravel, spattering darker spots amid the dust.

Lapolla pulled his service automatic from its holster.

"Don't know why *I* have to do it," he muttered. "You're supposed to be the deputy."

Billy watched long enough to be sure that Lapolla was aiming on a trajectory that would carry the ricochet away from the sheriff, himself, and the car, then stepped well away. Lapolla's hand was shaking so badly when he pulled the trigger that Billy feared he might actually miss.

The report made Billy cringe. Even now, two years later, even with a shot fired not in anger but in mercy, Billy felt the surge of terror he had experienced during his near-fatal shoot-out with Avi Posner. He had survived that incident with holes in his body and with his dignity and confidence ripped to shreds. Awareness of a desire to keep on living that exceeded his courage, his self-esteem, and his pride had been forced on him in that murderous exchange of gunfire, and he had pleaded, defecated on himself, and finally shot through the body of his dying partner to save himself. Before Posner had shot him, Billy had known no fear. Since then, it seemed to him, he had known little else, at least where guns were involved. Life had become a matter of pushing himself into and through one fright after another, and the constant effort not to quail, not to turn and run and hide forever in his room seemed to sap all of his strength. I couldn't even put a dog out of its misery, he thought with disgust. When he turned back to face the situation, his wounds twinged and tugged at him as if activated by his own sweat, or fear.

They donned gloves and wrapped the dog in a blanket and placed it in the trunk of the car. As they drove away, Billy glanced in the rearview mirror and saw a man emerge from the field in the receding distance. It was already too far to make out the man's features, but he saw him place his hands on his hips and stare after the squad car, planted as squarely and obstinately in the road as the dog had been.

CHAPTER TWO

B illy slipped the department cruiser into his garage, a fading, crumbling building constructed during the Depression, when one car was the most a family could hope for and concrete flooring was a wasteful luxury. The weight of many decades had compacted the dirt to the hardness of asphalt, but it had done nothing positive for the structure itself. Time and wet and rot had given the side boards a scalloped effect where they touched the ground. Half air and half wood turning green with algae, the skirting flirted with the dirt like the tattered hem of a pioneer's dress. Another thing I'll have to tend to eventually, Billy thought. If he stuck around. If he sent down roots again in this hard country. Although he had grown up in

Falls City, he had spent more time away from it than in it, touring the nation's cities with the Secret Service, scanning rooftops, running alongside open cars, interviewing the lonely, the frustrated, the criminal, and the half-mad who wrote threatening letters to the president, the vice president, the First Lady. He had returned after Posner had nearly killed him, not by choice but because he had nowhere else to go, and once home again, he had found that the roots he had left behind in this small town in farm country ached with nostalgia. But they were like phantom limbs, amputated twenty years earlier yet still throbbing with pain. He had no real place here, he knew, and yet he wasn't sure he had a place anywhere else.

The house was on Lane Street, two blocks from his sister Kath's house, the house where he had grown up. The proximity meant nothing special. There was no place within the city limits where he would have been more than a fifteen-minute walk away. He thought it was an ugly house. Dirty stucco exterior with the appearance of paper ground under heel on a sidewalk, gritty, nubbly, grubby, and worn. A porch with a low, looming roof dominated the front of the building and gave the house a scowling, foreboding face. The place was too small and unimpressive to be haunted, but it certainly made an effort to look angry and annoyed. . . . So much work to do—if he stayed around.

He could hear the bedroom air conditioner humming as he approached the front door. It had come with the house, and it whined and rattled as if aggrieved at the imposition Billy put upon it, but it kept the bedroom cool at least and gave him a refuge from the heat. He didn't mind the noise of the machine. Complete silence in an empty house reminded him a bit too much of death, and he was all too familiar with that. It was a subject he knew too much about.

He never locked his door, the result of an accurate sense of security, one of the benefits of life in such a small town. Besides the low crime rate, he knew that he had another protection. It would require a particularly brazen thief to burglarize the house of the deputy sheriff, and since most local thieves were teenage boys sowing their oats in safely criminal fields, they were characterized more by stupidity than brass. If ever a man is granted a special dispensation of personal security, it's a small-town cop, he thought.

Something hung from his doorknob. At first glance, Billy took it to be a notice from the postman, but as he approached, he saw it was a length of cord. There was no message attached; the cord was the message in itself. Billy gingerly removed it from the doorknob and held it up. It was a perfect miniature hangman's noose.

He glanced around, hoping to catch sight of children tittering in the bushes. The house was shaded by nonproducing apple trees in the backyard and a shaggy sycamore in front, so the interior was always dark and the wood shingles in wetter weather wore emerald moss. Judicious pruning would be another of Billy's chores if he ever found the motivation. There were plenty of places for a person to hide, but he knew in his heart that he was alone and that the noose was neither joke nor prank.

He turned on the light in the kitchen and placed the noose on the aged wooden table. The cord was puzzling. It was not one strand but three, each as thin and light as string, twisted together to form a sort of cable. Each of the components was itself an even smaller cable, which had been created by the manufacturer from some type of synthetic cotton. At first, Billy could not imagine what the cord had been used for before being cut and woven into a noose, but it looked familiar. The end of the smallest cables had been sliced crudely; then a knot had been formed in each end of the larger cables to keep it all from unraveling. The resultant cord was still very thin and light, an unusual and awkward choice for forming a hangman's knot, but the knot itself was perfectly done. Billy slipped it around his finger and pulled. It tightened, as it was designed to do, in an irreversible grip. No hanged man's desperate fingers could undo such a knot as long as weight was applied against it. The cord was looped around itself in the traditional thirteen turns and then tucked away within its own folds. There's nothing remarkable about a well-crafted knot, he reflected. Any Boy Scout could probably have done it as well, but no Boy Scout would have left it to dangle from the deputy sheriff's door.

Billy entered his bedroom and closed the door to keep the cool air in. He tossed the noose on the bed as he changed from his sweat-soaked clothes, pacing back and forth while he undressed, keeping the grisly cord in view, eyeing it cautiously, as if it were a live and dangerous thing.

There seemed no way around the fact that it was a sign of ill will, at the very least. He had heard that nooses had undergone a resurgence as a malign greeting in recent years, appearing in the lockers of unwanted workers, hanging from door lintels to greet unwelcome newcomers in a neighborhood. It was less flamboyant than a burning cross on the lawn, less grisly than the severed horse head on the pillow in Mafia myth, but more intimately chilling. A chillingly discreet reminder of malice, like a hoarse whisper in the ear in a darkened room.

Somebody is a bit annoyed with me, he said to himself. Someone is a bit aggrieved with the good deputy, unlikely as that seems. He tried to think of anyone who might be particularly angry with him, especially anyone whose grievance might be fresh. Although vengeance was said to be a dish best enjoyed cold, in Billy's experience, it was far more likely to be served up when the insult was new and the blood still hot. It was part and parcel of the sheriff's job to step on people's toes, and it would require a tightrope walker far more nimble than Billy to avoid the occasional misstep, but he could not think of anyone he had offended seriously in the past few months.

He looked at the noose again, and this time the aspect that struck him most was the size of the thing. Small enough to encompass nothing larger than his wrist, yet perfectly proportioned; it reminded him of the work of a hobbyist. It could have been fashioned by someone who built model airplanes or ships in bottles—if any craftsmen still did those things in the computer age. Did this man have miniature guillotines, as well? A workroom full of tiny headsman's axes? It was not as if somebody had grabbed a length of rope and fashioned a noose in the heat of the moment. Whoever it was had taken some time and trouble, suggesting a cold-blooded detachment that was frightening in itself. And all this for what? A greeting? A warning? A memento?

Dressed now in shorts, sandals, and a T-shirt, Billy regarded the noose one last time, wondering what to do with it. Finally, he put it in his pocket, where he could finger it as a talisman and ponder its meaning. The noose's creator would be pleased, he reflected, to see me paying so much attention to his artifact. He got what he wanted.

* * *

Twilight in a Nebraska summer was lengthy enough to be a time division in itself, equal to morning, noon, and night. The sun hovered on the horizon like a tiresome guest on the doorstep, lingering long past its welcome. Night was the only relief they had from the heat, and even that was illusory, as many lay sleepless through the night, too hot to sleep, and, after days of it, too tired to sleep.

Billy drove to Joan Blanchard's house on Fourteenth and Harlan, grateful for the air conditioning in the car for even this short distance. By nature, he was a walker, happy to traverse the town on foot in most weather. He took a small pleasure in treading sidewalks that were unchanged since his youth, each step infused with nostalgia. It was also useful to his work to be available for any home owner or passerby who cared to chat and drop a word or two of gossip en passant. He was, after all, Billy Tree, local legend, the boy who had made good in the world and yet returned home, where he continued to excel. This cloak of celebrity invited loose talk from others, especially, it seemed, tattling chatter, small tokens of disapproval of their neighbors, which they dropped in his ear as offerings, aligning themselves with Billy on the side of righteousness and order. By receiving the coinage of small-town information, he remained knowledgeable and still more available to them in their minds, as if acceptance of their gossip made him a party to it, binding them more tightly together. Who, after all, did not want to be friends with the local law? One never knew when it might come in handy. Billy was aware of their motivations, mixed and unreliable, and took advantage of them. Law enforcement was not a noble profession, however noble the practitioner, and a lawman's worst enemy was silence.

But today he drove, parking his car in the alley behind Joan's house and approaching via the rear door. Although he traded professionally in rumor and speculation, he didn't care to be the object of it himself. Nobody was really fooled, of course; true privacy in Falls City did not exist—the town was too flat and open. But discretion was valued; it did not do to flaunt a peccadillo. It was assumed that Billy had once called on Joan as a lover and now as a recalcitrant, dilatory suitor—those Irish men, famously slow to marry, don't you know—but in truth, Billy was still living apart from her because of

Joan's reluctance, not his own. Their passion, so fierce in the beginning that it threatened to grow hot enough to cauterize itself, searing their hearts and sealing them off from all infections of society and custom and convention, had ultimately proven insufficient to overcome common sense. Billy, however innocently, had been indirectly responsible for the death of Duane Blanchard, Joan's divorced husband. Joan and Duane's son, Will, still lived under her roof, and his presence kept Billy out of the house as effectively as a bolt on the door.

When he saw her, his heart quickened, as it always did. She wore her beauty so casually. Today she was clad in cut-off blue jean shorts and a halter top of a darker blue, which appeared all the bluer against the deep bronze of her skin. Joan tanned like a native of the Mediterranean, although she was of the same Germanic stock as most of the residents of the town. Women are at their loveliest at forty, he thought. So rich and ripe and bursting with seasoned sexiness and yet so relaxed with it that they appear to have forgotten its importance entirely.

She was on the telephone and she smiled distractedly as she opened the door, a reflex of courtesy that held the same tepid warmth one might offer the mailman on his daily visit. What if she becomes simply accustomed to me? he said to himself. What if her heart no longer soars? He felt his own heart dip as he thought it.

"Be careful," she said into the phone. "I know, but be careful. . . . Do it for me, then. . . . No, I can't come. I can't watch it. . . . I love you."

Something about the way she hung up the phone told Billy that she had not heard an expression of love in return. For a moment, she looked shattered.

"That was Will," she said, leading him into her living room, where she had been sorting laundry before the phone call. Billy perched on the arm of the sofa while she folded clothing. "He's riding both bulls and bucks tomorrow at Salina."

"He made it in with the big boys? First time, isn't it?"

She nodded, giving more attention to the clothing than it required. At seventeen, Will had followed in his father's footsteps and had taken to rodeoing as a serious, albeit part-time, activity. Joan had not drawn an unrestricted breath since he started.

"He'll do well, I'm sure," Billy said.

She cast him a sidelong glance, then returned to her chore.

"If he doesn't kill himself," she said.

"He won't kill himself."

She looked at him again, more directly this time, and her face collapsed into sorrow, then reformed itself so quickly, he almost missed it.

"Oh? Good to hear it."

"He's as tough as . . ."

"His father?"

"I was going to say an old boot," Billy said.

Duane Blanchard, Joan's ex-husband and Will's father, had died while trying to execute Billy in the waters of the Little Muddy for the offense of dating his divorced wife. Although Billy had not been the direct instrument of Duane's death, it seemed that Joan had never forgiven him—not for the man's death so much as for all the complications that had ensued. Or rather, that a resentment had grown steadily ever since, getting worse with time, until now it hovered over both of them like a dark cloud. Neither mentioned it. Will was not so reluctant. He hated Billy outright.

"When are we going?" he asked.

She shook her head. "I can't watch him. He'll have to break his neck on his own."

"It's his first time in a big show. He ought to have someone there."

"He shouldn't be there in the first place. I'm not going to encourage him."

Nor could she stop him. Mother and son maintained a steely silence in Billy's presence, as if determined to keep him out of their life together, but he had come in on the end of some of their shouting matches and overheard the opening salvos of others as he walked to his car. The boy was turning into his father, his behavior teetering on the razor-thin balance between rambunctious and openly delinquent.

Billy removed a towel from her hands and took her in his arms.

"Hi," he said.

It took her a moment to yield to his embrace.

"I'm sorry," she said. "I get so worried."

"I know. . . . Come on." He tugged at her arms.

"What?"

"Just come with me. I'll help you fold the clothes later."

"I don't need any help. Where are we going?"

"Where's your sense of adventure? We're taking an outing."

Billy was puzzled by her reluctance to go with him. When he first knew her, she had been eager for anything, happy to flaunt convention, more daring than he to try something, anything, new. He remembered how Pat Kunkel, the former sheriff, had referred to her as "possible," a woman who would talk to anyone, no matter how inappropriate others deemed it; friendly, flirtatious, quick to seek a good time. Her openness to others had driven her ex-husband murderously mad with jealousy, although her transgressions were more imagined than real, mostly superficial. Mostly. Whether or not anything happened, it always seemed "possible" with Joan . . . and now Billy was having trouble tugging her out of her house at night. How much of it was concern for her son, and how much of it just him? Billy wondered. Was he boring her? Restlessness was a dangerous state for someone as volatile as Joan. It might encourage eruptions.

"What's the matter, you expecting somebody to stop by?" he asked.

"No. Why do you say that?"

"Come on, Joanie. A small adventure."

He had planned to tell her about the noose. He had become accustomed to sharing things with her, but her mood was so low now that he didn't want to worsen it. They drove to the east of town and Billy pulled the cruiser off the road beside a field of corn. Getting out of the house seemed to cheer her up, and she gripped his arm playfully as they walked to a spot out of sight from the road.

"I hope you're planning what I think you're planning," she said.

"You are a bad and wicked girl," he said. "Keep it up."

"I'll do my best to keep it up, but it's your job to make sure I stay bad and wicked, Sheriff—so you can keep it up," She slid her hand inside his shorts to emphasize her meaning.

He sat down beside the corn, out of view from the road but only feet from the field. He held her hand, and eventually, feigning reluctance, she sat beside him. The moon was rising, usually a spectacular sight in a land so flat and treeless that it came up over the horizon looking huge and brilliant. With neither tree nor building to serve as a yardstick of comparison, the moon of the Great Plains crept up over the edge of the earth with such size and brilliance that it looked only another field away. Joan had seldom known it otherwise, but Billy had spent fifteen years in cities where a rising moon was not even visible until it appeared over the rooftops, and it still presented a great spectacle to him.

He held his finger to her lips even though she was not about to speak.

"They say you can actually hear the corn growing at this time of year," he whispered. "I've always wanted to see if it's true."

They lay back, watching the moon slowly ascend and diminish and listening for the sound of growth amid the chorus of insects. Bats soared and dipped silently overhead, gathering their nightly banquet, and in the farther distance frogs groaned and croaked their messages of love. Except for the occasional whine of tires on asphalt, the town of Falls City was somnolent before its bedtime, borne down at last by the torpor of the day.

"Chiggers," Joan said, scratching her leg.

He shushed her again and when she was quiet, he thought he could hear it, the sound of nature stealthily extending itself throughout an entire field of green. It was a subliquid sound, long, low, and continuous. Like the noise a swimming fish must make to another fish underwater, Billy thought. Inaudible to humans, and more sensed than heard. Not a sound, but an awareness of motion. Like somehow feeling that a man had straightened from a crouch in a pitch-black room, a knowledge that air, or water, or darkness had been displaced, that something infinitesimally slow but inexorable had expanded itself. Or maybe just a sudden perception that something huge and very close was alive. As if a feature of the landscape, a rock or hill, had been breathed into animation. No more noise than an opening eye and yet all was transformed.

It was creepy.

"Hear anything?" Joan teased.

"Not really," Billy said, embarrassed by his imagination, his romanticism.

Joan rolled atop him. "You deal with the chiggers for a while," she said. She maneuvered his shorts to his knees as she put her lips on his.

Billy's response to Joan was always the same, headlong and immediate. Her embrace unlocked something in his chest that sent a liquid heat throughout his being. Her kiss, her soft, blood-warm lips, made him feel as he were letting himself go into free fall, as close to a swoon as he would ever experience. The sex he could control, fast or slow, teasing or direct, hard or soft, whatever the occasion called for, but the emotion was always the same, yielding and complete.

She sat upon him, already wet, letting her own imagination work while he was contemplating growing corn, he realized, and took him fast and mechanically. A tension fuck, he thought. A quick and total release for the nerves. And very effective for both of them. At the end, she collapsed atop him and he held her tightly, wanting to cling to her love for a bit longer.

"I'm sorry I'm such a bitch," she whispered.

"You're not."

"Oh yeah. Oh yeah."

"Why?"

She wouldn't answer.

"I love you, Joan," he said.

"I know it," she replied. Billy wondered if he heard a suggestion of regret in her voice, or if it was just as imaginary as the growing of the corn.

CHAPTER THREE

It was late when Billy left Joan and walked to his car; the spilled light from the house was blocked by the huge shadow of the garage, so that he approached the alley semiblind, his eyes not yet accustomed to the gloom. He sensed the presence of the man before he could actually see him. He was standing by the driver's door, more a shape than a man, one more patch of darkness against the background of dark. When he moved slightly, Billy flinched, startled.

"Hello," Billy said. His tone was as much a question as a greeting.

"Um-hum."

"You scared me."

"Not yet, I ain't."

The man's voice was low and carried the thick accent of a country black man, a voice better suited to the piney woods of the Carolinas than Nebraska.

"You made a good start at it," Billy said. As his eyes adjusted, he could make out the man more clearly. He was tall and thick through the chest and shoulders, although how much was substance and how much the play of shadow, Billy could not say. The whites of his eyes and teeth seemed preternaturally bright. Billy glanced back at Joan's house and saw the interior lights go out.

"Don't imagine you scare that easy," the man said.

"Oh, yes. Jumpy as a cricket."

"Dat right?"

" 'Tis indeed," said Billy. When nervous, he would sometimes adopt an Irish brogue, thick and phony as a bad actor's, a habit he had tried to break. He heard himself using it now.

"Can I do anything for you at all?" Billy asked.

The man hesitated, and Billy imagined him wondering what sort of buffoon he had come upon in the alley, talking like a bloomin' eedjit.

"What you got in mind?" the man asked finally.

"Just being polite," Billy said, controlling the accent. "I assumed you had some reason for leaning on my car in the middle of nowhere."

"Resting."

"A good idea, with the heat an all."

"And not the middle of nowhere. This where you at."

"Temporarily."

Billy made a step toward the car door, expecting the man to move, but the other only shifted his weight and inched around to face Billy more directly. It was an adjustment Billy knew well, the practiced move of an athlete checking his balance. Or a fighter about to throw the first punch. If the man had any weapons, Billy could not see them in the dark.

"Been seeing your woman?"

"Was that just a wild guess on your part?"

Surprisingly, the man smiled and his teeth flashed in the gloom. "How I did?"

"You did good. I was, indeed, just seeing my woman."

"You nervous?"

"No more than usual."

"You nervous 'cause I near your womans?"

Womans? Was the man putting him on? Did anyone really talk like that?

"Some folks get nervous, I near their womans."

"Some people aren't even comfortable with themselves. I wouldn't take it personally."

"A good woman a comfort to a man."

"You're right. A good woman is solace and comfort to a man, although I'm not sure it's fashionable to say so," Billy said. "Let's keep the sentiment between ourselves."

"My dog a comfort to me."

"Well, less emotional variance with a dog. It's not apt to change its mind about you."

"But somebody took my dog."

"Did they? Maybe it wandered off. Dogs do that sometimes."

"You saying my dog change his mind about *me*? You say it my fault?"

The man rolled his shoulders like a boxer, and Billy shifted his footing slightly to present only his profile as a target for the first punch. If a punch were coming. As the man shifted his weight in response, Billy noticed a certain stiffness in one leg. If it came to it, Billy would concentrate his attack on that side.

"Where at my dog?" the man asked. He pronounced *dawwaag*, as if it had two syllables. Although Billy was no expert in linguistics, it sounded to him as if the accent was changing, sliding ever more southward, oozing from the piney woods into the bayous of the Mississippi Delta. It occurred to Billy that the man's cornpone mushmouth might be no more authentic than his own spurious brogue.

"What did you say?"

"Where at my dog?" the man repeated.

"I'm not sure I understand you."

"You got my dog?"

"I don't have a dog."

"Ain't studyin' *yo* dawwaag. Where at *my* dawwaag?"

In less ominous circumstances, Billy would have had difficulty suppressing a laugh at the dialogue.

"Do you find this conversation a little disjointed? Because I'm not certain why you're telling me about your relationship with your pet."

"Not a pet. A dog."

"All right, but why tell me?"

"You the one to tell."

"Am I?"

"You the man."

"Uh . . . which man is that?"

"Man for me."

"What's your name?"

"What your name?"

"I'm Billy Tree. And that's a sheriff's car you're leaning on."

"So you Billy Tree."

"I am. And what's your name?"

"You hot shit."

"Thank you."

"That what I hear. Billy Tree hot shit. Everybody say that."

"Just step away from the door, please, sir."

With insolent slowness, the man eased away from the car, and this time the stiffness in his leg was pronounced.

"Thank you. . . . What's your name?"

"Name Odette. You as good as they say?"

"Nowhere near. We have a communal misperception here. I'm not hot shit. Lukewarm shit at best."

The man chuckled in a deep, threatening way. Never looking away, Billy opened the car door and stood with it between himself and the man. The interior light flooded out and Billy could see the other's face for the first time. It was difficult to tell his age, but the bald head was clearly the result of shaving, not advanced years. If intelligence could be read in facial features, this was an intelligent man, not the backwoods yokel he sounded like, but Billy knew that intelligence revealed itself in actions, not surface details. There was something vaguely familiar about the man's appearance, but he could not place it. The man wore overalls and no shirt. Bare feet would be the only thing required to complete the outfit of a local rube, but Odette was wearing heavy work boots.

"You got a last name, Odette?"

"Everybody got a last name. Less they a slave."

"And you're no slave, are you, Odette?"

Odette chuckled again, a sound that made Billy want to take a defensive position.

"Not hardly."

"So what's your last name?"

"Collins."

"Do I know you, Mr. Collins? You look familiar."

"You know me now."

"Well, Mr. Collins, I'm sorry your dog is missing. If you see the police in the morning, they might be able to help you. And you can put up a few posters. I don't know if that ever helps, but it can't hurt."

"Ain't studying no poh-lice." He said the word as if naming something vile.

"Good luck with the posters, then. Now, if you'll excuse me, I'm through for the night." He started the car, but Odette remained where he was, watching Billy intently.

"Do you need a lift somewhere, Mr. Collins?"

"Don't need no lift. . . . You sure you big enough to pick me up?"

"Well, I know where to get help."

"You likely need it."

Billy turned on the headlights and saw Odette Collins even more clearly. The man was no taller than Billy, but thicker, as if another half of a body had been compressed into the existing one. I would likely need it, Billy agreed silently. I would likely need all the help I could get.

"Good night, then, Mr. Collins."

"I see you again, Billy Tree."

"I took forward to it, Mr. Collins."

Billy drove away, then made a slow circle around the block to see if the man had remained by Joan's house. When he cruised back through the alley minutes later, lighting the dark niches with the car's spotlight, there was no sign of Collins. Billy realized that he was very relieved. At least some of the sweat that had broken out on his body was not caused by the heat.

He found the man again on Harlan Street, walking slowly north, his hands in his pockets, the slight sheen of perspiration on his scalp and shoulders shining in every streetlight. *Walking* was scarcely the word; the man was ambling, like a lazy boy kicking clods down a country road, but dragging one leg slightly, as if the knee did not bend. He's not afraid of being seen, Billy thought. In fact, he's guaranteed to be noticed. There weren't many people on the streets at 11:30 on a weeknight, but those who were out could hardly miss him. Black men were scarce enough in Falls City; black men with shaven heads, looking like weight lifters in overalls, were nonexistent. Until now.

Billy could not drive slowly enough to stay behind him without giving the appearance of escorting him to the edge of town, so he turned off of Harlan Street at his sister's house, parked the car, and followed Collins on foot, staying well back. Some who saw him might assume Billy was out for a late-evening stroll—he was only a few blocks from his house. If they connected him with the unexpected black man shambling a hundred yards ahead of him and assumed that the acting deputy was fostering their safety and well-being, that was all right, too. In truth, Billy was not following Collins as a lawman— the man had broken no laws that Billy knew of, and, given his conspicuousness, he seemed highly unlikely to do so in the near future— he was following him for his own peace of mind.

Collins walked to the town limits, passed the detached liquor store that squatted there like a darkened bunker at a border crossing, and approached the motel, an open-ended rectangle of rooms flanking a swimming pool. Billy had never seen an adult in that particular cube of water, but then, Falls City was not a place to visit for recreation. Several men sat around the pool in lawn chairs under the stars, dipping now and then into a picnic cooler for another beer. He could hear the clink of ice against glass even from a distance. Truckers, most likely, Billy thought, maybe a salesman or two, but more likely workingmen, judging by their clothes and caps. The men watched Collins approach, watched him pass them by without a glance in their direction, then enter the motel office. Billy heard a guffaw from the men, then scornful laughter. It was not hard to imagine what they were saying.

Billy eased into the shadow of the liquor store and made himself comfortable leaning against the wall. Neon lights did not flash overtime in Falls City. Signs did not glow throughout the night. When shops closed, everything about them shut down, so Billy was wrapped in darkness as he kept watch and waited. One of the men got to his feet and gestured toward the motel office. He was tall and burly and louder than the others, perhaps drunker, probably showing off for them, too. There was no mistaking the angry bravado in his voice, although Billy could not distinguish individual words from that distance. The man was large enough that he was probably used to getting his way in shouting matches, and the beer had made him fearless. He waved an empty beer bottle menacingly in the air a few times, gesturing toward office, this accompanied by an encouragingly hostile undertone from the others. What was personal curiosity is about to become professional business, Billy thought. Unless Odette Collins proved more of a diplomat than he had in the alley.

Part of the hostility would be from the beer, of course. Or at any rate, the alcohol would allow it to surface. Billy wondered how much of it was a response to the clothes, as well. Would the beer drinkers be so easily incensed by the sight of a black man in a business suit? How much was culture, how much race? Decades of rhetoric and genuine social improvement had done little to change the underlying prejudice in many Americans, Billy knew. Disrespect, even contempt, was always simmering in their hearts, and the closer a person of color came to fitting one of the many negative stereotypes, the more quickly the scorn emerged. In some, it would take the form of violence, because that was the means of expression most readily available to them.

Collins emerged from the office with a key in his hand and passed by the pool, heading toward one of the rooms, again not looking at the men. Billy heard the big man say something quick and sharp, then saw Collins turn his head as if he had been slapped. Billy shoved off the wall and hurried toward the motel.

The two men regarded each other, a few yards separated them. Billy realized the big man was huge, nearly a head taller than Collins, and heavy, with too much flesh on the bones, like a weight lifter who has stopped working out. Bill heard the big man speak again, something abrupt and ugly. Collins replied with a low, humorless chuckle, and Billy quickened his pace.

One of the other men by the pool laughed, and the burly man snapped his head toward him angrily, then unleashed a torrent of invective at Collins. As Billy approached, he could make out individual words, but they didn't matter. The big man could as well have been barking hysterically like a dog whose yard was invaded. The man raised the empty beer bottle over his head and waved with his free hand. Collins took a slow step directly toward the big man, a step dangerous in its deliberateness. The big man roared more curses and shook the bottle threateningly over Collins's head.

Too late, big man, Billy thought. If you were going to hit him, you would already have done it, and Collins has read that. He's not going to be bluffed. Few men actually know how to fight. They scream at each other like monkeys and pound their chests, hoping all the while to avoid actual contact. When they do throw a punch, it is wild, leaning backward, ineffective. A man who knows what he is doing in a fight has no reason to fear someone who doesn't, no matter the size difference, no matter the brandished beer bottle . . . Guns are different, however. Guns can kill you no matter how cowardly the wielder. Billy knew all about guns.

"Whoa," said Billy, breaking into a run. Neither man acknowledged him, although one of the others turned his head. They were all out of their seats now, eager for action and beginning to crowd in toward the combatants.

"Hold on, hold it."

Collins took the final slightly dragging step and drove his forearm against the big man's chest. Collins's left arm was in the air to deflect the beer bottle, but it never descended. The big man recoiled from the strength of the blow, as if hopping backward. He fell into the swimming pool like a deadweight, not enough air left in his lungs to yell.

"Hang on, hang on," said Billy as he approached the pool. "Everybody just hold it right there."

He pointed a finger at Collins, who grinned at him, then turned to face the others.

"Who the fuck are you?" one of them demanded.

"I'm a deputy sheriff. Everybody just stay where they are."

"Sheriff, bullshit."

Billy glanced down at himself. In shorts and a T-shirt, he didn't look much like a lawman.

"Out of the way, asshole," said one of the men, although he made no move to advance toward Collins. They're glad I'm here, Billy thought. They're neither drunk enough nor angry enough to mess with Collins now, unless he had his back to them. But Collins made no attempt to move away, just stood there with an infuriating grin.

The big man flailed his way to the edge of the pool and started to climb out by Billy's feet.

"Gonna kill you, motherfucker," the big man muttered in Collin's direction. Billy waited until he was halfway up, then put his foot in the big man's chest and pushed him back into the pool.

"Just settle down. Everybody take it easy."

"Whose side you on?" one of the men yelled.

"I'll put you all in the pool, if that's what I have to do to calm you down. Now everybody just ease off."

The big man grabbed the side of the pool and jerked himself halfway out again. Billy pushed him back into the water once more.

"Use the other end of the pool," Billy said. "I don't want you any closer than that to this man . . . Mr. Collins, do you have a room in this establishment?"

"I do."

"Why don't you go to that room now?"

The big man splashed his way to the shallow end of the pool and stood there. "I'm going to kill both of you," he said.

"Not this evening, though. This evening, you're going to your room, you're going to dry off, and then you're going to sleep it off."

"The fuck you say."

"It's that or stay in the pool. Because I'm not going to let you out otherwise." Billy strode purposefully toward the shallow end. The big man moved to the edge, slowed by the water. He was halfway up when Billy pushed him. This time, the man made an ineffectual swipe at Billy's foot as he tumbled back into the water.

"You can't do that," one of the other men protested. He made a tentative move toward Billy.

"Don't move another inch," Billy said.

"Fuck you." The man looked around at his companions for courage, then started to move forward. Billy grabbed the man by the shoulder and propelled him toward the pool. His foot took the man's legs from under him and the man fell facedown in the water.

Billy turned to the others. One had lifted a lawn chair over his head.

"Now what if you miss?" Billy asked. The man blinked at him, taking in the possibility. "Have you considered what I will do to you if you miss?"

The man lowered the chair a few inches. Billy knew it was over. In combat circumstances, hesitation is loss.

"Or, worse, let's consider the repercussions if you don't miss. You've just struck a deputy sheriff. Until right now, none of you has done anything except be stupid and rude to a fellow human being, which, let's face it, is part of the human condition and not punishable by law. But if you swing that thing, I'll not only arrest you; I'll bounce your face off the concrete first. . . . Now, put the chair down and sit in it."

The man lowered the chair to the ground and sat on it.

"I was gonna . . ." he offered.

"It's too hot for this, guys. It really is." He turned toward the big man in the pool and pointed a finger at him. "When do you figure it's going to rain?"

"Huh?"

"When do you figure it's going to rain and break this damned hot spell?" The idea was to disrupt their focus on their anger. It didn't take much to dispel a menace. Not unless the participants were really committed, and these looked like they wanted an easy way out.

"Answer me," he said sharply.

"I don't know."

"Give me your best guess. A day? A week? When is it going to rain?"

The other man in the pool spoke. "I heard by Tuesday it'd rain."

Billy turned to the man in the chair. "Tuesday? What do you think? Tuesday?"

"Yeah, maybe."

"Because, guys, I'll tell you, I don't know if the crops can take much more of this, but I know the humans can't. Just look at yourselves. It's the heat that made you act like this, wasn't it? . . . Wasn't it?"

"It's too damned hot," said the man in the chair.

"Hotter than hell," said the big man.

"Fucking A," agreed the other.

Behind Billy, Odette Collins laughed.

"Mr. Collins, I ask you again to go to your room, please."

"This too much fun," said Collins.

"Why don't you throw his ass in the water?" the big man demanded. He stood now in four feet of water, avoiding the edge.

"That be interesting," said Collins. He folded his arms and grinned even wider, looking as if he would welcome an attempt by Billy. Not tonight, Billy thought. Not without a stout club and a pair of handcuffs.

"Mr. Collins is cool enough, I think. Besides, he's going to his room, aren't you, sir?"

"Who the hell are you anyway?" the big man asked.

"I guess you missed the introductions because you were trying to keep from drowning. I'm acting Deputy Sheriff Billy Tree."

"You're Billy Tree?" asked the other man in the pool.

"I thought you'd be a whole lot bigger," said the big man.

"He is a little disappointing, ain't he?" said Collins.

Billy turned to Collins once more. The man's teeth gleamed very white in the light of the single bulb hanging above the pool.

"Did I remember to say please, Mr. Collins?" Billy asked. "Please."

"Shit, you put it that way . . ." Collins turned and walked toward his room. His shoulders shook with laughter.

"How's it feel in there?" Billy asked, turning back to the others. "Is it as cool as it looks?"

They considered the question for a moment, bewildered.

"Yeah, it is kinda cool."

"Great," said Billy. "It's just what we all need." He took two steps and launched himself into the water. He could hear Collins, laughing now with genuine humor, up until he closed the door to his room.

They aren't malicious men, Billy thought as he walked back to his car. Just dumb and thoughtless and a bit too eager to follow their own bad impulses. Remind them of their decent side, or give them a chance to let their decent side return, and they are all right. Sometimes he thought that was the very essence of his job. He reminded people of who they ought to be.

His last conscious thought before he fell asleep was that dumb and thoughtless and a bit too eager to follow their own bad impulses was also a pretty good description of a murderous mob.

He could not recall later whether it was when awake or dreaming that he remembered how quickly the lights had gone out in Joan's house. She could not have been in bed so soon. Turning off the lights was the only way to see through the window. The idea occurred to him with a chill that Odette Collins had been waiting in the dark behind Joan's house for the most logical reason . . . Not to see Billy. To see Joan.

Lawton squeezed his body atop the hundred-pound sacks of potatoes in the pantry. His sister tried to maneuver the sacks around him, to cover the hole he had created in his haste, but they were too heavy. Instead, she slid some of the huge cans of tomatoes across the floor and into the gap. She could still see his face peering out. He gave her the goofy smile he reserved for the times when he wanted to make her stop crying, but she could see he was frightened, no matter how silly he acted for her benefit.

"Don't you worry 'bout this," he said, his voice hushed. "This goin' be all right."

"What are you doing?" she demanded, trying not to panic. He was *supposed to be the one who was brave. She was too young to have to be brave.*

"Jus' a game," Lawton said. "Jus' a game."

But it wouldn't be a game if any of the white folks came in and found him atop the potatoes. She knew that; she did not have to have that much explained to her.

"Close the door, then go on and git," he said. "Don't stay around. Don't be anywhere near me. Don't let them get you all mixed up in this . . . Go on, now, git."

She hesitated, her eyes brimming with tears, although she did not fully understand what was happening. He had explained some of it in hurried, garbled syntax as he sought a place to hide, but it made no sense to her why anyone would do what he said they had done, nor why her brother was being sought.

"Git!" he hissed angrily as she continued to stare, wide-eyed at him, his fear apparent to her.

She closed the pantry door and left the kitchen, as he had commanded, but still she heard the men burst in from the back way, heard them call out to one another in rushed and furious voices, shouting questions and directions. She made herself as small as she could and squeezed into a corner of the long hallway, her hands over her ears to block out the frightening sound of irate men, but still she could hear them. She heard the cry of triumph go up as they opened the pantry and found her brother. She heard his pleas, almost gibberish, they were so fast and frightened, heard their sharp retorts, the slide of tomato cans, the rocky thud of potatoes hitting the floor, the sound of bodies resisting one another. More men hurried into the kitchen from the back way, and she could distinguish her brother's voice only as a kind of yelp, rising above the voices of the white men like a scared puppy whimpering in the dark.

She did as he had told her: she stayed away from it all, never showed her face to the enraged white men. None of them had ever hurt her or even frightened her before this. Everyone there had been unfailingly kind to her, treating her with the condescending amusement that an eight-year-old girl seemed to elicit from adults. They smiled at her, some patted her head, and some asked her questions about her name, her age, where she was in school. Often, they would place coins in her hand, so often that she was no longer astonished when it happened, so often that she saw the looks from the other workers change over time from happiness for her to resentment and envy. When she made mistakes, dropped a fork or brought the wrong dish, the white people never scolded her, as they sometimes did with the older workers. They continued to smile and pat her, as if she were a good-luck piece. Still, despite their beneficence toward her, she knew to be cautious around white people. They were creatures of caprice, kind to the young and the very old, potentially dangerous to all the black people in the vast middle years. At eighteen, Lawton was vulnerable to that danger. She had seen him around white men, treating them always with the kind of placating deference he would use when forced to manipulate a large animal that could crush him with a sudden shift of its bulk. She did not need Lawton to tell her to stay away from them when they were like this. Her age, her little-girl cuteness would not protect her brother.

She heard the scuffle of feet, the crash of furniture falling, and then crockery shattering on the floor. She did not need to see to know that Lawton was struggling against their grip, using that strength that to her had always seemed monumental to break free from their clutches. The back door swung open violently on its hinges and there were more angry voices, stalled for the moment as Lawton clung to the door frame with feet and hands and fingernails. With her eyes squeezed shut and her hands over her ears, she could still see and hear it all. A final yelp from Lawton was the last she ever heard of his voice. Sometimes she thought it was her name he had called out, sometimes the name of someone else. Sometimes just a cry of terror.

CHAPTER FOUR

O n Fridays, Billy drove ten miles out of Falls City to Rulo, a
hamlet perched on the edge of the Missouri River like a
cardboard box on the lip of a drainage ditch, just waiting
for one rain too many to sweep it to disaster. There was a roadhouse
there where the bank had eroded away, leaving a full foot of flooring
poking over the abyss—a toe of a building, all set to test the waters.
Wooden stairs dug into the bank led down to a floating dock, aged
timbers held together by weed and algae, surface slick with the residue
of freshwater snails, and it was there that the local fisherman landed
with their catch. They were lapsed farmers, really, men who knew how
to run a skiff and bait a dragline and make a decrepit outboard motor

continue to cough and sputter and hold them in place against the current. Like most other farmers in Richardson County, they supplemented their incomes as they could, and dragging the depths of the Big Muddy for bottom-feeding catfish was as good a way as any, and better than some.

The catfish were a once-a-week specialty, a holdover from Catholic meatless Fridays, a tradition that had long since forgotten its origin. The farmer/fishermen tossed them from their boats into a basket and they were taken immediately to the kitchen, fresh as an otter's midday meal, monstrous, ugly, slick with protective ooze, sprouting barbels thick as car antennas. Billy thought they were the most delicious fish in the world. Breaded, seasoned, fried in deep fat that had served the same function before, then served with lemon, salt, and pepper, they were as rich in flavor as anything that lived in the water. Billy had tried aquaculture's cultivated catfish fillets and found them as bland as mass-produced chicken. The Rulo catfish tasted of the river and grease and something wild, and Billy would eat one per week, fastidiously picking bones from his mouth and drinking a beer at a scarred table made of planks and sawhorses. In the summer, he ate outside under a huge oak tree, sharing the picnic table with a few other customers, assorted ants and insects, and most of the bees in that part of the county as they swarmed around the side dish of inedible coleslaw and crawled through the beer foam. It was not an experience available in the city, any city that he had known, and he rated it as a culinary treat equaled only by sweet corn picked from the stalk just ten minutes before a very brief flirtation with hot water—another treat not available in the city. There have to be some reasons I'm still here, he thought, and this is certainly one of them.

The call came as he was squeezing the last of the lemon into a water glass, creating a Rulo finger bowl to cut the grease. He wiped his hands on the old newspaper that served as a tablecloth and listened to Gina Schul, the woman of all work, whom Lapolla referred to grandly as their "dispatcher."

"He's in a swivet," Gina confided in a half whisper. Billy assumed Lapolla was within earshot in the next room.

"A terrible place to be," said Billy.

"That's what he says. He wants you to hurry back."

"Siren hurry, or no dessert hurry?"

"You wouldn't eat dessert there, would you?"

"Gina, I am a man of no refinement. I would."

"I'll bet their pie tastes like mud, just like those fish."

"You would not bet *me*, however, for I am a cautious man and I suspect I would lose."

"You know how catfish feed, don't you?"

"Gina, I'm trying to digest."

"Christ, let me talk to him," Lapolla said in the background. Then, into the phone: "Billy, come on, man. He's giving me all kinds of grief."

"Who?"

"Judge Lyle Sunder. He's yelling at me like it's my fault."

"Deny, Bert, deny. You were home in bed and I'll swear to it."

"It's not funny, Billy. He keeps telling me to get you on the case . . . like it's something I couldn't deal with myself. He's a nice-enough guy, but he doesn't like me."

"I thought he was friend to all," Billy said. "Which is why he has continued to get elected for the past forty years."

"Well, sure, the voters like him, but what do they know about anything?"

"We'll find out when you run for election yourself, won't we, Bert?"

"I been meaning to talk to you about that, Billy."

"You can have my vote if you let me stay for dessert. They've got peach cobbler."

"Take it with you."

"Cobbler is a dangerous dish to eat while driving. I do my own laundry these days, remember."

"Please, Billy. Christ. You'd think someone cut his dick off, the way he's yelling."

"What happened?"

"Somebody gave him a noose."

A top a hill elevated just enough to provide a commanding view of its surroundings, in a former cornfield that had been first seeded, then, when that proved insufficiently lush, sodded with imported grass, sat Judge Lyle Sunder's house. Constructed of red brick, flanked by two large transplanted maples, and fronted by a scrim of shrubs, it sat atop its rise like the shiny bulb on a clown's nose, conspicuous, isolated, and a bit ridiculous. The judge's lot of land was just outside the city limits, overlooking the town but not actually part of it, which was a good working description of the judge's position, too. His location brought him under the jurisdiction of the sheriff and not the local police.

Billy picked up Lapolla at the department office and drove him East on Twenty-first Street, past the last of the new houses, and onto a long driveway with an elaborate wooden sign that read SUNDERLAND.

"Does the name Odette Collins mean anything to you?" Billy asked as he turned onto the judge's asphalt road.

"No. Should it?"

"It does to me, but I can't remember what."

"Who is he?"

"He paid me a visit last night. A black man with a shaven head, about my size and age, but thick, strong-looking. Real Deep South accent, like he had a mouthful of tongue. I had trouble understanding him . . . But I got his message."

"What was it?"

"He didn't care for me."

Billy pulled the car into a crescent-shaped parking area in front of the house.

"Hard to imagine," said Lapolla.

"He convinced *me*."

Judge Sunder met them at the door and acted as if Lapolla were not present.

"Billy, nice to see you," he said, shaking Billy's hand. In his mid-sixties but still moving with much of the grace and vitality of youth, Sunder radiated the bluff hardiness that many people would long for in a father. Assumed wise by virtue of his position as judge, he nonetheless had a sparkle in his eye and a midwestern lack of affectation. When he smiled, he looked as if he meant it, and when he made eye contact, he seemed to concentrate all of his attention on the other person. It was small wonder that the man was continually reelected. The female vote alone would carry him, Billy reflected. Poor Lapolla didn't stand a chance of getting elected if his opponent had any of Sunder's skill.

"I'm glad you could come. Got a little problem here."

"So the sheriff tells me."

"I had a break-in last night."

"Just discover it?"

"I was in Omaha. Little judicial review matter. You know. Walked into my study today and there it was."

Sunder opened the door to the study, a large room with wooden paneling, a desk covered with papers, and walls lined with trophies and plaques. An ornate crystal chandelier dominated the space, and hanging from the chandelier, the first thing to catch an entrant's eye, was a hangman's noose.

"See that?" Sunder demanded.

"I do."

"That's how I found it. Just like that. Hanging there like Sweet Jesus."

"Um." Billy surveyed the room after a cursory glance at the noose. Sunder called it his study, but it looked as if he used it to study himself. Trophies, plaques, engraved ashtrays, statuettes, ribbons, medallions, framed pictures, seemingly every award, honor, or memento he had ever received in a life now well into its seventh decade had been saved, preserved, and displayed.

"You don't seem surprised," said Sunder, disappointed.

Billy was not. The noose was exactly like the one he fingered now in his own pocket, neatly crafted, lethal, and miniature.

"Sheriff Lapolla explained it to me ahead of time," Billy said.

"You ever see anything like that?"

"I may have."

"What the hell does it mean?"

Billy continued to inspect the room. The judge appeared to be a man who liked to luxuriate amid his trophies in private. The blinds on all the windows but one were drawn. Billy looked out at the brilliant green of Sunder's transplanted lawn. Like the world's biggest putting green, Billy thought.

"It's a threat," Lapolla said, hanging back in the doorway.

Sunder ignored him.

"What do you think, Bill? It's a message of some sort. Should I take it seriously?"

One of the shelves had been knocked from the wall. A clock lay on the floor. An ancient golf ball rested a few inches away, a huge smiling slice on the cover.

"Is the room always like this?" Billy asked.

"I didn't touch a thing. I saw that noose and called you right away."

"Do you usually keep one window blind up and the others down?"

"No, I keep them all down. . . . You spend your life on the bench, a courtroom of lawyers staring at you, you come to appreciate a bit of privacy at home. . . . I figure he came in that way."

Billy noted that the window was unlocked. He studied the blind for a moment, then turned to the clock on the floor. Billy bent and looked at the timepiece. The glass front had been shattered, the hands arrested at 11:37.

"I figure that's when he broke in," Sunder said.

"Hum," said Billy. He nudged the clock with the back of his fingernail. It was a cheap alarm clock with a round, bulbous face of the type popular thirty or forty years ago.

"Family heirloom, was it?"

"I won that baby at a carnival," said Sunder. "One of those machines with the crane in the glass box. Must have spent twice what it was worth getting it."

Billy glanced at the judge. It seemed a strange waste of time and money for a man the judge's age, but then Sunder hadn't always been the age he was now, Billy reminded himself. Not so strange for a man in his twenties, maybe demonstrating his skills to a woman.

"And you kept it?"

The judge shrugged. "It's part of my life. All of this is part of my life." He swept the room with his hand. "You accomplish something, you ought to remember it. You ought to prize it. Seems foolish just to walk through life without memories . . . Doesn't have to be big. Doesn't have to be important to anybody but yourself." The judge wandered about the room, pointing out his treasures, his voice suddenly thick with nostalgia and a hint of wonder at his own successes.

"This was for second place in the school spelling bee, sixth grade. Doesn't sound like much now, but it was a proud time. Big moment in my young life . . . Your father was there; your uncle Sean would have been, too. Got this pinned on me in school assembly, right in front of everybody in North School."

"How'd my father do?" Billy asked.

"Your dad was not an academic," Sunder answered diplomatically. "But he was a good man, Billy. A fine friend."

Billy could not recall anyone who wasn't already several sheets to the wind describing his father as a good man. James Tree, or "Lord Jimmy," as he was known to every bartender and liquor salesman in the country, had been a drunk and a failure. Or at least that was the way Billy remembered it. No one had ever convinced him otherwise.

"Here's one from the Four-H club. Best rooster."

"You get a prize for best rooster?" Lapolla asked.

"Of course," the judge said dismissively. He held a blue ribbon in the air as if it were made of gossamer. "Beat out Rex Walgrim."

"This was when?" Billy asked.

"I'da been twelve. So, 1945? Your uncle Sean was a Four-H boy, too, you know."

"Hard to imagine Sean as a rooster boy." In truth, it was hard for Billy to imagine his uncle with anything other than a beer bottle gripped in his heavy fist, as if he wanted to choke it. Full of beer and bluster, he could kill a chicken with his breath alone. Like his brother, Lord Jimmy, Sean was ending his years in booze and cheap sentiment, wrapping himself in the flag of an Ireland he never saw and the imagined ethos of a people he didn't know.

"Calves," Sunder said. "Sean raised calves."

Lapolla inspected a stone that had been cut surgically in two.

"This is a whatchamacalit," said Lapolla.

Sunder removed it and placed it back on the shelf.

"A geode," he said. "Found it just south of Indian Cave."

"You can buy these in souvenir stores," said Lapolla. Billy wondered at his lack of tact.

"I *discovered* mine. It's a rare find."

Sunder picked up the golf ball and made a motion to put it back on the shelf that had fallen. He fingered the ball absently, at a loss for what to do with it now that it was out of place.

"My first hole in one," Sunder said when he saw Billy looking at the ball. "Only hole in one, I should say. . . . This probably all looks a little—what's the word—self-indulgent to you, I imagine."

"Not at all," Lapolla said hurriedly, realizing his gaffe of moments before.

Sunder continued to ignore Lapolla and focus his attention on Billy.

"*Self-congratulatory* is the better word, I guess," Sunder continued. "It probably looks pretty pathetic to you, Billy, what with all of your real trophies, your medals—what was it, a special presidential citation for courage?"

Billy remembered the deputy director of the Secret Service pinning the medal to his hospital gown, spouting fulsome praise while fluids dripped into Billy's veins and his self-esteem seeped out. The cowardice of his "heroism" haunted him still. He had thrown out the medal while recuperating from his wounds at his sister's house, but Kath had retrieved it and squirreled it away with the athletic trophies and all the rest of his triumphant youth. Had he known she would rescue it? Had it been just another cowardly display passing as courage?

"I don't keep them," Billy said.

"That's a mistake. The day will come when you'll want to be reminded," Sunder said. "Especially with a history like yours." He waved a hand around the room. "I get pleasure just from this sad stuff."

There was something sad about it, Billy thought, although Sunder clearly wanted him to deny it. Why seek approbation from me, he wondered, when Lapolla is ready to lick his boots for him if he would so much as acknowledge his presence? Because I withhold my approval and Lapolla does not, of course.

"Anything missing?" Billy asked. Sunder seemed slightly surprised to have his attention brought back to the matter at hand.

"Missing? You think it was a robbery?"

"I don't know. What do you think it was?"

"What about the noose? Isn't that what it's all about? It's a warning, a threat. . . ."

"A prank?"

"Do you think so?" Sunder cocked his head to regard the noose, as if seeing it in a new light. "Seems a lot of trouble for a prank. Well, you're the expert."

"Not really. This is more Sheriff Lapolla's line of expertise. What do you think, Sheriff?"

Billy was determined to make Sunder recognize Lapolla's superior position. He might be an incompetent, but he's my incompetent, Billy thought. I don't want anyone disrespecting him but me.

Lapolla shifted nervously, uncomfortable under Sunder's sudden gaze.

"Well, it might be a prank all right," he said. "Or, like I said, it could be a threat. Hard to say. . . . You just never know with this kind of thing."

"Have you ever seen this kind of thing?" Sunder asked.

"Well . . ." Lapolla thrust his hands in his pockets, then pulled them out again. "I've been in the department quite awhile now, Your Honor."

Sunder twitched his lips into a smile that withered as soon as it was born.

"So you think it's a robbery?" he said, turning back to Billy.

"Only if something's missing. How's the rest of the house?"

"Nothing disturbed at all, not that I could see at least."

"Did you check your safe?"

"I don't have a safe. I don't have anything that needs special protection, I live a simple life."

Billy grinned. "Well, you've got all these treasures, don't you?" He indicated the ribbons and medals and plaques.

"I do," said Sunder seriously. "I do have these, but they're of value only to me. I know that. I can't imagine a thief would want anything in here."

"Would you know if anything was missing? Do you have an inventory of all this?"

"Only in my mind."

"Let us know if you come up with anything that's missing."

"What I don't understand is, who would be fool enough to break into a judge's house in the first place, and just to put this . . . this thing in his study?"

The same guy who was fool enough to put one on the door of the deputy sheriff's house, Billy thought.

"I hear there's a black man in town," Sunder said as if in answer to his own question.

"There are several."

"I mean a new one."

Billy nodded. "There is."

"You might start there."

"Because he's black?"

"Because he's a stranger, because he might not know this was a judge's house."

"We'll check him out for sure," said Lapolla.

"You aren't suggesting racial profiling, are you, Judge?" Billy asked.

Sunder regarded Billy for a moment as if he had just arrived from an alien world.

"Of course not," he said finally. "I'm a county judge. I must adjudicate fairly for *all* of our citizens. I don't have a prejudiced bone in my body."

"Prejudice isn't in the bones, Judge."

Lapolla tugged on Billy's sleeve. "Billy . . . Billy . . ."

"And I don't know any man without some," Billy continued. "Myself very much included."

"You admit to me you're a prejudiced man, Deputy?"

"I admit to you that I'm a prejudiced *man*," said Billy. "I am not a prejudiced deputy."

"A fine distinction."

"It's one we all have to make, it seems to me."

"Well, it's not one I have to make, I'm happy to say. I regard myself as absolutely color-blind, have to be. I've trained myself that way. The law demands it, and the law is a stern master. . . . Now, if you don't feel right about checking out the whereabouts of this stranger in our town last night, I suppose that's up to you. I'm not telling you how to run the Sheriff's Department."

"You'd have to talk to the sheriff about that anyway. I'm just a acting deputy."

"We'll check him out for sure," Lapolla said again. "I'll do it myself."

"He has an alibi," said Billy. "I know exactly where he was last night."

"Oh? Where?"

"He was with me," said Billy.

"Oh? How's that?"

"I was swimming," said Billy.

"Friend of yours, is he?"

Billy grinned. "Can't say I know him real well as yet. It was just a very hot night. Several of the guys were already in the pool, thought I'd join them. Sort of a gesture of solidarity, if you know what I mean. Show them the law is their pal."

"I see," said Sunder, although he clearly did not. "Well, I suppose that's good politics. You'll do well in the election."

"I won't be in the election," Billy said as he saw Lapolla's face fall. "I'll be voting for Sheriff Lapolla."

Sunder offered another smile that died aborning. "Of course. . . . Now, we don't have any lingering misunderstanding, do we, Billy? I was in no way suggesting racial profiling of any kind. In fact, let me be doubly clear: I oppose it and I counsel you against it. If I hear of it happening, I will be obliged to take legal steps."

"That's very clear, Your Honor," said Lapolla. "No one was suggesting anything of the kind. . . ."

"Well, I was, Bert. It seemed to me that first the judge said 'black' and then he said 'checking out' where he was last night. I'm glad he's taken the time to correct me on my misunderstanding."

"You are a pisser, Bill," said Sunder. "Everybody told me you were. You got a peculiar way of looking at things. And then with all that Irish blarney, a man never knows when you're serious and when you're pulling his leg."

Sunder smiled broadly and Billy grinned back.

"Ah, sure, 'tis the Irish in me, don't you know."

"Lord Jimmy was a charmer, too," Sunder said with what sounded like admiration. Billy knew better.

"Tell me, will you need this?" Sunder continued. He indicated the noose, his finger wavering inches away, as if he couldn't wait to swing it back and forth.

"Why?"

"Because I'd like to keep it."

"You bet, Your Honor," Lapolla volunteered hastily.

Sunder lifted an eyebrow doubtfully and glanced at Billy for confirmation.

"You don't think you'll need it for evidence?" Sunder asked. His tone was that of a parent turned suddenly stern.

Lapolla looked uncertainly at Billy.

"You'll keep it on hand for us, won't you, Judge?"

"I'll take excellent care of it," said Sunder. He added doubtfully, "You don't think you can get fingerprints off of it?"

Lapolla squinted, miming serious thought.

"Hum . . ."

"Too small, huh?" Billy offered. "You'd only get a partial print at best."

"Absolutely too small," Lapolla said gratefully.

"What about DNA?" Sunder asked. "That stays on a thing forever, just about, doesn't it?"

"I'd have to read up on that," Billy admitted.

"I do, too," said Sunder.

"But I don't think this is a case where DNA is all that important, do you, Sheriff?"

Lapolla picked up his cue quickly. "No, I don't think DNA is something to worry about here."

"You're the boss," Billy said.

The acting sheriff beamed.

"So . . . that's it, then?" Sunder asked.

"How do you mean, Your Honor?"

"What do you think? About the noose? Is this something I should worry about? Forget about? Is it a prank? A warning of some kind? A threat? What's the deal here, Bill?"

Billy shrugged. "It would help if we knew what he stole."

"I'm not sure he stole anything. Why do you think that?"

"He went to the trouble to break in, not that it was all that hard, but it was certainly risky. If he just wanted to give you the noose, he could have left it on your doorknob, for instance. Or put it in your mailbox. I'd say he took something, or was looking for something to take at least. Until we know what that was, we don't have much to work with."

"I'll do an inventory, but I can tell you right now there's nothing in here that's of much interest to anybody else. . . . Of course, he might not have known that when he broke in."

"Well, do that inventory anyway, just to make sure. Otherwise, I don't know what to tell you. I don't think he'll be back, do you, Sheriff?"

"No . . ."

"Oh, I'll be ready for him if he comes back," Sunder said. "Don't worry about that. I don't think he'll want to be crawling through my window a second time."

esus, Billy, what was that all about?" Lapolla asked as they drove away from Judge Sunder's hill.

"A criminal investigation, I think, Bert. Do you suppose he even saves his old toenail clippings? The guy's got a souvenir of everything that ever happened to him."

"You accused the judge of being a racist."

"Not a racist. You have to combine prejudice with power to make it racism. All we saw there was prejudice."

"Well, whatever that means. And hell, what's so wrong with checking out this black guy?"

"Nothing. So long as we don't do it just because he's black."

Lapolla gave him a sidelong glance.

"You are kidding, right?"

"To tell you the truth, Bert, I don't exactly know what the hell I'm doing a good portion of the time."

Lapolla looked worried. "Oh, don't tell me that, Bill. I'm counting on you knowing."

I do know what I'm doing, he thought. I'm covering my tracks with this display of righteousness. My first reaction to Collins was distrust, and that was just because of his skin, no question about it. *I* checked him out immediately, so would anybody else in this county, so why am I attacking the judge for doing the same? Do I think by announcing my own prejudice that somehow makes it right?

"The judge likes you anyway," Lapolla said. He shook his head uncomprehendingly. "I don't get it. You say things to people sometimes, you'd think they'd want to paste you in the mouth, but they just love you for it. It's like they think everything out of your mouth is a compliment or a joke or something charming. . . . Me, they don't even hear. It's like I'm not there. And I'm *careful* to say the right thing. I mean, I make an effort, Billy. It's like you make an effort to piss them off, sometimes, and they act like you're joking. . . . Are you joking? You're not, are you?"

"I'm not joking. It's just the charming lilt in my voice."

"The lilt, huh? I guess I don't have one of those. Whatever it is, the judge likes you, no matter what you said to him."

"I don't care if he likes me or not," Billy said. And that isn't true, either, he thought. I want them all to like me, just as Lapolla does. But I'm too proud to admit it, so I say things to antagonize—but then I finish it with a grin and a bit of brogue to take the curse off it. "Charm," they call it. And maybe they call it that because it's easier to say than "confused hypocrisy."

"Well, I care, but he hates me."

"No, he doesn't, Bert."

"He does. How about that crack about you running for sheriff?"

"He was just paying me a compliment. Good politicians do that—they butter everybody up."

"He doesn't butter me up. He didn't give me any compliments."

"Probably doesn't think of you as a constituent so much as a fellow officeholder."

"Uh-huh . . . Are you planning on running for the job, Billy? I mean, you can tell me. I don't blame you if you do."

"No."

"You'd be good, you'd be a real good sheriff. Probably better than me."

"Nonsense. First of all, I don't want the job; I'm only here now helping you out because you asked me to. We both agreed this was just until the election. Then you can appoint real deputies of your own . . . or keep the others you got now, whatever you choose. Right?"

"People talk to you different, Bill. I see it. Everybody knows what you've done and everything. You're the one they want. You could win in a landslide."

"Can't win if I don't run, can I?"

"I was just saying . . . I'd understand if you did. No hard feelings."

Billy touched Lapolla's shoulder for emphasis.

"Sheriff . . . you're the sheriff."

Lapolla beamed again and exhaled in a gust of relief.

CHAPTER FIVE

W ith the acting sheriff back in the department office, Billy drove north on Harlan again, telling himself it was just part of his routine patrol, but when he reached the motel, he turned off the road. From his vantage point next to the office, he could see the room that Collins had entered the night before, his laughter taunting Billy for his antics in the swimming pool. Uncertain what he hoped to learn, Billy watched the room for a few minutes, even though he assumed Collins was no longer there. And if that was the case, where was he? Should it matter? Billy was not concerned about the whereabouts of the other men who had been at the pool last night. The assumption was that they were at work, on the road, going on about their lives, vanished into the pond of humanity, just so many more little fish. What made Collins special? All he had done was to ask Billy about a dog, then defend himself against an obstreperous drunk by pushing him into the water. If he had not been a black man, would Billy have felt threatened by his appearance outside Jane's house? If he had not been a black man, would Billy be here now? The answer in both cases was clearly no. But Odette Collins could not vanish into the pond of little fish, because all the fish in Richardson County were white. Odette had no more chance of being ignored or forgotten than the only raisin in a dish of tapioca. And if that's racial profiling, Billy thought, then I'm guilty of it. And it is, and I am.

Let it ride, he told himself. Let the man find his dog and let me go on about my business. But when he backed his car onto the road, he headed north on Highway 73, then west on 4, toward Humboldt and the strong gravitational pull of both curiosity and nostalgia.

Dick Mulhaus lived on a farm south of Humboldt, close to the north fork of the Big Nemaha river. The countryside was febrile with green, a frenzied beneficiary of the irrigation from the healthy water table next to the river. Fed energy by the fiery sun, cooled and slaked by the irrigation, the crops responded with frantic growth. Cornstalks towered like small trees, much higher than usual, blocking off the view of the countryside, even the roads. There were accidents at the draftsman-sharp ninety-degree intersections in this part of the county, oncoming traffic obscured from a driver's vision by the forest of corn. And it was a forest, Billy thought as he drove through a stretch of plants so high it seemed almost like a tunnel. Or a jungle. A very carefully nurtured and controlled man-made jungle with enough stored energy locked in roots and leaves and grain to feed and fuel half a nation and much of the rest of the world, as well. When the time came, when economics and technology and politics converged propitiously, every scrap and calorie and molecule of this great bounty would be used for something other than feeding cattle and making corn syrup. Billy had listened to futurists talk about the phenomenal riches stored in an acre of corn, of plastics and fuel and fiber potentials created by sun and water and chlorophyl so great that it would dwarf the current industries already thriving off it. Heady speeches they were, talking of energy independence from a field of susurrant green and a world of products bent, shaped, and extruded from recombined extracts of the same plant, or one of its many variations. Some of it was here already, some probably pipe dream, and some yet to happen. If they had managed to do all they had done with the humble soy plant, he thought, it was not hard to imagine they could do even more with a plant that grew so fast that you could hear it.

Dick Mulhaus was waiting for him on the front porch of a house so closely hedged by crops that it looked like an island afloat on a sea of green. A tall man, close to seventy, giving in to excess weight, but still light on his feet, he greeted Billy with the kind of enthusiasm that he had come to expect since returning to Falls City. There was a look of anticipation in the man's eyes, as if he thought Billy might say or do something extraordinary and memorable. At times, Billy felt like passing out cards like the deaf mendicants in restaurants and airports: *I do no tricks. I am overrated. Look for nothing special here.*

Billy was dripping with sweat by the time he'd reached the porch. The perspiration irritated the scars from his bullet wounds and made them itch. He extended his hand.

"Hey, Coach."

"Billy Tree. Damn it all, it's Billy Tree."

"That it is. How you doing, Coach?"

They stood smiling at each other for a moment. There was some thought of an embrace, which they both rejected.

"Still on top of the ground," said Mulhaus. "You're looking good, look like you could still drive it hard to the basket if you had to."

"If nobody was guarding me."

"You were always modest, Billy ... As good as you were, you could afford to be."

They sat on the porch steps, side by side, and Billy felt as if he were on the bench again, next to the coach, receiving the necessary wisdom for the game. Mulhaus touched him repeatedly, a hand on his arm, his shoulder, a pat on his back, with the easy familiarity of one athlete to another. He could tell the coach was excited to see him again.

Corn surrounded the farmhouse, taller than either of them. Now that he was out of the car, the plants seemed to press in on Billy as if almost menacingly alive, as if they were not plants at all, but alien animal life, the kind that advances only when you're not looking.

"You ever hear corn grow?" he asked.

Mulhaus gave him a searching look, then, to Billy's surprise, he said, "Some nights, I take a lawn chair and sit out next to a field— this is usually a night I've had words with the wife and maybe a beer or two too many, so I don't put any stock in it, but . . . yeah, some-times I think I hear it growing."

"What does it sound like?"

Mulhaus shrugged uneasily. It was not a topic he was accustomed to talking about. "To me, it sounds like a really tiny moan. You know how growing pains will make a kid groan and whimper sometimes? I figure with all the fertilizer and the water and the new seeds and this kind of sun, we're forcing these plants to grow awfully fast. It's got to hurt." He shrugged again, trying to diminish what he had said.

They sat in silence for a moment, both listening for a signal from the corn. They heard only the rustle of insects and the whine of tires on asphalt far away.

"It's good to see you, Billy," Mulhaus said at last. He slapped Billy's knee.

"You, too, Coach."

"You were the best I ever had. Far and away the best. The best I ever saw."

"I think your memory's playing tricks."

"You won the state championship for us damned near single-handed."

"I had a good coach."

"Pfff. I would have had to be one god-awful coach not to win with a player like you. You gave me a lot of good memories, Billy."

Billy nodded and smiled faintly. He was constantly encountering people who expected him to remember himself as vividly as they did, not realizing that his twenty years away from Nebraska had erased his memories of all but the most salient events and characters from his past. What remained for him was a generalized nostalgia for the place itself, the low-key easiness of a semirural lifestyle, even the weather, hard as that was to believe at the moment. But the people did not live in his mind the way he did in theirs. He was the local legend, after all, not they, and it was a cloak of distinction he found harder to bear by the day.

His defense for the embarrassment of such moments was charm. Charm and a polite evasiveness.

"I wonder what ever happened to me?"

"We all know what happened with the Secret Service and all, protecting the president. Saw you on television."

"I did a little running beside the vice president's car. I was never really with the president. . . ."

It was a correction no one wanted to hear, and Mulhaus was no exception.

"I forget where you went off to school, though. I just know it sure as hell wasn't U of N. They've never had an athlete good as you."

"Cornell," Billy said. "I went to Cornell."

"Where is that, exactly?"

"Upstate New York."

"Ivy League?"

"Yeah."

"Not exactly a basketball power, though, are they?"

"Not at all. Thought I'd get an education, since they were good enough to offer it along with the scholarship."

"You got injured, as I remember."

"Blew my knee out, first week. May have been the best thing that ever happened to me."

"You could have been another Larry Bird. . . . Well, a shorter one. Mark Price, maybe."

"There's only one Larry Bird," said Billy with a respect both men shared. "And I wasn't half as good as people remember. I seem to get better every year."

"I know how good you were. I was there. . . . You run for sheriff, you got my vote, Billy."

"I'm not running for sheriff."

"Hell, I'll write you in, then. . . . What brings you, Billy?"

"Thought I'd like to see you."

"Yeah, yeah. What else?"

"I have a name stuck in my mind and I think I know it, but I can't quite remember it. I'm pretty sure he's an athlete. I thought maybe you'd remember."

"Who is it?"

"Odette Collins."

"Whoa, that goes back a bit, doesn't it?"

"Do you know who he is?"

"Oh, sure. It's not like Nebraska's got that many homegrown professional athletes. Not that he's homegrown, exactly. He was from Omaha Central." Omaha was like another country to those who lived in the vast interior of the state. There was Nebraska, with its farms and ranches and small towns, and then there was Omaha, a real city with a real *inner* city, crime, racial problems, and all the rest, clinging like a hulking and unwelcome interloper to the shore of the Missouri River. Its population and industry skewed the entire state away from its agricultural nature, tilting things its way like a giant on a play-ground teeter-totter. The city was resented and mistrusted and its citizens, particularly its nonwhite citizens, were considered somehow less than Nebraskan.

"Right, he played for Central," Billy said.

"Terrific football player at the U. Was in the pros there for a couple years. . . . Played basketball for Central, too. But I'm surprised you don't remember him. You burned him for thirty-seven points in the championship game."

"Of course. That was Collins."

"Well, he was one of them they tried to guard you with. They used a zone, too. You don't remember that? I'd of thought for sure you'd remember that game."

"Must be my advancing age," Billy said, but he knew it was not. Memory needed exercise to function well, but since leaving Falls City for Cornell and then his years in the Secret Service, Billy had delib-erately *not* exercised the memories of his youth. Too many of them featured Lord Jimmy Tree, as drunk as he could manage, being deliv-ered to the door late at night by a policeman either too sympathetic or too fruitlessly enamored of Billy's beautiful mother, Annie; of Lord Jimmy still sleeping on the floor at midday when Billy brought home playmates; of Lord Jimmy and his brothers braying about legendary Irish courage while they goaded the boy into dubious battle with cousins and neighborhood children. For many years before the onset of puberty turned his fists and feet into truly dangerous weapons that neither cousin nor neighbor nor passing stranger wanted to risk, Billy had been raised like a fighting cock. For his own good, they said. So he could withstand the blows of a hostile world, for the greater glory of the Irish-American community, or just for the entertainment of his beery father and uncles, he was pushed into fights with anyone they could dragoon into the job, usually older, bigger kids who started with sympathetic reserve for the little boy, then found themselves struggling desperately as Billy tore into them with a skill and ferocity beyond his years. The uncles would cheer his triumphs, sneer at his tears, and push him back for more battle while Lord Jimmy looked on, a drink in hand, proud as any Guatemalan cock trainer with his prize rooster. By the time Billy reached his teens and began to add muscle to his quickness and cunning, the uncles' fighting cock was well on his way to becoming a pit bull.

At a reunion for the extended Keefe/Tree clan, following the fried chicken and potato salad and bottle after bottle of beer, they formed a ring and sent their fourteen-year-old protégé into combat against an eighteen-year-old cousin twice removed, a red-haired, freckle-faced, two-hundred-pound football player, as Irish and redoubtable as any mick champion right off the boat. Billy took out the boy's knee with his first move and was in the process of pounding his squalling face into the dirt with a grip on his ears when they pulled him off. The bigger boy was helped to his feet, where he puked from the pain and fainted.

Billy found his father passed out under the picnic table, where he had slept throughout the fight. He nudged him awake with the toe of his boot. " 'Twas a fair fight," said Lord Jimmy, blinking himself awake. From that moment on, Billy turned his athletic abilities to more civilized sports and began his experiment in selective amnesia.

After leaving the coach, Billy slid into his car and felt the lump of the noose in his pocket pressing against his thigh. He reached for his keys and rubbed his fingers against the synthetic smoothness of the cord, the tangled complexity of its loop. Was the hangman's knot a gift—or reminder—from someone from that past that he had worked so hard to forget? Someone whose grievance was beyond salving by Billy's smile or charm? Apparently, it was someone he shared with Judge Sunder, which might mean that someone was expressing dissatisfaction with the local legal system, but then why had Billy been the only member of the department to get a noose? Why not Lapolla? Or was there some other connection between Billy and Sunder? But the judge was a man he scarcely knew, although Sunder had claimed to be friendly with his father. Just what that meant was anyone's guess, and Billy assumed it was just a bit of political politesse on Sunder's part. Being friendly with the town drunk meant no more than petting the local dogs. How far back into Lord Jimmy's past would one have to go to find him without a bottle in his hand? Billy shook his head to clear the thought. He resented having to think about it.

CHAPTER SIX

L ike any man with a permanently guilty conscience, Lowell Briggs, the motel operator, tried with fulsome eagerness to accommodate the law, but he could find no record of Odette Collins ever having been in his establishment. According to the card filled out by the occupant himself, the man in Collins's room the night of the event by the pool was one Wilson Pickett of St. Louis, address indecipherable, no automobile registration listed.

"No car?" Billy asked.

The motel operator looked at the registration with wondering incomprehension.

"No car?" Briggs said as if laboring with a foreign tongue.

"Looks that way," Billy said, grinning at the operator's display of incredulity. The man turned the card around and squinted at it as if decoding ancient scripts. "Hard to credit, isn't it?"

Briggs tapped the empty space on the card.

"Huh," he offered.

"Supposed to get a vehicle ID there, Lowell."

"Don't know what happened."

"Could be he walked?"

The operator regarded Billy closely to see if he was joking, or offering an out.

"You think?"

"This a black male, late thirties, shaven head, dressed in overalls?"

"That's him."

"Can you read that home address, Lowell?"

"You know, I can't."

"Wasn't Wilson Pickett a pop singer?"

"Really?"

"One of those guys, you hear his name in a compilation of hit songs from the sixties or seventies on late-night television."

" 'A compilation of hits,' Billy?"

"I'll stand by that wording."

"So you mean I had a celebrity singer in my place?"

"Uh, no, Lowell. I don't think this is the same guy. I think this was a guy who gave you a false name, a home address you can't read, and no license number for his car."

"Celebrities sometimes like to go anonymous."

"No, Lowell."

"Just saying."

"Tell you what, Lowell. Seeing as you didn't do real well in getting the appropriate information this time around, if this guy shows up again—"

"Wilson Pickett?"

"The guy with the bald head, whatever name he happens to be using . . . if he shows up again, you give me a call. Right away."

"Right away?"

"Right away. You can get his autograph later."

"He looked kind of shifty."

"Shifty, huh?"

"You know how they do."

"Who?"

"They got that attitude, you know? That 'in your face' stuff, makes you want to pop them in the snoot."

"Did you want to pop Wilson Pickett in the snoot, Lowell? You never struck me as a masochist."

"You know what I mean."

"Not really."

"You can't trust them . . . I'm not saying all of them."

"Just some of them."

"Yeah."

"Just the ones you can't trust. . . . How do you know you can't trust those?"

"You can smell it on them. . . . You mad at me, Billy?"

"Do I sound mad?"

"You look a little miffed."

"You can't smell untrustworthiness, Lowell. You can't smell anything about a person's character. Unless you've got a nose like a hound."

"It's a figure of speech."

"It's not one I care for."

"I'm just saying there's something about those people. You know what I mean."

"No, I don't."

But of course he did. That's what made him angry, not Lowell Briggs's prejudice, but his own.

"What'd he do, Billy?" Briggs asked as Billy pushed through the glass door into the waiting wall of heat.

"So far . . . he gave false information on a motel registration."

Billy could hear the mocking smile on Briggs's face; he did not need to turn to see it. It was the "So far" that gave him away. The same presumption of guilt shared by Briggs and probably everyone else in the town. Whatever Odette Collins/Wilson Pickett was up to, it was assumed to be no good, and no amount of exposure to the world, no sermonizing, not even time spent with black partners could totally erase that assumption.

Feeling a little dirty, Billy turned the car south, toward Kansas.

* * *

The boy had grown to look startlingly like his father, and at first glance, Billy had to convince himself that he wasn't looking at Duane Blanchard himself, seventeen again, lean and with that absence of body fat that people call "raw-boned." Cheekbones as sharp as his elbows, the skin so taut across his face, it looked like the bones might pop through. Will wore a brown Stetson low on his forehead, hiding half his face. It was meant to appear cool, no doubt, rugged and insouciant in the traditional cowboy way, but Billy thought it just made him look mean and untrustworthy. The flamboyant western shirt boasted pearl buttons and extra stitching around the pockets, but it was at least a size too big for him. Billy wondered if it had belonged to his father. The blue jeans were old and faded, or manufactured to look that way, and frayed on the ends, where they creased over the cowboy boots. As he sauntered toward the chute where he would board his mount, hands tucked into his rear pockets in an emulation of casualness that he could not have felt, Will Blanchard looked as if a strong wind would blow him away—and as if you'd cut your hand if you tried to catch him.

Duane Blanchard had looked just like that—and had turned out like that, too, with a streak of evil that went beyond mean. Billy could often not look at the boy without conjuring visions of his father battling with him in the river, each blow of his lead-weighted gloves further loosening Billy's grip on consciousness, his thin-lipped mouth taunting, then snarling with the exertion of the next punch. With an effort Billy dispelled the memory. Who was he, son of Lord Jimmy Tree, to blame Will for Duane? The sins of the father were buried with him, or so he fervently hoped.

At 41,000 souls, Salina was a large town for this part of the country, and they turned out a boisterous, vocal crowd for their rodeo. The same riders and mounts, ropers and clowns had appeared in towns less than half the size, with audiences smaller still, grinding out a semiliving with their sweat and risk and outdated, untransferable skills. Will had done well to make the draw in a site like this. It would have been a spot much contested, Billy realized. Whether or not he had talent would be difficult to judge in a single ride—how much skill could be displayed in five seconds aboard a furious bull?—but Billy was certain the boy had a high degree of determination and sheer cussedness.

He was on a Brahma named Widow Maker (there was one in every rodeo), and it came out twisting wildly, like a two-ton cat stung by a bee and chasing its tail at the same time. When it bucked, it seemed to take Will by surprise, and he flew off, his right hand suspended over his head for a fraction of a second with a balletic grace that looked like part of some eccentric choreography. The bull considered mashing Will into the dirt of the arena but missed the first strike as the boy rolled quickly away; then it was distracted and gave a clown perfunctory chase before stopping in the middle of the stadium, looking around aimlessly at the audience in the bleachers, then at the dust that its hooves had just stirred up, perhaps trying to recall what it had been so angry about seconds before.

Will's ride on the bronco was better than on the bull, but not good enough to get him into the money. Afterward, Billy found Will pulling off the glove on his gripping hand, and he fought back another memory of Duane's weighted gloves, hard as brass knuckles.

"Good rides," he said. "Almost made it on the bronc."

Will was startled to see him there. The dust that coated his face was streaked by rivulets of sweat, giving him the appearance of a man as yet imperfectly formed from dirt.

"That horse wasn't a great ride," Billy said, giving the boy time. The better the horse bucked, the more points a rider scored. No one sought easy mounts.

Will hitched at his pants. "Might's well been riding a dairy cow."

"Luck of the draw, I guess."

Will's eyes looked past Billy, searching.

"She couldn't come," Billy said, hoping the boy would not ask for details.

"What are you doing here?"

"Felt like a rodeo. Thought I'd see my favorite rider go at it big time."

The boy blinked at him, then squinted and adjusted his hat lower.

"Just showing the flag," Billy said. "Thought you'd like a little support."

"I don't need that," Will said.

"Everyone can use a little support," Billy said. "Nothing wrong with a rooting section as you go through life."

"Not you. I don't need it from you."

Billy did not know how to respond. He looked away from Will's unfriendly gaze, focusing on the boots of a passing barrel racer. He was not unaccustomed to animosity—no one liked being arrested—but not from someone he was trying to befriend. Not from someone so young. Not as directly as a spit in the face.

"A good crowd . . ." Billy stumbled through some meaningless chatter, trying to recover himself. He could not believe how much the boy's remark had hurt him.

"So, don't bother to come. All right?"

"I'm on your side, Will. . . ."

"I haven't got a side. You're fucking her, not me."

Will turned and walked away, already affecting the half limp, half roll of his profession.

Billy leaned against the fence for a moment, his face burning. It was a very long ride home.

The photographer stared stupidly at first, not really believing what was clearly before him. He lowered the camera to check with his naked eye what the lens was telling him. Unlike the men in the crowd, he had not been born and bred in farm country. He had arrived recently from Chicago, hoping to establish a career for himself with his camera, and he had no knowledge of the harder life they led. Although of good size and an athlete in high school only the year before, he often felt ineffectual and effete around these men with horny hands, these strong and sinewy men whose muscles were formed by labor, not exercise. Even the more intelligent among them, the bankers and attorneys and doctors, seemed to have grown up with shovels and axes and pitchforks in their hands—he was the son of a tailor and had studied the clarinet at an age when these men were heaving bales of hay over their heads, swinging weight as easily as he did sheet music. He had missed the war, too, and although they all told him he was lucky, he knew that he was not, that he had missed a chance at initiation into manhood that could never be acquired in any other way.

He had to fight his stomach, which wanted to betray him. He focused on the body of the black man that was still swinging slightly, the pendulum motion winding down long after the twitching had stopped. None of the men seemed queasy; only the boys who stood on the fringe of the crowd, closest to him, appeared to be troubled by the sight. The smallest of them had been weeping and another, obviously his brother, had his arm around the smaller boy's shoulder, trying to comfort him.

The photographer took a picture, hurriedly, as he remembered why he had raced out from the town. It was a bad one; he knew it even as he snapped the shutter—too fast, poorly framed. He thought of the great war correspondent photographers whose work he had so admired. They had managed with shells bursting around them, with men dying right and left, showing a courage and a nerve that shamed him.

Some of the men closest to him became aware of his presence, and then those next to them, and soon a ripple moved through the crowd. Within a moment or two, everyone had turned to face his camera. He felt such a surge of power. Him, they were all focused on him, these older, stronger, superior men. With a wave of his hand, he beckoned them closer together, and they obliged, moving instinctively toward the center of the frame, the hanged black man. Someone next to the victim seemed to understand the problem of motion blurring the picture, and he held a hand against the black man's leg until he stopped swinging and hung straight as a plumb line.

He snapped the shot, then two more in quick succession, desperate to get it before they lost interest. When he lifted his eye from the viewfinder, he knew that he done it. He had captured the shot of his life, frozen it in time, a scene as heroic in its own way as Capra's photo of the Spanish soldier at the precise instant he was hit by a bullet. There was an artistry to it that most people did not understand; they thought it was dumb luck to catch the exact action at the exact moment, but he understood and felt that he had been blessed.

CHAPTER SEVEN

T he next obscenity waited in an envelope on his porch. It had been addressed in pencil simply to "Tree," delivered by hand and dropped on the porch. Or carefully placed perhaps.

Billy put it on his kitchen table. It was a six-by-nine-inch envelope, available virtually anywhere. He dug under the sink until he found a pair of yellow dish-washing gloves. He tugged them on, then held it to the light and saw the shape of a postcard within. Nothing else—no explosive device, no scorpions or poison darts. Why then did he fear it was going to blow up in his face? Why such trepidation about something so innocent? The noose had upset him. If this new delivery had to do with the noose, and he assumed it did, was it not intended to upset him still further? Wasn't there an escalation in matters like this? . . . What matters like this? he wondered. He did not know what the noose was all about, and he certainly wouldn't know anything more about the envelope until he opened it. He fought down an urge to toss it in the wastebasket and forget all about it. Instead, he carefully pried open the metal fasteners holding it shut. The flap was not sealed, which meant that no one had licked it. Everyone understood about DNA these days, it seemed. Or thought they did. Not that anyone in the county had the resources to apply the relevant technology in the first place, not without miles of forms and weeks of waiting.

He lifted the envelope and tipped its contents on the table, where it sat like an unanswerable insult.

It was a postcard, as he had thought—or rather, a copy of a very old postcard that had turned yellow with age. The copy captured the look of age accurately, the cracking and discoloration applied to new paper stock. Billy looked at the picture, winced, then turned it over. The reverse side was blank, no space for an address, no dotted rectangle for affixing a stamp, nothing. Someone had copied the picture but had never intended to send it through the mail. Not that it would have been delivered. The picture itself made that illegal.

Reluctantly, Billy turned the postcard back to the side with the picture, holding it by its edges, as if it were a piece of filth. Like a child who had been told not to look, he tried to keep his eyes away from the awful central image, but they would flit there of their own accord, then recoil as if scalded. He couldn't look and he couldn't ignore it.

No physical signs of age were necessary to tell him it was an old photograph. More than anything, it was the hats that dated the event—wide-brimmed fedoras, the kind he saw only in old movies and newsreels, the kind he associated—he didn't know why—with Harry Truman. Many of the men wore white shirts and neckties, ties so short that they looked as if they had been cut in half with a scissors, loosely and clumsily knotted. Those without ties wore their shirts buttoned to the neck. Even some of the boys sported neckties. It was an age of greater formality, which seemed to be reflected in their erect posture, as well. Those in front stood with their chests thrust forth, obviously posing, and those in the rear ranks craned their necks and tilted their chins, straining to get into the picture and acting as if it were as important to see the camera as to be seen by it. But ultimately, the fashions would have made no difference, for it was the faces themselves that seemed to come from another age: sunburned skin, eyes looking wider and brighter against the darkened flesh, and haircuts that knew nothing of razor cuts or gel or styling. Ears seemed to protrude more than they did today; cowlicks were untamed; Adam's apples stuck out. They were who they were, and made no effort to hide it. Long faces, high cheekbones, square foreheads, hair and eyebrows fair—they were Germans by ancestry, English, Scandinavian, the people who had settled the plains before the sprinkling of Irish and Mediterranean peoples who had drifted west after World War II. They were the parents and grandparents of the people Billy had known all his life, hovering somewhere in time between immediately recognizable and too far in the past for him to relate to at all.

Many of them beamed at the camera, as if proud to be there, proud of the occasion. There was certainly no sense of shame, no hint of guilt. They were just ordinary people, happy to be present at a spectacle.

Finally, Billy forced his eyes to take in the central focus of the picture. Dangling from a tree whose branch was barely visible at the top of the frame was a young black man, a rope around his neck. His face pointed directly skyward, as if seeking a final glimpse of the sun. Because of the camera angle, his bare feet seemed to hover directly over the head of an oblivious local burgher, looking as if a slight extension of his toes could provide him with relief from the awful mortal tension of the rope. Or, if the viewer believed in such things, as if the hanged man's spirit were rising directly from the crowd and ascending to heaven. Billy could find no comfort in such a thought; there were no angels in this picture, nothing to glorify a triumph of the human spirit. The people in the happy crowd were witnesses, perhaps participants, at a lynching, and there was something about the young black man that indicated that he was only very recently dead. He was dressed as the others were in white shirt and dark pants. If he had ever worn a necktie, it was replaced now by the unforgiving hemp of the noose.

Billy broke away, unable to look any longer—not only because of the sight of the hanged man, although that was bad enough, but also because he had seen dead men before, even one frighteningly close to this. The painful memory of Walter Matuzak came to mind, his Secret Service partner suspended from the ceiling by a loop of piano wire, swinging and twitching like a marionette gone wild, while Avi Posner, smiling with his dragon teeth, shot from behind his body, doing his best to kill Billy as he lay on the floor. But Walter had been murdered by a madman. This young man had been killed by the good citizens of some rural town, someplace not unlike Falls City. Perhaps even worse than the lynching was the indifference to murder, the self-congratulatory appearance of the onlookers. Common people, simple men, merchants and farmers, by the look of them, totally unaware that they had done anything wrong and unaffected by the corpse that hung within a few feet of them. It looked, Billy thought with repugnance, as if they regarded the young man as not human at all, but just another hanging side of beef in a community that was inured to the results of butchery. The only novelty in the scene for these men was not the body they had watched die, but the camera that recorded their presence.

Billy went outside, feeling the need for air. Sitting on the porch, he watched the stars blink out one by one as dark clouds roiled across the sky. The cicadas and frogs had long since lapsed into silence, and the only sound was the wind that had ushered in the clouds moving distressfully across the face of the town. Thoughts of evil assailed him.

Who would send him such an ugly thing? Or perhaps that was the wrong question. What reaction had the sender hoped to get? Did he want Billy to feel a sense of unease? He had succeeded. Did he want Billy to feel a dread that something worse was going to happen? Again, he'd been successful. But did he want Billy to do anything? If he was trying to torment Billy, would it be sufficient for the sender to assume that he would be successful? It didn't seem quite enough. The man was taking a risk, after all. Someone might have seen him deliver the card and the noose, Billy might find out who he was— although in reality, Billy had no clue how to do so—and would the man find some abstract fulfillment sufficient to warrant the hazard?

Billy felt threatened by the anonymity of the two deliveries, but what if they were not threats, but warnings? Was someone trying to tell him he was in harm's way? If so, why take such a roundabout and uncertain way of doing it? Billy wondered if Judge Sunder had received a copy of the postcard, as well. But even if he had, that would not help Billy understand things any better. He didn't know what his connection with Sunder was in the first place, other than their mutual involvement with the law. It was not as if Billy had apprehended someone and the judge had sent him away to prison and now he was back, lusting for vengeance. Such an idea was luridly attractive in its simplicity, but it had not happened. Billy had been in his current position for little over a year, and the worst thing he had dealt with had been traffic accidents on the county roads.

He was unable to go back inside his house; it seemed haunted by the presence of the postcard. Ignoring the cloying heat, he walked toward Joan's house. She would be asleep, no doubt, but if she weren't, he would tell her about his visit to the rodeo, omitting the hurtful nature of his encounter with her son. If her mood was right, they would make love. If she could use sex to relieve her tensions, so could he.

The wind was his only companion in the sleeping town, pushing at his back, urging him along. Billy had spent many nights on patrol cruising slowly through the neighborhoods, the only car on the road, the only soul still awake, and usually it made him feel like the town's protector, keeping harm at a distance with his vigilance. Tonight, it made him feel like a part of that harm, whatever it was going to be, a tainted, haunted man, forced to walk the streets pathetically alone and under cover of darkness, a man who had somehow drawn trouble to himself.

By the time he reached Joan's house, the clouds had covered the face of the night sky entirely and the rumble of distant thunder could be heard in the north. Although he would not have thought it possible, the humidity had risen. His shirt clung to his body and he pulled it away periodically, shaking it to create a breeze next to his skin. Joan's house was completely dark, as he had expected it to be. Disappointed even though he was not certain that he was up to coping with the vagaries of Joan's humors at the moment, he sat wearily in the aluminum rocking chair that served as her porch furniture. The nylon webbing groaned slightly under his weight and a board on the porch creaked in protest.

In the north, the first strike of lightning was visible as a diffuse illumination obscured by layers of cloud. The thunder, when it came, was muted and distant. Billy rocked gently, enjoying the sense of rhythm created by the squeaking board. His back was to the house and his eyes went first to the empty road, the town's lifeline to the world, now lifeless, as somnolent as the citizens, and then to the sky, where he watched the inexorable approach of the storm, each flash a little brighter than the one before. The wind had picked up and was beginning to make more aggressive sounds of its own as it whistled against the reeds of telephone lines and rattled the leaves of bushes and trees.

He had relaxed, awaiting the storm and enjoying nature's show, when he heard a noise from the house. Something low, not unlike the distant thunder, and then a voice—or rather, a human sound, a half moan, half mew. Will was still away at his rodeo; it had to have come from Joan. A pause, and then it sounded again, longer this time. At first, he thought it was Joan reacting to a dream, but it soon developed into the unmistakable metronomic noise of her lovemaking, each sigh more protracted, a mix of pleasure and strain, as if she were pulling the joy upward with a bodily effort. He could picture her head thrown back, her teeth clenched, her whole body quivering with tension. There was nothing placid about her lovemaking; she attacked it as though it were an embedded treasure to be wrenched from both of them by effort and persistence. Normally, he thrilled to her noises as they filled his head and egged him on to greater endeavor, but now they struck him with alarm. He should not be here; he should not be listening.

He told himself to leave the porch, walk away from the house, and leave her with some privacy and himself with some vestige of dignity, but he was riveted to the chair, straining to hear. Even the growing light display did not distract him. The storm was moving rapidly toward the town, the lightning strikes coming one after the other now, illuminating the heavens like a strobe, but Billy did not see them. He was looking only with his inner eye, picturing Joan thrashing on the bed, nearly snarling now with effort, and urging someone on. He had sensed from the beginning that she was not alone, and now a man's voice had entered the mix, also subverbal, muted yet surprised, as if startled by the onrushing pleasure.

Billy felt a chill as he realized what he was hearing. There was no sense of outrage, no impulse to burst into the bedroom and wreak havoc. He felt a deep sinking of despair and humiliation. His Joan was "possible" after all.

An enormous clap of thunder struck the town, startlingly close. Billy looked to the sky and realized with surprise that the storm was upon them. A block away, a light went on in a house as a sleeper was shaken awake by the great noise, and from behind him came the sound of Joan crying out. The first drops of rain fell with audible plops, huge and cold and thinly spaced, like commas punctuating the enveloping noise. Billy rose and left the porch, stepping into the storm.

He walked to the back of the house to see whose car was parked in the alley. The rear window of Joan's car reflected the lighting flashes through the eye-level window of the garage door, but there was no other vehicle to be seen. Had she driven him here, or did he live close enough to walk? Everyone in town lived close enough to walk. By the time he turned back toward the house, the rain began in earnest. His instinct was to run for cover, but there was nowhere to run except back to the porch, and he knew he could not shelter there.

Ashamed of himself, he moved to the window of Joan's bedroom. There was nothing to hear now, and any but the loudest of voices would be obscured by the noise of the rain. If they were still in there, if they were moving about, if they were whispering endearments into each other's ears, he could not tell. He did not look in—the humiliation of being caught as a Peeping Tom would be too much to bear. Even the act of spying on her, whether he was caught or not, would do too much damage to his self-esteem, or what there was left of it after this assault.

Unless he wanted to wait all night outside her house, there was nothing for it but to walk home in the rain. He went slowly as the water pelted, then flooded down, forcing himself as a kind of penance to walk slower the harder it fell. It made him feel like a complete fool, sloping home in disgrace like the village idiot, too dumb to come in out of the torrential rain, the crashing of thunder matching his mood completely.

He had gone only a few blocks when he caught sight of a motion in the light of a streetlamp on Stone Street, which ran parallel to Harlan. It was just a flicker of a shadow moving through the light, but he knew it was a man on the run. Joan's lover, streaking for shelter.

Billy ran to Stone Street and looked north, into the heart of the storm, but saw only a sheet of water, dotted here and there by streetlights. In the distance, now several blocks hence, a darkness seemed to move quickly through the light, but it was too far away to make it out clearly. He wanted to believe that it was nothing, that the whole episode was nothing, a cruel trick of his own imagining. Already upset by the postcard of the lynching, deceived by the roar of the storm, he had heard things that hadn't happened, seen things that never were. Suddenly, a bolt of lightning struck immediately overhead and the entire town was illuminated as if by a gargantuan flashbulb. Frozen on Billy's retina was the shape of a man, running, undeniable.

For a moment, Billy gave chase, even though he was several blocks behind, but futility and humiliation weighed him down and he stopped, peering into the waterfall, as the dark shape of the man disappeared entirely. Whatever point there was for the man to run, it could not have been from any hope to stay dry. Billy was soaked from scalp to socks.

The man was running out of territory. Whoever he was, he was still sprinting past Twenty-second Street. Within another two blocks, he would reach the elementary school, and after that the edge of town. Billy tried to think who lived in that section of town, a man young enough and fit enough to make the run, old enough to be his cuckolder. There were a few, and he knew them all. It was a humbling business to ponder whether Joan would prefer any of them to him.

CHAPTER EIGHT

K ath discovered her brother sitting cross-legged on her front porch when she came downstairs in the morning to make her coffee. The rain had washed away the heat and there was an autumnal crispness to the early-morning air, but Billy had removed his shirt and was bare-chested, his head leaning back against the siding, his eyes closed, like a supplicant waiting for the sun.

"Tough night?" she asked. Since Billy's return to Falls City two years ago, Kath had grown accustomed to the eccentricities of his behavior. She tried to take them as matter-of-factly as he did himself, even though they often offended her sense of order. Nothing about the men in her life had turned out the way she would have planned it, and her brother was no exception.

"I've had better," he said. His eyes were still closed. He sniffed the air.

"Coffee?"

"Please," he said.

Kath took the opportunity to study the scars on his torso. After he was shot, she had nursed him back to health in his old bedroom in this same house and had seen them many times, but they were less angry than they had been, and they frightened her less now that she knew he was all right. The scars had become part of the landscape of his body, red puckers and ridges amid the topography of flesh, muscle, and hair. The worst was a hogback that meandered a full eight inches, from beneath his belt to well above his navel, a permanent zipperlike reminder of where the surgeons had gone in to mend his perforated colon.

She did not ask why he had come to her like this—Kath did not demand explanations of her men—but she knew he turned to her when he was troubled, and the thing that troubled him most in his new life was that woman. Kath always referred to her that way, "that woman," namelessness conveying contempt more completely than obloquy.

She gave him towels, coffee, and breakfast, but she would not give him comfort. Like a mother with an ill-behaved child, she went through the motions of nurture but withheld the warmth. If he wanted to talk about his woes, he would have to initiate the topic; she was not going to do it for him.

Billy knew he was loved, although often disapproved of, and the proximity of that love was all he required at the moment—and all that he expected. He could not speak of Joan's betrayal to his sister without hearing an "I told you so," even it were tactfully left unsaid. There would also be an element of disloyalty on his part were he to say anything against Joan to someone who disliked her so intensely. He was not ready to do that. Fidelity was all he had to cling to at the moment.

* * *

His message machine was blinking admonishingly, reminding him that he had not checked it the previous night, but had left the house right after viewing the postcard. The postcard was still on the table, its image a reminder of malice. He turned it facedown and tended to his messages. The first was from Joan.

"Billy, don't come by the house tonight. I've gone to Auburn to baby-sit for Margie's kids." Margie was Joan's younger sister. "I may stay overnight. I'll call you when I get back. . . . Bye."

He played the message again, listening for the lie in the voice. If she was a good liar, he wouldn't hear it; he knew that from his years of conducting interviews for the Secret Service. Only the nervous liars gave themselves away. The professionals had already convinced themselves of the truth of their misstatements before the words left their mouths. Even polygraphs were gullible for a really good liar. Billy had no idea how skilled a liar Joan was. This was the first time he had caught her at it.

". . . I may stay overnight. I'll call you when I get back. . . . Bye."

The slight hesitation before the farewell, the uncertainty of how to end the message—therein lay Billy's best hope for rationalization. Was it a moment's doubt that had caused the slight flutter? Had she considered taking it all back, telling him the truth? Or had she been selecting the proper valediction for a message that would make possible her infidelity? Had her few words been enough, or had she pondered the need to embellish, wondering if a more elaborate cover story was required? Had she thought of concluding by saying, "I love you, Billy" but found the words sticking in her throat? Had she been seeking details to embellish her tale, or grappling without success for the endearment that might somehow show her affection as well as regret?

Billy listened once more, worrying the place that hurt, hoping the pain would make the deeper wound go away. It didn't work.

The second message was from Lowell Briggs, the motel operator. It had come in late the night before, about the time Billy'd been dealing with the postcard. There was no need to guess whether Briggs was nervous or not, because he'd made no attempt to hide it, but Billy did not think it was because he was lying.

"Billy, uh, Sheriff Tree, this is Lowell Briggs over to the motel? We got another black man here. This one is named . . . Otis Redding, but, huh, here's the thing—he looks like the other guy. Sort of. I don't know, I'm no expert, but he's the same type of guy, you know? The shaved head and everything? But he's got a different name, so, I don't know. But you wanted me to let you know, so I'm letting you know, sort of, I mean—I don't know. He's here anyway, or he was. He checked in about half an hour ago, but then I got a call from my wife and sort of forgot. . . . This is Lowell Briggs at the motel, by the way."

The third call had come in sometime while Billy was standing in the downpour, watching the retreating figure of the running man disappear into the darkness. The first few words were an indecipherable jumble; then Billy recognized the voice of his Uncle Sean.

". . . your jail. I'm fine, boyo. Don't you worry about me, tough as nails. Can't kill a Tree, you know, hard as the fucking rocks of Ireland. . . . If I'd seen him coming, he never would have laid a hand on me. . . ."

It was a familiar bluster of boast and self-serving sentiment, Sean's staple when in his cups. He frequently called Billy when he had driven away all other listeners, ranting drunkenly about his exploits, recent and long past. All hollow, as far as Billy knew. If Sean had accomplished anything of note in his life, it was managing to keep his farm intact for forty years with no visible means of support. It was a family trait, Billy thought ruefully. Sean's older brother, Lord Jimmy, had done the same, somehow putting bread on the table, with enough left over to drink himself unconscious most nights.

". . . supposed to see him when it's that dark?"

Billy realized he had not been paying attention. It was the only way to get through his uncle's tirades, and Billy had come to prefer hearing them over the telephone. At least he did not have to look at Sean's ruddy complexion stoked to the point of combustion by alcohol, his eyes alternately squinting and opening wide as he tried to hang on to his thoughts by the strength of his facial muscles. It was all too painfully reminiscent of his youth.

Another voice intruded suddenly.

"Billy, it's Schatz." Deputy Sheriff Douglas Schatz, usually the duty officer for the midnight-to-eight shift. "He's at the office when you can get here."

"Don't tell your aunt!" Sean bellowed from the background.

"He's not arrested," Schatz said. "He's been assaulted."

"Ambushed! He jumped me from behind!"

Billy heard a brief struggle for control of the phone, then Schatz's voice again, fighting to remain patient. "As soon as you can, please." Schatz hesitated, looking for a means of emphasis. "Please," he repeated plaintively.

Don't you want to see him, Billy?" asked Lapolla.

Dealing with his uncle in a hungover state was no better than listening to him bluster when drunk, but Billy did not feel it politic to offer details to the acting sheriff. It was family policy to deny what was public knowledge.

"Tell me our side of it first," Billy said.

Lapolla chuckled at "our side."

"Rubin, the bartender down at the Sportsman's, says Sean left there about eleven o'clock last night. No drunker than usual. Able to drive, according to Rubin."

Billy had been on some of those late-night rides with his uncle. Sean always managed to avoid most living things, but his truck attested to frequent contact with the inanimate. Sean was blessed to be living in a part of the country where there was very little traffic at the hour when he normally wended his way home.

Lapolla continued. "Sean says he was almost to his pickup when the perpetrator jumped out of the shadows and hit him with a blunt object. Sean fought back and says he nearly knocked the guy out."

"He's a scrapper, our Sean," said Billy, unable to keep a trace of the mocking brogue from his voice.

Lapolla shrugged. "His knuckles are a little scraped. He must have got in a punch or two anyway. He thinks there might have been another man involved."

"No other way to explain his losing a fight. Numerous assailants."

"I know. Still, maybe so. Anyway, somebody gave him a shot or two, that's for sure. Took his wallet and ran off, left Sean on the sidewalk."

"No witnesses, I suppose."

"At eleven last night? With that storm? What idiot would be out on the streets?"

What idiot indeed, agreed Billy silently.

"Sean made his way back into the Sportsman's and Rubin called the police, who brought Sean to us."

This was hardly the first time that Sean Tree had fallen to the mercies of the local police for numerous variations on drunk and disorderly charges, nor was it the most imaginative excuse he had come up with to cover tripping on the curb and lying in the street, baying at the moon. Why, Billy wondered, was everyone taking it more seriously this time?

"Why didn't they keep him?"

"Well, he *is* your uncle. Also, they think the crime is going to fall under our jurisdiction."

"Why?"

"The perpetrator is out of the city limits."

"Are we sure there's a perpetrator? Sean's fought a few phantom opponents in his time."

"We're sure."

"And how do we know this?"

"He gave us an accurate description, for one thing. The perpetrator is at the motel, which is just over the town line."

"He's at the motel waiting for us, or what?"

"Lowell says he thinks he's in his room. Whether he's waiting for us, or sleeping, or whatever the hell else they get up to, I don't know."

"Bert, what the hell are you talking about?"

"The assailant was a black man with a shaven head. Lowell's got one checked in out there. You know any others in town?"

A man running in the rain, a man Billy had feared was fleeing Joan's house. But the man had been on Stone Street. The Sportsman's Bar was on Stone, as well. Billy didn't know if he was relieved or just more confused.

"I've seen a lot of black men with shaven heads."

"In Falls City?"

Billy shrugged. If the motel registration cards were correct, there had been two in a few days. Otis Redding and Wilson Pickett. It seemed highly unlikely that they weren't both Odette Collins, but it was an assumption he didn't care to cede to Lapolla.

"Could be. Why not?"

"Why not? I agree, Billy. This is a lovely community; you'd think blacks would leave the ghetto in droves to come here."

"Is he from the ghetto?"

"You know what I mean."

"So why haven't you gone to the motel to question this guy, Bert?"

"I was waiting for you. You know how to talk to these people."

"Don't you watch television, Bert? You just say, You're under arrest, motherfucker. Spread 'em."

Lapolla glanced quickly around the office, as if expecting to see an audience of horrified matrons with children.

"Jees, Bill. Language."

"Sorry, Father Bert. I was just trying to give you a demonstration."

"Gina's in the other room," Lapolla said, lowering his voice.

"I've heard it before, Bert," Gina called from the switchboard. "Shocking, isn't it?"

Lapolla shook his head. "She *listens*," he whispered with disapproval. He pointed at his ear, as if Billy might not have understood him.

"Unlike us," Billy said.

"You know what I mean."

"I'm afraid I do, Bert. Most of the time."

"Anyway, I thought you might want to talk to your uncle before you go to the motel."

"I might. I'd hate to have you arrest a man with a shaven head when my uncle really saw a pink elephant."

"Me? I'm not going to arrest him. Why should I arrest him?"

"Because you're the acting sheriff?"

"Bill, I got all this stuff. . . ." He waved his hand at the debris on his desk.

"Just remember the magic word, Bert."

"Please?"

"No . . ."

"Motherfucker," Gina called from the other room. Her laughter ran all the way down the corridor as Billy walked to their single barred cell.

Sean sat in the corner, as if wedged there by a strong wind. His eyes were abnormally wide-open and he looked like he was viewing a parade of ghosts, but Billy recognized it as the way Sean dealt with the first few minutes of a hangover. For a man who had awakened in the state so many times, he always seemed peculiarly surprised at his distress. He's not very clear on cause and effect, my uncle, Billy thought.

"How are you, Sean?" The door of the cell was open, but Billy preferred to talk to him through the bars. "You're looking a mite . . . wan."

"Wan, is it? Bejesus, I'm not feeling wan, that's for sure." His eyes came into focus and he squinted at Billy. "I'm feeling like they went after me with a bag of bricks last night."

Sean gingerly touched the welt on his right cheekbone. A matching lump adorned his forehead just above his eye.

"Who's they?"

"There was a bunch of them, that's for sure."

"A team effort, was it?"

"The bastards."

Sean waggled his right fist, proudly displaying the scraped skin like notches on his gun. He could have done that walking on his knuckles, Billy thought.

"I gave as good as I got, let me tell you. You don't take a Tree down without a fight."

"It was a famous victory for you, then."

"He'll remember me," Sean said grumpily. He checked his teeth with his thumb, then lifted his shirt for more self-examination. Billy had trouble looking at his uncle unclothed at the best of times. The ugly bruise above his heart did not improve matters any.

"He got you a good shot there all right," Billy said.

"I think it was a brick."

Or where you fell against the curb, thought Billy.

"Who was it, Uncle Sean?" He looked away from his uncle, studying the floor until the older man lowered his shirt over the soft pale skin. We Trees need more sun, he thought. Nature did not intend for the Irish to go topless. He wondered if he looked like that to Joan, then was immediately annoyed with himself for bringing her to mind.

"I only saw the one," Sean was explaining. "An evil-looking monkey."

"You were attacked by a monkey?"

"You know what I mean. He was a fucking ape. Biggest, blackest ape you ever want to see. Give me the terrors just to look at him, bald as a billiard ball and his head coming to a point. . . ."

"What did he say?"

"Say? Who knows if he could talk? And who could understand it if he did? You know how they are."

Why does everyone assume I'm an expert on the subject? Billy wondered. They didn't, of course. They assumed *their* knowledge was correct, based as it was on popular stereotype and prevailing prejudice. What they assumed of Billy was a predisposition different from their own. He had worked with "these people," lived with them in the cities, and from time to time expressed a sympathy toward them that he seemed to be daring his listeners to refute. More than anything, he didn't seem to be afraid of "these people," which was puzzling to a population raised with virtually no direct, personal exposure to any group but their own. They had learned what they knew of blacks from television, an education based on fear and contempt. They took Billy's overt manner for a facade, a bit of posturing akin to better table manners and a familiarity with opera, also necessary adjustments to living in a more sophisticated world. Underneath it all, deep in his Nebraska heart, they believed that he was just like them, disdainful and intimidated by color, and their reminders of "You know what I mean" were calls upon that basic understanding. The part that bothered Billy the most was that they might well be right.

"How big was he, Sean?"

"Fucking huge, Billy. Like a house."

"My height?"

"God no. A head taller. And wide as a barn."

"You were attacked by a black giant, Sean. Did you notice a bean stalk anywhere?"

"You don't believe me?"

"Faith, Sean, I think you do exaggerate a bit," Billy said in his brogue.

"It's a sad day when my own nephew doesn't believe me." He struggled to his feet, easing his back up the wall but never losing contact with it.

"I didn't say I don't believe you."

"Remember when I taught you how to box, Billy? Remember that? We cleared a space in the barn and I let you beat on me, just to get your confidence up?"

Although Lord Jimmy was only two years older, Sean had seemed younger by a generation. Not yet a prisoner of alcohol, he'd taught his nephew not only how to fight but also how to hunt, shoot, fish, throw a ball, and even how to tie a necktie. All the while, Lord Jimmy watched from the sidelines, a bottle close at hand, slowly nodding off. Billy remembered the ginger of Sean's hair—most of it now gone or turned to gray—the way his flesh glowed with exercise, so that the freckles stood out even more, the stentorian roar of his approval as he cheered Billy on. He had seemed a giant to the boy in those days before the bottle. Who was he to chide his uncle for seeing giants now?

"I remember," he said, meaning more than Sean knew.

"You didn't doubt me in those days. You did what I told you—ah, you were a grand pupil, Billy—that's why you turned out the way you did."

I turned out to be a quasi-official, sort of part-time deputy sheriff in an agricultural county slowly drifting into poverty and oblivion, Billy thought. And Sean is proud of it. Of course he doesn't see me that way; he sees a decorated Secret Service agent, a star athlete. A once and future hero. That was the thing about families: They clung so desperately to their delusions. They made up their minds early, and neither time nor facts could alter them. Lord Jimmy was a drunk, Annie, his wife, a saint, Billy a hero, sister Kath long-suffering, and Sean the paragon of uncles. Why can't I have the decency to still see him that way? Billy thought. He had come to look too much like his older brother. Billy could not help but see Lord Jimmy superimposed on the blurry features, the distracted eyes.

"I don't doubt you, Uncle Sean. I'm just trying to get a description I could use."

"You haven't called me that in years."

"Is that right?"

Sean lurched toward Billy, walking as if on nails, and embraced him suddenly. Billy was taken off balance, and he slumped against the bars, nearly dragging them both to the ground.

"You're a good boy," Sean said, patting his back. "Always such a good boy." He sounded close to tears. That was Sean's way, tough enough to gnaw off his own leg rather than cry from pain or loss, but as full of moisture as a squeezed sponge when easy bathos was involved. You could bang him on the head with a board and get nothing but abuse in return, but give him a tale of an orphan who befriends a stray dog and he'd blubber all day long.

Billy disengaged himself and started down the corridor, embarrassed by the sentimentality and also trapped by it. He was off now to interview the only black man in town in order not to insult an uncle.

"Oh, he did say something," Sean called after him. "I remember now."

"What?"

"Something about a dog."

Billy stared at his uncle for a moment before returning to Lapolla's office.

CHAPTER NINE

I haven't seen him all morning," said Lowell Briggs. "I've kept my eye out for him, but he hasn't shown his ugly mug outside the door yet." He nodded vigorously to indicate how diligently he had been working for the law.

"So he's in the room, then, you figure?" Lapolla asked.

"He wouldn't slip past me, you can bet on that. Not since I realized you were after him."

"Not after him," Billy corrected. "We just want to talk to him, not arrest him."

"Although we might arrest him," Lapolla said. It was as much a question as a statement.

"If it turns out he's a giant with Sean's wallet in his possession, then, yes, we might have to arrest him," Billy conceded.

"Oh, he's your man all right," said Briggs. "You can't very well miss him. It's not like he's going in disguise."

"I do believe he's going by an alias, though, Lowell," Billy said. "Unless you think this is really Otis Redding."

"Well, I couldn't say."

"Or is it Wilson Pickett?"

"You know how they look."

"So, in a manner of speaking, he could be in disguise after all, couldn't he, Lowell?"

"I didn't want to stare at him, you know, so I didn't get the best-possible look at him."

"You're staring at me, Lowell."

"I'm just *looking* at you, Billy."

"That ought to be good enough in most cases."

Lapolla stood by the door of the office, nervously eyeing the row of rooms. "You think he's alone?"

"Alone?"

"You know, Lowell. Alone. Anyone else with him?"

"I hadn't . . . uh . . . He's only registered for one."

"Might he have a guest?"

"Around here? Where's he going to get a guest in Falls City? Who'd go?"

"Just get the key," Billy said.

Lapolla was alarmed. "Are we going in?"

Briggs offered a key dangling from a pink plastic lozenge, but Billy waved it away.

"You bring it. You're the one who has the right to go into his room."

"Why would I go into his room? What would—listen, this is your deal."

Billy drew a deep breath and grinned widely. "Guys . . . I don't think he's in there chewing on human bones. That's a different giant. This man may be one of two dead rock and rollers, or he may be a former athlete, or he may be a man who assaulted my uncle while in search of his dog, or he may be none of those—actually, I don't know if Wilson Pickett is still alive or not. I hope he is—but at any rate, all we're going to do is knock on the door and ask this guy a few questions. If he's not there, maybe Lowell will enter for a little housekeeping. Okay?"

"I never said anything," Lapolla complained.

"What a minute," said Briggs. "You think Wilson Pickett might have killed himself in my room?"

"Lowell, Wilson Pickett is an alias. He and Otis Redding are famous rock singers from several decades ago."

"Not that famous," said Briggs. He appealed to Lapolla. "You ever heard of them?"

Lapolla did not answer. They walked past the pool, and Billy knocked when they reached the motel room's door.

"What if he's in there but won't come out?" Briggs asked. "What if I open the door and he's still in there?"

"You'll excuse yourself and withdraw," Billy said.

Billy knocked three times and waited for a reply each time. Finally, he turned to Briggs and with a little gesture invited him to open the door.

"Coming in," Briggs said loudly. "Housekeeping."

"That should do it," said Billy. Briggs had some trouble opening the door because he was standing to the side, presumably out of the line of fire. They watch too much television, Billy thought. They suffer fear that is taught to them by screenwriters and actors. When no rain of semiautomatic fire burst through the door, Briggs opened it and went inside. After a moment, Lapolla followed. Billy saw all that he needed from the doorway. The room was small and simple. Either the man was hiding under the bed or in the closet or he had exited through the bathroom window, which was wide-open.

"When is checkout time?" Billy asked.

"Eleven."

"I believe he's checked out," said Billy.

Lapolla exclaimed, "Whoa!" and retreated from the bathroom, holding his hand over his nose. Briggs rushed in immediately with proprietorial zeal. After a moment, he, too, recoiled.

"What a stink!"

"Smell that, Bill," said Lapolla, gesturing toward the bathroom.

"Why is it that when somebody says something smells bad, they want everyone else to take a whiff, too?" Billy asked.

Neither of his listeners was in the mood for speculation. They both waved him on.

"These people are animals," said Briggs. "I don't care what you say, you go around smelling like that . . ." The consequences eluded articulation and he settled for shaking his head in disgust.

"Smells like something died in there," said Lapolla, eager for Billy to experience it.

Reluctantly, Billy stepped into the tiny room. He realized immediately that the open window might have been for ventilation rather than egress. Lapolla was wrong, he thought. It did not smell like something had died. He knew the sickeningly sweet odor of putrefaction, and this was nothing like it. This was a much more familiar stench.

A T-shirt was bunched up in a corner of the tub, still wet after someone's attempt to wash it out. Water had done nothing to remove the stains. There was blood and something green and the dull brown of feces, as well as a few colors Billy could not easily name or identify. It reminded him with a visceral rush of his own garments when they took him to the hospital, riddled with holes and leaking from every one, covered in the shit and gore of his own body. There were no bullet holes in this shirt, however, at least none that Billy could see without handling it, which he was not going to do. The shirt smelled awful and would probably continue to do so after a proper washing in a machine. He wondered at the frugality of someone who would try to salvage such an eminently discardable garment. Unless, of course, there was something on the shirt that needed removal even before it went into the trash.

"Think we ought to bag it?" Lapolla asked. "Send it to a lab maybe?"

"Why?" Billy gazed out the open window, still troubled by the memory of himself after his shooting. Mewling and squalling like an infant, he thought. Out of control, out of courage, out of dignity. His body perforated, his self-esteem shredded even more. The wounds had all healed, leaving lumps as a reminder. The marks on his psyche seemed never to mend.

"Evidence?" Lapolla asked.

"Of what crime, Bert? You want to send this to Omaha on spec? They won't thank you for that. Assault isn't good enough to waste their time."

"Why would you want to bag pig shit?" Briggs demanded. "That's it for me. That's the last time I accommodate these people. I'm going to have to fumigate this room now."

"It looks to me like he was trying to clean himself up," said Billy.

"After doing what? Rolling in the hog wallow? And besides, I ain't no Laundromat."

"What's this?" Bert had knelt to look under the bed. Gingerly, he pulled out a sheet of bubble wrap and a roll of tape. The wrap had been cut raggedly along its length.

"Did you see him carrying anything around, any kind of package?" Billy asked.

Briggs shook his head.

"Looks like he had something he wanted to take good care of," said Billy.

"He must have took it with him."

"Well, yes, Lowell, I think he did. What kind of luggage did he have when he checked in?"

"Luggage?"

"Did he have luggage? Couldn't have been much, since he didn't seem to have a car."

"I can't remember if he had any. I don't think so."

"Don't most of your guests have some kind of bag with them, Lowell?"

"Well, not all of them. Unless you mean that other kind of bag." Briggs smiled unpleasantly, then realized that he might be incriminating himself in some way. The smile vanished precipitously. "We get some of that, but, hey, you know, we don't encourage it."

"How about a limp? Did this man have a limp?"

"You mean a . . . limp?"

"A hitch in his gitalong. You know what a limp is, Lowell. Did he walk funny, like he had a stiff leg?"

"No."

"Would you remember?"

"Well . . ."

"Because he had a pronounced limp when I saw him."

Briggs sucked on his lower lip. "He must have had a limp if you saw it. I just don't recall it. . . . Oh hell!"

Lapolla looked around nervously, as if expecting some further fright to leap from behind the door.

"What?"

"He didn't pay," said Briggs. He took a deep breath, then sighed with the air of someone whose faith had been betrayed. "You just can't trust them, can you? I'm sorry to say it, but you just can't trust them. I'm not a prejudiced man, you know that, but come on."

Billy regarded Lapolla, who was nodding slowly in agreement, convinced of the fairness of Briggs's conclusions as well as his self-assessment. Not a prejudiced man, Billy thought. And he truly believes it. He wondered if he was the only one who admitted to himself that he was prejudiced. It was easier to deny it, of course, because then there was no obligation to struggle against it. It was like cowardice, he realized. If Billy'd had the good sense to deny that he was a coward, he could have continued to bluster and boast like everyone else. But since he'd confessed to his fears, he felt that he had to grapple with them. It was a conflict that sometimes rendered him immobile. Thinking, he decided, was a dangerous thing to do.

He drove south on Harlan, slowing to a crawl as he approached Joan's block. As the school nurse, she had very little to do in the summer, so he hoped to find her outside. He sucked in his breath with his first glimpse. She was kneeling in the flower bed that bordered the front porch, her back to the road, but as he came abreast of her house in the car, she rose and stretched her back, one hand holding a trowel, the other pressed against her spine. She turned to face the road, totally unself-conscious about her bare legs, her bare midriff, the sweat that made her neck and chest glisten in the sun. God, she's lovely, he thought. Born to be looked at and admired and coveted. She caught sight of him and waved. Billy wanted to pull the car to the side, run into her yard, embrace her, confront her, something, anything, to break this terrible sense of longing and betrayal he felt when he saw her. But he could not. He found himself powerless to do anything except swivel his eyes to the road and pretend he did not see her.

At the edge of town, he made a U-turn, prerogative of law enforcement, and headed slowly back. He did not want to go. He felt like a boy being forced to fetch the switch for his own punishment, but he was powerless to stop himself. She was still in the yard, closer to the road now, as if expecting him. She waited with her hands on her hips, one of her favorite postures, stern and sexy. As he approached, she lifted her hands, palms up, a gesture of curiosity. He glanced at her, away, and then back at her, unable to meet her eye, unable to speak. He hoped she would read his silence as disapproval, forgiveness, anger, love. She tipped her head to one side, watching him pass, baffled. Billy wished he could muster outrage, wished he could mask his pain with fury, but all he felt was a sinking sense of loneliness and loss. He needed to speak to someone about his pain, but the only one he wanted to talk to was the woman who had hurt him.

Billy spent the afternoon in the town library, using the high-speed Internet access, a nicety not yet provided by county funds for the Sheriff's Department. He went first to microfilmed copies of the *Falls City Journal*, to no avail. If there had ever been a lynching in Falls City, it was never reported, but he had not expected the search to be that easy. Nonetheless, he had a sense that the incident captured on his postcard was at least regional, if not local. Lynchings had occurred everywhere in the country, at one time or another, and most of them in the South, but there was something in the faces of the men on his postcard that told him they were his people.

His Internet search revealed that Billy's was but one of many postcards of lynchings. They fluttered and waved at him electronically like tattered flags, the photos worn by age but still displaying a sense of righteous, almost patriotic, pride in their grisly accomplishment. People had arrived in dozens, sometimes hundreds, to pose next to dangling victims like proud hunters beside the prey they had put on display. One of the slain had been barbecued like a side of beef; several had had their headgear put back on, as if dressed for an outing in top hat and hemp necktie, mocked even after death. In a display of urgent improvisation, one man had been stretched from beneath a hastily constructed tripod of poles, demonstrating the vengeful resourcefulness of the citizens of the treeless prairie. Another man had been flayed mercilessly, so that his back looked as if it had been scored by a hot grill. A woman hung from a railroad trestle, her audience assembled above her, and the enterprising photographer had captured it all from a boat.

They were hung in pairs, hung in trios, dangled from trees, saplings, anything high enough and close enough to do the job. Whipped, set on fire, tortured in ways only hinted at in the photographs, they were all caused to die by slow suffocation, their weight and the noose combining to strangle them. It takes a long time to strangle to death, and it was not hard to imagine the frantic writhing, the jerks and twists and final spasmodic twitchings of their deaths, all done in a public dance, to the delight of the onlookers.

Billy was sickened, as much as by the living as the dead. Their faces screamed of righteousness, and he knew that most would have proudly justified the killings not only by an outraged sense of justice, too impatient to abide the slow and uncertain motions of the law, but also by religion. They had believed it was God's work they were at, and these witnesses to mob murder would have gone to church, many in the same Sunday finest that they had worn to the killing affair, satisfied in their souls that God's will had been done.

He had been wrong in thinking that only the men and the boys in the postcard on his kitchen table were his people. They were all his people. Violent, dangerous, and very pleased with themselves, certain they were the Lord's anointed because, irrefutably, God had given them the dominion, the power, and the sheer numbers to do what they wanted to whomever they wished. And it was no coincidence that they all chose to do it to the same people.

After looking at the pictures, he found a list of all the known lynchings over the last two centuries. They numbered in the thousands. The last reported incident was Perry Small in Alabama in 1965; Billy worked backward from there and found what he dreaded, in a listing for 1948. The *Omaha World-Herald* and the *Kansas City Star* had both covered it in sketchy detail. Lawton Mills, described as a male Negro whose age was estimated to be mid-twenties, was lynched in Sabella, Kansas, on August 27. Although never arrested or formally charged, Mills was said to have raped and then beaten to death a twelve-year-old girl from the area. There was mention of an eyewitness, whose name was withheld. The witness's testimony had apparently been compelling enough to incite the locals to string up Mills on the spot.

Was it the lynching captured on his postcard? Billy knew Sabella; it was a town slightly smaller than Falls City, an occasional destination when he was a teenager because of the leniency of the Kansas law governing drinking age. Although not much of a trip now, he imagined that on the roads of the time, it would have been about an hour's drive in 1948.

Had whoever wanted to intimidate Billy purposely chosen a photo of the lynching in Sabella? Or was it simply a postcard that had fallen into his hands at a time when he wanted to torment the acting deputy sheriff? Had the sender come across the postcard after leaving the noose—a serendipitous event, the way that such things often happened? Or had the noose been sent first as a deliberate precursor, in order to prepare Billy for the horror of the postcard? If that were so, had Judge Sunder received a postcard as well? . . . Or was the proximity of Sabella just a coincidence? There was no indication on the postcard of where the lynching had taken place, no date, no name of the victim, and thus no way to know whether it was Sabella or not. No way for the sender to know, no way for Billy to be sure. Perhaps the proximity of Sabella was just a coincidence . . . He wanted to believe that. He wanted to think that he had been singled out for harassment by any means that fell conveniently to hand, just as pranksters and vandals took targets of opportunity. None of it really had to *mean* anything. . . . But he knew it did. Coincidence was just a little too easy. The postcard had been sent for a reason, just as Billy had been selected to receive it for a reason, and the reason most probably lay hidden within the postcard itself.

Sunder was having dinner when Billy arrived, and he dabbed at his face periodically with his napkin, as if afraid some telltale sign of his meal was migrating across his face.

"Postcard? What kind of postcard? I get a lot of mail."

"This was a different kind of card," Billy explained. "You'd remember it."

Sunder touched the corner of his lips with the napkin and shook his head. "No . . . I didn't get anything special. What kind of postcard are we talking about here?"

"A picture postcard."

"Maybe I'll get it in the next mail," Sunder offered.

"Maybe. Let me know if you do."

"I can't very well let you know unless I know what it is, can I?"

"You'll know," Billy said.

"You're acting damned mysterious, it seems to me. If you've got something to tell me, just come out and say it . . . It's got something to do with the noose, hasn't it?"

"I don't know," Billy said. "I don't know what it has to do with anything. I don't know what the noose is all about, for that matter."

"I haven't had any brilliant insights, either. Just that somebody doesn't like me, I guess. . . . I can live with that. What progress are you making on my break-in?"

"To be honest, none. Did you do a little inventory of your study yet?"

"How's that?"

"You were going to figure out if anything was missing after that break-in. Have you done that yet?"

"Not systematically. I'm not sure I could, actually. I mean, how do you know if part of your life is missing unless you know what exactly to look for?"

"Could I take another squint at the room myself?"

"Sure . . . You think you can figure out what he snipped out of my past?"

"I'm not sure I can figure out much of anything; I just don't know where else to look."

The judge's study had been restored to order. The fallen shelf was up again, the cheap alarm clock ticking. Next to it was the golf ball with the smiling face. Above the shelf were two empty hooks awaiting new trophies.

"Do you have things in any kind of order?" Billy asked. "You know, alphabetical, chronological?"

"Not really," said Sunder. "Things are just where they seemed to fit, you know."

"Where's the noose? You saved it, didn't you?"

"Yes, I did."

Sunder waved his arm at the area of the wall just to the right of the door, where the most recent trophies seemed to be. Billy noted a citation from the Elks Club and another from the local Odd Fellows, both lauding the judge for his good works and citizenship. Next to them was the noose, hanging on a picture hook nailed to the wall.

"Not exactly the place of honor," Billy said. He nudged the door open a few more inches and the noose disappeared behind it. Someone entering the room would not see it, although the judge could when seated in his chair with the door closed.

"That's where it fit," said the judge.

"You're running out of room for your trophies," Billy said, looking around the room again, grinning. "I guess that's the mark of a rich, full life."

"Oh, I'll find more room. I'm not through living, not by a long chalk. . . . And you know, Billy, if you ever think about running for sheriff, you ought to talk to me. I know a good deal about how things are put together in this county."

"I'm not thinking of running."

"You ought to, though. Those of us who can lead, should. Otherwise, well, with all due respect to your friend Lapolla, things don't get run as well as they might."

"I have no interest in running. We have an acting sheriff right now, and I intend to support him when he runs for election."

"You mean you'll support him if he's the best candidate, or you'll support him no matter what?"

"Until I see who else is going to run, I'm going to assume Bert is the best man for the job."

"Except for yourself."

"You're a hard man to convince."

Sunder smiled. "Only when I need to be. You just let me know when you decide to run. I know a little bit about electioneering; maybe I can help out."

One of the senior workmen found the body behind an equipment shack, nearly stumbled over it and cried out with alarm, he was so startled. When he knelt and saw who it was and what had happened, he called out in earnest, screaming, "Hey! Hey! Hey!" again and again, not knowing what else to say about what he had discovered. Other workmen came first, then, slowly, all the men within hearing distance. Still others, seeing the growing crowd, realizing by the agitation that something unusual was afoot, left their meals and their games and wandered over, until eventually virtually every man on the place was there. The man who had made the discovery had been replaced in his position close to the body by those more aggressive and accustomed to command. He told his story to little knots of men, how he had come around the corner and nearly stepped on it, but as he lacked details, his tale was not enough to hold them for long, and eventually he was passed back from knot to knot to the periphery of the crowd. Far more interesting speculation was going on next to the body, where the closest knelt in a tight circle, almost as if out of respect, while others stood behind them. These were men accustomed to death. Most had survived the carnage of the recent war and all of them, even the wealthy and professional, had beheaded chickens behind their kitchens as children, assisted in the slaughter of hogs and cattle, hunted and skinned rabbits, squirrels, and deer. They were not squeamish about blood or death itself, but there was something very unsettling about a dead twelve-year-old girl, something out of nature. She could have been the daughter of any of them, and the awkwardness of her splayed limbs, the rip in her dress, garish as an open wound, sickened them at first, then enraged them.

"Who was with her last?" one of the men close to her demanded, rising to his feet and facing the crowd. "Who saw someone with her?"

The men looked at one another, found it impossible to believe of anyone they knew. On the outside of the crowd, where they had been craning to see, the boys shifted uneasily, looking at one another. They were noticed. They were her age, or close enough, still children. They would know; they would have secret knowledge of one another that no adult could penetrate.

One of the men close by turned to them and thrust his face at them, dark and accusatory. "Who was with her?"

They shifted their bodies, frightened, casting glances back and forth. The youngest of them seemed about to cry. Another man put his hand on the youngest's shoulder, shaking him slightly. It was an age when adults still felt they could discipline a child, anyone's child, a time and place where consensus in these matters reigned. The man squeezed the youngest boy's arm with work-callused fingers.

"Who was with her?"

The youngest looked to the boy next to him, an older copy from the same mold, the same eyes and mouth and nose, and began to weep. The older boy put a protective arm on his brother's shoulder and tried to pull him away from the man.

"Who?" they demanded. "Was it you?"

The older boy lifted his arm and pointed to Lawton Mills, who stood by the equipment shack, apart from the others, almost as if hiding.

Lawton shook his head violently.

"Not me," he said.

"What do you know about this, Lawton?" demanded the man in the center, next to the girl's body.

"Don' know nothin'," said Lawton. "Don' know nothin' 'bout it."

He began to move from the crowd instinctively and at that point one of the men rose with the body in his arms. Her dress rode up and they could see the suntan marks on her stick-thin legs, the exposed white flesh screaming with vulnerability and innocence. They could see the horrible wound on her temple where the blood had dried like a clump of mud. A cry of fury rose up from the men and they looked away from her, unable to bear the sight of the guiltless slaughtered, and sought out Lawton.

Startled by their cry of anguish, Lawton began to run. It was a fatal mistake.

CHAPTER TEN

Will was home again when Billy went to see Joan. Sprawled on the sofa, he was watching television, a bag of chips in one hand, his little finger hooked around the long neck of a beer bottle, the remote control in the other, a look of world-weary boredom on his face. Billy wanted to tell him to be careful or his features would set that way permanently, but he knew Will would not find it funny. He found nothing funny about what Billy had to say. The boy's eyes flickered upward briefly as Billy passed, and he aimed the remote control at him, clicking it repeatedly, as if he could remove Billy from the airspace.

Joan was startled when Billy walked into the kitchen, where she was doing the dinner dishes.

"Oh," she said. "I wasn't expecting you."

Billy wondered if things had changed so much that he had to make an appointment to see her now.

"Thought I'd stop by and see how it went last night," he said, keeping his place in the doorway. Normally, he would have embraced her by now. Usually, she would have held her arms open with mock impatience if he hesitated at all. "Well, kiss me," she would say if he had not already done so. The "you fool" was left unsaid. Tonight, she turned only halfway to him, presenting him with a semiprofile before returning to the sink.

"How'd it go?" Billy asked after a pause.

"How did what go?"

"Whatever you were doing last night."

She kept her back to him.

"Baby-sitting?" she asked.

"Okay. How was the baby-sitting?"

"The baby-sitting was fine."

Joan's sister had two boys under the age of ten, and Joan usually referred to harnessing their volatile energies as an exercise as exhausting as trying to herd cats.

"No problems?"

"No. They were fine."

"How was the driving?" he asked, hating himself for trying to trick her.

"What driving?"

"Didn't you have to drive back to Falls City from Auburn in that storm?"

She turned fully now and looked at him searchingly for a moment.

"The driving was okay. . . . Are you all right, Billy?"

"Me? I'm fine."

"I'm trying to listen to my show in here!" Will called. Billy advanced into the kitchen and stood within a few feet of Joan.

"You seem a little funny," she said.

"Just work stuff," he offered.

She tilted her face up to his, arched an eyebrow questioningly.

"So what was that silent treatment when you drove by today?"

"What do you mean?"

"You drove by twice. I waved. Nothing. You ignored me, for some reason."

"I didn't see you."

"Uh-huh."

"Guess I was preoccupied."

She looked at him with the patience one might reserve for a child determined to withhold the truth. There seemed so little point in lying; he didn't fool her for a second and he only made himself feel bad.

She shrugged, forgiving him.

"So? Kiss me."

It surprised him that her lips felt so soft and inviting despite her having betrayed him less than twenty-four hours earlier.

She turned back to the sink, smiling to herself.

"What's going on at work that's got you acting this way?"

Billy put his hands on her shoulders.

"Do you remember Odette Collins?"

Her shoulders tensed and he could feel her catch her breath.

"Odette Collins?"

"Yeah. . . . Remember him?"

"Why?" she asked after a pause.

Wrong response, he thought sorrowfully.

"Oh, he's been on my mind. He played for Central against us in the state championships."

"About a million years ago."

"An athlete never forgets," said Billy.

"You spend your days thinking about old basketball games, do you, Billy?"

"Not usually. Odette's been in town. . . . Have you seen him?"

"Why would I see him?"

Billy stood beside the sink so he could look at her face. She glanced at him angrily.

"He's a black man, Joan. You'd know if you saw him."

"I know he's black." She fixed him with her eyes now. "So what?"

"So we want to question him."

"For being black?"

"In part, I think, yeah. Just for being black in Richardson County."

"Shame on you."

"It was a joke," he said lamely. Or an attempt at turning the truth into a joke.

She continued to scrub vigorously at a carving knife that she had been clean minutes ago.

"He may need an alibi," Billy continued.

"For being black?"

"For a charge of assault."

He saw that she was surprised, although she quickly hid it. She finally placed the knife in the drainer, then made an elaborate moment of wiping her hands dry and replacing the towel on its hook.

"Why do you do this, Billy?"

"Do what?"

"Play at being a cop. What satisfaction do you get out of harassing people?"

Billy was stunned. "I don't harass anyone," he said.

"You're harassing me."

"I was . . . just discussing the day."

"Oh, was that it? I sensed a deeper meaning."

"What deeper meaning could I have—unless you can give Odette Collins an alibi for his whereabouts at eleven last night."

She glared at him.

"Just when the storm started," he added.

"Leave it," she said softly.

"What?"

"Leave it, Billy. Just leave it."

"Joan, we can talk about anything. . . ."

"No, we can't," she said sharply. "Don't always be a sheriff. Just leave it."

"I wish I could. . . ."

"You heard her," Will said ominously from the doorway. Billy turned, to see the boy a few feet behind him, his square shoulders almost filling the frame. "She said leave her alone."

"She said leave *it* alone," Billy replied.

"Leaving is a good idea. Why don't you just do it?"

"Take it easy, son."

"I ain't your son. I sure as shit ain't your son."

"Will, please . . ." Joan said. "Please."

"I got it, Mom."

"No, you don't 'got it.' Just go back to the other room."

"You want him out of here, I'll get him out for you."

She put her hands on her son's chest and gently pushed. Will gave ground reluctantly, his eyes glaring at Billy with every inch of retreat.

"Why don't you go, Billy?" she said softly after Will was out of the room. "Just let him cool off."

"I might need to cool off, too," Billy said. Despite himself, he had felt his adrenaline surge in response to Will's challenge. His reaction frightened him. A battle with Joan's minor son was hardly the thing he needed to solve his problems with her. His hand shook as he placed it on the kitchen sink.

"Is that how we're going to leave it, then?" he asked.

"You'd be really smart to drop it," she said.

"I'm not sure I can. . . . I came by here last night."

She closed her eyes for a moment, seeking strength and patience.

"Didn't you get my message that I wouldn't be here?"

"I got it this morning. I was in Salina when you called."

"Salina?"

"I went to watch Will in the rodeo."

"Oh, Billy . . . Why?"

"I thought he should have some one there on his side. It just seemed right."

"Billy . . . Billy."

"He told me not to come anymore."

She sighed, as if there were no appropriate words.

"I'm sorry," she said finally.

"For which?"

She shrugged her shoulders. "How much do you want? I'm sorry for my son's rotten behavior. I'm sorry I was in Auburn when you came by last night. I'm sorry you have that hurt look on your face right now. . . . I wish you'd leave."

He exited the house by the back door. The front door meant the living room and another encounter with Will. Billy was not certain he could stifle the urge to break the boy in two this time. It took all the self-control he could muster at the moment just to walk away from Joan with some dignity. It had turned out she was quite a good liar after all. She stuck to her story even when they both knew it wasn't true. Cling to the element of doubt, make your interrogator question his certainty. Force him to prove his version of things. Of course she had one advantage over her interrogator that most would not have—he did not want to call her a liar to her face. It was the sort of accusation that left marks. And she had another advantage, too. Billy desperately wanted to believe her.

He walked from her house into the alley and from there to Fifteenth Street where he turned left, retracing the route Odette Collins—or someone—had taken after fleeing Joan's bed. Stone Street was half a block away, the Sportsman's Bar another three. A running man could make it in a couple of minutes. Where had Billy caught sight of him? Billy had run to get a better view and intersected Stone Street at Nineteenth Street. The Sportsman had been behind him, Sean lying on the ground, by his account, but Billy had never looked behind him—his focus had been to the north, where the running man had been barely visible through the downpour. So did Collins have the time to run from Joan's house, accost his uncle, take his wallet, pass some remarks about a dog, then keep on running and be nearly out of sight before Billy made it to Stone Street? He would have had to be running very fast, and Sean could not have put up the valiant struggle he claimed—which Billy had not believed in the first place. He would have had to take Sean as a target of opportunity. See him, rob him, punch him several times, hard enough to raise considerable bruises, then keep on running. It hardly seemed the action of a man moving at that speed. But it was possible. And if Billy tried to prove it was possible, if he found Odette Collins and questioned him and Odette offered as an alibi the fact that he'd been in bed with Joan at the time of the assault . . . Unthinkable. It would destroy Joan. On the other hand, if Odette was seized by chivalry and did not offer Joan as an alibi, could

Billy allow him to deny it and thus convict himself? How much easier never to find Odette Collins in the first place. If he was on the run, let him stay that way.

Even as he contemplated it, Billy knew it would not happen. If Collins were lucky enough to have found Joan, would he be fool enough to walk away and never come back? Billy certainly couldn't. He couldn't walk away from her even now, when common sense and injured pride screamed at him to do just that.

Billy returned home to find the postcard snarling at him from the table. He retrieved the noose from his pocket and flopped it down next to the photo. The instrument of evil and its hideous result. Why was it so often lynching? he wondered.

Why the rope when there were so many ways to kill a man? Why go to the trouble to construct a tripod when they could simply have cut the man's throat, shot him, bashed his brains out with a rock? Another glance at the postcard told him the reason. A hanged man was above the crowd, where everyone could bear witness. A dangling moral lesson, a visible reminder of one's place in society. An affirmation to the whites of their collective power and justice, a warning to the blacks, hoisted high for all to see. Was it also because the lynching was a simulation of official justice? A demonstration of the public will, and therefore sanctified? And perhaps because it was a communal effort by necessity—difficult for one man to hang another without assistance—and thus the onus was removed from any single partici-pant.... Or maybe it was just more fun than a firing squad, he thought. Maybe the sons of bitches just enjoyed it.

He moved a table lamp from his bedroom to the kitchen and went over the postcard with a magnifying glass, looking for some indication that the photo had been taken in Sabella. Part of the roof of a building was visible in the background, the slope of it too shallow to be a barn or farmhouse. Even with the magnifying glass, he could find no sign or any lettering that might identify the building as a shop, as he had hoped. Billy had the feeling that the lynching had occurred in town, perhaps even the town square, but he could find nothing concrete to confirm the suspicion. The roof was long, running across most of the frame, so the building must be sizable—or must have *been* sizable, he reminded himself. This had happened fifty-two years ago, and it was quite possible that the structure had long since been torn down. If all he had to go on was part of a roof, a trip to Sabella was not apt to prove fruitful. He moved the glass slowly down from the roof and across the blank and featureless side of the building that provided the backdrop for most of the space above the men's heads. He searched the horizon formed by the heads and hats of the men in the back row, searching for some landmark that might be useful. A man with a full mustache craned his neck to see the camera, and just next to his hat, filling a gap in the flattened perspective that put his face next to the hanged man's foot, was something neither head nor hat. Billy moved the glass forward and back, seeking a focus that would clarify the image. He turned the photo to the side, then upside down, trying to put the object into a perspective that he could interpret. It looked like a piece of cloth, like a handkerchief perhaps, and wrinkled when captured by the camera, as if in motion. An attempt by someone at the very rear of the crowd to be noticed, waving a dark handkerchief as if at a departing ship? Or a wag signaling surrender on behalf of the dangling corpse?

Billy continued his search and, at the very edge of the photo, he saw part of a window. Again, it was distorted by the flat perspective, so that it appeared to be atop the head of one of the men, although in reality the building must have been thirty or forty yards away. There, looking out the window, little more than a tinted blur, was a face, or a shape, given the surroundings, that Billy interpreted as a face. It was darker than that of the men, as dark as that of the hanged man himself. Was another black man viewing this obscenity committed against his race? Billy stood from the table and paced through the house.

It was as if he had never really looked at the picture until he had noticed that witness, he realized. The victim was facing in that direction. Had he made eye contact with the witness as the noose was fitted around his neck? Had he still seen him while he struggled for breath? And what terrors had the witness felt? . . . That, of course, was the point of the exercise. Or part of the point.

Billy looked at the faces of the spectators anew, studying each in turn with his magnifying glass, as if he might discern the appearance of the man's soul if he looked deeply enough. One of the men was missing a tooth in the front of his mouth, so that his grin at the camera made him look like the quintessential yokel. If only they had all looked like that, Billy thought. Half-witted, parodies of rednecks, men from whom you could expect no better. But they didn't look like that; they had faces of distressing normality. It was as if a random sampling of the citizens of Falls City had been cast as Nazi executioners—and all of them fit the part. Despite the occasional smirk or gloat, they appeared remarkably businesslike, he thought. Sober, serious, average men who might have been assembled for a group photograph in front of some community project they had helped to build and with which they were justly pleased—the courthouse, a hardware store, a lynching.

A number of teenaged boys were on the outer fringe of the men, which put them closest to the camera. A couple were smiling at the camera, the others looking as serious as if it were their class picture. Two boys were separated from the others, standing close together on the other side of the frame. One of them was smaller and younger than the others, perhaps not yet a teen, and he looked slightly cowed by the situation, but not so put off that he didn't want to have his picture taken. The older boy next to him wore a cloth cap and a white shirt with stripes and his eyes did not face the camera, but looked somewhat to one side, as if he saw something everyone else had missed. With a chill, Billy moved the glass forward and back on that face.

With a gasp, he heaved himself up from the chair as if the face had suddenly winked at him. The chair skittered across the kitchen and toppled against the wall.

"No."

Billy looked anxiously around the room, seeking an explanation for what he had seen. He fingered the noose, tossed it nervously in his hand while standing over the picture. The added distance did nothing to change the face of the boy with the cloth hat. The features are shadowed, he told himself. There's no way to be sure; you're filling in the gaps with your imagination. He retrieved the chair, sat again, and squinted at the boy's face. He was just a boy somewhere in his early teens, frightened but trying not to show it, and masking his fear with a most serious mien. At least he was frightened, Billy thought. The only one in the picture who seemed to have sense enough to be frightened.

Billy sat for a long time, letting his eyes lose focus so that the photo was there but not there, its particulars blurry and indistinct. He had seen all he could take for the moment, at least all he could take in with his eyes. Now his mind took over and he tried to insert himself into the scene, tried to see that distant time with the vision of a teenager. Five decades ago, two generations, several sea changes away in racial relations, political correctness, mutual understanding. A completely different age, as distant as the Gay Nineties in many ways, before Kennedy and King, before the growth of agribusiness had crippled the family farms, before Vietnam and Watergate had brought cynicism to the American soul. A time of innocence, America still flush with victory in a righteous war, a simpler, purer time, when naïve American hearts still believed they had the right to slaughter a human being whenever the spirit moved them. A world away? Or a membrane away? He thought of Lowell Briggs and his insistence that he still could not tell "them" apart, Sunder's immediate assumption of guilt of the new black man in town, Lapolla's suggestion that a special language was needed for communication. Billy wondered if the changes of the decades amounted to much more than a thin tissue of official, governmental politesse. There were no lynchings anymore, but how much would it take for the custom to be revived? Manners had been improved, but had hearts been changed? . . . And how much of Billy's rage at Odette Collins was simply because he had cuckolded him, and how much because he was a *black man* who had cuckolded him?

Billy put the postcard back into the envelope in which it had come, then placed that envelope in a larger one of his own. For a time, he contemplated hiding it somewhere so that no visitor would stumble across it, as if it were pornography or a secret document.

The phone rang, and Billy reacted with a shock of guilt, as if he'd been caught in the act of something shameful.

"You kill my dog?" a voice demanded.

"What?"

"You kill my dog, Sheriff?"

"Who is this? Odette?"

The voice on the phone chuckled, a low, mirthless, ominous sound.

"Where are you?" Billy asked.

He was answered by the dull drone of a dial tone. The caller had hung up. Billy puzzled over the call for a moment, then ran out of the house.

The only reason for someone to make a nonsensical call was to check on his whereabouts, Billy reasoned. If he was home, then he obviously wasn't . . . where? He drove to Joan's house, resisting the temptation to turn on the siren. There was no traffic at this hour of the night, in any event, but Billy's frantic mood yearned for the accompaniment of electronic screams.

He cut the lights and glided to a silent stop at the opening to the alley behind her house. From where he sat, he saw no lights. His chest was heaving with urgency, but there was nothing to do about it. He's not there, he told himself. He's playing with you, but he's not in her house, not tonight, not with Will there. Turning off the interior lights, he stepped out of the car and eased the door closed. The alley was familiar territory, and he walked through it confidently despite the darkness. As he approached the back of her house, his stride slowed and he found himself on his toes. Creeping, he realized with embarrassment. The word seemed unpleasantly appropriate. Creeping because I'm a creep. A panicked, jealous, ridiculous creep.

He stopped at the spot where he normally parked his car and studied the house, half-expecting Odette to materialize out of the darkness as he had done previously, speaking inanely about his dog. It was clear to Billy that their first meeting had been no accident, that Odette had not come seeking the sheriff. He was there for Joan, waiting for Billy to leave. How many nights had he been here in the dark, lustful and expectant, biding his time until Billy went home, the unsuspecting cuckold?

Rage swept over him abruptly, pushing aside the shame and humiliation. For the first time, he allowed the full fury of his anger to seize him, and it was all he could do to keep from screaming aloud. He wanted to kill the son of a bitch, wanted to do it with his bare hands, rip the life from him for daring to put his black paws on Billy's woman. Shaking with adrenaline and frustration, he returned to his car and sat there until he was in control of his breathing before pulling out into the night once more.

CHAPTER ELEVEN

J udge Sunder wants us to arrest your pal—you know, what's his name," Lapolla said accusingly.

"What pal?"

Lapolla turned the arrest order so that Billy could read it from across the desk. "The monkey from the motel. Shaven head, 'African American.'"

Billy glanced at the description on the arrest order. The man's height was given as five nine to six three. Build medium, weight one hundred and seventy to two hundred and twenty.

"That should be vague enough," Billy said. "Why is he my pal?"

"You said you knew him, didn't you? You said the man was threatening you."

"He wasn't threatening me," Billy said.

"That's what you said."

"I may have said he was kind of scary—but so are you with your shirt off."

"That's not funny."

"That's what I'm saying. Scary, Bert."

"You said he offered to pound on you or something."

"I believe I said I got the impression he didn't like me, but that's not against the law; it's just a character flaw." Billy read from the order again. " 'May answer to?' That's what you write about lost pets. Who's responsible for this order?"

"Judge Sunder."

"Sunder issued a bench warrant because of the incident—whatever it was—with my uncle?"

"No. Theft of services from the motel, because he scooted out the window and didn't pay. The judge hates that kind of thing. It undermines the fabric of society, he says."

" 'Theft of services'?"

"Theft of any kind. He's a tiger about that. He'll throw their ass in the town jail until they rot, unless they pay up."

"Except for this villain. Since the motel is in our jurisdiction, he'll throw his ass in *our* cell until it rots."

"As soon as you find him and bring him in."

Lapolla tilted his head to one side and regarded Billy for a moment.

"You look kind of funny, Billy."

"Do I?"

"Like a ghost walked over your grave or something. You okay?"

"Fine. . . . I had a tough night."

"You all right with this?"

"Which?"

"Arresting this rock singer or whatever he is. You okay with it?"

"Why wouldn't I be?"

"Sometimes, you know . . . Sometimes you get on your civil rights high horse or something."

"I may have dismounted from that particular horse in this case, Bert."

"So you're okay with arresting him?"

"I am very okay with that," Billy said. "I will gladly lock his ass up for as long as Judge Sunder will allow."

"A little revenge, huh?"

Billy looked at him blankly.

"For him pounding on your uncle the way he did," Lapolla prompted.

"Oh . . . right. For Sean."

"A little payback," said Lapolla. He winked broadly. "All perfectly legal."

"A little payback," Billy agreed. The legality of it didn't trouble him terribly much at the moment.

The quickest route to Tecumseh lay through Auburn, and Billy reached there by noon, agitated and at war with himself. The town lay open and sprawled on its back, basking in a perfect summer day with the sun bright but the heat moderate and the humidity drained from the air by the recent rain. Billy would have preferred it dark and stormy to match his mood. It seemed a shame to ruin a lovely day by dragging his own miasmic cloud into it.

Margie Duerfeldt, Joan's sister, worked with her husband at the local Dairy Queen, of which they were the franchisees. Billy pulled into the parking lot surrounding the hut wearing the familiar red sign as a crown. Margie scurried out the back door of the hut, wiping her hands on her apron. Joan was prettier; all the facial bones that had aligned themselves so perfectly for her were just slightly askew in her sister, and the result was not beautiful, but pleasant; not striking, but comforting. Although Margie was not heavy, there was a softness to her face that made Billy think of her as an animated throw pillow, perfect for cuddling. Easy to fall asleep on, he thought, but in no way exciting. Which is probably just as well, he reflected. Joan was exciting and he had come to spy on her. It was hard to imagine Margie inspiring jealous espionage.

She was alarmed at seeing him and started talking before Billy's window was rolled down all the way.

"Billy, I saw you pull in. Is something wrong? Is Joan all right?"

"Fine, she's fine. Nothing's wrong."

She sighed deeply. "It's the police car that does it—well, sheriff's car. I never see one without . . . you know."

"It makes most people feel instantly guilty," Billy said, grinning. She stood back enough to let him open the door, although she kept her hands on the open window. "Sometimes I get up in the morning, see it sitting in my driveway, and wonder, What have I done now? I'm sorry if I scared you."

"No, no . . ."

He hesitated until she released the window before he closed the car door.

"Everything's all right, though?" she asked.

"It's a good thing I don't drive a hearse," he said. "Can you imagine how people would react to me then?"

"It's not *you*, Billy. Everybody's always happy to see you." She slapped playfully at his arm, as if he had been teasing her. It was a kittenish gesture, one her sister might have used, but Joan's hand would have lingered a second, he thought. And her touch would have burned. Not just him. Any man.

"Scary uniform, too," Billy said.

"No, it's just . . . you know."

"It's a curse," he said. "On the other hand, when people see *your* uniform, I bet they want to give you a hug."

She looked at herself, as if surprised to see what she was wearing.

"No . . . Oh. You're such a flirt, Billy," she said approvingly. "I don't know how Joan puts up with it."

"A very tolerant girl, your sister." He felt the grin on his face begin to strain and pretended to a sudden interest in the sky. It was important not to let any of his bitterness about Joan come to the surface.

"She's wonderful," Margie concurred. He knew she meant it. Her adoration of her older sister was obvious and undisguised. Billy understood it perfectly. Resentfully. "What brings you to Auburn?"

"Just thought I'd stop by and say hello," he said. He forced his grin to broaden and split into a smile.

Margie shifted uncertainly for a moment, then stretched upward to kiss his cheek. She smelled pleasantly, as always, of vanilla.

"Well, hello," she said.

"And I thought I'd get a cone while I'm at it. There's no better ice cream in the whole state."

"Sure. Come on in."

She led him into the back of the hut, her plump behind wriggling beneath the white Gore-Tex uniform trousers as she walked. On Joan, it would have looked sexy, he thought. On Margie, it was cute.

He sat on a stool behind the service counter and licked a swirled mound of ice cream while she worked. "Where's Hank?" he asked.

Margie looked up abruptly, as if she could not work and speak at the same time.

"He's in Tarkio," she said, naming a town in Missouri.

"I didn't know."

She nodded her head and continued to bob it up and down to confirm her statement.

"His sister has a problem with her gallbladder. They don't know how bad it is yet. He's there a lot these days."

"I see," Billy said. "So that's why you needed Joan to baby-sit."

"What?"

"That's why you had Joan over to baby-sit, so you could go to Tarkio."

She appeared flustered. "Is that what Joan told you?"

Billy licked the ice cream, taking his time. It was almost cruel to question Margie. She was so devoted to her sister—and such a lousy liar.

"Maybe I misunderstood her," Billy said. "I thought she was baby-sitting with your boys the night before last. . . . You know, the night of the big storm."

"That was a terrible storm, wasn't it? But it really cleared things up. It's beautiful now."

"It sure is."

He continued to lick his cone while looking at her, letting his eyes do the interrogating.

"The boys just love her," she said, returning abruptly to her work, as if she had just remembered the urgency of making ice cream.

"Who can blame them?"

"You're awfully sweet, Billy," she said, her back now to him. "And Joanie knows it. She appreciates you so much. Don't think she doesn't."

"Nice to hear."

She looked at him again, twisting her neck. "No, really. She understands how lucky she is."

Billy struggled to keep his face neutral. It felt as if it might crack and fall off like dried mud on a fence post.

"And after all she went through with that terrible Duane. He was such a bad man, Billy, you don't know—well, yes, I guess you do know." She sighed, and Billy could see moisture gathering in her eyes. "You two are so lucky now. What you have together is so good and so rare . . ."

He let her prattle on about the horrors of Joan's marriage to Duane Blanchard for a time, Margie covering her unease with nervous sentiment. Billy felt like a bully, forcing her to tap-dance to cover for her sister. It was obvious enough that Joan had not been to Auburn to baby-sit. And what had he expected to happen—that Margie in her innocent goodness would convince him that he had not heard Joan with another man that night? That Odette Collins had not been the man fleeing in the storm? He had known the truth of the case from the moment Joan had been unable to deny it. His obsession to tie up all the loose ends—or to give Joan any possible out—had only managed to make Margie lie for her sister, to their mutual embarrassment.

"Well, I'm off to Tecumseh," he said when he had finished the cone and she had come to a break in her monologue.

"Tecumseh? Why Tecumseh?" she asked with ill-disguised alarm.

"Got to see a man about a dog."

"But you're not sheriff in Tecumseh, are you, Billy? You can't arrest anyone there."

"I'm not sheriff in Auburn, either, but they let me drive in to visit with you."

"No, be serious."

"You're right, I can't arrest anyone outside of Richardson County. I'm just trying to locate somebody, and I think I know where to look."

She preceded him to his car, walking backward, half-impeding his progress.

"Does Joanie know you're going to Tecumseh to see . . . this person?"

"No."

"Are you sure this is a good idea?"

"Margie, I haven't had a really good idea since I decided to resign from the Secret Service. Why change things now?"

She stood with her butt against the car door, her arms across her bosom, blocking his way while trying to appear casual. And so she knows Collins is in Tecumseh, Billy realized. Joan has told her of her affair with him—she just neglected to prepare her for the baby-sitting lie. How many others know? he wondered. How many others looked at him with pity, or derision? Had it spread to the extent that he could no longer walk down a street without being the object of guilty amusement? He suddenly wanted to be away from Margie's eyes.

"I have to go, Margie. Thanks for the ice cream. Give my best to Hank."

She lowered her head as if shamed. He put his hands on her shoulders and maneuvered her away from the car door.

"Don't hate me," she said.

"I don't blame you, Margie. You were doing what you should have done."

She surprised him by leaning forward abruptly and kissing his cheek for the second time.

"Thank you," she said so softly that he could barely hear her. And then she added, "I know you don't mean that, but thank you anyway. . . . Always be this nice to Joanie."

A bitter chuckle burbled forth unbidden.

"Right," he said.

*   *   *

His cell phone rang before he was more than a few miles out of Auburn. Joan's voice was tight and angry. He could visualize those full lips turned inward into a livid, disapproving line, like a scar of disapproval.

"What do you think you're doing?" she asked.

"My job."

"Since when does your job involve scaring my sister?"

"Scare her? I didn't scare her. What are you talking about? We had a nice conversation. Did she say I scared her?"

"Leave her alone."

"I said hello; she gave me an ice-cream cone. . . ."

"She said you were grilling her about the night of the storm, when I was baby-sitting for her."

"Margie would not use the word *grilling*."

"You think you know here so well, do you? She said you kept at her, asked her where she'd gone that night, if she was in Tarkio."

"Why would any of this scare her?"

"Maybe because you walk around with a gun on your hip and a great big badge."

"My holster's empty; you know that."

"What business is it of yours where she was that night? Does it matter to you whether she went to Tarkio or went to a movie by herself?"

"You don't think it concerns me?"

"She said you were looking at her funny, too."

"Hey, I can't help my poor face. . . ."

"Don't try to charm me, Billy. If you have questions about my sister, you ask me, not her. She's got enough to deal with as it is."

"My questions aren't about her, Joan. They're about you, and I'm not sure I have any questions left."

"I don't know what that's supposed to mean. Is it true you're going to Tecumseh?"

"I'm on my way."

He could hear her take a deep breath, inhaling through her nose, the way she did when trying to keep control. The sides of her nose would turn white as the nostrils flared. It was as clear a demonstration that her patience was near an end as a semaphore. Her chest would rise and, despite whatever he had done to arouse her displeasure, he would find himself furtively admiring her breasts. When she was angry, it just made him want to make love to her. Normally. Three days ago. Now her anger made him want to respond in kind.

"Why?" she asked finally.

"I'm looking for somebody."

"What if I told you not to do it?"

"I'd ask why. Why don't you want me to go to Tecumseh and look for somebody, Joan?"

"Just because I told you not to."

"Then I'd go ahead and find him."

"You'll just make people unhappy," she said. "What do you hope to get out of it?"

"I'm just doing my job."

"Stop being such a *cop*," she said as she hung up the phone.

CHAPTER TWELVE

A s he crossed the line into Johnson County, Billy radioed the local Sheriff's Department to advise them of his presence. It was a courtesy they extended to one another, not only to explain the anomalous presence of an alien squad car cruising their county but also to forestall any jealous territorial reactions. Billy did not want a zealous local deputy swooping down on him at the wrong time and demanding an explanation of his activities.

Billy's escort met him on the highway a few miles from his destination. The Johnson County patrol car was pulled onto the shoulder and a deputy leaned casually against the hood with his head back, as if sunning himself, although he still wore his sunglasses. Billy drove onto the shoulder behind the other car and shook hands with his counterpart, a short man with a nose most charitably described as "interesting."

"Deputy Ralph Morgan," he said, extending his hand.

"Billy Tree."

The deputy's eyebrows arched briefly in a flash of recognition. "Oh, yeah? How's it going?"

"It advances, as they say in France," said Billy. "And how does it go for you?"

Morgan either did not understand Billy's comment or did not care. "You know Schatz?" he asked.

"Deputy Schatz? Sure. Friend of yours?"

Morgan extended his lower lip as if pondering the question, but when he spoke again, he said, "You want to see the meat works, is that it?"

"I thought I'd like to take a squint, see how they make sausage."

"They don't make sausage there," said Morgan. "They slaughter hogs, cut 'em up, saw them into pork chops, hams, ham hocks, trotters, shoulders, picnics, pig's knuckles, baby back ribs, chitlins, scrape and precure the hides, do something with the insides I never wanted to ask about—nothing they don't use except the squeal. But they don't make the actual sausage there."

"Sounds like you had the tour."

"We've all had the tour. Once. Once is plenty." He shivered for emphasis. "A hellhole, if you ask me."

"No sausage, though?" Billy asked, grinning. "Might as well turn around and go back home, then."

Deputy Morgan blinked, tried a smile to see if it was appropriate, then gave it up.

"If they make sausage, it's new to me. I haven't been in there for over a year, but, like I said, I'm not about to go back unless I have to. They might make sausage now. Anything is possible."

"How long has the plant been in operation?"

"Little over a year. Sheriff made us all take the tour when it first opened, just so we knew what was going on. Lot of new people working there, not exactly natives, if you know what I mean. The kind of people

you could sell those chitlins to—whooee, man, who'd eat a pig's guts?—
and the Mexicans. . . ." He shook his head incredulously. "Man, I don't
know what those people eat, and don't tell me, either. . . . These are not
the kind of people you want making your sausage for you."

"I was just joking about the sausage," said Billy.

Again, Morgan didn't hear or didn't care.

"Some pretty desperate characters in there. . . . Well, you'll see.
Ex-cons, literates, that kind of thing."

" 'Literates'?"

"Most of them, I'd guess. If you could read or write, you'd find
some better way to make a living, wouldn't you think? Some people
don't seem to mind working under those conditions, I guess."

"These are transients, are they?"

"They don't live around here, not if we can help it. Most of them
get bused in every day from Omaha. That must be least an hour
commute both ways. How'd you like to drive an hour just to work
neck-deep in pig shit?"

"I don't think I'd drive more than half an hour for that. Forty-
five minutes, tops."

"I'll take you there, tell the supervisor you want to look around—
it's not exactly a tourist attraction, so you'll need an introduction—
but I'm not going in with you."

"I get the idea it's not real pleasant in there," Billy said.

Morgan looked into the distance, his gaze skimming the surface
of tall corn, as if seeking the answer to human behavior on the horizon.

"The things these people will do, you give them a little money,"
he said.

" 'These people'?"

"You don't see any white boys working on that slaughter floor,
let me put it that way." Morgan waited a moment, checking Billy's
reaction. "You know what I mean," he added.

Billy smiled wryly. "Alas."

"Right," said Morgan with finality, as if a deal had been concluded.

*　*　*

They approached the slaughterhouse from the east, driving past acres of holding pens, where thousands of swine awaited their deaths. From the road, they looked like so many humps, a geological phenomenon in pink, with black-and-white spots, crammed together by glacial action and undulating slightly, as if his gaze were affected by heat waves. It was only when Billy cracked a window that he knew the pigs were undisputably alive—and protesting. Their squeals seemed to rise in unison, like the roar of spectators in a stadium, thousands of individual voices, each with its own version of discomfort or complaint, concentrated into a single sound.

The smell struck him immediately after the sound, a stench of thousands of hogs voiding themselves in terror, adding their contribution to the thousands that had gone the day before, and the day before that. It was the stink that had brought him here, the odor of the T-shirt left behind in the motel bathtub, magnified thousands of times. Lowell Briggs had identified it instantly and correctly. Billy could see workers in a few empty lots clearing the concrete with high-power hoses. He glanced to his right and saw the tree line marking the path of the North Fork River, less than a thousand yards from the slaughterhouse's holding pens. However they treated their waste, it seemed impossible that some of it did not leach eventually into the North Fork. Did all the fecund greenery of the irrigated land originate in the belly of a swine?

The approach road swung in a long loop to the front of the slaughterhouse, and Billy was struck at first by the scarcity of cars in the huge parking lot. Those who drove to work could be numbered in the tens. To the side of the building, not immediately visible from the entrance to the lot, were the rows of buses, dozens of them in yellow and blue and several in the institutional gray of the penitentiary. Morgan told him the slaughterhouse was open around the clock, seven days a week, and the waiting buses would be filled every eight hours by one shift of workers and replaced by another coming in.

"The manager will do just about anything you want, within reason," said Deputy Morgan, leading Billy into the outer lobby of the plant. "He's so scared of the law, he'd probably go to his knees and give you a love lock if that's what you wanted."

"I'm not apt to ask for that," said Billy. "I have a touch of homophobia."

"Oh, yeah?" Morgan examined Billy for a moment, trying to detect the affliction.

"It's not catching," Billy explained. "What is he so scared of?" Billy asked.

"Well, shit, half his workers are illegal. Drop a dime to the immigration people and you'd lose most of your Mexicans in a heartbeat. There'd be a stampede out the door like somebody set fire to the place." Morgan chuckled, amused by the vision. "Red-hot Mexicans whooshing by. Put all those tacos to good use for a change." He offered a few hand gestures to emphasize his point. "Whoosh . . . whoosh."

"Got it."

"I never cared for tacos or any of that recycled food the beaners eat," Morgan said, floundering a bit, not certain he'd retained the thread of his argument.

"Apart from your culinary differences, do you have any trouble with the Mexican workers?"

"Trouble? No trouble in *my* county, because they're never actually *in* my county. They're here, cutting meat, and that's it. The whistle blows, back into the bus and they're out of here. They're Omaha's problem, not mine."

"Does the same go for your black workers?"

"As long as they stay on the bus, I got no problem with any of them. As long as they stay on the bus and in this shithole here, they got no problem with me."

"Equity," said Billy.

"What?"

"America's social system working at its best. You stay out of my yard and we'll get along fine."

"You were a fed, weren't you?" Morgan asked.

"To my lasting glory, I was in the Secret Service. Mostly, I protected the vice president."

"That asshole."

"No, not that asshole, the other one. And the one before that. I worked the protection side, off and on, for the three previous administrations."

Morgan took a minute, trying to work out the shifting lines of succession. He summarized his views of the seconds in command succinctly. "A bunch of assholes."

"Granting varying degrees of assholedom, I would have to agree with you."

"And you were ready to take a bullet for that collection of . . . assholes?"

"Actually, jumping in the line of fire doesn't come up too often. Usually, you jump on the vice president *after* they've taken a shot at him. Because if you knew they were going to take a shot and had time to get in front of the vice president in the first place, you probably had time to figure out a less personally punishing way of dealing with the problem. Like going somewhere else. At least that's my guess. It never came up for me, because no one cares enough about the vice president to go after him."

Morgan nodded. "And now you're here."

"Go figure," said Billy.

"Life's a pisser," said the deputy. He held open the door, then retreated as Billy walked into a stench of ammonia strong enough to make his eyes tear up.

"Clear's your sinuses right up," the plant manager acknowledged when he saw Billy blinking. "Kind of a shock, first time. You get used to it. We use an awful lot of ammonia and chlorine to clean up."

Now it smells like astringent manure, Billy thought to himself. Pig shit with a kick. The manager, a large man with a mole under one eye that looked at first glance like a tick feeding itself to satiety, led Billy onto the cutting floor. True to his word, Deputy Morgan had left Billy at the door and not entered.

"We can look for his name on our employee list afterward. Everyone has valid identification, or we don't hire them, you understand." Billy did not respond because he was stunned by the sight before him, but the manager took his silence as doubt and hurried on. "I'm not saying that someone might not have slipped under our radar; that could happen. We're not in the business of checking each item of identification, after all. It's kind of scary how easy it is to get a phony driver's licence or Social Security card these days, but, naturally, we do all we can to verify their identity. Within reason." The cutting floor was vast and noisy, and the manager was shouting to make himself heard.

"Right," said Billy, wishing the man would shut up so he could concentrate on the sight before him. The building was the size of an airport hangar, and more than a thousand people dressed in white smocks and hairnets and plastic hard hats wielded knives in green-gloved hands as they cut hog flesh. They stood at assembly lines, bent over at the waist, hacking and slicing with amazing speed at the butchered slabs of pork passing relentlessly in front of them.

"Of course, the turnover rate is very high. Most workers don't last more than eight, nine months," the manager bellowed in his ear. "We have more than twenty-five hundred new hires every year."

They advanced into the bowels of the cutting floor. The workers wore green or yellow hard hats. Supervisors were clad in bright orange coveralls of the kind the manager had required Billy to put on before they entered. His helmet was the same color as his jumpsuit. The orange men moved among the green and yellow workers, pausing now and then to lean close and yell at an individual. The workers being yelled at seemed not to respond, perhaps not even to hear over the roar of the moving lines and a thousand knives clicking against bone. It looked to Billy like a science fiction movie about a nightmarish future when humanity was reduced to automatonlike status under the control of the orange men.

"Under those conditions, a few are bound to slip past us, despite all due diligence," the manager roared.

Billy realized that ignoring the man was just making him more nervous. He turned to the manager, put a hand on his arm, and offered his biggest smile. "No problem," he said, moving his lips in exaggeration. Smiling in the middle of such a nightmare was not easy.

Most of the knife-wielding workers, men and women, were Hispanic. Short people, dwarfed by their overseers, their dark eyes glazed by the repetition of the work. They did not lift their gaze to note the passing of Billy and the manager. Billy thought he remembered a scene very like this one, involving white-clad Mexican Indian peasants laboring in a demonic gold mine—a filmmaker's horrific vision of the domination of the Aztecs by the Spaniards.

As the visual shock wore off, Billy realized that the cutting floor was cold. He gave a shiver, more in acknowledgment of his new awareness than from an actual chill.

"We keep it around forty-five degrees in here," the manager said. "Retards bacterial growth. And makes it more comfortable for the workers."

Billy wondered how comfortable the workers found it to be performing endlessly repetitive hand motions with sharp knives when their fingers were cold. He had seen no one yet who looked remotely comfortable, only dazed.

There was a sprinkling of black faces among the sea of brown, but few enough that Billy could scan them quickly.

The manager seemed to be attempting to read Billy's mind. "Most of the African-American workers are on the killing floor," he said.

"Why is that?"

The manager's eyes widened; he was obviously flustered. It was not the type of question people asked while on the tour.

"It pays more," he said, adding quickly, "and they're better at it."

"Better at killing?"

"They seem to be able to handle it better. . . . We're very proud of them."

"African-Americans can handle killing better than other people? I didn't realize that."

The manager smiled uncertainly. The mole under his eye seemed to twitch. "The Mexicans aren't strong enough—and they don't like blood. And the African-Americans all speak English," he added lamely.

"Imagine," said Billy.

They went against the flow of the assembly line, walking past the men and women hacking away at progressively larger pieces of the hog, until they reached an area where the entire animal, gutted but whole, swung through a shredded plastic curtain on a line of overhead hooks. Here, there were black men who eased the carcasses from hook to conveyer belt and made the initial cuts, severing the beast into its largest component parts. As electrical saws and slicers cut through joints and spinal column, bloody bits of gristle and chips of bone flew against their goggled eyes. The men had the grim, stunned, gore-speckled faces of spectators who had been standing too close while a high-caliber bullet blew someone else's brains out.

The noise was deafening, and the men wore the same padded ear protectors as airline baggage handlers. Any communication was done by sign language, but no one looked up or acknowledged the presence of Billy and the manager. The pace of the assembly line was too fast for anything but work. The curtain flapped like a tongue as corpse after corpse issued forth from the great maw of the killing floor.

The manager looked on proudly for a moment, then drew the number 8 in the air with his finger. Billy shrugged his lack of comprehension. The manager smiled and waggled a finger in the air, counseling patience. He led Billy through a door and into a closet that housed more of the cutting tools the men were using on the line. The noise was lessened there, but still very loud. The manager leaned toward Billy's ear.

"Eight million shoulders last year! That's a hog every forty-five seconds!"

He positioned his face directly in front of Billy's, urging approval with his eyebrows. Billy struggled not to focus on the mole. He wondered how often people helpfully informed the manager that he had a little something under his eye before realizing their mistake.

"Terrific," Billy said without enthusiasm.

"Every forty-five *seconds*," he repeated, thrilled with the information.

Billy gave him a thumbs-up. Pleased with his conversion, the manager preceded Billy out of the closet and through a pair of automated doors onto the killing floor.

The stench of pooled warm blood, overpowering, nauseating, rose above the odor of ammonia and pig shit. Billy squinted against it, as if the smell were strong enough to invade through the eyes. He saw a train of hogs, just inches from one another, hanging upside down by shackles on their hind legs. They lurched past him on the cog-driven chain from which they hung, long tendrils of blood trailing from their muzzles and snouts. He shifted his gaze away from the dead beasts, only to find living brutes, electrically stunned but still breathing, being hoisted into the air by a machine. Black men in white smocks covered with a clear plastic outer coat cut the animals' throats with long knives, and a gush of blood, propelled by gravity and a still-beating heart, spurted forth into collection tubs. Like everything else emerging from the hogs, it would be put to commercial use.

There was something alarmingly human about the hanging pink-skinned corpses. The complete indifference of the men to the carnage that surrounded them reminded Billy of the scenes of lynchings he had viewed in the library the day before. The parallels were imaginary, more whimsical than real, but still he could not shake the sense that he was witnessing a photographic negative of the pale Sabella farmers clustered around their dark-skinned victim. It was unsettling, claustrophobic, and redolent of danger. All those knives, all that blood—how easy to lose respect for life in general, how simple for a worker overstressed, unsensitized, and dehumanized by the pace of killing a hog every forty-five seconds to snap and turn his knife on the jugular of the closest human.

Gagging and nervous, Billy needed to get off of the killing floor. The manager leaned into one of the cutters, roaring criticism into his ear. The worker listened sullenly, then turned a look of such baleful disdain at the manager that Billy wondered if the manager realized how close he was to being hung from one of the overhead hooks himself. He searched for the nearest exit, leaving the manager to deal with problems of his own making. The difference between me and the manager, Billy thought, is one of assumptions. The manager's experience of life leads him to assume that he can mess with an angry man with a knife in his hand and suffer no consequences. I assume otherwise. The manager had never seen a man snap under pressure and turn homicidally mad. Billy had. It was not something to forget, and it changed one's perspective forever after.

An exit sign glowed dimly red, reinforcing the hellishness of the atmosphere. Billy saw the door swing outward as a white-smocked figure hurried from the floor like a ghost summoned from the pit to do its evil works in the larger world. In his haste, the departing worker had set some of the hanging porkers swinging, and as Billy hurried past them, he saw the spray of blood they sprinkled on the floor. Reaching the exit door, he heard a noise behind him. He turned in time to see another worker slip on the blood, grab a hanging corpse to right himself, and bring it collapsing down atop him. Several more hog bodies were involved in a small chain reaction, each of them landing on the downed man, more than two hundred pounds of bone and flesh atop him. While some of the men rushed to help their fallen comrade, the manager waved his arms, gesticulating wildly. Billy half-heard, half-lip-read the manager's urgent message: "Keep the line moving! Keep the line moving!"

The worker from the killing floor who had preceded him out of the exit had already skirted the holding pens crammed with the hill-ocks of protesting pork and was running toward the highway. He discarded his plastic overcoat and then his hard hat and hairnet as he ran, finally ripping off the white smock and dropping it among the weeds next to the highway. He treated the highway like a practice track. Turning south, he kept on running in a line as straight as a draftsman could draw it, his legs fluid, his arms swinging easily in concert, gobbling up the distance in a pace that looked as if he could maintain it for a long, long time. Heavy work boots appeared to be no impediment. A gifted athlete, Billy thought. A trained and talented athlete who runs as easily as he walks.

"So long, Odette," he murmured. Considering the hellishness of the abattoir and the presence of those throat-slitting knives, Billy was very grateful that Odette had seen him first. He had already met Collins in a dark alley and hadn't cared for that very much. He would have liked a confrontation on the killing floor even less.

When Billy returned to his car and made his way along the long loop back to the highway, Collins was gone, and there was no point in speculating where. Any cornfield among the thousands of acres accessible within a few minutes' run would suffice to swallow him as absolutely as the ocean. If only the man would disappear as completely from my life as he did from the road, Billy mused, knowing it was wishful thinking.

The long drive home gave him more time to think than he would have wished. What he needed now was action, something fast and violent that didn't require thought, speculation, or long, labored re-flection. He wanted to smash somebody in the mouth, and at the moment he was not too particular whom it might be, although some-one small and slow was preferable, since he wasn't looking for a workout, just a release. He envied Collins his run into oblivion. Exhausting himself in the enervating heat and humidity was a poor substitute for a physical explosion, but it was an acceptable one at least. Brooding over Joan was not.

He drove automatically, letting the towering stands of plant life funnel him homeward while he tried to concentrate on Odette Collins. If Collins had a car, he would have run for it, not taken to the highway on foot. That was consistent with the motel operator's belief that he had arrived at the lodging on foot, as well as the fact that the two times Billy had seen him in town he had been walking—or running. So how did he get around? Probably via bus to the slaughterhouse in Tecumseh. But from the slaughterhouse to the motel in Falls City? Billy had to wonder how often the locals would pick up a black hitch-hiker with a shaven head, reeking of pig. There would be some long, dry periods between rides. Which meant that he had prearranged transportation. Someone to pick him up—where, here? On the highway, or at the slaughterhouse? Someone to drive him to the motel, where he could cleanse himself. Someone who dropped him off at the outskirts because she didn't want to be seen with him in public. Someone who didn't offer her own shower for him to use because it was not safe. Someone who saw him on the sly. . . . Billy blinked and tried to focus on the road, avoiding the obvious conclusion to the sequence.

He switched on a country-western station and sang along at the top of his lungs, howling noise instead of lyrics all the way home.

CHAPTER THIRTEEN

S ean Tree went first to an ATM machine and checked his balance, as he did every month. There, as it had been for so long that he could scarcely remember the stretch of years, was the regular deposit. It had been there when he was an active farmer, the monthly remittance often making the difference between solvency and debt, and it had been there after he had given up the endless labor of farming and turned to the solace of the bottle. The amount had grown through the years, adjusted sporadically for inflation, never a huge sum, but always enough to keep the wolf from the door or to keep his credit active at the Sportsman's Bar and the liquor store. Sean thought of it as his lifeline; it had pulled him from deep waters many a time. So many times, in fact, that he considered it his due for a life lived by certain rules. A just reward, nothing excessive, only what he deserved. He never wished it to be more; it was enough, and Sean was not a greedy man. If his actions of the last few days had merited recognition, he did not expect an increase in the monthly stipend. He was acting to preserve it, after all, not to pump it up. Sean had his failings, but he was never tempted to strangle the goose that laid his monthly golden egg.

He withdrew enough to keep him in liquids for a week and proceeded to the Sportsman's. He vowed as he did every day that this time he would not drink too much, that he would have just a few to quench the thirst, fight the chill, and leaven the evening with a bit of conviviality—and what was the harm in any of that? Sure. None at all, but he would not overdo. He would get home under his own steam and at a reasonable hour so he could spend a bit of quality time with his lady wife. Filled with his usual predrink sense of propriety and happy resolve, he even briefly considered a bit of fun in bed with her upon his early arrival at home. As he crossed the street, he indulged in a quick fantasy of putting it to her in the kitchen, making her squeal among the assiduously scrubbed pots and pans and porcelain. And sure, Sean was just the boyo to do it, too. He'd made many a woman squeal in his time, and many more had wished he had . . . although he'd been a faithful husband, by and large. Unlike some he knew, Sean had hewn to the straight and narrow, and the few little slips scarcely counted at all. He was human and a man, after all. And a healthy, virile man at that. But his peccadilloes had been just that, dalliances that never lasted more than a year or two. They always parted friends, the women disappointed, of course, and Sean relieved, but he never lied to any of them, never let on that he could offer them anything but his big willie—which was more than enough for any woman, not that he cared to boast about it, or needed to. Actions spoke louder than words, and Sean's prowess was legendary, he liked to think. Or at least among those who'd had occasion to know. He hoped to God that the word had spread no further; he would hate to have a reputation as a licentious man. As was so often the case when thinking about sex, Sean was whipsawed between lusty braggadocio and hypocritical virtue to the extent that he was left confused and disenchanted. It was probably just as well, he reflected, that he had actually given up sex many years ago. Not that he might not make a comeback at any moment, mind. He was still as good a man as ever he was.

By the time he reached the comforting gloom of the bar, the sexual moment and its attendant jumble of emotions had passed and, after the second beer, so had the vow to get home early.

Hours later, he drove home slowly, as always, singing "Will you go, lassie, go?" loudly in his whiskey tenor. It was a song that came to him only when in his cups and thus had become a nightly ritual. His eyes teared when he reached the bathetic chorus, but he sang bravely through it. When he saw the sheriff's car, he blinked his lights, honked, and waved his hand, thinking it might be his nephew. The squad car swerved onto the shoulder, prudently giving Sean that little extra space his truck sometimes required on the trip home. It wasn't his nephew, Sean saw, but that nighttime fellow, Schatz. Well, and a good man he was, too. Not the brightest bulb in the fixture, but a fine listener, as Sean had had occasion to know, having bent the man's ear on more than one instance while sharing a ride home in the squad car or taking advantage of the hospitality of the local cell.

Sean's pickup pulled off the dirt road and into the driveway of his farm like a veteran horse seeking its stall. The left rear wheel caught the edge of the culvert, but not enough to matter. He pulled up next to the house and sat for a moment in the cab of the truck, the lights still on, engine running, while he finished the song. Sean hated to quit a song in midverse; it would haunt him afterward, demanding to be finished with the respect it deserved.

He leaned forward slightly to turn off the ignition and douse the lights, nagged by the awareness that there was something yet to be done. Something he had to do to complete his obligations. Service the wife? He was a bit overdo there, had to get around to it soon. His head swam pleasantly and he rested it momentarily on the steering wheel. It wasn't the wife, something else. Something clever he had to do. And he was just the man for the job, too. Sean was nothing if not clever. He made a sly face in the dark of the cab. God, he was a funny fellow. Merriment burbled up, filling his chest, and he had to laugh at how clever and funny he was. Still the thought nagged him, swimming around in his brain, just out of reach. He put his head back on the steering wheel, closing his eyes so he could think the better, and if he caught a little bit of sleep, there was nothing wrong with that, either. Who deserved it more than he did?

The first bullet ripped through the window and the space where the driver's head should be, and the second bullet passed in front of the first and exited through the windshield. The third and fourth shots hit the outside of the cab with solid whaps, sounding like someone was after the truck with a baseball bat. The final two shots were aimed too rapidly and badly, one of them missing the truck entirely and lodging in the side of the barn.

Billy was doing push-ups on his living room floor when the phone call came, punishing himself until his muscles burned and quivered in surrender—a vain attempt to exhaust himself so that he could sleep. His body would succumb, but his mind would not shut off, and he welcomed his aunt's measured midnight invitation.

Billy checked the truck first to be sure that the attack on Sean wasn't just another alcoholic experience, then listened to his uncle with as much patience as he could muster. As always, the tale was told with more detail than absolutely necessary, most of it having to do with various accounts of Sean's many, and questionable, virtues.

"Who do you think would want to kill you?" Billy interrupted.

Sean was not easily deterred from his path. "Too cowardly to come at me face-to-face," he blustered.

You would rather be shot while you watched? Billy thought. Been there, done that, didn't care for it. Don't think I'd recommend it, Sean.

"A man is known by his enemies," Sean said, picking up on Billy's question belatedly.

"And who are yours?"

Sean lowered the lid on one eye, implying dark secrets. "Fucking legion," he said proudly. "More enemies than you can shake a stick at."

"Leave off, Sean," said his wife disgustedly. She had been pouring black coffee into him for the past two hours, to little observable effect. Billy wondered if his aunt Adley were not one of the enemies who might wish Sean dead, at least from time to time. "You haven't got any enemies. All you've got is creditors."

"That's all you know about it. A powerful man attracts enemies like lint."

"And so he might," she agreed. "But you're not one of them."

Sean regarded his wife darkly. It was hard to imagine what he was thinking of earlier when he'd contemplated slipping her a stiff one amid the pots and pans. She'd as like brain him with one of those pots as tolerate his approach from the rear.

"Fat chance," he said.

"What are you talking about now?"

"I haven't lost my mind entirely, you know. There'll be no waltzing around this kitchen anytime soon, I can promise you that."

Adley looked at Billy in despair.

"He's gone," she said. "You'll get nothing useful out of him until he sleeps it off."

Sean grasped at another thread swinging through his mind. "I think it was that black fella," he said.

Billy made himself wait a moment before pursuing the lead. He was entirely too eager for it to be true, he realized.

"What black fella is that, Sean?"

"The one who attacked me." He ripped his shirt open, displaying the bruise on his chest, now turning yellow. It stood out obscenely against the pale white of his flesh, while the companion bruise on his cheek was largely obscured by the perpetually florid flush of burst blood vessels.

"He came at me from behind," Sean said. He brandished a fist, the knuckles still scraped from the encounter. Billy leaned forward, suddenly struck by the pattern of the bruises. Whatever else had happened the night of the storm, no one had attacked Sean from behind and hit him repeatedly from the front.

"From behind," Sean repeated to his wife.

"Sure he did," said Adley. "Cover yourself. No one wants to look at you."

Christ, was it any wonder he had a nip now and again? The woman didn't even recognize the marks of heroism when she saw them. Nor appreciate the manly torso, neither.

"I nearly had him," Sean continued. "He ran, the coward. . . . They'll always run, you know. Stand up to them and they'll always run in the end, isn't that right, Billy?"

"Why do you think it was the black man, Sean? Did you see him?"

"See him? We were face-to-face, trading blows like fury. . . ."

"I mean tonight. Did you see him shoot at you?"

Sean paused, struggling to restore things to their proper order. "Tonight, was it?"

"Somebody shot at your truck tonight, Sean," Adley said, her tone now patient and helpful. "If he was shooting at you, he wasn't a very good shot. But it did happen; I heard the shots myself. Billy wants to know if you saw that black man with the gun."

"I want to know if you saw anyone with a gun." How easy it would be to plant a story in Sean's mind. A few words of encouragement now and Sean would be convinced it was the truth and swear to it until he was blue in the face.

"He was shooting at me?" Sean asked. He remembered the story about the attack on the street, but he didn't realize there was a gun involved. He looked to Billy for guidance.

"Maybe we'd better do this in the morning, Sean."

"I could use a little drink," said Sean. "Just a short one."

"Go to bed," Adley said sharply.

"Could I have him for a moment alone?" Billy asked.

"You can take him with you, for all I care," said Adley, but she did not leave the kitchen.

"Who do you think might have shot at him?" Billy asked.

Sean tapped his nose and winked at his nephew in an indication of great, and secret, knowledge.

Adley gripped the neck of her bathrobe and shook her head.

"You'd have to care an awful lot to come out here in the night and take a shot—take a lot of shots—at him, wouldn't you? Who cares that much about him? Look at him." She cleared a throat suddenly tight with emotion. "Who cares enough about him in the whole world? Just me."

"I—"

Adley cut him short with a hand in the air.

"I know, Billy, you're good to him; you're a good nephew—but I'm the only one alive who loves him enough to kill him."

She left the two men alone at the kitchen table. Sean fixed Billy with a benign smile, which was the usual precursor to passing out. Billy glanced out the window, seeing nothing but his reflection against the background of the black night. If someone were still out there, hoping to finish the assassination, he could have done it at any time in the last hour. Billy knew the shooter was long since gone, but he still felt uneasy.

Billy placed the postcard of the lynching on the table in front of Sean.

"Sean, pay attention now."

Sean's smile widened, but his eyes did not focus. Billy patted his cheek. If he was ever going to get Sean to respond with candor, it would have to be when his defenses were down.

"Who is that?" Billy asked. He put his finger under the face of the older of the two boys who huddled together on one side of the frame. "Who is it, Sean?"

He tapped his uncle's face again and directed him to the postcard. Sean blinked repeatedly, as if trying to kick his mind into action.

"You know who that is," Sean said.

"Who is it, Sean?"

"You know, lad."

"Tell me. Tell me who it is, Sean."

"It's your daddy, boy. That's my brother Jim."

As if relieved of a great burden, Sean put his head on the kitchen table and fell asleep.

CHAPTER FOURTEEN

In the morning, Billy found Carl Wittrock, an uncle by marriage, sitting on the sweeping front porch of Sean's farmhouse with a .388 Magnum Winchester rifle on his lap. A shotgun was propped against the wall behind him. Wittrock had a baseball cap tipped low on his brow to keep the sun from his eyes as he scanned the road and the access over the adjoining fields. He looks like an advertisement for NRA paranoia, Billy thought. Except in this case, the paranoia seems justified.

"Billy Boy!" Wittrock piped as Billy stepped onto the porch. Although Wittrock's own heritage was a mix of square-jawed Germans and long-Americanized English, he had transformed himself into an

Irishman like the Trees, as ardently foolish about the auld sod as Sean himself. Billy thought he looked like a sheep masquerading as a goat, but he never mentioned it to his uncle. To the family, Carl Wittrock's blood had become as emerald green as all their own. If three or four generations of dilution and intermarriage in America had not weakened their Irishness—in itself a minor miracle of suspension of Mendel's law—then who was to say that Uncle Carl's transformation to one of Erin's own could not have been brought about by sheer willpower? Neither Gregor Mendel nor Watson and Crick had the last word on these matters in the Tree clan.

"You appear to be well armed there, Uncle Carl."

"That I am, Billy lad. Keeping watch, don't you know, while Sean gets a bit of tucker."

Billy noted the "tucker" but did not comment. Carl was wont to toss the odd bit of English or Australian slang into his conversation, thinking it to be straight from Dublin. Since no one else in the family was genuinely Irish, either, and had no firmer grasp on Irishisms than Carl himself, they did not question the provenance of anything he said that they did not understand. The meaning was usually clear enough, in any event.

"I'm going to have to wake him up, I'm afraid. We have a little unfinished business."

"You'll want to avoid his first breath or two," said Carl. "Fiercely foul."

"Thanks for the tip."

"Had the pleasure myself once or twice. Smells like the devil's own asshole."

"Nice."

"I believe it aged me."

"I'll come at him from a distance, then," said Billy.

"He tends to thrash about a bit, as well. Watch the flying arms." Carl had accompanied Sean on more benders than either could remember and knew whereof he spoke. Although he could match Sean drink for drink when he was of a mind, Carl had not developed either the Tree weakness or the Tree dependency. At this stage of his alcoholism, Sean could get drunk on two beers, as much from eager anticipation as the spirits themselves, but Carl could imbibe prodigious amounts and still appear sober. The only indication of intoxication was Carl's increasingly slower speech, as if he were selecting every word with the caution of a politician in mid-lie.

"Have you found the villain who shot at him yet?" Carl asked.

Billy was grateful for the "yet." The chances of finding the villain did not seem particularly high.

"Not yet. I'm going to take a look around right now. We'll let Sean sleep it off a bit longer."

"Just as well."

"You'll be careful not to point that thing in my direction, won't you, Carl?"

"I'm always careful with a gun," said Carl.

"That's what they all say," said Billy, who knew that loaded guns bred incaution and "unloaded" guns were virtual incubators of recklessness.

Billy determined the direction from which the shots at the truck had come by inserting a pencil into the holes, then walked in increasingly longer arcs, studying the ground. The shooter must not have been too close, or he would not have missed. Too far and he would not have had much hope of hitting his target—and the number of shots indicated a serious desire to succeed.

If Sean had been hit, much less killed, there would be a team of forensic experts from the state patrol to do the job Billy was doing now. As it was, the case was nothing more than someone taking potshots at a truck belonging to a famous local souse. Some might contend that Sean had done it himself, plugging away at his own truck while under the influence—a thought that had occurred to Billy, as well.

The ground was still soft from the recent rain, so finding the footprints was not hard. The shooter had walked around like a nesting dog before taking a kneeling position next to a fence post about forty yards from the truck. He would have used the post as a gun rest to steady himself. It was not a particularly difficult shot from this distance, assuming there had been enough light spilling from the house to illuminate Sean. Evidently, there had been, because the shots had come close enough to shatter the windshield. Perilously close to the driver. Assuming the driver was behind the wheel, of course. Assuming he wasn't out here, shooting at his own truck. Billy had no clear idea of *why* Sean would be shooting at his truck and claiming another attack, but he could not shake the notion from his mind. The pattern of bruises on his uncle's chest and face—revisited during the unwelcome display at the kitchen table—had stirred Billy's suspicions. As had the fact that Sean had emerged from a truck peppered with bullet holes and yet had only a few scratches from shattered glass to show for the near miss. It could have happened as Sean recounted it, of course, and Sean had certainly demonstrated an amazing streak of luck in avoiding serious injury during his years of alcoholic motoring.

Whether it was Sean or someone else, the gunman had not much cared if the traces of his activity were found. Empty shell cases, still redolent of gunpowder, were littered around an area a foot or two behind the fence post, where a bolt action would have ejected them. Billy gathered them into a plastic evidence bag and slipped them into his pocket, then got down on his hands and knees and examined the footprints more closely.

They were a disappointment, a fact he hated to admit to himself. The prints were not those of Odette Collins's heavy work boots. It would have been so convenient if it had been Collins, that would have wrapped most of his problems into one neat package and tied them with a ribbon of revenge. But these were the deep heel indentations of cowboy boots. A great many men in the area wore cowboy boots, but Collins, on the two occasions when Billy had noted his footwear, did not. He had worn work boots the night Billy encountered him behind Joan's house, and he had worn work boots when he fled from the slaughterhouse and hotfooted it down the highway. To assume that he had made his way to Falls City from Tecumseh in work boots and then somehow acquired cowboy boots before coming out to snipe at Sean was stretching things a bit too much, even for someone who wanted to put the man behind bars and let him rot.

And *would I* go to the trouble he went to? Billy asked himself, squatting over the boot prints. Travel to Falls City after eight hours in that bloody hellhole, check into the motel, shower and cleanse myself, walk through the dark to meet Joan? He laughed bitterly. Of course he would. For Joan, who wouldn't? For a woman like Joan, what else might a man do? Frame a rival, for instance? How hard would it be to get Odette Collins's boot print out here by the fence post on his uncle's farm? Or simply wait for the next rain to eliminate the existing prints? How hard to convince Sean that he had seen Odette with a rifle, firing away—he was already thinking as much without prompting from Billy—and how hard thereafter to convince a jury? Around here? With a defendant who traveled by foot and killed hogs for a living and had skin the color of good walnut furniture and a head shaven in that threatening way? How hard? All it would take was a little imagination, a little work—and a total lack of conscience.... And what has my conscience done for me lately? Billy wondered.

As he stood and stretched, he thought about rubbing out the cowboy boot prints with his toes. For a woman like Joan, what would a man not do? . . . But he could stop right there. There was no woman like Joan; there was only Joan herself. He had never met another who affected him so, whose every changing mood worked on him with such devastating effect. So the question was even more direct. What would he do to keep Joan?

Billy did not know the answer, but he was astounded at himself for asking the question. He left the boot prints as they were. There was no point in doing anything until he had Collins in custody, and he had the bench warrant to justify that. If he decided to fake some work boot prints, he had better know what size they were, at the very least.

Get any clues?" Carl asked when Billy returned to the porch. As far as Billy could tell, his uncle had not stirred while he was gone. The chair was still tipped back on its rear legs as Carl converted it into an impromptu rocker, and the DeKalb Seed cap was still pulled down so low that Carl appeared to be seeing through his nose. Provided anyone was obliging enough to approach the house from the direction in which Carl was looking, he would see them.

"I did some powerful sleuthing all right," Billy acknowledged. "It appears to be a left-handed man of medium height and weight who smokes expensive cigars, drinks cognac of an evening, and received his education in India."

"How do you know all that?"

"Elementary, Carl. I made it up." He glanced at the cowboy boots on his uncle's feet. "Does Sean ever wear boots like that?"

Carl studied his boots for a moment, apparently surprised to find them encasing his feet.

"Beats the hell out of me."

"Me, too. We're not very observant, Carl. Men, I mean. Did you ever notice that? A woman would be able to tell you what Sean wore and if he ever changed. She'd remember what she was wearing on the same day, too."

"You lost me," Carl said.

"I've been doing that lately," Billy said. "Losing people. I'm getting downright careless about it."

"Well, you got no worries on this end, Billy. I'll hold the fort while you do your investigating."

"What will you do if you see someone coming, Uncle Carl?"

"What will I do?" Carl patted the stock of the rifle. "Right between the eyes."

"Easy as that?"

"You know it."

"Show me."

"Show you? What do you mean?"

"You see that fence post where I was checking things out? Imagine that's the villain, coming back for another try at Sean. Show me what you'd do."

Carl raised the rifle to his shoulder. "Bang."

"You'd do it like that? Sitting down?"

"No. You know what I mean."

"Show me, Carl. Can't have you holding down the fort unless I know how you're going to do it."

With the air of humoring his nephew, Carl rose to his feet, widened his stance, lifted the rifle to his shoulder again, and sighted it on the fence post.

"Want me to shoot it?"

"If you feel the spirit move," Billy said.

Carl squeezed off a round. "Got it," he said triumphantly.

"Nice shooting." Carl had missed, as Billy knew he would. A bullet would have made a sound as it hit the post, and the post would have shuddered. If Carl aimed at things that way, standing, the least stable of all positions, the approaching villain could jump up and down and wave his arms and be as safe as if he were home in bed. Carl had not knelt, nor had he used the chair or the side of the porch as a gun rest. He had missed the post, but he had also pretty quickly eliminated himself as a suspect. As would most men in the county, of course. They owned guns, hunted now and then, but that did not make them good shots. Whoever had shot at Sean was good, just not quite good enough. Or at least sensible. From that distance, shooting that way, Carl might well have missed the truck entirely.

"Do me a favor, Carl."

"Sure."

"Keep an eye peeled—but don't shoot."

"Why not?"

"We can't justify executing the man yet. He doesn't have your deadly eye. So far, he's only shot a pickup."

After Billy entered the house, Carl wondered if it was important that he understood only about half of what his nephew said. The boy was always referring to something else, but Carl seldom knew the reference. Before reaching the conclusion that it did not matter, Carl's mind wandered to a better question. Why, he wondered, had Sean decided to shoot up his own truck?

Sean slept in a spare small room adjoining the master bedroom, from which he had moved, or been evicted by Adley, years earlier, for reasons Billy did not care to speculate upon. There was little furniture and few signs of occupancy other than the bed and an aged floor lamp. Clearly, Sean was not one to read himself to sleep. Adley kept the room spotlessly clean, but there was nothing she could do about the miasmic air that accumulated from Sean's breath during the night. An open window did not appear to help, for the room smelled of stale beer processed through the human stomach. Billy understood what Carl had meant when he warned him about waking the man.

Billy searched for cowboy boots and found them on the closet floor; standing beside the bed was the footwear Adley had removed after she and Billy maneuvered Sean from the kitchen table—a scuffed pair of brogans, work shoes, not boots. Billy took one of the cowboy boots to compare it with the prints by the fence post, just in case, and shook his uncle by the foot.

Sean awoke with a start, flailing his arms, as Carl had warned. For several seconds, his expression was one of sheer terror. I wouldn't want to have his dreams, Billy thought. But then again, he didn't want to have his own, either.

"Good morning," Billy said.

"Jaysus, Billy! You give me a terrible scare."

"Sorry. . . . It's morning."

"You'd wake a man to tell him a thing like that? It's morning every day."

Sean moved his tongue energetically about his mouth and under his lips with a flapping sound. It was not hard to see why Aunt Adley was no longer sharing a bed with him.

"I've got a few more questions for you," Billy said. Sean dragged his fingers down his face, then put himself through a series of eye exercises, rolling them strenuously from side to side and up and down while holding them as wide open as possible. Billy looked away until the gymnastics were over, hoping that his uncle would not find it necessary to do a full inventory of all his body parts before getting out of bed.

"Questions about what?" Sean asked. He stretched his tongue to its full length like a Maori warrior.

"Last night's incident."

"Last night? . . . Last night . . . Refresh my memory there, would you, Bill?"

Billy sighed wearily. It was going to be uphill all the way.

"Someone shot at you, or at least at your truck."

"They never!" Sean exclaimed.

Billy was unable to resist a touch of his phony brogue. "Aye, Sean, they did and all."

"The little buggers!"

"I don't think it was a team effort. Just one man with a thirty-aught-six. You don't remember any of it, I suppose."

"Give me some hints, Billy. I don't always grasp the events of the night before right away."

"I'm not going to implant a memory for you. Try to think about it; if any of it comes back, we'll talk."

"Shooting at me?"

"Or your truck. Maybe just your truck. No one would want to shoot *you*, would they?"

Sean investigated both ears simultaneously, producing a loud liquid sound. Billy winced and wished himself elsewhere.

"Only the odd husband now and then." He winked broadly, then quickly changed to a serious mien. "And that was years ago. Not a word to your aunt, mind."

Who would believe it anyway? Billy wondered. Sean's sounds alone would drive any woman from the room, screaming. And this is my blood uncle, what I may turn into in twenty-five years, Billy thought. Unless I see the transformation coming and have the good sense to blow my brains out first.

Billy put the postcard of the lynching on the bed next to Sean and pointed at the boys in the front of the crowd.

"If that's my dad, who is this?"

Sean sucked in his breath and pulled away from the photo.

"Where did you ever get such a thing?"

"Somebody gave it to me. Who is that little boy in front, Sean?"

"Your father? Who? Where? That's not Jimmy. That's not your father, Billy. What in God's name would your father be doing in such a situation?"

"Last night, you told me it was my father. It certainly looks like him, but I never knew him as a boy. *You did.*"

Sean shook his head. "Not your father. Christ, Billy, don't you see what's going on there? Don't you see that horror hanging from the tree there? What would your father be doing there?"

"You tell me."

"It's not him.

"Last night, you said it was. You didn't hesitate."

A look of sudden understanding passed over Sean's face. "Oh, Billy, last night . . . I drink, Bill."

"I've heard that rumor, Sean. But last night, I believed you. You were very certain about it."

"No."

"What was my father doing there?"

Sean shook his head again.

"I wasn't given this at random," Billy said. "Somebody dropped it on me for a reason. This happened in Sabella in 1948. My father would have been fifteen years old. Just like this kid. And you would have been twelve, Sean." Billy put his finger underneath the face of the smallest of the boys. "Just like this kid. He's about twelve, wouldn't you say?"

"Take that out of my face. I don't know who these people are. I don't know why you think I would."

"I think that's you and that's my dad."

"Oh, no. You're dead wrong there." Sean averted his eyes and tried to rise from the bed. Billy touched his chest and sat him back down.

"I think you know about this, Sean. Tell me. Tell me what this is about. Why did he give me this and a noose?"

"They gave you a noose, too?"

"Yes. Why? What does it mean? Who's 'they'?"

"In the name of God, Billy, I don't know. I'd tell you if I knew, wouldn't I? Why would you think me and your father'd be mixed up in anything as shameful as that, no matter how old we were?"

"Because you were. Here's the photo to prove it."

"It's not me, sure, it's never me."

"You know what I can do, don't you, Sean? I can give this to the FBI and they can run one of those computer enhancements on it and they can show me exactly what this little kid—you, Sean—would look like today, fifty-two years later. Those things are so accurate, I'll be able to fit it on your face like mask."

"Naw, you couldn't, sure you couldn't."

"I'll have it in two days. One for you, one for my father. We'll even throw in some for the rest of those boys. . . . They do them in three dimensions, too, you know. We can make a latex mask of it, slip it on your face like they do in the movies. You won't be able to deny it then."

"I've got to go to the bathroom, Billy." Sean struggled to his feet, squeezing past his nephew.

"But the problem is, the FBI will be involved in it then. Once you get them into it, they never get out until they're finished. Do you want that, Sean? Or would you rather just tell me about it now?"

"There's nothing to tell," Sean murmured.

"Yes there is, Sean. Somebody's got something to tell, or I wouldn't been given this piece of filth as a present. What is it, Sean? Tell me."

"I know nothing about it. You got to believe me."

"I 'got' to believe you? You know who says I 'got' to believe them? Desperate people, people who know I don't believe them and their ass is in trouble. Is your ass in trouble, Sean? . . . Of course it is. Someone's trying to shoot it full of holes—and let's not kid ourselves, it's not an angry husband, is it?"

Sean pushed his way past Billy and into the hallway, where he darted quickly into the bathroom.

"You mustn't shout at him, Billy."

Adley stood at the end of the hallway. Listening for how long? Understanding how much?

"I wasn't shouting."

"You were shouting."

"He's lying to me."

Adley snorted. "He lies to me now and then, too, believe it or not. He means no harm by it. He just tells little lies to keep from hurting people's feelings."

The Tree family definition of charm, thought Billy. Never offend by telling the truth when an artful lie will serve. Lord Jimmy had swaddled his family with "little lies," chief among them being the classically simple "It wasn't me." "It wasn't me who stole the money from your purse." "It wasn't me who was too drunk to come to the game." "It wasn't me who lost another job." "It wasn't me who started it." "It wasn't me"—fill in the blank.

Billy stepped away from the bathroom door as he heard the uncertain trickle of an old man urinating. He had been forced into a far too intimate embrace of his aging uncle in the past few days. They said that a doctor should not operate on a member of his family, that a lawyer should not take on one as a client. Nor should a sheriff investigate a case involving his relatives, Billy thought. Too involved, no objectivity. All the little quirks of humanity that you shouldn't even notice suddenly drive you crazy. You wouldn't shout during an interview of anyone else unless you decided it was the right tactical maneuver, and when you did shout, you would know it—you wouldn't need your aunt to tell you.

"Remember, he loves you," said Adley.

"I love him, too," said Billy, wondering if that wasn't also one of the Tree family little lies. Or was strangling emotional enmeshment what was meant by love? And in the category of little lies, should he include his threat to get the FBI to make a computer-aged photo? In the first place, the Feds were not about to waste valuable computer time on a non-case such as this. In the second place, Billy didn't think those computer enhancements were worth anything. They looked impressive but were not particularly accurate, and after forty-eight years had passed, any mask he made of one would fit Sean about as neatly as a Halloween disguise bought from the drugstore. Sean didn't know any of that, of course. Like so many others of an abiding superstitious bent, he had switched his belief in little green men to the white-coated practitioners of science. They worked in mysterious ways and produced wonders to be marveled at. Or feared, in this case. Assuming Sean had anything to be afraid of. Billy was bluffing. He could not identify any of the boys in the photo with certainty, and Sean's reaction could spring as much from a lifetime habit of generic guilt as from any specific truth. Billy was guessing, and he hoped he was wrong. He did not know what consequences might spring from the presence of his father and uncle at a lynching half a century earlier, but whatever it was, it would not be something to be proud of.

"I'll have to talk to him again," he said, easing past his aunt in the narrow hallway.

"Billy, there's no harm done," she said.

It was only on the drive back to town that Billy realized he did not know if his aunt meant no harm had been done in the shooting of the truck, or something deeper.

CHAPTER FIFTEEN

A t the end of the day, he drove to Joan's house instead of walking. He had no intention of staying, or even getting out of the car; he did not trust himself or his resolve were he free to embrace her. He knew that neither jealousy nor righteous indignation was as strong as his desire for her, given prolonged proximity. She came out on the porch as soon as he arrived, as if she'd been sitting by the window, waiting. Her arms were folded across her chest in the classical sign of matronly disapproval, but she wore her cutoff jean shorts, and her shapely legs, tanned to the color of dark honey, seemed to be sending him an entirely different signal. The stretch of skin showing at her midriff did not look so forbidding, either. How can she dress like a teenager and get away with it? he wondered. How can she look so good when most would just look silly? Billy stayed in the car with the window rolled down, his head out.

"Are you going to make me yell?" he asked.

"Are you going to make me walk over to you?"

"I was hoping you would."

"Why don't you get out of the car and come to the porch like a civilized person?" she asked.

"Because I don't trust myself out of the car," he said.

"Why is that?"

"Now we're at the point where you probably don't want me to be yelling so all the world can hear," he said.

Joan stared at him for a moment, then put her hands on her hips and stared some more. She wore a man's white shirt knotted at the waist, with the sleeves rolled up. The new position of her arms tightened the cloth across her breasts and exposed even more of her bronzed stomach. Oh, hell, he told himself, just grab her and take her to bed; you'll feel so much better. . . . It was a near thing, but he wouldn't let himself.

He could see her make a decision. A little grin creased her face and she stepped off the porch as if to say, All right, I'll play your silly game. But when she reached the car, her arms went across her chest again.

"Better?" she asked.

"The closer to you, the better, always," he said.

The grin moved up just one side of her face, which was a good indication of how much of his flirting she was willing to succumb to. About half. She didn't want to remain angry with him; she didn't want to let the anger go too easily, either. There was a pleasure in being the wronged party.

"So what don't you trust yourself about?" she asked.

"You. Looking at you weakens my resolve."

"You're looking at me now."

"You ought to see the state of my resolve. . . . Of course, resolve isn't everything in life."

"You're cute when you're full of shit."

"I must be absolutely gorgeous, then," he replied.

"Just short of absolute." She gave him a full smile, the first. "You do look awfully cute. Kind of lonesome, though."

"It shows?"

"You've got those sad eyes. You always look a little lonesome—well, not always. . . . Will's rodeoing over in Kansas tonight, you know."

He had not known. When Will was away, they took to her large bed, a luxury compared to his own Spartan litter. The sex seemed better there, although he could not have said why this should be so. Maybe it was the mutual sense of themselves as teenagers rolling illicitly in the parents' bed that did it. When Will was gone, they both dropped their more mature, tutorial roles and about twenty years' worth of restraint in the process.

"I'm not coming in," he said.

"What's got into you, Billy? What's wrong?"

He could barely suppress a bitter laugh.

"Gee, I can't imagine."

"Come in the house and tell me about it," she said, suddenly warm. She put a hand on his arm, and he wished he had lashed himself to the mast.

"We had a fight, that's all," she said. "We've had them before. Let's just get over it. I hate being mad at you. It's not as fun as it is being mad at somebody else."

"I just came to give you a message."

"Give it to me inside."

"I can't do that, Joan. I'm not that forgiving a person. I wish I was, but I'm not. I wouldn't feel right in that house or that bed after what happened the other night."

"You know your problem, Billy. You're too moral. The rest of the world doesn't always govern itself according to their morals. They're just people; we're all just people. Except you, sometimes."

"I'm not that moral," he protested, as if it were an accusation.

"You may not know it," she said. "But you are. You're the most moral man I know. It was one of the things about you I fell in love with. I never knew anybody else who really ran his life according to his principles—it was very attractive, especially considering the people

I'd had to deal with in my life . . . but it's not always easy to put up with on a regular basis."

"Morality? I didn't know that's what I'm upset about. I thought it was—"

"I know what you thought. Just relax about it," she said. "Give everyone else a little more breathing room. I'll boil the sheets."

"Here's some breathing room. Or maybe just a warning. If you see Odette Collins, tell him to turn himself in to the Sheriff's Department," he said.

"What are you talking about?"

"There's a bench warrant out for his arrest. He's also wanted for questioning in an assault case."

"Leave him alone, Billy."

"I can't do that."

"He hasn't done anything."

"To who? He's done an awful lot, if you ask me. But some of it isn't against the law. We just want to talk to him about the stuff that is . . . I'm telling you, Joan, because I don't want to see you get hurt by this. If he gets arrested while he's . . . visiting . . . in your house, you'd never live it down in this town."

"So don't arrest him here. No one else knows he comes here," she said.

"But I know it. It doesn't take more than that."

"Just look the other way, Billy. Do it for me, if for no other reason."

"Jesus, Joan. I don't know who or what the hell you think I am."

"Don't be so righteous about it. That's exactly what I'm talking about."

"If he won't give himself up, then tell him to leave. Leave Falls City, leave the county, just go away and stay away."

"You're running him out of town, is that it, Sheriff? I didn't know you could do that sort of thing anymore."

"Only if he's smart enough to leave. . . . All right, there, I've told you. I've warned you, and that's already more than I should have done. I can't help either one of you any more than that. If I see him, I'll arrest him. If I learn where he is, I'll go after him. Clear?"

"You going to get up a posse? How about tar and feathers? Or maybe just a simple lynching."

"Lynching?"

"Nothing fancy, just tree and a rope on the town square."

"What do you know about it, Joan?" he demanded, his voice rising.

She looked at him curiously. "Know about what?"

"Lynching, goddamn it! Have you seen it?"

"What's the matter with you? Seen what?"

"The lynching! Where did you get it? Who gave it to you?"

"What are you yelling about? I don't know what you want from me."

"Neither do I anymore," he said.

As he drove away, Billy knew he had handled the encounter badly. He should turn the car around right now, whip a U-turn on Harlan, and take her into the bedroom and make peace with the most ardent display of sex he could muster. Even throw in a bit of his anger with her to spice it up. It would break the tension and give them a chance to start over, if there was ever to be a chance after Collins. She took it so blithely, so matter-of-factly, that beneath his pain and outrage, he wondered if there was any chance he was overreacting. Could they really view this betrayal so differently? Could she not exhibit at least some hypocritical guilt? If she asked his forgiveness, he would forgive her immediately. Clearly, she wanted to make up, but could she possibly believe he would slip between the sheets soiled by another man without a murmur of protest? And what did morality have to do with her sleeping with Odette Collins? Billy wasn't morally outraged about that; he was wildly jealous and deeply wounded by her betrayal. Surely he had a right to that. True, they had never exchanged vows, but it had hardly seemed necessary. Were there not some underlying assumptions about fidelity that were shared by everyone in the culture? He wondered if there was any truth at all to what she was saying about his moral posturing. Was he any more moral than anyone else? How moral was it for him to be considering how to frame Odette Collins for shooting at Sean?

And what the hell did she mean about his sad eyes anyway? Lonesome? That was the first he'd heard of that.

Billy had little use for a car of his own. If he went anywhere in the town, he usually walked, and the primary reason he ever left the town limits was official business, at which times he used the squad car. He did own a car, however, and after dark, he drove it out of his garage and toward Joan's house. A great advantage to being so seldom seen in it was that no one associated it with him. He parked it in the alley that ran behind Joan's house, wedged in next to a pair of trash cans and a discarded sofa. Three doors away from Joan's house, he could see if anyone approached her place via the alley, as Collins surely would, if he came.

There was nothing sophisticated about it, but for Falls City it would pass as a stakeout. He sat in the passenger seat to give the impression of someone waiting for the driver, and he wore a baseball cap. Nothing sophisticated about his disguise, either, but in the dark, from a distance, it would break up his silhouette and at least give Collins pause. In any event, it was less conspicuous than sitting in the sheriff's car, hunched behind the wheel. He slumped in his seat, put a tape of Irish ballads on his Walkman, and settled in for a lengthy stay.

Although he shunned or mocked most of the family's slavish attachment to Irish culture, he had not turned his back on the music. The doleful laments, the defiant cries, and the sugary love songs all still had the power to move him like no others. For reasons he had never bothered to examine, he could be moved to tears by an Irish tenor crooning about his mother or roused to outrage by a tuneful slaughter of patriots facing down the British several centuries ago. There was so much history in Irish music, implanted like battle standards in the lyrics, the names of heroes and martyrs, the proud listing of the losses and routs, the forced emigrations, the famine and starvation and the endless "Troubles," and, above it all, the pride and furious refusal to bend to the tyrant, echoing again and again in individual voices living and losing their loves against the background of the great communal struggle. And all of it accompanied by the insistent drum of the bodhran, the eerie skirling of the pipes, the ceaseless sawing of the fiddle. He found the instrumental music irresistible, the musicians chasing their complex, repetitive Celtic rhythms as if the devil himself were at their heels. There was nothing remotely as affecting in present-day American music, had not been since the passing of folk music. But the Irish still used their folk forms and traditions, having found a vitality in them that was not drowned by synthesizer or electric guitars.

Listening for the second time to tale of brave Brennan on the moors, Billy saw the lights of a car in his rearview mirror. Deputy Schatz pulled up next to Billy. There goes the stakeout, Billy thought.

"Jesus Christ, Billy, where have you been? We've been trying to get hold of you all over the place."

"I've been right here."

Schatz looked around quickly, trying to determine where exactly "here" was. Billy was known to do some strange things—Lapolla called them "unorthodox," but they seemed strange to Schatz—but the acting sheriff was very glad to have him helping out, and the word in the department was to overlook the little oddities. Still, Schatz had to wonder sometimes.

"We called. I went by the house, tried the radio. . . ."

"Any luck at all?"

Now that was the kind of comment Schatz found peculiar. Was he joking or what? Billy always had a bit of turn to his lips, like he was fighting a grin, but who knew if that meant he was making a joke, or laughing at you? Everybody was always calling him "Charming Billy." Charming. What the hell was that about? Maybe he was better with women.

"You weren't there," said Schatz.

"Ah. So what brings you out on a night like this?"

See, there wasn't anything special about the night, either, so what was the point in that comment? Why not just ask what was up? Sometimes Schatz felt like playing along, showing a half grin himself, and sometimes he didn't. Sometimes he just wanted to cut the shit and get right to it. Right now, he just wanted to cut the shit.

"Somebody took a shot at Judge Sunder," he said.

"Oh boy. . . . Was he hit?"

"I don't know for sure. Lapolla went over there, and he sent me looking for you."

"Where was this?"

"At Sunder's house. That's where everybody is now."

"Tell them I'll be right over," Billy said. "I'll go home and get the squad car."

"Why not drive over in this?"

Billy did not answer, just clambered into the driver's seat and backed out of the alley.

She walked past them for the third time in as many minutes, the cotton print dress swishing loosely around her legs, her sandals slapping against her heels with every step, pursuing some imaginary errand that kept her going in circles.

"Hello, Alice," said one of the boys.

She stopped, as if surprised to see so many boys all together, as if they hadn't been there that day and every weekend all summer long.

"How do you know my name?" she asked.

"A little bird told me."

"I bet," she said, wishing she had something clever to add. She had wanted them to notice her, of course. Wanted them to speak to her. But

all of the witty and alluring things she had thought to say had vanished in an instant. She cocked her hip to one side in a gesture she had seen in the movies.

"Hot enough for you?" asked the smallest of the boys. He tittered as if it were a smart rejoinder and looked to the boy next to him, obviously his older brother, for approval. The older brother was the cutest of the bunch, she thought, the one she would like to talk to, but he wouldn't even look at her, just kept studying her bare legs, as if there was anything of interest in a girl's shinbone.

She ignored the smallest of the boys because he was too young, probably no older than she was herself, and it would not do to dignify his remarks with an answer, or to give the impression that he had laid any claim on her.

"What you all doing?" she asked.

"Working," said one.

"What's it look like?" demanded another.

"Looks like you're just sitting, polishing that bench," she said. She did not understand why the note of defiance always entered her tone when she spoke with boys these days. That wasn't how she felt, wasn't how she felt at all. Her mother would tell her just to listen. That's what men liked, she always said—a woman who would listen to them. But how was she supposed to listen if they never said anything? Or spoke only to one another with nudges and winks? As if she didn't know what they meant. When they acted like that, sniggering and slitting their eyes and poking one another, they were about as subtle as a stack of cow pies.

She waited for a moment, hoping one of them would make an effort at a conversation, even though she didn't know how to start one herself. Let one of them say something that she could actually listen to and she would curb her tongue. Several of them went back to tracing patterns in the space where their feet had worn the grass down to bare dirt. The older brother, the cute one, finally lifted his head and looked her in the face. She looked directly at him, too pleased to be coy and shy about it the way you were supposed to be, and he smiled. It was the very best smile, she thought, and she felt her throat tighten just looking at him looking at her. She was glad he didn't say anything, because she knew for sure she couldn't speak right now, couldn't make any sense of words at all with that radiant smile beaming at her.

She must have looked as foolish as she felt, must have been standing there with her mouth open and her eyes bugging out, because another of the boys started the nudging and winking, waggling his eyebrows and making everything dirty. The older brother shut down his smile and cast his eyes back to the study of her legs, and it was like a light had snapped off.

Lawton Mills came walking toward them in the distance, looking always a little too relaxed, a little slack. He made her uncomfortable; she didn't like either the way he looked at her or the way he avoided her eyes. Worse, she didn't like the way she looked at him sometimes, the way she felt just watching him work in the sun. At eighteen, he was not yet a man, but not quite a boy, either. Not quite someone she could talk to—not that she would anyway. Her father would have her hide if he heard of her lollygagging around, talking to a black man.

"See you," she said finally, wanting to stay for the boy with the smile but wanting to hurry off before the sniggering began in earnest, or before Lawton joined the crowd.

"Not if I see you first," said the younger brother, again looking for approval of his wit and finding little. The others were too busy watching her stride away, studying the way her butt twitched under the cotton, the way the little muscles in her calves flexed and released as she walked.

"She's asking for it," said one of them.

"She's just a kid," said another from the vast remove of three years.

"Kid, shit, you see those tits?"

There was no argument with anatomy, at least none the boys knew about. It was conventional wisdom that early development was associated with, if not provoked by, a looseness of character.

"Tits," repeated the youngest, showing off, hoping to get a rise.

They watched her sashay past the big house, turning on the bench, twisting their necks to follow her with their eyes. They saw her pause as she approached Lawton, saw them exchange a few words. She slapped the air with her arm, perhaps aiming at Lawton, perhaps not. He jerked his head, seemed to laugh, and she walked on, past the equipment shack.

The boys returned to their contemplation of the dirt, keeping their thoughts to themselves, except for the youngest, who was not stirred by the girl the way the others were. He continued to clown, looking for *attention, until his older brother cuffed him rudely on the shoulder and told him to shut up.*

After a minute, one of the boys stood and stretched his back.

"I'm going to take a whiz," he said, and ambled off in the direction in which Alice had gone.

CHAPTER SIXTEEN

J udge Sunder was in his bathrobe and slippers and looked shaken
but still powerfully in control of himself. Like a man who has just
emerged unscathed from a car wreck caused by someone else—
still frightened, awash in adrenaline, but looking for the person responsible, Billy thought. Or, more to the point, he looked like a man
who had been shot at and missed by an inch or two and was more
interested in shooting back than diving for cover. Billy admired the
attitude, but admiring it did not mean that he found it wise. Personally, he thought he would be hiding and simultaneously shouting, "I
give up." It was not an affectation of cowardice. Billy had been shot
at. He knew.

Billy wandered the judge's study, where the shooting had occurred, letting Lapolla deal with the questions. Sunder kept trying to involve Billy, looking to him for reaction when not actually addressing him, but Billy ignored him. He wanted Lapolla to occupy the man while he tried to think. There were two bullet holes in the wall opposite the one window in the room with the blinds up. Broken window glass covered the floor several feet into the room. Billy put pencils into each hole, trying to determine the angle of entrance. The pencils were not parallel to each other, but one was parallel to the floor. Billy sighted back along that one toward the window, past the judge's swivel chair.

"You were in the chair?" Billy asked, interrupting.

"I've just been through that," Sunder said. His residual fear was coming out now in annoyance. "Or weren't you listening?"

"I wasn't actually. I can have Sheriff Lapolla fill me in later if you're rather not go through it again."

Sunder studied Billy for a moment, wondering if the deputy was trying to provoke him, or just being deferential in the extreme. He decided the former but also decided to let it pass.

"I was in my chair, kind of half-dozing, I suppose. I don't usually work this late. I felt a tug on my sleeve, and then the window exploded."

Sunder lifted his arm. A bullet had gone cleanly through the loose material in the armpit and the terry-cloth lapel, less than an inch from the chest. The difference between being hit and missed seemed to be whether the judge was inhaling or exhaling at the time of the shot.

Billy whistled soundlessly.

"The judge is a very lucky man," said Lapolla.

"Luck doesn't begin to cover it," said Sunder. "Blessed, I'd say."

"One lucky man," said Billy, reinforcing the acting sheriff. Lapolla rolled his eyes. "What did you do?"

"When?"

"After you realized you were being shot at."

"I hit the deck," Sunder said. "I crawled out of the room, then went to the phone and called you." He shrugged slightly as if to ask, What else?

Billy gestured toward the shotgun resting against the desk.

"When did you get the shotgun?"

"All right, I got it before I made the phone call. For all I knew, the son of a bitch was going to break down the door."

"You can understand that," Lapolla offered helpfully.

"I suppose so," said Billy. "Although I would have run out the back door and would still be racing, myself. You'd find me halfway to Auburn by now. You're a brave man, Judge."

The judge puffed out his chest slightly but made humble noises. "Just protecting myself."

"As you have every right to do," said Lapolla.

"I know I have a right to do it," said the judge testily. "That's not in question. I just hope the son of a bitch comes back so I can exercise my right."

"The problem there is that he gets to take the first shot; otherwise, you're really not justified in shooting him in self-defense," said Billy.

"You presume to tell me the law? I can blow his nuts off if he steps on my property, and never do a day of time. A wise officer of the law wouldn't even take me in for questioning after this provocation."

"Ah, well, a *wise* one. You ask a lot."

Lapolla jumped in quickly. "Did you get a look at the assailant, Your Honor?"

Sunder turned his attention to Lapolla as if to an annoying child.

"Of course not. It was the middle of the night. I was on the fucking floor. If I'd got a look at him, don't you think I would have blown his head off?"

"Yes, sir, I believe you would."

"You better believe I would," said Sunder.

Billy stared out the shattered window into the night, trying to determine the angle of the other shot.

"Any idea who would do this?" he asked.

"None."

"Do you have any enemies, Your Honor?" asked Lapolla, shaking his head as if such a notion were ridiculous.

Sunder snorted. "Enemies? Of course I've got enemies. I'm a *judge.* You can probably count everyone I've ever ruled against and everyone I've ever sent to jail."

"Yes, sir, I can see that. Can you imagine any of them actually taking a shot at you?"

"Several dozen," he said dismissively. "Billy, you have to assume it was whoever shot at your uncle, don't you? Someone has gone homicidal and is sniping at targets of opportunity is my guess."

"I'm going out to the yard," Billy said.

Sunder glared at Billy's retreating back, then turned toward Lapolla, who flapped his hands in a gesture of conciliation.

"What does he have against me?" the judge asked plaintively.

Billy found the spent cartridges easily enough, their casings glittering in the flashlight beam a few yards from where his estimate had put them. The lawn was thick with grass and he could tell even with the beam of his light that there would be no footprints this time. He stood at the spot, forty yards from the house, looking up the hill at the light in the shattered window. He extended his arm like a rifle and aimed, then dropped to one knee and repeated the action.

Lapolla joined him as he trudged back up the hill toward the corridor of light coming from the window. They reached the window and Billy played his flashlight beam around the thin border of shrubbery.

"The judge thinks you don't like him," Lapolla said.

"You're the sheriff; he should be dealing with you. I don't like him acting like you're not in the room and addressing everything to me."

"I don't mind."

"I do. It means he thinks I'm enough of a jerk not to notice, or not to care. . . . Look in there, Bert. Do you see any work? Anything on the desk that looks like a legal paper? Any books?"

"So what?"

"He said he was working when he was shot at. What was he working on?"

"Does it matter?"

"No, I don't care what he was doing in his own study. Jerking off, for all I care."

"Bill, Bill, Bill . . ." Lapolla half-whispered his dismay and gestured to demonstrate how close they were to an open window.

"I bet he was, in his own fashion. I bet he was in there fondling his memorabilia, reliving his little triumphs."

"What does that have to do with anything?"

"Nothing at all. Just my keen powers of observation."

"Okay, okay," said Lapolla, trying to hush him. "What are we looking for here?"

Billy sighted, using his arm as a rifle again, then lowered his arm to the windowsill and sighted once more.

"What are we doing?" Lapolla asked.

"Plane geometry," said Billy.

They drove in their separate cars back to the department and met in Lapolla's office.

"So, how do you see this, Bert?"

"Pretty straightforward . . . don't you think?" Lapolla asked cautiously.

"I mean the sequence. What's your take on that?"

"The sequence? How do you mean?"

"The timing of things. I'm sure you've had some trouble with that."

"Well, some, yeah," Lapolla said, stalling. He knew that Billy only used him for a sounding board and that he would probably be as surprised by any Lapolla insight, as would Lapolla himself, but he was so sincere in his phrasing, so convincing in his deferral to the acting sheriff's opinion that it made Lapolla nervous.

"Somebody fired two shots into the room, but they came in at different angles. One was from approximately forty yards away, at about the angle you'd expect from a kneeling shooter. The other bullet came in almost dead straight. The house is on top of a hill. You can't shoot dead straight into it if you're downhill, not unless you're on a ladder. The only place you could be is right outside the window. . . . Agreed?"

"I'm listening," said Lapolla.

"So, what was the sequence of those shots? That's my question.

Did the shooter fire from forty yards away and then go up to the house and shoot again?"

"Sounds like it."

"Why would he go up to the house?"

"To finish him off."

"Finish him off? Bert, he hadn't even started. The judge wasn't hit."

"As close as, damn it. Couldn't have missed him by more than an inch."

"True, but the judge wasn't incapacitated. He still had his wits about him, I assume. . . ."

"I imagine old Judge Sunder always has his wits about him."

"I imagine so, too. So a shot comes through his window. He feels the bullet go through his bathrobe, hears it smack into the wall. What does he do—just stay in his chair while the shooter sprints forty yards uphill to finish him off? I don't think so, do you? If I took a shot at Judge Sunder and missed, I wouldn't go anywhere near the house, because I'd know he'd be waiting for me with a shotgun and a handgun and probably a few knives, as well."

"So he shot from up close and then again from farther away," said Lapolla.

"He shoots from close range, misses, runs downhill forty yards—I assume he's running, but maybe he's strolling—and then turns around and takes a parting shot. If he can't hit the man from right outside the house, what makes him think he'll get him from that much farther away?"

"So you're saying neither way makes any sense," said Lapolla. "I see your point."

"Well, yes, I'm saying it doesn't make sense. That doesn't mean it didn't happen, because obviously it did. Maybe he shot up close first, then ran. Sunder looked out the window and presented an irresistible target, so he figured, Why not, and popped off another one. Except Sunder didn't say he did that, and frankly, I don't think he's dumb enough to stick his head out the window to see who's shooting at him. Maybe I'm wrong."

"So maybe Sunder was in shock or something," Lapolla ventured. "He sees the window fly into a hundred pieces, realizes he's been shot at, and all of a sudden it's like he's paralyzed. He stays where he is just long enough for the perpetrator to run up and shoot at close range. He nearly gets shot this time, and that snaps him to attention or something and he falls behind his desk or whatever and the shooter realizes he can't get him. . . . Except the judge said the first shot hit his arm, didn't he?"

"And he dropped to the floor. . . . Of course, he might not be the best-possible witness. You're right about that, Bert. Glass is flying. Someone's shooting. Your mind isn't necessarily getting all the facts right under those circumstances."

"I'll tell you one thing, Billy. I'm not going to be the one to tell Judge Sunder he doesn't have his facts right."

"I don't imagine he hears that too often in the courtroom, does he?"

"So what do you make of it?" Lapolla asked, pleased that he was now the one asking Billy for answers.

"I don't know," Billy admitted. "It might have been two shooters, one long-distance, one close. That would account for the time difference."

"Hum," said Lapolla. "That would account for it."

"But I don't quite get it, do you? Is the second guy there to cover for the first after he takes the close shot and runs? Why would you need two men for the job?"

" 'Need,' Billy? That makes it sound like some kind of hired job."

"It does, doesn't it? That hadn't occurred to me until I said it."

Lapolla doubted it. He knew that *he* had no clear idea of what he meant until he heard himself say it, but he assumed Billy was always at least a couple of steps ahead of his mouth.

"I was getting comfortable with the two shooter theory until I realized how much it complicates things. I'm not sure that it even makes any sense at all," said Billy.

"Why not?"

"Two shots were fired. . . . At least we found only two bullet holes. And I found two shell casings at the site forty yards from the house."

"Right."

"Right? So where was the casing from the shot someone took with the rifle on the windowsill? There wasn't one."

"I gotcha."

"Then explain it to me. Did the window shooter pick up his shell and drop it down by the lawn shooter? Or did the lawn shooter fire one that didn't even go through the window, in addition to the one that did? That would account for his two shells at least. One shot at the window, one off the mark so much, it didn't enter the room. The window shooter could have pocketed his and gone off with it. That's assuming the window shooter and the lawn shooter are two different people. Which makes no immediate sense. But if they were the same man, why clean up after himself at the window but leave the shells on the lawn?"

Lapolla shrugged. "He shoots while standing by the window, thinks he's killed Sunder, pockets the shell, walks down the hill, turns and sees Judge Sunder in the window with the shotgun. Knowing Sunder, he probably hears him first, yelling at him. He panics, thinking he's about to get shot himself, so he fires twice. The first one is wild, misses the whole house, for all we know. The second goes through the window and into the wall. Since he's scared now, he doesn't stay to pick up the shells; he just takes off."

"Bert, you're a genius."

"Yeah. Well."

"But if one of those shots goes through the window where Sunder is standing, how come Sunder isn't hit?"

"That's the one that goes through the bathrobe, damn near hits him."

"Very good."

"But?"

"Did I say 'but'?" Lapolla waited.

Billy obliged. "But Sunder said he felt the tug on his robe, the window exploded, and he fell to the floor on the first shot. So the shot that nearly hit him had already been fired before he got the shotgun and presented himself as a target by standing in the window."

"Hell, Billy, I don't know. Maybe the tug on his robe wasn't from the first bullet. It might have been just a piece of flying glass he felt. He thinks some kid has tossed a rock through the window, so he grabs his shotgun, stands there yelling. The man on the lawn fires again—"

"And misses everything."

"And misses everything because he shot too fast; he was scared. Then he shoots again and nearly kills the judge."

"That would seem to cover it," Billy said after a moment.

"Good. . . . So, there you go."

"It doesn't trouble you that the judge didn't tell it that way?"

"Look, Billy, I respect the judge. As much as I know about these things, he's actually a pretty good judge. You don't hear the lawyers complaining too much. He keeps getting elected; everybody else speaks highly of him . . . So I say this with no disrespect, but I think he's a big bag of wind, so full of himself, he's about to pop. Can you imagine keeping Four-H ribbons from 1910 or whatever? So if he did do something like what I said—think it was just a kid throwing a rock as a prank and did get stupid and stand silhouetted in the window and practically beg somebody to shoot again—do I think he'd admit it to us? Never. Not in this lifetime. He's too big a cheese to admit he did something wrong."

"We're in agreement there," said Billy. "So you think it was just a random shooter taking potshots at targets of opportunity?"

"What motive would anybody have to shoot at either your uncle or the judge? I figure, look, they both live in isolated areas, so the shooter could be fairly sure he wouldn't be seen. Perfectly easy to just slip away into the night. . . ." Lapolla let it trail off, having nothing further to add. In truth, he had no clear idea of what was going on at all. "So I don't think we need two shooters to explain how it happened at all. Just a bad shooter and a witness who is . . . not being strictly accurate."

"No, you're right, Bert. Just one rather inconsistent shooter who isn't overly bright or very accurate with the rifle, that would do it."

"Probably he was drinking anyway. If you're out taking potshots at people, you're probably drunk or high to begin with, don't you think?"

Billy nodded. He wondered where Sean was when the shots were being fired. Or if anyone could ever crack Aunt Adley's alibi for him. How hard was it to imagine Sean, pissed and feisty as usual, taking shots at his truck for reasons known perhaps only to himself and his vehicle, then realizing he had just established a modus and an alibi for settling old scores? Had he and the judge ever tangled? Given Sean's history of financial failure and intemperate actions, it was hard to imagine that they had not. Was it hard to think of Sean, at the end of his career, out to right some wrongs in the best Irish revanchist tradition? Counting, perhaps, on the fact that even if discovered, his nephew, Charming Billy Tree himself, now acting deputy sheriff, would see him through? It was so easy to imagine that Billy felt gripped by a sense of despair. Sean, drunk, muttering self-justification, pleased with his cleverness, stalking old foes with shaking hands and lousy marksmanship. Who would he go after next, and how long before he got off a lucky shot and actually hit someone? How could Billy help him then?

"So how do you think Odette Collins or Otis Redding figures into this?" Billy asked abruptly.

Lapolla stirred papers on his desk and pretended not to be confused. There were times when the best thing to do with Billy was to ignore him. Listening to him think out loud could be troubling, and it occurred to the acting sheriff that they had trouble enough as it was.

"Uh . . . not sure, Billy."

"You don't think he's behind it?"

"Well, it didn't leap right out at me, but I see what you mean. . . . He is the new element in town. . . ." Lapolla cast about frantically for connections and brightened when he found one. "He did attack your uncle before, stole his wallet. That would give him Sean's address. . . . He probably heard there's a bench warrant out for him, Judge Sunder issued that warrant. There's your connection, easy as that. I should have thought of it myself."

Easy as that, Billy thought. Give a little direction, or misdirection, as the case required, and the dogs of the law were off and running. Once unleashed, it was hard to make them change direction. Collaborating facts would be accumulated, inconvenient facts ignored, and a case would develop all on its own. He knew how the process worked. It was like making crystals—introduce a seed into a body of water at the right temperature and, bang, the whole thing threw itself together without further assistance. Proper conditions, a tap on the tray, and you had gone in an instant from a fluid situation to solid ice. There's nothing flexible about ice; it has already made up its mind.

Billy did not remember actually making the firm decision to frame Odette Collins; it seemed to have happened on its own. But he realized he had better get started before Sean made too much of a mess to cover up.

CHAPTER SEVENTEEN

Adley met him at the door of the farmhouse, her finger to her lips to shush him.

"You're very early," she said.

"Never went to bed."

"You need your rest, Billy. You're not that young anymore."

"You have me there," he agreed, grinning. "Longer in the tooth every day."

"I'm serious. You men seem to think you can carouse and carry on all night long, every night, and it will never catch up with you. But it will."

"I wasn't carousing, Aunt Adley. I was working. Doing my great sleuth act."

She put a hand on his cheek and pulled him into an embrace.

"You're still my favorite, I don't care what they say," she said.

She was on the porch and Billy two steps down, so she pulled his face onto her bosom. She smelled of talcum powder and lilac, and her breasts were ample and soft. For a moment, Billy wanted to pillow against them longer. He straightened up, embarrassed.

Looking at her, he wondered if their eyes had made contact in a new way for just a flash. He had always regarded her as his uncle's wife, no blood relation, to be sure, but that was a meaningless distinction when he was growing up. She was one of the cadre of older women who did their best to cosset him and cushion the sharp edges of the uncles, part of the generation of his very own nurturing females, scarcely distinguishable from the mass, slightly spryer than the grandmothers, slightly more permissive than his mother. Older then by a gap in age that was unbridgeable, unthinkable, she was simply older now. Sean was her senior by several years, so Adley was still in her fifties, although Billy did not know precisely where. The younger woman was still visible now and then in the planes of her face, the promise of youth still capable of flashing through the aging facade like sunlight off a windowpane, a brief, startling revelation.

For whom did she scent herself with lilac? Sean? She seemed a full generation younger than Sean now. The travails of living with an alcoholic had not shown themselves in her appearance the way being one had done to Sean. Billy was no longer of an age when he considered the fifties or sixties as ancient. Who knew what his aunt was capable of? Loving, certainly. He'd been the recipient of plenty of that in his time. Making love? Why not, and if not with Sean, then with whom?

"You look like you need it," she said.

"Pardon me?"

"You look like you need some coffee."

"Oh . . . Yes, please."

To hide his discomfort, he did what he always did: He turned on the full Charming Billy grin, a beam of teeth and lips that suggested pleasure, well-being, and a beguiling hint of mischief.

Adley smiled back, a warmer, accepting smile, and she rumpled his hair with one hand before turning and leading him into the kitchen.

He paused for a moment on the porch, stalling for time while pretending to stretch and study the results of the morning sun on the tin roofs of the outbuildings, shimmering like the aftereffects of an ice storm. Christ, he thought. My aunt is a woman. And a vital, attractive one at that. Where the hell have I been while this happened?

He studied her while she moved about the kitchen. She wore blue jeans with a wide belt that sported an even wider silver buckle. A checked shirt tucked in at her waist, which, although certainly not slim, was discernible. The jeans were shoved into cowboy boots with a red-and-black geometric design. Her hair was cut to shoulder length and worn in a style that Billy thought he recognized as fashionable a few years back. Either she was immune to gray or her hair had been colored to a believable shade of brown. He knew enough to look for roots but saw no discoloration. If anyone had asked him yesterday whether his aunt wore makeup, he would have scoffed, but now he noticed a bit of blush fading unevenly into the neck, and lining around the eyes that was subtle but definitely not natural. The overall effect depended on how you looked at it. She could have been a farm wife conscious of her appearance but ready for chores and the life of a farm, or she could have been a woman discreetly on the prowl, ready for a bit of line dancing and whatever else arose. The difference lay in her expression—and the eye of the beholder, Billy's eye at the moment, was puzzled.

She poured coffee and sat with him at the kitchen table. They talked in the same easy, desultory way of long-time acquaintances who are not really paying attention to each other, but Billy's imagination was aflame. He tried not to stare, but he could not keep his eyes off of her. She was an adult changeling, a woman of possibility inhabiting the body of a woman of predictable stasis. Had she always been like this? he wondered. Had he been so blind, or had something transformed her? Could his new awareness really have sprung from a misdirected hug, or was this a new Adley?

His speculation was interrupted by the sound of garotting coming from the next room.

"Carl," she said. "The boys were out together last night."

Billy tipped back in his chair and saw Carl on the living room sofa, twitching slightly in the transport of a dream, and snoring in brief, startling gasps.

"Well, I'm off," she announced, taking her cup to the sink. "There's plenty of coffee, but don't take it all. They'll need some when they get up."

"Where are you off to?"

She smiled provocatively. "I have a life, you know."

I believe you do, Billy thought. Who would have thought?

"What shall I tell Sean if he asks?"

"He won't ask," she said.

As Billy turned his head, she bent and caught him with a kiss close to his ear.

"You be good, Billy," she said.

"You, too."

"Oh, I'm too old to be any other way, don't you think?"

Honestly, no, he thought. He put his hand to the spot where she had kissed him. Christ on a crutch, he thought, and didn't get much beyond that.

Billy woke the men and herded them into the kitchen, where they slumped over cups of coffee with the hangdog look of the perpetually guilty.

"Quite a night, was it?"

"A grand night," said Sean. "Your uncle Carl's a terrible man with the bottle."

"Huhn," Carl offered.

"Where did you two wild men go? The Sportsman's?"

"Oh, we were around. You know how it is. Here a little, there a little."

"Carl?"

Carl lifted bleary eyes. So we're back to the two gunman theory, Billy thought. Sean and Carl, drunk as stooges, playing Irish patriots perhaps, shooting wildly at the judge and giggling and cursing each other for incompetence.

"Where'd you go, Carl?"

"Not sure I remember."

"Do you remember going to Judge Sunder's house?"

"No."

"Why would we be going there?" Sean demanded. "His Honor is a tight fist with a drink. There's no fun to be had in the house of Sunder, and that's for sure."

Carl chuckled and massaged his temples. "The house of Sunder," he repeated.

"You don't much like Sunder, do you?"

Carl shrugged.

"We like the judge fine. Why shouldn't we?" Sean asked. "He's a fair man. You can't deny it. Say what else you will, Lyle Sunder plays you fair. And you can't say better than that about a man, now can you?"

"Somebody shot at him last night," Billy said.

"No! They never did! Tell me he's all right; tell me he's not dead, Billy!"

"That's a fine bit of overreaction, Sean. The judge is fine—the shooter missed him. But whoever it is had better be very careful in the future. He's a very angry man right now."

"But he's all right, then? Thank God."

"I didn't know Sunder meant that much to you."

"We don't wish anybody dead, Billy," said Carl.

"That's not quite the same as not wishing anybody harm, though, is it? . . . What kind of relationship have you had with the judge other than being in the Four-H club together?"

"The Four-H club? I wouldn't know anything about that. I've had some dealings with the man. You know how it is."

"How would I know how it is? I've only been in this town for two years. What were your 'dealings' with Sunder before I came back? Did he have anything to do with the loss of your farm?"

"His Honor? What would he have to do with the loss of my farm? He's on the bench; he's no farmer. Only an idiot would want this place. It damned near killed me working these acres. I was glad to sell them and keep the house."

"You declared bankruptcy, didn't you? Was he the presiding judge in that case? Did he give you bad terms, Sean? Do you feel he helped to sink you?"

"You have the wrong end of the stick entirely. Lyle Sunder has never done me a bad turn in all my life. He was as good a friend to me and your father as you could ever hope to have."

"Is that right? You socialize with him a lot, do you, Sean? You and this great old friend have dinner together now and then? Does he have you and Adley over to the house, give you a tour of his memorabilia room? Sit around by the fire, you and the judge, sipping cognac and smoking big cigars? You and Adley go on vacations with him?"

"I don't know what you're going on about. Do you understand this, Carl?"

"Nope."

"How about you, Carl?" Billy asked. "Are you a bosom buddy of the judge's, too?"

"I can take him or leave him alone," said Carl. "Seems all right. Kind of a snob maybe. Pretty full of himself."

"He's a man of accomplishment," said Sean.

"Is that right? Well, one of the things he accomplished was dodging a bullet that missed his heart by an inch or two last night."

"Luck of the Irish," said Sean.

"He isn't Irish. . . . There were two men involved."

"Were there? Can you imagine? Who would they be, then, Bill? We know you're on top of it. He's a bulldog for solving things, Carl. Once he gets his teeth into it . . ."

"A real terrier," said Carl.

"Are you still standing guard on the porch, Carl?"

"Right after my coffee."

"Can't be too careful," said Sean.

"Indeed. With all the shooting going on around here . . . You must be afraid they might pop you through the window right now, Sean."

"They'd better not try it. Besides, who'd want to be shooting me?"

"I don't know yet. They did try once already, though, didn't they? You do recall that."

"Oh, that's right, I suppose. It was a vague sort of night, that one."

"Where's your rifle, Carl?"

"I left it—well, I don't remember exactly."

"See if you could find it for me, would you? I need to speak to Sean alone for a moment anyway."

Carl shuffled off slowly and Billy asked Sean to stand.

"Take off your shirt."

"My shirt."

"I want to see your manly form. You wanted to show me the other night."

"Did I?"

"Take it off, Sean."

Sean removed his shirt and held it with both hands in front of his crotch. "Not in top shape at the moment," he said, uncharacteristically self-conscious.

"Still a fine broth of a man," said Billy. The bruise on the left side of his chest had been reduced to a dull brown, matching the one on his right cheek. Billy jabbed his left fist toward Sean's face, stopping just short of contact, then followed it immediately with a pulled punch with his right hand to the chest. Sean's arms flew up, defensively but late.

"Reflexes are a bit slow, Sean. But they still work, I see."

"Were you looking to spar a few rounds? I'll need some breakfast first."

"No, I was just wondering about your bruises there. You took quite a pounding in both places. But precisely in both places. Did you notice that? He hit you in almost the same spot, several times. Was he that fast? Couldn't you get your arms up at all? Doesn't sound like you, Sean, just stand there and let him hit you again and again in the same spot. Was it left, left, left, then right, right, right? Or the other way around?"

"I don't see what you're driving at."

"Don't you? Either someone was holding your arms and he was taking target practice or you got those bruises some other way."

"What are you talking about? I was fighting for my life. Of course I didn't just stand still. . . ."

"You know the only explanation I can come up with for that pattern of bruises? . . . See if this looks familiar to you."

Billy slapped his own right cheek several times with his right hand, his arm working like a piston, then he repeated the process on his own chest, his hand going naturally to the left side.

"It's hard to hit yourself on the right breast with your right hand—and you are right-handed. But easier to hit your right cheek with your right hand—you don't have to worry about your nose."

"You're not saying I did it to myself? Tell me you're not saying such a thing to your own uncle."

"Anything you want to tell me, Sean? Off the record, just between nephew and uncle? Because I'd rather not have to play the deputy sheriff if I can avoid it. . . . No? . . . How about last night? You and Carl and your grand activities. Anything you'd prefer to confess to me now, as a member of the family, rather than later, when I'm wearing my badge."

"You've been drinking early, haven't you, Billy? It's not a good thing, and I'm the one who would know."

"You can tell me later, after you think about it and realize I can still be your friend, but not too much later. . . . I have no love for the black man with the shaven head who supposedly attacked you, either. I'm not even going to say that what you did was wrong, because I'm not here to judge you—not yet. What I am saying is, if you want to make life harder for the man, you've got to do it in a much smarter fashion, because if I can figure it out, so can somebody else."

"I've heard you. Can I get dressed now, or do you want to go a couple of rounds for real? Keep on insulting me and we will do that, my lad."

Carl entered the kitchen, hands up in a gesture of futility. "I can't find the rifle," he said.

"Why doesn't that surprise me?" Billy asked. He stepped onto the porch and let the screen door slam shut behind him. A couple of naughty boys, high school kids on a bender, clumsy and ineffective in their murderous intent, and as unconcerned as any spoiled brats, certain they could get away with anything because of their cleverness and dumb luck and beery charm. Not that I am any better, Billy thought. What kind of an idiotic statement had he just made concerning his willingness to frame Odette Collins for his uncle's lunatic behavior? Thank goodness it was only Sean in the room; he wouldn't be apt to remember it anyway. But who was the man who had said it? Was that Billy Tree, the man Joan had said was too moral for his own good? Was that the man universally respected and looked up to because of his heroism on the playing field and in life itself?

You haven't actually done anything yet, he told himself. It isn't bad thoughts that make you a bad man. It's evil actions. Thus far, he had taken no actions. He hoped circumstances would not provide him an opportunity to do so, because he had come to believe that his moral stance heretofore had only been a matter of convenience. It had cost him nothing to do the right things in his life, because that was what he was inclined to do in the first place. Now he was inclined to do something wrong—what was more, something that he could easily get away with—and morality felt like a very feeble restraint. He hoped that Odette Collins had the good sense to head for the high timber and stay there. It seemed the only way to keep Billy a good man.

CHAPTER EIGHTEEN

B illy gave Gina Schul the bullets they had dug out of Judge Sunder's wall to send to the crime lab in Omaha, along with the ones that had come from Sean's truck. He had little doubt that ballistics testing would show they had come from the same gun. The same gun, no doubt, that Carl and Sean had hidden away after their foray at the judge's house. They were not clever enough to toss it in the Missouri River; he was fairly certain of that. They would have squirreled it away someplace they considered safe. Or if they had been Sunder, they probably would have hung it on their wall as a reminder of another escapade survived. Why waste a perfectly good weapon, after all?

"Given up shaving?" Gina asked.

"Bad night," said Billy. He ran a hand across the stubble of beard. "But a brighter morning for having seen you."

Gina responded with a slow grin.

"That's what they all say," she said. There was a pleasantly wicked quality to Gina that Billy responded to, a suggestion of readiness for mild devilment that belied her pudgy, matronly appearance. It reminded him of Joan, he realized. And of the Aunt Adley he had glimpsed anew less than an hour ago. A certain knowingness coupled with forgiveness of folly. The admonition "Don't do anything I wouldn't do" would provide a great deal of latitude coming from either Joan or Gina. And from Adley? She had certainly tolerated a lifetime of misbehavior, but he had always assumed it was because of an inherent saintliness. There could be another way to survive it, he realized. A little hair of the dog approach to the problem of a wayward spouse.

"You know my aunt Adley, don't you?"

"I know her to nod to. Why?"

"Do you know her car?" In some parts of the country, the question would be ludicrous. In a small community like Falls City, however, people knew one another by vehicle as well as face, name, and attitude.

Gina thought briefly. "I see something gray. Four-door sedan, recent model."

"You sound like a police report."

"Surprise, surprise."

"Ninety-six Oldsmobile."

She nodded in confirmation. "Right. I know it when I see it anyway. Why?"

"Let me know if you see it around town, would you? . . . Just between us."

"Not official business, then."

"No. Just between us."

Gina grinned. Decidedly wicked, thought Billy.

"Stalking your own aunt, huh? Billy, you have a very suspicious nature."

"No, I just . . . I'm planning a little surprise for her birthday, don't want her to know."

"You don't lie enough to be good at it, Billy."

"It's probably nothing."

"I hope it is something, for her sake." She seemed to relish whatever possibility had come to her mind.

How little we know about them, Billy thought. We spend our lives trusting them, thinking we're outwitting them. It's because of all that nurture, he realized. They make us feel good, so why should we suspect they could also make us feel so bad?

"We got the report back from the vet," Gina said.

"What report?"

"That dog *was* rabid."

"What dog?"

"The one you and Lapolla shot a few days ago. You took it to the vet; he says it was rabid. You did the right thing."

The dog. He had forgotten about it completely. Odette Collins in the dark alley behind Joan's house, asking about his dog. "*You* got my dog?" It had seemed so strange a remark, so out of context, no wonder Billy had made no connection at the time. Then later, on the phone, without identifying himself, "You kill my dog?" Could the dog Lapolla had shot be the one Collins had been talking about? Billy had supposed it to be some kind of threat, some coded blackspeak. Was the man really just asking about his pet? Looking for his dog in the middle of the night, on foot, in the alley behind Joan's house? No, he was not looking for his dog; he was looking for Joan. Well, he had found her.

"He wants to see you about it."

"Who?"

"The vet. Doc Stiles. He says you ought to know about the dog."

The local veterinarian was actually in a partnership, one that reflected its clientele. Two of the vets specialized in large animals, spending their working days on the surrounding farms, tending to the livestock. Doc Stiles specialized in smaller animals, the cats, dogs, and other pets that constituted the patient list of any urban veterinarian.

Like most vets, Stiles had entered his profession because of a love of animals, and that love had not diminished after twenty-odd years of practice.

"That animal was abused," Stiles said, controlling the quiver of anger in his voice with difficulty.

"How do you mean?" Billy asked.

Stiles glanced at the file on his desk. The dog itself had been incinerated once the rabies was diagnosed. "Multiple fractures of the ribs, various bones in the feet, left rear quarter, tail, skull . . . you name it. Over the years, that poor animal went through hell."

"Over the years?"

"The fractures weren't new, but boy, I didn't have to look far to find them. Just had to palpate the bones and I felt like I was reading braille—bumps of mended fractures all over the place. Not to mention the scars."

"Now that you mentioned them, Doc . . ."

Stiles shook his head, remembering something painful. "His whole body at one time or another. Bites from other dogs would be my guess. You brought him in. Did you notice his ears?"

"Not really."

"Practically lace, they'd been chewed on so much. Up in here—" Stiles stroked his clavicle angrily, then his neck—"and here. That's where a dog would attack. But here, too, all the way around his neck. That's a choke chain. You got to use it a lot and real hard—I mean real hard—to cause a permanent ridge like this fella had. . . . I don't know if you're a dog lover, but this was enough to make anybody sick."

"What, uh, what are your conclusions here, Doc? Give me a little guidance."

"Guidance, shit. I'll tell you flat out. This dog was used in fights, deliberately, repeatedly. And after that trauma was seared into his soul, he was turned into an attack dog. It wouldn't have taken much to convert him; he probably hated the world by that point anyway."

"Does this have anything to do with the rabies?"

"Not directly, unless he got it from a bite from another dog, one that was already infected. More likely, he got it from the bite of some rabid racoon or rat he was killing. I'd almost say he got it from his owner, who must be one sick sadistic son of a bitch, but that would be confusing the issue. Considering the life this poor dog led, rabies might have been a blessing—although it's a terrible way to go. Do you know who it belonged to?"

"No. Maybe. I'm not sure."

"I suppose you ought to warn him in case he was bitten himself, but, frankly, it would serve him right. . . . I say that as a human being, not as a physician."

"I understand."

"The son of a bitch. . . . There are laws on the books against this kind of mistreatment, Billy. Find the asshole; I'll testify on the dog's behalf."

A s Billy entered unannounced, Lapolla looked up guiltily and hastily placed something in the top drawer of his desk. Casually, he partially closed the drawer during their conversation, as if his hand worked without the direction of his conscious mind. Billy wondered if he had happened upon the acting sheriff perusing his office pornography.

"Jeez, Bill, try to knock."

"I did try, Bert. I missed."

"What?"

"Joke."

"You know . . . your jokes . . ."

"Ah, but they amuse me, that's the thing, even if I have no future as a stand-up."

Lapolla was still easing the drawer shut, acting for all the world like a man with nothing to hide. Billy fought back an urge to rip the drawer open and grab Bert's hidden shame, dangle it by its centerfold, and peruse the acting sheriff's sexual predilection. He was feeling mean. But not that mean. God knows what Bert, or any man, responds to, he thought. Billy did not want to view Lapolla's mammoth-breasted or shelf-assed or animal-loving dream girl. There were a whole lot of things he didn't want to know about, and when a discovery was forced upon him, he ended up paying a price for the knowledge. With Joan and his family put together, he had learned far too much in the past few days. Bert Lapolla's orgasmic delights would not improve his lot in life.

"Feel like taking a drive?" Billy asked.

"Where to?"

"I think I know where we might find Odette Collins."

"Really? Where?"

"Where we found that dog."

"What dog?"

"Glad to know I'm not the only one who's forgetful. The dog you shot because it was rabid. I think it might have been Collins's dog."

"You made me shoot it," Lapolla said hastily.

Billy grinned. "I did at that, Bert. When the shit hits the fan, you can blame it all on me."

"I didn't mean that."

"Joke."

"See? That's what I mean. How's anybody supposed to know that's a joke?"

"Watch me, see if I grin. I'm a sucker for my own jokes," said Billy.

"You're grinning all the time."

"That should tell you something," Billy said.

CHAPTER NINETEEN

They drove north through the fields of corn and milo and soybeans, each a sea of a slightly different shade of green. A huge mass of verdancy, distinguishable in its parts to the casual viewer only by the differing height of the plants, its color map was as noticeable as a change in topography to the initiated. The subtle variation in hue made the fields appear to have a texture one could touch with the eye. The fields were not fractals, endless clones on varying scales, but each a distinct entity, as unique in its place on the chromatic spectrum as a radio frequency on the electromagnetic dial.

Shortly after the village of Shubert, they turned east, toward the hamlet of Barada, then again onto the same gravel road where they had encountered the rabid dog. Four days ago? Five? It had been that same night that Billy's world had begun to tilt, and the acceleration since had been breathtakingly fast. These few days later, his world was topsy-turvy. His love was lost or stolen, his family suspect of murderous intrigue, his aunt transfigured—for better or worse, he could not yet say—and his long-dead father propelled back into his life in the most disturbing way. It's a wonder I'm not staggering around in a state of shock, he thought. Then again, maybe I am. If he was in shock, he wouldn't know it. He had raved for a solid hour after being nearly killed by Posner, more concerned with his dignity than his life, and it had not seemed like shock at the time. Neither does this, he thought, but maybe it is. Maybe shock is the only sane way to react to everything happening at once.

"About here, wasn't it?" Lapolla asked, slowing the car to a crawl.

Billy tried to turn his mind to the business at hand. "Yeah, about here."

"So? What now?"

"We start looking for roads that lead onto this one. A dog that sick could not have wandered all that far. He had to come from one of the farms close by."

"Unless somebody just dumped the dog out of their car and drove off."

"Assuming anybody was dumb enough to get into a car with a rabid dog in the first place."

But assuming people were dumb enough to do something was the very basis of law-enforcement detection. Anyone on any police force in the world learned within a week how dumb people could be. The level of their indiscretions, mistakes, and outright stupidity could never be underestimated. Most crime was spontaneous, an immediate, unthinking exercise of the basic instincts, be it to jaywalk, to stuff an extra supermarket item in a pocket, or to settle a barroom dispute with a sharp instrument, and the things people did in such unconsidered circumstances were frequently akin to licking a flagpole in sub-zero weather. What on earth were they thinking? The simplest answer was also the correct one. They weren't thinking. It wasn't necessarily that they were stupid all of the time. It took only a moment, a brief second of letting go of the anchor of rules and guidelines, and the high winds of selfishness could blow anyone into trouble.

"Do you think selfishness is the root cause of all crimes, Bert?" Billy asked as they drove slowly forward, seeking any paths leading from the gravel road.

"Uh . . . I'd have to think about it."

"All crimes are offenses against someone else, aren't they? Some individual, or the community, the state, the federal government. Haven't we constructed society so that none of us is supposed to do anything without considering everyone else first? We're like kindergarten teachers, telling everybody to 'play nice.' Isn't that what law enforcement is, at the very core of it all?"

Lapolla shook his head, amused.

"I don't know, Billy. The things you come up with."

"You can't swear or spit or run around naked, because somebody's sensibilities will be offended. You can't walk on your neighbor's lawn, or dump your garbage, or smoke indoors because—there's the road."

They had been steadily approaching the Missouri River and the land had begun to buckle and rise into hills. A long row of trees topped the ridge to the east, not the defeated and misshapen scrub oaks of the windbreaks, but full-grown oaks and maples and birch, which thrived on the steady supply of water sucked from the spongy earth along the riverbank. The path leading away from the road crested one of the hillocks and vanished on the other side.

"You think there's a house on the other side?" Lapolla asked. Nebraska farmers didn't build their houses right next to the road as the old New Englanders had done, but they did tend to stay close enough that they could get out of their driveways in case of heavy snowfall. Even with tractors at their disposal, it made no sense to be too far from access to the outside world. Lapolla's suspicion that there was no house over the hill was soundly based on local custom.

But it was wrong. They reached the top of the hill, and in the valley on the other side, completely hidden from the road, squatted a derelict of a house. Surrounded by weeds and a string of sumacs making their way from the river, the house was being quickly reduced to a state of nature itself. Strangler vines had claimed one entire side wall and were moving onto the porch like the tentacles of a devouring octopus. One of the porch columns had succumbed to rot and the roof tilted at a dangerous angle. The chimney bricks had been meticulously removed, only the tin flashing left behind.

"Nobody living *there*," said Lapolla.

"Maybe not living, but visiting."

"In there?"

"Look at the upstairs windows." Two windows were sparkling clean, while all the rest were nearly opaque with the dust from years of neglect. "That would be the bedroom."

Something a woman would do, Billy thought, thinking of his own house. Although he ran the vacuum cleaner occasionally, did the dishes, and generally picked up as required, any refinements were acts of volunteerism by Joan. Such as windows. She had minimal standards far above Billy's, and sexual ardor alone was not enough to make her forgo them. On more than one occasion, they had made it to his bed only after she had straightened and scrubbed to her own satisfaction. Billy assumed that it had to do with issues of control, but he was smart enough not to try to change it.

"Park it here," Billy said, putting a hand on Lapolla's arm.

The change in his tone alerted Lapolla, who braked abruptly. "What? *What?*"

"Nothing . . . probably. . . . I thought I saw something move upstairs. Let's just stay here for a minute and watch."

"What are we watching for?"

"I don't know, Bert. The last time I went through a suspect's door without knowing what was on the other side, I ended up with a dead partner and quite a few holes in my body." Unthinkingly, he put his hand to the scar that ran vertically on his abdomen. The scar tissue was raised enough to feel it through the fabric of his shirt. He thought briefly of Doc Stiles's description of the rabid dog. A body with lumps that could be read by a blind man. "So let's just sit for a minute. Either we'll see something or my nerves will settle down."

Lapolla anxiously took his eyes off the house just long enough to glance at Billy. The acting deputy revealed no signs of being nervous, and Lapolla wondered why he had said it. It certainly made *him* nervous to think of Billy being nervous.

"I could call for backup," Lapolla said.

"Well, there we have to deal with the old embarrassment factor, don't we?"

"Right." After a moment, Lapolla realized he didn't know what he had agreed to. "How do you mean?"

"What are we calling backup *for*? Do we have a serious situation here? Do we have *any* situation? What if we drag another car over here and there's nobody even in the house?"

"You said you saw somebody."

"I said I *thought* I saw something move. It might have been a squirrel." But it wasn't a squirrel and he knew it. It was a human, scuttling in the hurried, panicked way of the alarmed and guilty. There was danger in that upper window, and Billy's body knew it no matter how much his mind might feel compelled to consider alternatives. He had already broken into a sweat in the air-conditioned car and he could feel the tingle of adrenaline like a rasp upon his skin.

"There's a car behind the house," Billy said.

"I don't see it."

"I don't see it, either, but that's where it is."

"Okay."

They sat for a while longer, studying the house. Lapolla became aware of Billy's breathing. He was inhaling through his nose and exhaling through his mouth in very deep drafts. The exhalations sounded like a distant wind.

"I'll call." Lapolla reached for the radio.

"It's just me," Billy said. "We're all right. Bit of a flashback, I guess."

He had not had an actual flashback this time. Those had ceased to haunt him a year ago, horrifying scenes of his would-be assassin's snaggletoothed dragon grin that would burst like a flashbulb behind his eyes, or visions of the nightmare itself, Billy helpless on his back, his partner suspended from the ceiling by a piano wire around his neck, his feet inches from the floor and still twitching, and behind his bulk the maniacal Zionist Jacobin firing at Billy. Today's episode was nothing so extreme. This is just a jab of fear, he told himself. Like starting at a loud noise, his body was just preparing him for fight or flight. Flight would be my choice, he thought, because if I wanted to shoot at intruders, that upstairs window is where I'd be. . . . It was the prospect of guns that did it to him. The guns, always the goddamned guns.

He breathed deeply again, blew it out with extended cheeks, and essayed a smile for Lapolla's benefit. What would I do if I were alone? he wondered. Would I already be back over the hill and halfway home? What was this lunacy of pride that made him go against his instincts?

"Okay," he said. "Let's go get Mr. Otis Redding Pickett Collins."

"Are you sure?"

"I'd rather not get into certainty here, Bert. Let's just go do it."

The weeds in the space in front of the house were thigh-high and so thick, they impeded their walking. They lifted their feet as if wading through water. Saplings and small sumac scattered among the weeds gave the whole the impression of a dwarf jungle, and they the giants who bestrode it.

Billy advanced through the field as if against a small surf, his eyes scanning rapidly everywhere but always returning to the second-story window. Lapolla walked close beside him and a little behind.

"Move more to the side," Billy said. He shooed Lapolla away with a hand gesture.

"Billy, Billy, what are you expecting? Are they going to shoot at us? Let me call for backup."

"It's just basic procedure." Basic for survival, so that a gunman could not hit more than one man with a single burst of fire.

"You're scaring the shit out of me. Is there something going on I don't know about?"

"Not yet."

"Geez, see! What does that mean, 'not yet'? What's going to happen?"

"Nothing's going to happen. . . . If I yell 'down,' get down immediately. Don't ask me questions, just hit the dirt."

"Why would you yell 'down' if nothing is going to happen? What is it, what? I'm going back to the car to call for some backup here." Lapolla turned his back to the house.

Billy saw motion in the window, this time unmistakable in its intent.

"Down!"

He hit the ground before he heard the shot, a subdued pop accompanied by the sound of shattering glass.

"Billy? Billy?"

Lapolla remained on his feet, searching for his partner, his own gun half out of his holster.

"Did they get you, Bill?"

"Get down," Billy muttered, his face in the weeds.

Lapolla looked down at Billy's prostrate form. "The sons of bitches!" he yelled.

Voices came from the farmhouse. A man was screaming, "Whoa, whoa, whoa! What the hell are you doing?"

A woman replied, her words undecipherable but her voice high and panicked.

Billy rolled his head to one side and looked up at the window, where Joan stood, rifle in hand. From Billy's perspective, one jagged shard of glass hung down from the top of the frame like an icicle and seemed to cleave her face into multiple parts.

"Stop it. Stop it!" the man yelled.

"Throw down your gun!" Lapolla screamed.

Billy turned and saw Lapolla assuming the shooter's stance, his arms in a triangle, his legs spread, presenting about as large a target as possible, the only object above waist height for many yards. Billy grabbed at his heel and upended him. Lapolla landed on his back and his gun discharged, sending a bullet skyward and to the rear.

"No firing!" Billy yelled. "No firing! In the house, in the house! Don't shoot!"

Lapolla lay on his back, gasping for breath. It took him a moment to realize that the barrel of his pistol was resting on his heaving chest, pointing toward his nose.

"Are you alive?" he asked with a wheeze, moving the gun away from his face.

"Shut up," Billy said.

Lapolla could barely make him out through the weeds.

Joan's voice could be heard again. Billy could not discern the words, but the tenor and pitch were hers. Had she shot at them? he wondered. Or was it just a warning? And why?

"It was a mistake," the man was yelling from the house. "She didn't mean to fire! Just a mistake."

Billy and Lapolla lay still, hidden from sight by the weeds. Billy hoped Lapolla had sense enough to keep his mouth shut and not admit that his own shot had also been a mistake.

"Throw the rifle out," Billy called.

He heard the two in the house talking, their voices lower now, closer to conversational. He thought he heard them using his name.

"No, we ain't going to do that," the man said after a pause. "We'll keep the rifle . . . but we're not shooting at you, either. That was just a mistake before."

"Okay, then," Lapolla said.

" 'Okay, then'?" Billy hissed. "What was okay about it?"

"I thought for sure you were shot," Lapolla said with relief.

"Didn't I tell you to get down?"

"I couldn't let them shoot you like that."

"They didn't shoot me. Because I got down."

"Well, still."

"Shut up, Bert."

"Right."

"What did you see?" Billy asked.

"I saw a woman in the window. I don't know where the man is. It sounds like he's downstairs."

"Did you recognize the woman?"

"Is she someone I know?"

"That's what I'm asking."

"No, I didn't recognize her. Should I? Did you?"

"I was hiding in the weeds," said Billy. Oh, if only it were that simple. Right now, burrowing into the ground and estivating for a month or two seemed like a perfect solution. Had Joan really shot a rifle at him? His mind couldn't believe it, but his body had no doubts at all.

"In the house!" he yelled.

"Yo!"

"We're going to leave now."

"Good idea."

"Leave?" Lapolla hissed. "How can we leave? We can't just leave. What do you mean we're going to leave?"

"What do you want to do, have a shoot-out?"

"I want to arrest that son of a bitch. He *shot* at me."

"He shot at me, too." Billy noted that Lapolla had already transferred responsibility for the shooting to Collins, even though he must have seen the rifle in Joan's hands. He was happy to go along with that perception—if he could be said to be happy about anything in the current situation.

"I'm willing to live and let live," Billy continued.

"We can't just leave!"

"Why not?"

"For Christ's sake, Billy. I'm the sheriff." Lapolla sputtered. "He's got one gun; we've got two."

Take a shot at him and suddenly he's Lapolla the Tiger, Billy thought. Take a shot at me and I'm Billy Weasel, looking for a hole to creep into. We can't both be right.

"His gun is a rifle, yours is a pistol, and we have only one, because you know I don't have one."

"Right."

"And I wouldn't use it if I did."

"Why not?"

"Because it would be a pointless overreaction to the situation. It would be like eight city cops killing a man for pulling a comb out of his pocket. Because it's not the smart thing to do. . . . And because I'm scared silly."

"You're not scared, Billy."

"I am, Bert."

"Really?"

"I'm lying in the weeds, my teeth are chattering, and I'm struggling to keep the sphincter closed."

"Really?"

Billy was not sure if he detected triumph or incredulity in Lapolla's voice.

The man's voice came from the house. "So when are you leaving?"

"When we're good and ready, you pissant," Lapolla said. "What do you mean taking a shot at the sheriff of Richardson County? I'm on official business?"

"I'm on my way," Billy said to Lapolla. He started to crawl through the weeds toward the car. "You're going to get us shot at again."

"I told you, that shot was a mistake," said the voice from the house. "Anybody make a mistake. But that don't mean you can be coming in this house."

"I've got a warrant for your arrest. Come on out of there with your hands up," Lapolla roared.

"You got a warrant for whose arrest?"

"Yours."

"Who it say on that warrant?"

Again, Billy had the sense that the accent was applied. He swiveled around and raised his eyes above weed level, having taken cover behind a worthless tangle of a sumac no thicker than his wrist. He could not locate the man, and Joan was no longer visible in the window. He assumed she was now by Collins's side. He could not see Lapolla, either. The weeds were a perfect hiding place, but they provided no defense against a bullet. If the acting sheriff moved, the weeds would move, too. A few rifle shots fired into the center of the motion would do the trick. Billy did not know how Lapolla could fail to understand that.

"It says you," Lapolla said, continuing his unlikely dialogue while lying in the waist-high jungle.

"But who it *say?*"

"It says *you,* goddamn it. I don't care what name you're going by at the moment, the warrant is for your arrest. Now come on out of there or I'm coming in."

The man's voice dropped an octave, no longer semiplayful, but deep and menacing.

"Don't be trying that."

"I be trying whatever I want," replied Lapolla, falling into this seductive grammar. The temptation to mock it by emulating it was too strong. "Don't be telling me what to try. I'm the sheriff of Richardson County, and if I want to come in there and drag you out by the scruff of your neck, I by God will."

"It ain't got no scruff to my neck. I ain't no dog."

"You're a dog abuser, though, ain't you? I know how you mistreated that animal."

"I didn't mistreat nothing. I rented that dog to protect me out here. Wasn't mine. But you killed it, didn't you?"

"Don't be worrying about what I did and didn't do. Just come on out here or I'll come in and find your scruff, pal, don't worry about that."

The tough-guy talk sounded so forced and phony to Billy that he half-expected to hear Collins laugh at it. It was the kind of bravado men displayed when they were safe from actual physical contact, yelling at each other from their cars, strutting their stuff on the telephone. But Lapolla was not safe from physical contact, and he didn't seem to know that. If Collins took the rifle to the upstairs window, he would be able to see the sheriff's depression in the undergrowth like a crater on the moon.

Billy dropped his head back below the cover of the weeds and called out, "In the house?"

"Yo . . . that be the great Billy Tree now?"

"That's me."

"Thought you went home."

"That's what I'm trying to do. But I can't go without my sheriff."

"Take him with you; I sure as hell don't want him."

"You got me, like it or not, pal," Lapolla called.

"Bert, for God's sake, let me negotiate here."

"Yeah, Bert. Let the man negotiate. That's the great Billy Tree you're talking about. Don't be disrespecting him."

"Okay, we can drop 'the great.' I'm not feeling real great right at the moment. Let's just talk about a way to put an end to this."

"Go 'way and leave me be, that put an end to it. I ain't done nothing to you all."

"You shot at the sheriff of Richardson County, you black pissant! How's that for starters?"

"Bert, Bert!"

"Well, geez, Billy."

"What we got here, a couple of racist cops? My, my, I never would have thought."

"I'm not racist," Billy said.

"Neither am I," said Lapolla.

"You ain't racist. You liars."

A few weeks ago, Billy might have felt morally obliged to argue the point. Now it seemed that Collins was right about both accusations.

"You ain't racist, how come you be after my black ass?"

"I'm going to stand up now, all right?"

"Don't do that, Billy," Lapolla counseled.

"That all right. Can't walk away if you don't stand up first."

"Right now, you're wanted for theft of services."

"Theft of services? The hell is that?"

"You didn't pay your motel bill."

"You come out here with guns for that? You telling me you ain't racist?"

"My point is, that's *all* you're wanted for right now. If you fire at either me or the sheriff or threaten us in any way, you'll be charged with attempted homicide at least. . . . You can always just *pay* the motel bill."

"That's what I'm talking about."

"I didn't hear you talking about it," said Lapolla.

Billy saw the weeds move and realized Lapolla was creeping closer to the house. Madness.

"I'm standing up now," Billy called. "I'm going to stand up, get my sheriff, and go home. You come pay that motel bill and we can forget all the rest of this stuff."

"You keep saying you be standing up, but I still don't see you nowhere."

Billy rose to a crouch, then slowly straightened, his hands open at shoulder height, his whole body cringing in anticipation of the impact of a bullet. It was like waiting to be hit with a sledgehammer. He could see the thing being drawn back, practically feel the rush of wind that preceded the blow.

"Don't be putting your hands up. I didn't say to put your hands up. I ain't got a gun on you, so don't be acting like that."

Billy put his hands down. He felt his legs weaken beneath him.

They were so ready to collapse, his body so eager to fall back to the earth and hide.

"Okay," he said.

"Don't be forgetting your sheriff, crawling around like some kind of big-ass snake over there. Think I don't see him. Think black means blind or something."

Forget him? Billy thought. That was the only reason he was on his feet, exposing himself to anything the people in the house cared to do to him. Left to himself, he would have been more than happy to slither on his belly all the way to the car. At the moment, he hated Lapolla and wished to leave him to his own devices, but he forced himself to take one step, then another, eyes still on the house.

"Let's go, Bert," he said, standing over the acting sheriff, who was now on his back, gesturing frantically for Billy to go away, as if the man in the house didn't know exactly where he was already.

"Stay there and keep talking like I'm still here; I'll slip around back," Lapolla hissed as he started to move on his back like a soldier creeping under barbed wire.

"Get up, Bert."

Lapolla waved him away and kept wriggling. Billy grabbed him by the collar and yanked him to his feet.

"Don't make me keep standing here. I'm jumping out of my skin," he said.

"What are you doing?" Lapolla struggled uselessly against Billy's grip.

"Saving your ass."

Lapolla swatted at Billy's arms.

"Who in charge out there?" called the man.

"I want to get that son of a bitch," Lapolla said.

"Look like *nobody* in charge."

"Walk with me, Bert." Billy clamped a hand on Lapolla's arm and crab-walked away from the house, watching it all the time, keeping bullets away with his eyes, as if it made a difference whether he was shot in the front or the back. You just don't turn your back to a nightmare.

"This isn't right, Billy," Lapolla said. But he had quit struggling.

"Let's just get to the car before I piss myself, okay? We'll discuss it then."

"You're not really that scared. I know you."

"Keep your eyes on the upper window. When we get to the car, you drive. Go slowly over the hill, but when you get back to the road, take up a position on the road to Shubert. Watch for them to pass you, then radio for all the help you need."

"Where you going to be?"

They continued to walk sideways up the slope of the hill. Billy maintained his grip on Lapolla, not yet convinced he wouldn't go charging back to the house given the chance.

"Remember, don't stop anywhere they can see you before the Shubert road. They'll know they're trapped, and then we'll be right back where we started."

When they reached the car, Billy strained to keep from sprinting the final few yards. The last steps before reaching safety always made his back scream with dread. Billy ducked into the passenger seat and pulled the door toward him, holding it a few inches away from latching securely.

"You'll see me again, you black pissant!" Lapolla yelled, waving his fist.

"There you go racist again," the man called back.

"Bert, please. Get in the car."

"I don't want him to think he's getting away with anything," he said, sliding behind the wheel.

"Just drive us over the hill."

"The son of a bitch."

"I know. As soon as we're over the crest, I'm going to roll out. Just keep going—drive to the Shubert road and do what I told you. Please."

"I knew you weren't scared."

"Of course I'm scared. I've been shot before, remember? Please, Bert, wait until they pass you; don't let them see you before they hit the main road. . . . Okay?"

"You sure fooled him. . . . Where's he get off talking to Billy Tree like that? You ought to hand him his head."

"*Okay?*"

"Okay, sure. I was just saying . . ."

As they started down the hill, Billy rolled out of the car and flicked the door closed behind him. From where he lay on his back in the weeds, he could see Lapolla reach the base of the hill, adjusting his mirror to watch Billy before he turned onto the gravel road and headed toward Shubert.

Lawton saw the girl coming toward him, swinging those hips like an invitation to dance, her cute little self bouncing under that dress, dress thin as wet paper, sticking to her body here and there where she was sweating because of the summer heat, here a pattern of tiny flowers, there a damp spot made translucent with moisture, holding on to her body, refusing to let go, just like a man might hang on once he got hold of her. Lord. How could a father let his daughter out the house like that? Lawton ever had a child, she going stay a child until she wasn't one no more, not come sashaying out in public, busting out her clothes like her parents couldn't afford two more inches of cotton to cover up all that stuff the child had underneath. . . . Lord! Girl was no more than twelve, couldn't be no older with a face like that, face like a little angel in the drawings, pudgy little face, all baby fat and tiny teeth. . . . Did those little naked angels have teeth? He couldn't remember ever seeing any: Mostly just little rolls of baby fat on their pudgy legs and lots of times big old horns they was blowing on, horns bigger than they were . . . and wings, of course. They always had wings about big enough to lift a wren. There was a funny thing: Big angels had wings come down to the heels when all folded up and baby angels had wings about the size. . . . This Alice wasn't no angel, though. Still a baby in some ways, maybe, but that wasn't no baby's body trying to climb out that dress, and it wasn't no angel's body, either.

She was looking right at Lawton now. She had been glancing over her shoulder at all them boys, but she was almost on top of Lawton now and staring right at him. He didn't like the way she looked at him sometimes, and he sure didn't like it now as she approached him, tossing her head a little bit, brushing hair away from her face, jouncing around under that wet cotton. . . . Some people ought to do with their daughters the way the Lord did with poison snakes—give them some kind of marking so any fool could see to stay away from them. Paint them bright red, with big old diamonds, or give them rattles . . . although this girl was trouble plain enough, didn't need any more markings than that dress and all that firm, liquid flesh, like putting water in a balloon till it's full, slap it and it jiggle but come right back, good and solid if you put your hand on it. Lord, he had to stop thinking about all that. He was more than half-hard already, seemed like he'd been that way for most of the past four years.

"Hello, Lawton," she said. Little trace of something in her voice, always a little something hidden under her words when she talked to him. Teasing maybe? He was eighteen, a grown man. Who was she to be teasing him?

" 'Lo."

"You're sweating awful hard. What you been doing?"

She stopped like she wanted to have a conversation, but Lawton wanted none of that. He slowed just enough not to be rude.

"Working. What you been doing with those boys?"

"Pfff. I wouldn't be doing anything with those boys."

"Long as they know that," he said, still moving.

She took a playful swat at him. He felt the breeze of it against the skin of his arm. He grinned at her, jumping to the side just enough to show her he understood she was playing, but thinking, *Don't be hitting me, little miss. You got no business hitting me like I was one of them children on the bench. I ain't your playmate.*

Lawton kept going, making damned sure he didn't turn around to watch her walk away like those boys had done. That would be about the last thing he needed, to see that little jailbait heinie struggling to pop through that cloth, hips swishing, ass rolling back and forth like a couple of kick balls.

He stepped into the equipment shed, didn't really need to, told himself it was to get out of the sun for a second, but knew it was really just to take a deep breath, settle himself down. Being hard all the time was tough. Sometimes he felt like he was going to break right through his pants, and it didn't take nothing at all to set it off, anything, just a thought, and some of those thoughts—he was embarrassed even to name them to himself. What the hell did they have to do with anything? Why would he get hard thinking about some of that stuff? It made no sense—he wondered if anyone else felt the way he did, if any of those boys on the bench would get hard at nothing at all. Sometimes just a breeze seemed to be all it was, just the wind passing over his body. Sometimes just lying in the sun, feeling the heat on his. . . . He leaned cautiously around the corner of the shed and caught a peek of her from behind. *Lord, look at them legs, look at that butt, little triangle of sweat darkening the dress just there where the two halves . . . Lord! It made him want to . . . Lawton* turned his back on her and walked away.

"What you looking at, Lawton?"

One of them boys, standing in front of him, smirking like he knew exactly what Lawton was looking at, like they was just two of a kind, up to the same kind of thoughts, and nasty thoughts at that, going by the look on the boy's face. The boy couldn't have been no more than fifteen years old. What did he know about Lawton's thoughts? Lawton was a man, not no snotty white boy, and an out-of-town white boy at that, come all the way here just to take a job Lawton could do better, did do better when they give him the chance. Problem was, they never give him the chance. He could sit on that bench with them white boys all day long and the white men would pick some little runny nose instead of Lawton *every time, smiling at them children, leaning over, talking to them like they was uncles, giving them advice, discussing their future, all kinds of things that had nothing to do with the work. Lawton could sit there until his ass was full of splinters and the white men would choose every single white boy in the state before they picked him. Made him wonder if all white people were related in some way, if they all thought of themselves as being family. Or maybe that was just when Lawton was around. Like they was all family compared to him, who pretty clearly was* not.

"You best leave that little girl in peace," Lawton said sharply. His anger surprised him; surprised the boy, too.

"Who you talking to?" the boy demanded.

"Talking to you," Lawton said. He poked a finger at the boy's chest for emphasis, rocking him back on his heels. Harder than he had meant to do it. He wasn't even sure he had meant to do it at all. Just sometimes he got so tired of it all. Sometimes he got so mad.

CHAPTER TWENTY

———✦———

C rawling back to the crest of the hill, Billy hoped that Joan would have sense enough to turn the other way when she hit the gravel road. It would take a while, but she could wend her way home via the rutted local paths and never come into Lapolla's view at all. If she had sense enough to do it. The Joan he knew and loved would make the right decision, but this one, the woman firing at them, seemed to have no sense whatever. It made him think of the mad days of the revolutionary sixties, of Patty Hearst and the Symbionese Liberation Army, a middle-class white girl falling under the influence of men with agendas that had nothing to do with her. He did not know what had possessed her to fire at them, nor why she was hiding in this collapsing old farmhouse with Odette Collins, but he wanted to find out for himself, by himself, without the intrusion of the Sheriff's Department. If he could keep her safe from the law, he would. That did not make her safe from him, though.

He lay quietly just below the hilltop, lifting his head cautiously now and then, expecting their car to appear from behind the house at any moment. What could they be waiting for? Did they not realize he had given them the opportunity to escape? After a few minutes, he crept forward on his stomach, trying to disturb the grasses as little as possible. Behind him, the sun was setting, shining its rays directly into the house. The sun and the approaching darkness would both serve to disguise his approach.

He was within twenty yards of the house again, back almost to the point where Lapolla had prepared to launch his ill-considered assault, when he heard the first sounds from the house. The sun reflected like a fireball from the polished upstairs window, then went dark as the hill shut off the last of the rays like a curtain. Where he lay beneath the hill, Billy was already in deep shadow. They were speaking in harsh whispers and he could hear their agitated hissing, although he could not make out the words. They seemed to be behind the house. Billy listened for the car. If they left now, they might still have time before Bert decided to take matters into his hands again and come charging back heroically, guns blazing. He was not sure why he was still here. All he wanted was to see her get safely away. He knew only that he could not leave her to be dragged further into whatever lunacy had gripped her.

With increasing frustration, he listened in vain for the cough and roar of an engine starting. Come on! he shrieked in his mind. Get out of here!

The voices stopped and he heard the sound of running. Someone was hurrying through the underbrush behind the house, making no pretense about stealth. Was it one body or two? Was Collins waiting in ambush behind the house while Joan ran to safety?

Billy came up in a low crouch and hurried to the side of the house, pressing his body against the building's siding, making himself as small a target as possible. Two people reached the cover of the fringe of trees on the far side of what had once been a backyard, running past a collapsed swing set. Billy saw only Joan's feet as they slid through the trees, but the man paused and glanced back toward the house before stepping into the shelter of the trunks and branches. He held a rifle in his hand.

A cursory glance showed Billy that he had been wrong about the car he assumed to be behind the house; there was none. Which meant that they had arrived here on foot some way and were going back via that route now. They knew where they were going and he did not. Billy breathed deeply, steeling himself again for exposure across open ground. How easy for Collins to turn behind the nearest tree and take aim at his pursuer. He did not believe Collins wanted to shoot him. He could have done so many times over during Billy's slow exit to the car. But then Billy wasn't chasing him at that time; he was retreating. Now he was there alone, a single kill shot would take care of the pursuit. . . . He didn't begin to know how Collins thought. Believing Collins would not shoot at him did nothing to convince Billy's nervous system, which was causing him to twitch violently again.

Thinking he knew the mind of Odette Collins was dangerous enough, he realized, but was the man even Collins? The man with the rifle who might be waiting for him was the man from behind Joan's house, the man whose face Billy had seen only once clearly, in the lights around the motel swimming pool. But why had Billy assumed that Odette Collins was his true name and not another alias? Only because it was the name he heard first, he realized. Because it was the name of someone he knew, or had known twenty years ago, and then only fleetingly. In the end, of course, it didn't matter. A bullet had the same effect on flesh and bone no matter who pulled the trigger. And he was going after them anyway. He knew he could not ponder why or he would never do it.

He heard thrashing as someone stumbled through the trees and underbrush in the growing dark, but was it one body or two? Cursing in his mind, Billy set forth across the open field, crouched and running in a zigzag fashion. Halfway across, his nerves gave out and he threw himself to the ground. His limbs were trembling with fear so much that he needed a moment to control them. He crawled on all fours for a few yards and then, feeling ridiculous, rose to his feet and completed his dash to the trees. A great wave of relief washed over him as he leaned against a tree trunk, panting far more than the exertion warranted. Guns, he muttered to himself, guns.

Feeling better, he followed the sounds ahead of him as best he could. They were making no attempt at silence now. It was clearly outright flight, and they were heedless of pursuit. Billy moved quicker. He didn't want to lose touch with them, and he didn't want to get much closer, either. Neither did he want to twist an ankle on this treacherous terrain, nor bash his head against timber.

It took him a moment to realize that the only sound of thrashing through branches was his own. Somewhere ahead of them, they had either halted or found a clear path through the small forest that bordered the river. He stopped and listened until he heard their voices, far ahead now. Hurrying forward, he crested a small rise and found himself at an abrupt end to the woods.

They were visible a hundred yards ahead. Collins was twisting about, looking behind him, the rifle still gripped in his hand. Joan was moving forward with the near stagger of exhaustion, and Collins supported her with his free hand. They slowed to a walk and stepped onto an expanse of asphalt. The risen moon glinted off glass, and Billy realized that they had reached a parking lot. Only then did he understand where he was. Indian Cave State Park abutted the overgrown property he had just left. Collins and Joan had simply driven into the park as visitors, left their car, and walked through the woods to the derelict farmhouse.

There was no way that Billy could approach them fast enough without exposing himself on the open ground, and they were not going to wait for him to crawl to them. Joan was already in a waiting car. He heard their voices one more time before the car started and Joan drove off. She was gone; she was safe. Lapolla had not recognized her at the farmhouse, and if he saw her now, she would not be coming off the gravel road. There was no reason for him to associate her with the shooter. For the moment at least, she was out of jeopardy and her reputation was safe. Billy noted that it was not her car, but there was no time to ponder where Collins hid it when he went to Falls City, because Collins himself was on the move again. He jogged toward the river, the rifle dangling at his side, looking like a backwoodsman in a movie.

Billy struck off across the field, confident now that Collins was unaware of him. He lost sight of him for a time because of the intervening screen of trees skirting the riverbank. When he was clear of the trees, Billy saw him again in a clearing carved from the woods, where the state engineers had installed a dock.

Collins stood for a moment, a dark shadow, frozen, inanimate. Both arms were at his side, and Billy realized he was gripping the rifle by the barrel. For an insane moment, he thought Collins was going to shoot himself, but then the man snapped suddenly to life and spun twice, the rifle at arm's length. He released it in a high arc and it soared, spinning, before it splashed into the river. The water flew up, almost white in the deepening gloom, then subsided into ripples that were immediately dragged downstream by the current. Collins was already at the end of the dock. He studied the water for a moment, then walked to the end of the dock and searched the ground until he found some sticks.

Safely behind the cover of the trees, Billy squinted to make out what Collins was doing. The man tossed a stick into the river and watched as the river pulled it away. He kept his eyes on it until it was out of sight, then threw another into the stream. Contented that he understood the strength of the current, Collins sat on the end of the dock and removed his shoes, which he tied together by their laces and draped around his neck. He took off his pants and tied the legs together, something Billy had not seen since learning how to turn trousers into a flotation device during a preparatory course for lifeguards in high school.

Collins climbed down from the dock and strode into the river. Billy could see the water frothing around his legs as he held the pants upside down and eased them under water until they ballooned with the trapped air. With the makeshift life preserver under his chest, Collins pushed tentatively into the stream. He moved like a man unsure of himself, as if he were acting on theory and not any practiced certainty. Like a man who was no swimmer.

Billy watched in amazement as Odette Collins drifted with the current down the treacherous Missouri River, his head held above the water like a swimming dog by the flotation device, his body melding with the turbid brown liquid as all color faded in the dying light. Billy ran parallel to the river for a bit, glimpsing Collins's shaven head now and then through the trees as the moon glinted off the wet skin, but Collins was already advancing faster than a man could move through the trees and picking up speed as he left the shallows and was sucked into the faster course in midstream.

Billy stopped running and gave in to the obvious. Collins was either going to drown or get away. There had been only one moment when Billy could have taken him, that brief period between throwing away the rifle and entering the river himself, and Billy had been too puzzled by what was going on to act. What was Collins thinking? The river was tranquil enough at the moment, all of the runoff from the great storm having already passed through the drainage system, but it was a dangerous avenue at any time, and never a place for a man who was not a strong swimmer. How desperate must he be to use the river for an escape route? Or was he making some grand gesture to make sure that Joan got away scot-free? In the company of a black man, she would have been picked up immediately, assuming Lapolla had called in the situation. Alone, no one would give her a second thought. And Collins must have known that he could not hope to escape via the roads in any direction. Billy hated the idea that Collins might be taking the desperate way out to save Joan. If anyone was going to sacrifice for Joan, he wanted it to be him. This was not the time to develop any grudging admiration of Collins's chivalrous intent.

As he retraced his steps and approached the dilapidated house from which Joan had fled, Billy heard the cough and sputter of an outboard engine. He raced through the trees and underbrush toward the river and broke through to the bank in time to see a skiff vanishing in the gloom, its wake arching downstream. Collins's figure was just visible in the stern, his hand on the tiller, his face turning to look at Billy, then back to the river.

Furious at himself, Billy could only watch in frustration. Of course the man had a reason for taking to the river! Had Billy thought he was going to float all the way to St. Louis? In the fading light, cursing his stupidity, he located the marks in the mud where Collins had hauled his boat ashore and moored it to an overhanging bough. How simple. The river brought him practically to the doorstep of his trysting place. And no wonder he was never seen in a car.

CHAPTER TWENTY-ONE

Billy returned to the house from which Joan had fled and entered it with foreboding. The house was all but barren, a home for mice and squirrels and those that hunted them, and their scat and effects were everywhere, but there were signs that someone had been using the kitchen. Both ends of tin cans of beans, spinach, beets, and corn had been removed and the cans flattened. They were layered in a Hinky-Dinky shopping bag, awaiting collection. Bottled water and a toothbrush stood beside the sink; an open bag of dog food was under it. A rumpled bed made from an old blanket and newspapers showed where the dog had lain. The collar from which it had slipped was beside the bed and a few feet away lay the choke chain, clear reminder that the dog was not a pet, not a companion.

An attack dog was kept to protect something. What was there of value in this temporary hideout to warrant the trouble and expense of a dog? It certainly wasn't the house itself.

In the upstairs bedroom, some of the window glass shattered by Joan's shot crunched underfoot as Billy looked with amazement at a lovers' nest. A new mattress rested on an old metal bedstead—how had it been transported, installed? At what cost in secrecy? Sheets and matching pillowcases the color of a summer sky brightened the room, and an embroidered throw pillow—an unmistakably female touch— lay atop a multihued braided rug. Billy could not prevent himself from envisioning Joan walking through the filth and disarray of the house, then standing demurely on the rug, her feet protected from the splintered floor, while she disrobed. A towel was tossed over the back of a straight-back wooden chair, the only other piece of furniture in the room. Someone—Joan, of course—had picked wildflowers from the field and placed them on the floor in a tin can serving as a vase. They had already wilted and slumped, as if floral analogues to passion spent. The woman's touch—it made Billy's stomach lurch to see it, to imagine what was in her heart as she gathered flowers for her lover. There was no pretense about the arrangement in the room, no other niceties that could lead to a misconstruction of the purpose. Collins obviously spent time downstairs, eating from cans, but two people came to this room to have sex. Period. As trysting places went in Richardson County, it was a very private one. What it lacked in creature comforts, it made up for in security. Joan could drive into the Indian Cave Park, leave the car—it was not hers, where did she get it?—where it would not attract attention, walk through the woods, and meet Collins, who had come via the river, or had been waiting for her through the length of several hasty meals. Here they could recline at their ease without concern that campers would stumble over them on the ground or passersby glimpse them from the road. Billy wondered how much searching Collins had done to find this place. Was he scouting it out on the day his rabid dog had blundered onto the road in front of the sheriff's car? Or had he been living here for a time already? Dogs did not reach the final stages of rabies overnight, after all, and who would be mad enough to drive in a car with an animal that sick? How badly must the man have wanted to be with Joan to go to so much trouble?

Although it pained him to think of it, Joan's participation was easier to understand. She loved adventure; she was unorthodox enough to find the romance in this squalid undertaking—she might even have been the instigator. Billy recalled how in their early days together she'd been keen to make love to him in any and every unusual locale she could think of. She was always daring him to do it in semipublic places—in her backyard, under the stars; standing up against his garage, with his hand over her mouth so her cries would not alert the neighbors. Not that she cared about the neighbors' sensibilities—that was only Billy's concern. The wildness in Joan had attracted him, excited him, intimidated him. He wanted to think that he resonated sympathetically with the chord in her that made her always seem to be pushing against the boundaries of accepted behavior, but in truth, he did not. He was more conventional than she in many ways, more timid. Or maybe he just preferred making love indoors and somewhere soft once the frantic lubricity of the first six months abated. He was, by evolved nature, a slow and thoughtful lover, more concerned for his partner than for himself. His approach required a decent measure of both time and comfort. Joan responded to loving treatment, but she also wanted him wild, even close to violent at times. She wanted to see him consumed with his ardor for her, the ferocity of his need being foreplay enough for her. He remembered an incident in their first months together when they were in her car, engaging in light touching as they drove somewhere. She had pulled to the side of the highway and made love to him on the front seat, the two of them squirming and panting on the passenger side in broad daylight, bathed in sweat, Joan naked to the waist, her skirt bunched above her thighs. A Good Samaritan had pulled up next to them and asked if they needed help. He remembered more vividly than the sex the rich fullness of her laugh. There was no trace of embarrassment, no attempt to cover herself. "Do you think you could improve on this?" she had said, still laughing. The man, finally taking in the situation, had sped off, yelling something unintelligible back at them, but Billy had thought, for at least that second, that she would not have objected to his participation. She was, at times, simply more than a match for Billy, too energetic, too excitable, too open to experience. But, overmatched or not, he loved her, and that put him in the position of the boy who had the tiger by the tail—letting go was not an option. . . . It did him no good to think of any of that now; it only increased the ache that he thought could not get worse. In this trysting place, visions of Collins having sex with Joan bombarded his imagination. His sleek black ass, shiny as his dome, sweating and pumping as she writhed beneath him, glorying in his fabled black man's physical endowment. . . . Billy kicked the flower can across the room and through the broken window. It was worse because his rival was black; he could not deny it. He hated himself for it, but he hated Collins worse. With brutish effort, he dragged the mattress to the window and pushed the unwieldy thing out onto the weeds below. It hit the earth with a muffled thump, like an underground explosion that seemed to reverberate with a steady pounding. . . . It took Billy a moment to realize that he was hearing the sound of an outboard motor once more. He hurried downstairs and went outside.

Collins was on the far side of the river, close to the Missouri banks, where the current was weaker. He passed well upstream of his improvised dock on the Nebraska side before heading straight across the Big Muddy, letting the current sweep him sideways and downstream. Once he was within a few yards of the Nebraska banks, he killed the engine and let the river bring him to his dock, steering with an oar. It was a cautious approach, as quiet as could be managed, but Billy crouched in the woods and watched it all under the light of the rising moon. As he waited, he stripped a fallen branch of its twigs and leaves, shaping it into a streamlined club.

Collins back-paddled, slowing the skiff to a near standstill before rising in the boat and grabbing the overhanging tree limb. He stayed there, a few yards from shore, listening, his head cocked to one side like any wary prey animal trying to detect danger over the noise of rushing waters. His eyes searched the shore, passing twice over the spot where Billy squatted behind the trunk of a tree, his body only partially hidden. He was a step too far, Billy calculated. A sudden rush would have to take him around several trees and into the water, which would slow him drastically. If Collins reacted as quickly as his wariness indicated he would, Billy would not quite get to him. He needed the gap between the boat and shore to be closed by a yard or two. He could only wait for Collins to reach land.

Still, Collins hesitated, sensing something. His gaze turned again toward Billy as he tried to decipher the unusual shape in the gloom. Lacking the context of a whole body, a leg was not recognizable as a leg, a shoulder protruding from the trunk of a tree was not a shoulder, and a single eye without a head was not easily interpreted as human. He continued to stare, moving his own head to change his perspective, putting the disparate pieces together. Come in, Billy willed him. Come to shore.

Caution won the day, and Collins released the overhanging limb and sat quickly in the skiff, letting the water take him away. He had the oar in hand and was taking the first long stroke downstream before Billy burst from cover and raced the few steps through the trees and into the water. Billy swung the club in desperation as the water slowed his progress abruptly. The branch struck the outboard motor and snapped in Billy's hand. He lunged forward, diving for the boat, but his fingers barely scraped the side of the skiff before Collins dug heavily and expertly with the oar, pulling away.

After two steps, Billy had to swim, and he lashed at the water furiously, trying to keep pace. It was no contest; the force of the oar and the current combined carried the skiff smoothly away from him. He could feel the drag of his clothes, the heavy weight of his shoes as the water almost tumbled him onto his side. Collins worked impassively as he recalled quickly into the dark, and Billy found himself too far into the river, his energy consumed in the frantic, futile surge. He rolled to his back and kicked off his shoes, then settled into a slow and patient backstroke, taking what little sideways progress the current would grant him, inching his way back toward the shallows. After a moment, he heard the outboard motor catch and purr, carrying Collins swiftly to his destination, wherever that was, far from Billy's reach.

Collins muttered abuse at himself with every sway of the boat, every hiccup of the engine as the prop was lifted briefly above the water by the whimsy of the current. He had blown it; he had gone back too soon. He was too anxious, too fearful that they would find it. Billy

Tree would know now, or he would figure it out soon enough. Too soon for Collins to act. He should have waited, given it a day, come back by cover of night, let Billy think he had gone for good, or sunk beneath the turbid water of the river. Anything but what he had done, which was to call attention to his desperate need to return to the farmhouse. Now he had no choice but to lie low for a time and hope for the best. Not that fate had ever favored him with the best.

He had pushed Tree too far, made an enemy of him. The rage on the man's face as he attacked with the tree branch had astounded Collins. That was no lawman then. No one looking for a negotiated peace. Had Tree carried a gun, Collins would be dead now, he was sure of it.

CHAPTER TWENTY-TWO

W hen he reached Joan's house, Billy pounded once on the door to announce his presence, then walked in without awaiting a response. Will was slouched on the couch, watching television and devouring potato chips. He scrambled to his feet with a mouthful of crumbs.

"The hell you doing?"

"Where is she?" Billy demanded.

Will choked down the chips. "Did I say you could come in? You don't come in this house unless I invite you."

"I've got no time for your shit now, Will. Where's your mother?"

"You ain't got time for my shit? You better make time, 'cause that's all you're getting from me."

Billy stepped forward until he was toe-to-toe with the boy, crowding him back against the couch.

"Where . . . is . . . your . . . mother."

Will collapsed backward against the cushions, then scrambled up again, intimidated by a side of Billy Tree he had never seen, but determined not to show it.

"Baby-sitting," he said.

"Bullshit. Where is she?"

"Baby-sitting, I told you. For her sister."

"That's what she told you?"

"Not that it's any of your business," Will said, regaining some of his poise.

"Oh, your mother is my business all right. More than ever. When she gets back, tell her to call me right away. *Right away.* You understand that? She doesn't want to make me come looking for her."

"Big fucking deal you are."

Billy had turned to leave. He spun around so fast that Will once more took a step back and collapsed onto the couch. This time, he stayed down as Billy bent over him.

"Goddamn it, boy, don't be an idiot all the time. Get your head out of your pubescent ass and listen to me. I'm the best friend your mother's got, and I'm going to keep her out of trouble if I can, but she better not try to hide from me."

"You're the only trouble she's got," said Will.

"I wish that was true."

Will struggled to rise, but Billy pushed him back down and stayed over him.

"You tell her to call me as soon as you hear from her. Do you hear me? I don't care what time it is."

"Why don't you call her yourself and leave me out of it? She's at my aunt Margie's in Auburn. I already told you that."

"And I told *you.* Don't forget it."

Will bounced to his feet and followed Billy to the door. Once Billy was outside, Will called after him.

"You come in here like that again, I just might have to shoot your ass."

Billy turned and glared at the boy for a moment. It seems to run in the family, he thought. Father, mother, and son all want to take a shot at me.

"Be glad you're your mother's son," he said. "But don't press the advantage. I'm running out of patience real fast."

"You know where to find me."

"I don't want you, Will. If I did, I could slam that screen door on your fingers, kick your leg out from under you, and brain you with the table lamp."

Will jerked his fingers away from the door frame and checked the proximity of the table lamp, which was only a step inside the door.

"But I don't want you. I want your mother. Do her a favor and make her call me."

As Billy walked to his car, Will did a slower survey of his situation with the door and the lamp. What surprised him was that Billy had already figured out a plan of attack while he himself had not realized there were any weapons present at all. For the first time in two years, he wondered if some of the stories they told about Billy Tree were true after all.

At the gas station two blocks from Joan's house, Billy purchased road maps of Nebraska, Kansas, and Missouri, all of which abutted the Missouri River downstream from Indian Cave. He could have gone to the sheriff's office for the maps, but he did not want to risk facing Lapolla just yet, not until he could explain what was going on, what had happened, and his own foolish part in it. Lapolla would have to flounder in ignorance, just as Billy was doing. Right now, Billy understood nothing of what was going on, and he could not protect Joan until he had information. The sexual relationship was all too painfully clear to him, but why take a rifle to their tryst? Why fire at Billy and Lapolla instead of just running away, since they had an escape route well in hand? And why should Collins risk his life in the river for failure to pay a motel bill? Or for the noncrime of having sex with an unmarried woman? What did he think Billy was going to do, lynch him? . . . The innocence of the term, how easily tossed off as a synonym for any manner of mild mistreatment. It had lost its meaning in the last half century . . . or it had for Billy. Obviously not for others. It remained a deadly reality for others. Was that the point of the postcard and noose?

At home, he tossed the maps onto the kitchen table, next to the accusatory postcard. For the first time, he thought he saw a connection, not an answer, but at least a connection. He opened the Kansas map, smoothing the folds, then ran his finger down the broad blue line of the Missouri River. He stopped his finger at Sabella. His eyes moved to the postcard and to the face of the boy who became his father. Was it really his father and his uncle Sean staring at Billy through the transfiguring distance of more than half a century? Was it in Sabella where the hanged man rose above the crowd as straight and vivid as an exclamation point? . . . Was it Sabella that Odette Collins was heading for, bobbing on the flood like a fisherman's float? He could have gotten out of the water at any time, of course, docked his boat anywhere along the river. He could have acquired a car and headed back north. Hopped a train, walked away, left the water after a couple of hundred yards and hidden in the woods.

Nothing has to make sense yet, Billy told himself. The earlier one formed a theory about something, the sooner one could go seriously wrong. There might be no connection whatever between Collins and the postcard or Collins and Sabella, and Billy certainly had no working theory to connect them, at least none that he would want to articulate to anyone else. He would simply follow his instincts for the moment, and if they failed him, he would try something else. It was not what he would call a plan; it was just the only thing he could think of to do. In the morning, he would go to Sabella.

After three telephone calls had led him to the home of the sleeping sports editor of the *Omaha World-Herald* and he had made his request, he went back to Joan's.

From his stakeout position in the alley, Billy saw the headlights of a car turning into Joan's driveway. He glanced at the dashboard clock. It was after 3:00 A.M. He hurried to reach her before she entered the house and got Will involved.

She saw his shape hurrying toward her in the dark, and for a moment she was frightened, but then she recognized him and relaxed. Billy realized from her stance that she had been about to launch a kick at his vulnerable parts.

"It's you," she said. "What a nice surprise." She held out her arms for an embrace, but he kept coming, grabbed her by the biceps, and pressed her against the garage.

"You idiot! You goddamned idiot!"

"Hey," she gasped.

"What do you think you're doing? What the hell do you think you're doing? You could have been killed; don't you know that? Or you could have killed me."

She struggled against his grip.

"Let go of me!"

He shook her, reinforcing his control.

"Have you lost your mind over this Collins?"

"Let me go!"

"Don't you know what will happen to a woman around here who is sleeping with a black man?"

She tried to kick him, but her knee missed his groin, hitting his thigh instead. He pressed his weight against her, pinning her against the garage and immobilizing her.

"He's a human being." Inflected with contempt, her voice cut into his anger. She was morally correct. Racism was easy to indulge internally, difficult for him to uphold in the presence of someone who demanded more. And Joan, it seemed, was always demanding more of him.

She had ceased to struggle, but the fury in her face intimidated him. He had thought he wanted to hurt her as badly as she had hurt him, but now he feared that he had gone too far already. Whenever they fought, her anger cowed him and made him doubt himself, because he knew she was a better person than he was, less what people expected her to be, more of what everyone should be—free and open and courageous.

"I'm only trying to protect you from yourself," he said, already losing conviction.

"Let go of me."

"Joan, you've got to stop it. You're going to destroy yourself. You're doing insane things. . . ."

"Why do you harass the man? Why can't you leave him alone? Do you have any idea what he's been through?"

The screen door slapped shut, and Billy turned in time to see Will racing across the yard, brandishing a baseball bat. Releasing Joan, he held up one hand to stop Will, like a policeman at an intersection.

"No!" cried Joan.

If Will swung the bat horizontally, Billy knew he would have to take the blow, because right now he was shielding Joan, and if he moved, she would be hit full force. Will was aware of his mother's position as well, however, and he came at Billy with an overhand chop, trying to drive him into the ground like a fence post hit by a sledgehammer. It was not the way to use a bat, but Billy was not going to explain that now. Will had already lost the fight. All that remained was letting the boy know it without inflicting more harm than necessary.

Billy sidestepped easily. The bat hit the ground, sending a shiver through Will's arms. Billy disarmed him by stepping on the bat. It spurted out of Will's grasp as if greased, and Will started to straighten, stunned by the speed with which he had lost the advantage. Billy hooked one leg and sent the boy sprawling forward onto his face, accompanied by his mother's screams. When Will scrambled to his feet, he found Billy standing in front of him, gripping the bat in the middle with one hand, holding it horizontally so that it could deliver a blow from either side with a flick of the wrist.

"Let's just let it go there, boy. You were protecting your mother. I understand."

"You're going to need more than that bat," Will said. He dropped his arms to his side but curled his hands, beckoning with his fingers.

Probably saw that in some movie about a knife fight, Billy thought. Just about the dumbest way to position yourself that he could think of. The anger he had felt moments before had vanished with the initial attack, and now he was comfortable, alert, and ready, relaxed and dangerous, the way he always was in a fight. The only thing he needed to guard against now, he knew, was the adrenaline surge that, along with Will's general attitude for weeks, made him want to break the boy into pieces.

"Will, stop it," said Joan.

Will lunged forward and Billy stepped back and to the side. He made a jab with the bat that stopped well short of hitting the boy.

"Consider yourself hit," Billy said.

"Billy, please . . ."

Will snorted contempt and charged once more, grabbing for the bat, again in emulation of some idealized knife fighter. Billy evaded him and flicked the bat, stopping a foot short of the boy's head.

"That one would have hurt," Billy said.

Will paused, already out of breath, but still in his crouch. Tension, Billy thought. It can cripple you as fast as your opponent. Muscles are slow, breathing stertorous. You become fatigued in seconds, fighting yourself with every movement. Frequently, all Billy needed to do was stay out of reach for a few moments until his foe exhausted himself with effort.

Joan stepped in front of her son.

"Billy, stop it."

"I haven't done anything yet, I'm trying to discourage him," he said.

"This ain't a computer game, you asshole. You don't get points for saying you hit me."

"Will, stop it," said Joan. "He can break you in two if he wants to."

"Why, because he's the great Billy Tree?"

"Because he *can,* because he knows *how.*"

"Wrong thing to say," Billy said.

"I know how," said Will. He sidestepped his mother and lunged at the bat. Billy pulled the bat back and to the side, like a matador with a cape, and pushed Will off balance with his free hand. The boy stumbled over his own feet and hit the garage with his shoulder.

Uttering a muffled scream, Joan launched herself at Billy and reached for his face. He spun her with his free hand and held her from behind, hooking one leg so she could not kick back at him.

"If you hurt him, I'll never forgive you."

"You best go in the house," Billy said into her ear. "As long as you're here, he's going to have to keep coming at me to prove himself. Go in; give him a chance to save face.

"Let her go, you asshole," said Will, pushing himself off the garage.

"Will, just stop. He won't hurt you."

"Don't say that," Billy hissed.

"I know he's not going to hurt me," said Will. " 'Cause I'm going to kick his ass."

"Go in the house, or I'll have to hurt him just to make him stop," Billy said, keeping his voice low enough so that the boy could not hear.

"Come in the house, Will. Just come in with me right now."

"You go, Mom. I got business here."

"Billy . . . can I trust you?"

"How in hell can you ask me that now? I won't swim the Missouri River for you, but you can trust me."

He released her. She gave him a curious look and entered the house. Billy knew she would be watching from the window, of course, but at least she wouldn't be able to hear them.

He waited until the door closed before addressing Will.

"You don't have to keep this up. You made your point; you're a brave young man. We can just shake hands and call it quits right now."

"You wish."

"I don't want to embarrass you and I don't want to hurt you. I have a weapon, I have training, and I have a lot of experience. I'm very good at this, Will."

"Little old to be bragging, aren't you?"

Will began to circle Billy in his knife fighter's crouch. At least he's stopped wiggling his fingers, Billy thought. He's less apt to get one broken that way.

"What will convince you to stop?" Billy asked. "How about if I drop this bat and put my hands in the air? Is that surrender enough?"

"How about if I knock you on your ass and kick you around for a week?"

"That's not going to happen, Will."

"That's why we're here, to find out."

Will was making a series of feinting gestures, testing Billy's responses. Something else he saw somewhere, Billy thought.

A feint turned into a lunge, and Billy pivoted to one side, turning the bat to a vertical position and steering Will's questing arms away from his body. Foolishly thinking he had gained some advantage through momentum, Will wheeled around and leapt forward again, straight into the extended bat. He took the blow created by his own velocity directly on his chest and staggered backward. Billy had done nothing but hold the bat, fat end forward, and let Will run into it. He could have pointed it at the boy's face, had he wanted to, but he didn't expect Will to interpret what he did instead as an act of conciliation.

Billy took two steps backward, not wanting Will to feel challenged by proximity.

"Stop it, Will. Don't make me hurt you. I'll drop the bat and we'll both just walk away. Nothing gets solved this way."

"You drop the bat and I'll beat you with it."

Billy's options were few. There were not nearly as many ways to immobilize an opponent as there were to hurt one. The one-blow knockout to the chin, so beloved of movie directors, the single punch that left the sentry unconscious for the rest of the action sequence while the hero performed greater feats—that was the stuff of fantasy. He was more apt to break Will's jaw and teeth. A shot to the temple, even with only a fist, could kill him. Billy knew he could pin the boy to the earth easily enough, but that would only humiliate him—a result he wanted to avoid, in hopes of future reconciliation.

"Look, I'm quitting," Billy said. "You've done fine; I respect your efforts. I'm just walking to my car and getting out of here."

He tossed the bat into the dark, hoping Will could not get to it before he reached his car. Without waiting for a response, he turned his back and walked, rapidly but not running, toward the alley. For a second, he thought Will was going to be smart enough to let him go. Then he heard Will's boots as the boy came running after him.

Billy turned, crouched, and stepped directly into Will's path. The boy was surprised and swung wildly once over Billy's head, unable to stop his momentum. Billy turned his shoulder and threw one very short punch, designed more for accuracy than power, driving his fist into Will's stomach.

The boy continued forward with enough power to knock them both to the ground, but that was the end of it. Billy peeled him off and stood over his adversary, who was gasping like a fish out of water, unable to catch his breath.

"It'll come," he said, intending to wait beside the boy until he got his first clean breath before turning his back once more and continuing toward his car.

Joan exploded from the house and ran to her son.

"He wouldn't quit," Billy explained, knowing nothing would be adequate.

"Never come back!" she screamed. "Never!"

"Joan . . ."

"Never come back! It's over, *over!*"

And then her attentions were only for her son, who continued to gasp and gulp for air.

"It looks worse than it is," Billy said, but neither of them heard him.

When he reached his car, he sat in silence for a moment, hoping she would realize he had done the only thing he could, and that he had done it for her. Hoping she would run to him and beg his forgiveness—or just simply run to him, show him her defiance, yell at him, anything but look at him with the crushing glare of hatred he had just seen. After a moment, he drove away.

From the shelter of the house, she watched him go, saw his taillights blink, then disappear. Her arms still burned where he had grabbed them. She wanted to rush after him, to pound him with her fists, then shower him with kisses, but her arms held her back. She would not be handled that way again, never, ever again. A man would touch her lovingly, respectfully, or not at all. She would never again allow herself to be bullied and abused the way her husband had done, not by Billy, not by anyone. Her reaction to being grabbed that way had been immediate and visceral and had sprung not from Billy but from the years of being mistreated by Duane Blanchard. Knowing that had not tempered her reaction. She had felt instantly trapped by the harshness of his hands, panicked and threatened.

Behind her, Will was raging through the house like a caged animal, snarling his anger and muttering revenge. Billy should never have hit him. Wrong as Will was—and she knew it was his fault, for he had provoked and persisted—she could not allow anyone to abuse him, any more than she could allow herself to be abused. Even less. There was nothing she could do for her son now, not yet. If he was like his father, his anger would flare up briefly, then subside and sink deep within, stoking the seething cauldron of resentments that heated him day and night. She prayed he was not like his father, that he would not become a man obsessed with vengeance—but prayer had never availed her of anything before. . . . How she hated Duane, how his presence haunted her still, years after his banishment from her house, even after his death. What a price is extracted, she thought, for our rush to find a mate, confusing propinquity with choice, familiarity with affection. We pay for our mistakes with installments of misery for the rest of our lives.

She turned from the window to cope with her son.

CHAPTER TWENTY-THREE

⊰⊱

T he fax from the *World-Herald* was waiting for him in the office. Deputy Schatz was sleeping away the last of his night shift on the cot in the jail cell, so Billy tore off fax sheet and quietly slipped back out and into his car. Halfway to Rulo, he pulled to the side of the road and read about the career of Odette Collins.

Although he had played basketball in the state high school tournament against Billy, Collins's real sport was football. After starring at the University of Nebraska, he had joined the National Football League as a defensive back. In his second year, his knee had been rearranged by the force of a blow and he had spent months in rehabilitation. In his third season, his knee collapsed again, and by his fourth year, Collins was out of football, too soon to get his pension. His name was well enough known in the state for him to land a series of jobs in promotion where little was required of him other than a handshake and a ready smile for the cameras, but he had been only a brief star, not a legend, and in short order, his name was replaced by newer ones. Hooked initially by the painkillers prescribed for his knee, he shifted substances to a variety of drugs and finally to alcohol. It was a story all too familiar—an athlete pampered from an early age, idolized but undereducated, sinks into precipitous decline when the support of an adoring public vanishes. Hitting the heavier atmosphere of real life, he crashes and burns. It made Billy grateful that he had possessed the good sense to avoid big-time athletics. Collins's decline was deeper than most. The reporter's article documented failure after failure, treatments aborted, rehabs abandoned, the loss of family and friends. For a time, his name and fame had cut him some slack with local police—always friends of athletes—and minor crimes were overlooked or dismissed. Eventually, however, that cushion of goodwill was eroded, too, and Collins began to do jail time, finally spending four years in prison. He had hit bottom. Sobered, repentant, he emerged from behind bars a changed man, but not, as was usually the case, spouting the news of divine intervention that had shown him the way. His was a sterner call. The reporter had found him three years ago, doing seasonal work, helping with the wheat harvest. "It's what I'm good for," he had said without apology. "Grunt work. It's about my speed. It wears me out, helps me sleep, and I don't spend any time thinking about myself." Billy detected a whiff of the AA admonition against grandiosity. "I got to burn myself down to a nub before I rebuild. Get all the poison out." He had worked as a roustabout in an oil field, spent six months on a duck farm, the only non-Mexican in a crew of seventy, force-feeding the fowl whose livers would be used to make foie gras. He had built new stone walls for suburbanites seeking the "natural" look, then worked for three months in a rendering plant, scooping offal. Self-flagellation was the mode, hard labor the higher power. And was he burned down now? the reporter asked. Was he to the nub yet? What poisons remained? "Not there yet," Collins had confided. "Got one big one yet to get rid off. Then I can start being me."

Billy let the fax curl itself back into a roll on the passenger seat. One big poison left. The article was three years old, and Collins was still flailing himself at minimum-wage jobs. Had he reached the big poison at last? Was Billy part of the purgative that would cure him? Or part of the poison?

On a segment of the Missouri River where the water's course jutted into the land like a swollen knuckle on a boxer's hand squatted the town of Sabella, Kansas. Because of the natural quay, the town had once been a fueling and provisioning stop for riverboats, which could find easy anchorage against the Missouri's whimsical current, going both upstream and down. With the river traffic came considerable, albeit transient, wealth. Unlike Falls City, a town of comparable size, Sabella boasted a number of large Victorian-style homes, pride of the early years of the twentieth century, and the expansive grounds and gardens to go with them. A less pleasant side effect of the onetime heyday—again, unlike Falls City—was the section of ramshackle huts that had once housed the laborers necessary to deal with the river traffic. Poverty being always a reality, whatever the vagaries of wealth, the huts had never wanted for lodgers, although many of the fine and stately homes had long since been sold for taxes, subdivided, or converted into rent-producing commercial properties. The riches that had once been Sabella's remained now only like the artificial beauty mark of an aging vanity; the unchanging slum was the ugly reality.

"They get by," said the local police chief as he cruised through the rough neighborhood. His name was Harbart and he spoke as if his listener was doubting his every word and thus needed constant reassurance. "No, I mean they get along okay. Not bad people, most of them. You don't want to bunk down with them, but they're okay. All I'm saying is, they're not as bad as they look. Just poor, for the most part."

Billy nodded and looked out the window at the houses they passed. Poorer than the worst of Falls City's poor, poor in the sunken, pitted way that had no expectation of getting better. Black poor, Billy thought. Defeated, forced to surrender, and sullen, the poor of the inner cities across the nation, who expected no better and consequently would never get it, no matter how many advances were made by people of color everywhere else. Self-fulfilling prophecies, every one of them.

"Not a whole lot of trickle-down," Billy observed.

"No, what I'm saying, you don't get a whole lot of that here," offered Harbart, although he hadn't been saying any such thing.

Billy had been in Harbart's company for the better part of an hour, most of it in the police station, where the local chief checked on addresses and filled Billy in on the town's history and genealogy. As was usually the case with small-town law enforcement, the chief had been born and bred in the municipality he now served and knew as much fact and legend about the place as anyone else—and was not much better at separating the two than anyone else, either. True historians were thin on the ground in places this small, and the editors of the newspapers were often transients, trying to gain experience and work their way up to the cities—or veterans of the cities, trying to halt their further descent. But the police were there for the same reason Lapolla was there, steered into the job as much by opportunity for steady employment as actual attraction to the work. They might not be skilled at their craft, but they knew their town, their citizens, and most police work at this level was just a matter of asking the right questions of enough people until someone had the answer. Billy had followed the same procedure to get where he was now, cruising the lower levels of Sabella with the man who knew how to find the person he sought.

The residents of the streets regarded the police car with sidelong glances. It was not the wary glance of the guilty that Billy had seen so often in the cities, nor the angry stare of the defiant. There was something bovine about the attitude, as if they knew what the police could do to them but had no idea what to do about it.

They drove in silence, although Billy sensed that it made the chief uncomfortable not to be talking. He had declined the proffered offer of the tour of the stately houses, some of which were maintained in museum condition as proud testimony to the town's glory days, offering to take it with the chief after he had concluded his business. It had not set well with the man who wanted to show his town at its best to the visiting lawman. Billy understood the impulse. Civic pride was not a bad quality in a policeman, provided he did not come to believe the propaganda himself. Viewed from the ground level of law enforcement, civic virtue was at best a Platonic ideal, at worst an oxymoron.

Harbart broke the silence, apropos of nothing except a counterbalance to the surrounding squalor, by saying, "No, what I'm saying is, we have a great golf course. One of the oldest in the Midwest."

"Is that right?"

"You wouldn't think so, a town this size, but some of that old river money got together. There's clubhouse architects come out and study, the grounds. . . . You play golf?"

"When I retire, maybe," Billy said.

"Great game. Great game. Hardest game there is, even though it looks like the easiest. They used to have a professional tournament here, back in those days. Lloyd Mangrum played here. Dow Finsterwald, I think. . . . Didn't get Hogan or Snead, but hey."

"Nothing wrong with Lloyd Mangrum," Billy said, hoping he had repeated the name correctly. He had never heard of either Mangrum or Finsterwald.

"No, what I'm saying, nothing shabby about those two," Harbart said.

Billy knew that golfers had to be derailed early. Once they got up some steam about their sport, they were unstoppable.

"That would be before the lynching, or after?" he asked.

The joy of contemplated golf vanished from Harbart's voice and his face turned stony.

"The lynching isn't discussed around here," he said, then lapsed into a silence as if to prove the point.

A small boy burst from one of the houses, bounding toward the street. He stopped abruptly when he saw the police car, frozen into place except for his eyes, which widened and followed the car's progression past him. Billy watched in the side-view mirror as the boy returned to the shelter of the house. They may not talk about the lynching, Billy thought. That doesn't mean they don't still think about it.

"It could have happened anywhere," Harbart said. "Anytime. Don't kid yourself."

"Uh-huh."

"No, what I'm saying, a thing like that—terrible, of course. Just terrible—but you can't tar and feather a whole community. They were just people, doing what they thought was right. Wouldn't happen now, of course; times are different."

"Sure."

"Everybody gets along fine now. We had a black man who was, uh, parks and recreation commissioner awhile back."

"Really? Parks and recreation."

"This was awhile back. Did a good job, I think. Never heard any complaints."

"You have a lot of parks in town?"

"He moved away, though. Most of them do. Nothing for them here, just cleaning houses, septic work. Get somebody with some promise, some git-up-and-go, and they go. I think those that stay just do it because of the housing—couldn't get much cheaper—that and the clean living, you know. This is a wonderful town. People are happy to stay here. Everyone's friendly. Everyone gets along pretty much. . . . Don't know why they don't just tear these houses down, bulldoze them under. . . . You know, when they come free. I'm not saying evict anybody. Just wait till someone dies, then bulldoze the shack."

"Who owns them?"

"Well, they do. That's the thing."

"That would be the thing," Billy agreed.

"Still, without violating any property rights or anything, get rid of them. They're an eyesore."

"Where would they live then?"

"Who?"

"The people living there before you bulldoze their homes."

"No, what I mean, they'd go somewhere else."

"Somewhere else in town?" Billy asked.

"Where would that be? Why start the problem all over again someplace else in town?"

"Gotcha."

Harbart nodded agreement with himself for a moment, then pulled the car to a halt in front of one of the houses.

"That was the end of the tournament, of course. Couldn't get people to come back after that. Well, ran out of money, too, I suppose. Couldn't get prize money together after that."

"After . . ."

"The . . . uh . . . you know." Harbart bent over and peered past Billy toward the house. It was a two-story structure, and the continuing elevation of the second story floor to be as much a result of faith as physics.

"Paint holds some of these things up, you got to think," Harbart offered, as if reading Billy's mind.

"Maybe they've got a few dozen extra coats of primer on the inside," Billy said. "Because it looks like it could use some out here."

"You want me to introduce you?"

"I'll take care of it," Billy said. "You want to start building that rapport in an interview right away." He grinned broadly. "Charm over substance."

Harbart was a little confused by the statement, but he smiled in return. It was difficult not to, with Billy beaming at him that way.

"I'll make my way back to you afterward," Billy continued. "No need to wait for me."

"You sure?"

"Absolutely. Thanks for everything."

"Didn't do much."

"You did all you were asked, and I enjoyed the commentary, as well. Very enlightening. You've been as helpful and gracious as they said you would be." Billy stepped out and closed the door before Harbart could inquire who had been saying such nice things about him.

Billy waited on the sidewalk until the police car slowly crawled away. The surrounding neighborhood had taken on the aspect of a petrified forest: All motion had ceased, frozen as abruptly as the wide-eyed boy. He did not delude himself that all life within the houses had stopped, as well. He would be the object of everyone's attention, a white man stepping out of a police car, the Man incarnate. The basilisk had come to harm them with his very glance—no wonder they were hiding.

It's not supposed to be like this in America anymore, he reflected. But then, this wasn't a twenty-first century middle-class black neighborhood. This wasn't the breeding ground of tomorrow's college students and professionals. This was the detritus, the slag left behind after the purifying fires had powered the civil rights revolution, the affirmative action revolution, the big umbrella, rainbow-happy family of the Republican administration. These were the people who would never be changed, whether they rode up front on the bus or not. Their problem was not about buses or lunch counters or jobs or quotas. Their problem was about self-expectation. In immigrant communities, these people would be the ones who never bothered to learn English, the widows who dressed all in black half a century after leaving the old country, the super-orthodox, who clung to medieval ways in the midst of modernity. Some people could not be elevated beyond their station, Billy reflected, and some *would* not be. Their roots were too deeply sunk into the past to nurture from the present.

Billy listened for the noise from within the house as soon as he reached the porch. His knock on the flimsy pine of the screen door reverberated as if a tree had been felled in the surrounding petrified forest. And now I know what it sounds like when a tree falls and I'm the only one to hear it, he thought. It sounds hollow, as if the whole empty house exists for no other reason than to amplify the echo.

"Mrs. Mills?" he called. "It's Billy Tree, from Falls City. . . . I'm sort of a sheriff over there. I'd like a word with you, if I could. I won't take much of your time."

He did not expect his name to mean anything to her; he offered it only as a token of formal introduction, like showing her that his hands held no weapon. If she *did* know who he was, of course, it wouldn't be because of his days as an athlete. Whether that would make her more apt to come to the door, he couldn't say.

There was some life in the house; he could sense it. Years of conducting interviews for the Secret Service had made him as attuned to the nuance of human presence as a rent collector in a tenement. Sometimes just waiting was all that was needed to make people give themselves away. They thought they were frozen in place, that they were barely breathing, but they had no practice with the element of time. Muscles tightened and demanded relief, throats tickled, or noses itched. Playing statues was child's play for the first minute. After that, it took an expert, and few people had bothered to master the skill.

Eventually, they shifted weight, thinking they could do it without boards creaking. They cleared their throats, fighting back the tickle, thinking he would not hear. They did not understand that in artificial silence, clothes rustled when moved, cloth scraped against cloth, leather creaked. Furniture could be like a sounding board as cramping muscles demanded relief and buttocks were adjusted, backaches relieved.

Once he was convinced that she was there, Billy spoke again through the screen door.

"I don't want to inconvenience you, Mrs. Mills. I realize you've got things to take care of. I'll just sit here on your porch until you're ready to talk to me."

That usually worked. Sitting on their porch was like waving a flag to the community that the Man was on the case. If anyone had missed his arrival, they wouldn't be unaware of his presence for long. When necessary, Billy had camped on a stoop for over an hour, whistling, singing some of his favorite Celtic songs in an adequate baritone, chatting with passersby—for eventually, curiosity would revive the neighbors, even in a neighborhood as wary as this one, and they would stream by on newly discovered errands, often not looking in his direction, but taking him in like a strong and unwelcome odor nonetheless.

"I'll just be waiting for you out here, then, Mrs. Mills. Take your time. It's a beautiful day, so I don't mind a rest anyway."

He sat half-looking at the house, half-studying the neighborhood. The proximity to the river ensured the presence of trees, a luxury in Falls City, where anything taller than a few feet had been imported onto the prairie or carefully nurtured by some past generation of home owner. Here they flourished, giving the neighborhood a deceptively sylvan appearance. But there was nothing of the woods about the place. It was a strictly urban and man-made phenomenon, human beings huddling together when cramping was not necessary, crowding one another, as if afraid of open spaces.

He heard the footsteps, slow and shuffling, and rose to his feet.

"Yes?" asked a querulous voice.

"Mrs. Mills? I'm Billy Tree."

She was a stooped and heavily wrinkled woman in a cheap wig

that curled permanently at the neck like the coiffure of a Motown backup singer. Hastily arranged on her head so that it made her appear to be tilting to one side, the synthetic hair was of a color that may once have been auburn but had taken on earthier tones after decades of use. Billy tried to imagine a younger woman, any younger woman, thinking that this piece of artless artifice was an improvement on her own hair, be she bald as a teacup.

"Sister Mills," she corrected him.

Billy had given her the "Mrs." as an honorific; he knew she had never married.

"Sister Mills, I'd like to talk to you for a minute about your brother."

"My brother? Ain't got no brother. They a man say he my brother down to Kansas City, up to Omaha, but he ain't. I been shut with him for years."

"I don't mean your brother-in-law, Robert Collins. I mean your brother, Lawton."

She was staggered for a moment, as if Billy had cursed at her.

"Lawton dead," she said finally.

"Yes, ma'am, I know. . . . Do you mind if I come in?"

The interior of the house was a stew. A single rocking chair facing the television set offered the only unlittered surface in the living room. From a passing glance into the kitchen, Billy determined that things were no better there. A predisposition against housekeeping coupled with aging eyesight provided a fine layer of dust over all, accented in every corner by abandoned spiderwebs, darkening with time. The newer webs, maintained by their arachnid hosts, were harder to see. Chief Harbart had told Billy that she had made her living cleaning other people's houses, but obviously she took no busman's holidays in her own. Still, he had seen much worse. This was no youthful bachelor pad with dirty dishes on the floor and take-out containers under the seat cushions. There was no chaos amid the overcrowding; things had been put where they were wanted and where they were intended to stay, but there was a lifetime of them. Except for the difference in cleanliness, he was reminded of Judge Sunder's den jammed with memorabilia. Sunder's tchotchkes were all personal, Sister Mills the accreted bric-a-brac of found objects and employer discards garnered after sixty years of working for others. But the impulse to accumulate was the same.

She would not sit, nor did she make an offer to Billy to do so, so they stood, she with her arms crossed, eyes downcast. He removed a copy of the postcard from his pocket and held it toward her.

"I know this will be painful for you to look at after all these years, Sister Mills, and I wouldn't ask you to if it wasn't important."

She took it between thumb and forefinger and held it at waist level, never lifting her eyes. The muscles in her jaw moved. A few white hairs protruded from her chin and along the loose flesh of her jowls. The image of Adley, waist cinched in by the cowboy belt, looking very much a woman in quest of adventure, flashed into Billy's mind. Could she possibly be a contemporary of this old woman, who was desiccated and withered by the same years, vitality sucked out of her as if siphoned by a straw? She looked two decades older than his Adley, although they were no more than a few years apart in age. A few years apart in age—a world or two in life experience.

"That's Lawton," Sister Mills confirmed, extending the photo toward Billy. Her voice was flat and emotionless, as if he had asked her to identify a picture of a cow or dog.

"Yes, ma'am, I know it is. I was hoping you could help me out with some of the other faces."

"Don't remember," she said.

"Uh-huh. It's been a long time."

The ceiling creaked. Another statue forced to life by cramping, Billy thought. Or an attempt to hear better.

"You do remember this . . . I'm sorry, Sister Mills. There just isn't any way to word any of this as delicately as . . ."

"Go ahead on."

"You do remember this . . . scene?"

"Um."

"You saw it, didn't you? You actually saw it?"

"Um."

"Would you be more comfortable sitting?"

"I be more comfortable this over," she said.

"I understand." For a moment, Billy considered telling her that she did not have to endure the situation at all. She had no need to talk to him, as he was out of his jurisdiction. She could tell him to leave her house, and he would go with almost as much relief as she would feel.

"That's you in the background, the face in the window, isn't it?" He pointed over the shoulder of one of the male bystanders to the suggestion of a face in the distance. She did not bother to look at the photo again, just nodded her head almost imperceptibly.

"I know how ugly it is," he said, pulling the picture away. "Where was this taken? Where did this happen?"

"Here. Sabella."

Billy's voice had fallen to a level as low as her own. They were speaking in murmurs now, almost like lovers, joined in a mutual distaste of the specter of an event that might be reawakened by too much noise.

"Where in Sabella?"

Billy had done a tour of the town on his own before seeking out the police chief and had found no tree, no background that fit the photo. He had assumed they had vanished with the years.

"Golf course."

"The golf course? This happened at the golf course?"

"Um."

"Was Lawton a golfer? . . ." He realized immediately the stupidity of his question. "Did he work there? Did you work there?"

"Lawton work on the greens and that. Sometimes caddy. I work in the kitchen."

An eight-year-old girl, working in the kitchen. At least some things have improved, Billy thought. The ceiling creaked again.

"I see. I'll ask you to look at the picture just one more time, Sister Mills." He carefully covered the image of her brother hanging from the tree with his thumb and held the photo in front of her. "Do you know these boys?"

"Um," she said. She had not bothered to look, Billy noted. Either the scene was forever fixed in her mind's eye or she had seen the picture recently. "They caddies."

"Caddies? They were all caddies?"

"Sometimes."

It had not occurred to him. An hour's ride by car from Falls City, given the roads that existed in 1947? How had they managed it? Would it have been easy for teenagers to hitchhike in those days? Easier than today, certainly. Surely fear of injury at the hands of strangers had been less than it was now. Back then, paranoia was still just a concept for psychologists, not a national attribute. And for blacks? Fear of injury at the hands of a crowd of familiars seemed like common sense. At least in Sabella two years after a war fought to make the world safe for democracy.

"Do you know who the boys were?" Billy asked. He dreaded the answer.

For the first time in the interview, she looked directly at him, her expression puzzled but stern, as if wondering why he asked, determined not to be toyed with.

"I know," she said. There was a new firmness in her voice. Some things she would yield to discretion, and some not.

Billy could not look at her. He felt himself blushing with disgrace.

"I know who they are. I know where they live," she continued. "I knowed about them ever since. I ain't never going to forget them."

Billy forced himself to look at the photo again. Had he missed something despite the hours he had studied it?

"Do you know everyone in the picture?"

She shook her head. "Ain't studying all of them," she said. "They mostly just trash, having a look at sorrow. No shame in any of they faces—you see that? But I ain't studying them. I know some, though. Some I even work for, clean they house."

"You worked for them before this . . . happened?"

"After."

He could not imagine it, working in the house of her brother's assassins, probably passing through the rooms as invisible to the occupants as Lawton Mills's ghost.

"Clean they house," she repeated, thinking he had not understood the arrangement.

"I see. That must have been very hard for you."

She fixed him with her gaze again, and he thought he saw the barest hint of a mocking smile.

"Most of life's hard," she said.

The floorboards overhead groaned loudly, but she gave no sign that she noticed.

"You need anything else?" she asked.

"Why the boys?" Billy asked. "Why have you been 'studying' the boys for all these years?"

"You best ask them," she said.

"My father's dead," he blurted, as if it might provide him with absolution.

"I know," she said, offering no hint of sympathy.

Billy could not stop himself from pursuing the obvious. Any pretense that this was an ordinary interview had ceased as soon as he had asked about the boys in the photo.

"Was it my father? Was that him?"

He pointed at the picture, pressing hard with his finger, trying to eradicate the identification. A fullness came upon his sinuses and his eyes itched. He realized that he was close to crying.

Her tone softened. "Wasn't your father then," she said. "Wasn't nobody's father, nobody's son, just a white boy from out of town. Jimmy Tree. Falls City, Nebraska."

"Did you know him?"

"Didn't know him. Knew about him."

"Did your brother know him? What did he say about him?"

"Lawton didn't talk about those boys. Probably didn't much think about them. Why should he? White boys from out of town, come to take work Lawton could use, carrying clubs. They carry clubs; Lawton shine the shoes. Why should he talk about them? You think they friends?"

"No, ma'am, I don't imagine they were friends. I imagine they treated you and your brother the way white people treated black people in those days. Not very nicely. Those were ugly times, and we're all ashamed of them."

"Um."

"Or we should be," Billy added.

"*Should* don't cut the wood," she muttered. "That all?"

"Is there anything else you want to tell me?"

"Didn't ask to tell you that. Didn't ask to talk to you at all."

"I know. It can't be easy for you, looking at this filth again and again, but I appreciate your doing it for me."

"Ain't no again and again. I ain't be studying that picture."

Billy paused.

"Well, you have, though, haven't you?" he asked softly. He smiled with understanding. He was coming back to himself, recovering from his sense of humiliation, summoned by the old woman's lie. "You've seen this postcard many times, haven't you, Sister Mills?"

Eyeing the floor between their feet, she said nothing, her head bowed in stoic, sullen pose, like an animal prepared to bear whatever burden was laid upon its back. It was a posture Billy had seen many times among the guilty.

"Haven't you? You're very familiar with it. You know who is who without even looking. It's been more than half a century, Sister Mills, but you know what boy I'm pointing to without so much as a glance. . . . You said that's you in the background? How would you know that if you haven't seen this picture from this angle?"

He absorbed more of her silence as it came at him in waves of speechless acceptance.

"You haven't been completely honest with me, have you, Sister Mills?"

The old woman said nothing, did nothing, just stood, head bowed. Billy was reminded of movie scenes he had seen of horses or camels in a dust storm. They simply hung their heads and endured.

"Have you seen Odette lately?" he asked, watching.

"Odette?" she said carefully, as if trying to construe some sense from meaningless sounds.

"Your sister's son. The boy you raised until Robert Collins took him away."

"Got no truck with Robert."

"This is his boy I'm talking about. . . . You must remember him, Sister Mills. He's the one you've been studying this picture with, isn't he? He's the one who made a copy and put it on my porch, isn't he? Was that your idea? And the noose? Was that your idea, too, Sister Mills, or was that something Odette dreamed up on his own?"

Mute, suffering stoically the indignities of the oppressor, Sister

Mills turned half away from Billy, as if his words were the lash of a whip.

"I don't know what you planned to happen, Sister, you and Odette. . . . But I've been living with this picture ever since I saw it. It pains me to look at it; it pains me to think about it. It pains me to believe that's my father there. Is that what you wanted? You want to make me feel bad because my father happened to be in town when your brother was lynched?"

"Not just lynched. He murdered. My brother murdered."

"Well, yes, if you want to make that distinction."

She turned to him suddenly with a defiant glare, startling him. "Lawton Mills was murdered," she declared. "That my distinction."

"All right. I understand that."

"You understand that? You *think* you understand that. You the sheriff? You the sheriff?"

"What is it, Sister Mills? What do you expect of me? Look at those men; they must all be dead by now. There's nothing to be done about them now. I understand that your pain is still alive, but *they're* not. Your brother's killers are not alive. What do you want from their children? What do you want from *me*? Guilt? You have it; you succeeded. I feel guilty."

"Don't want your guilt. Don't want your pain."

"What do you want?"

"You the *sheriff*," she said indignantly. "You the *sheriff*."

"What can I do at this late date, Sister Mills? What do you expect me to do?"

"Spect? I spect you to do just what you doing. Nothing at all. You *his* idea, not mine."

She stepped away from him and sagged into a chair, as if her moment of animation had drained her of the last of her strength.

"His? What do you mean I'm '*his* idea'? Odette's? I'm Odette's idea?"

She turned her face away from him and studied a spot on the wall.

"It was his idea to bring me into this? Why? What does he expect from me? I wasn't even alive. Neither was he."

"You alive *now*," she murmured.

"What does he want me to do?"

Billy spoke some more, entreating her to understand, but she had finished the interview and took no more heed of him than if she were a stone. Oddly, as he stumbled to a conclusion, Billy felt that he had failed *her*.

"Well, thank you for your time," he said at last. "I won't bother you any longer."

He paused at the door. "I do have a message for Odette, though."

"Don't know nothing about that," she said, coming out of her silence.

"Well, he might just pop up . . . You don't need to worry if he does, Sister Mills. I have no jurisdiction here."

"Ain't need it so far," she said beneath her breath.

"Just tell him his dog was rabid."

"Odette ain't got no dog. How he going keep a dog?"

"Well, he had one for a day or two. He says he rented it as a watchdog. Somebody had mistreated it pretty badly before that to make it an attack dog. It was sick and we shot it. He should know in case the dog bit anybody. They should see a doctor right away if it did. If Odette was bitten, it's a terrible way to die."

"He ain't got bit," she blurted.

Billy paused, looking toward the ceiling, awaiting any movement.

"I'm relieved to hear that. I'm sure you must be, too. But if his dog bit anyone else and Odette doesn't inform that person, he might be liable for criminal charges."

"That ain't his dog. He just borrow it for a couple days, like you say. He wouldn't mistreat nothing. Why you can't just leave him alone?"

"Because he wants to be part of my life. He started this; he's the one who gave me a noose and a postcard. I'm '*his* idea,' you said. I didn't ask for any of this."

She turned away again, reverting to silence.

"Tell Odette I'm not very smart, I'm not a great detective, and I'm having trouble figuring out what he's up to . . . but I don't usually give up on a thing, either."

She twitched slightly but gave no reply. Billy let himself out the door, feeling ashamed of himself. He had been feeling that way a lot lately, he realized. Under these conditions, there didn't seem to be any way to conduct himself that he could be proud of.

Someone was following her. She wasn't sure which one, but she could hear him, hear his footsteps, hear his breathing. He was walking faster than she was, gaining on her, panting a little with the effort. She smiled to herself, pleased that someone had come after her. She didn't know which one she would prefer, Lawton or the boy with the brilliant smile. Well, not Lawton; that wouldn't be right. She was just pretending with herself when she thought that; it didn't count. It wasn't like she really wanted it to be Lawton or anything like that, because that wasn't right and everyone knew it.

He was making noises with his mouth now, the kind of sounds you made to a dog or a cat. Boys did that to her sometimes, just to annoy her, she thought. And because they didn't know what to say. She knew they wanted to say something to her, but they couldn't talk well. Almost no boys could talk well. They could only say stupid things and clown around and act silly. It made her wonder why she even liked them sometimes.

She turned around to face him when she knew he had almost caught up with her. It wasn't the person she expected and she was surprised, just as he seemed surprised that she had turned on him so abruptly.

"You oughtn't to do that," she said.

He had been prepared to say something, been rehearsing it all the time he was following her, and she could see that she had thrown him off completely by talking to him first.

"Do what?"

"Make that noise. You oughtn't make that noise to a person."

So of course he made that noise again, as loud as he could. She hoped they got smarter as they got older, because most of them seemed just too dumb to get by on their own when they were this age.

"You're not very nice, are you?"

"How would you know?"

"I can tell."

"I am so."

"I don't think so," she insisted, although he seemed as nice as most.

"Well, I am."

"Prove it," she said.

"That's what I'm going to do," he replied.

"How?"

"I'm going to cool you off. That's a nice thing, isn't it, hot as it is?"

"How you going to cool me off? You want to be my fan?"

"You got too many clothes on; that's why you're so hot," he said. He wiped sweat from his nose and blushed at his own audacity.

She thought he had wanted to say more, but he stopped entirely and just stared at her. He's scared himself, she thought. He said something he knows he shouldn't have said and now he doesn't know what to say.

"I don't see you taking your clothes off," she teased. "You look hotter than me."

"You want me to take my clothes off?"

"You do what you want; it's none of my business if you run around buck naked. . . . But I ain't going to stay here and watch."

"I'm going to take your dress off for you," he said.

"No, you ain't."

He looked her up and down, really staring hard, like she was naked already, it seemed to her. She didn't like being looked at that way, so hot and cold at the same time like he had the right to do that. She didn't mind when they snuck a glance; they all seemed to do that, but then they had the decency to be embarrassed. He wasn't embarrassed anymore; he'd stopped blushing. She realized for the first time that she should be frightened.

"I'm leaving," she said.

"Don't."

"I was right—you're not nice." But she couldn't make herself leave. She knew she should, because he was looking a little crazy. You never knew what boys might do. They got crazy so easy, running around like apes, yelling, what all. Darryl Woodard had started throwing things at her once, sticks and clods of dirt, for no reason at all, and right when she'd thought he was going to be nice. She had run away from him and didn't stop until she looked back and saw him crying. When she returned and asked him what was wrong, he started throwing things again. She never did figure that out.

"I'm just going to give you a little breeze," the boy said. "I'm going to fan you after all."

And he stood right next to her and began blowing on her. It was the strangest thing. Just blowing on her skin, her hand, her arm, her neck.

"Feel good?" he asked.

Well, of course it felt good, cool and tingly and better than a fan almost, but she didn't think she should just stand there and let him do it. He lifted her arm and held it straight out and blew on all the exposed skin from her fingers to the middle of her bicep. It reminded her of something she had seen in the movies, although there it was a man kissing the woman's arm, not just blowing on it.

"Feels all right," she conceded.

"How's this?"

He bent down and blew on her knee just below where the dress stopped. She pulled back a step, but he held her leg.

"What's the difference?" he asked. He glanced up at her, then fell to his own knees and lifted the hem of her dress and blew on her thighs.

"Hey!"

She tried to pull away, but he clung to her leg and then he put his hand up there where he was blowing.

"Cut it out!"

"You like it," he said.

"I don't." She twisted and pulled, got loose and tried to run, but he held on to her dress and the cloth tore. She stopped abruptly, looking at the rip in her dress. How was she ever going to explain that to her mother? He stopped, too, for just a moment, as if he realized how serious this all was now, but then he was at her again, more urgently than before. He gripped both legs, as if tackling her, and she fell on her bottom with a grunt. He scrambled onto her, forcing her flat onto the ground, pressing his body on hers.

"Stop it!" she said, striking his back.

"You like it," he insisted. "You like it."

CHAPTER TWENTY-FOUR

A forest of black faces awaited Billy when he emerged from Sister Mills's house. He had heard none of them converge; they had waited in silence and seemed to have sprung from the earth. An inner circle of men parted slightly, offering him an opening into their midst. A second ring of women surrounded the men and, in the distance, as if dispatched for safety, children formed the periphery of—what, witnesses? participants? Billy could think of them only as parties to an action that had not yet occurred, one that was just waiting for him, the catalyst, to make it happen. He scanned them briefly, hesitating on the slight elevation of the cinder block that served as a stoop. It seemed that he recognized the scene in some primal way, a gathering of angry villagers about to storm the monster's castle, an incensed mob demanding justice, placard-wielding strikers swarming around a scab, other scenes from his cinematic memory imprinted since early youth, but with a stark difference that it took him a moment to recognize. In those filmic scenes, the angry populace was always white. This one was black, and they were waiting for *him*. He saw no anger—no fists were raised above the crowd; no shouts were heard; their expressions were as much curious as incensed—but he felt the threat nonetheless. All eyes were on him, and in a movie he would have made a stirring speech from his elevated position, something brilliant and inspirational to turn the tide. Or, as it occurred to him fleetingly, he might also yell, "Follow me!" and lead them to the castle. As it was, he could think of nothing to say; it took a good deal of effort to stifle an impulse to turn and run. Not that there was anywhere to run except back into the house. Instead, he moved forward.

The circle parted and he stepped into it. Then it reformed around him immediately, so that he stood encompassed by bodies, all of them facing him, staring at him as if he were something novel and alien. No one touched him—indeed, all the men were at least an arm's length away—and although the inner circle shifted constantly, accommodating itself to the pressure of those behind, who were eager to see, it did not press in on him.

"What you want?" asked one of the men. He was a small man, much shorter than some of them, and he had to tilt his chin upward to speak to Billy.

"How you doing?" Billy said, smiling. "Nice day, isn't it?"

"Nice for what?" The man had one lazy eyelid, which drooped occasionally, as if one side of his face were taking a nap.

"Oh, just about anything you want to do, I'd say." Billy looked up as if taking in the sky. "It's a good day to meet the neighbors, for instance."

One of the surrounding men gave in to the pressure from the people pressing behind him and moved half a step closer. The circle closed in on Billy.

"What you want here?" the man repeated. "You ain't from here."

"What I don't want is to have to arrest you or anyone else for assault."

"Ain't assault you," another man said, already nervous. It reminded Billy that this was not a riotous mob, certain of its purpose. They were unsure, disparate, and tentative—or he would have been disposed of already.

"One more step and you will," Billy said, turning directly to the man who had spoken.

The spokesman called his attention back. "You ain't no po-lice here. You don't be arresting people."

The outlying crowd surged again, inspired by the belligerent tones of the spokesman, and the inner circle gave yet more ground. Their bodies were almost pressing against him now, and Billy felt a wave of claustrophobia. The inner circle of men was not in charge; the man with the droopy eyelid was not in control. They would not be able to withstand the larger numbers of the people behind them even if they wanted to. Billy could be squashed and trampled underfoot without malicious intent on anyone's part.

"I'm asking you to get out of my way now," Billy said. "Let me pass."

"Ain't nobody hurt you."

"You're obstructing my way."

The small man grinned unpleasantly. "Ain't you happy, this 'nice day'? Don't you wan' meet the neighbors no mo'?"

The inner circle shifted again, readjusted, and Billy had barely room enough to turn around. He felt sweat forming under his arms, and his impulse was to lash out, to smash the little man in the face, and the next man, and the next, until he had fought his way to the open street. But of course there could be no worse course of action— they would bury him in a minute.

A very large man to Billy's left suddenly spoke loudly. "You all right in the house, Sister Mills?"

The spokesman glared at Billy.

"Bes' hope she all right."

"She's fine," Billy said, hoping she had not chosen this moment to take a nap.

There was no response from the house.

"What you do to her?" the spokesman demanded.

Billy concentrated on the little man. There was no point in arguing the welfare of Sister Mills. The crowd was not there for a debate, and it seemed unlikely that anything Billy said or did would have any effect on anything except his dignity.

"Sister Mills," called another voice.

Billy spoke in a hiss to the spokesman, whose face was almost touching his own. "When it starts, I'm going to grab your nuts. If I go down, your balls are coming with me."

The little man recoiled instinctively, but there was no place to go; he was as trapped as Billy himself.

"Kiss 'em good-bye," Billy said.

A murmur ran through the crowd, and at first Billy thought that Sister Mills had appeared behind him, whole and unharmed, but the tone turned to one of alarm and rancor. A red light flashed in a familiar pattern through the tree branches overhead, and the crowd began to disperse like smoke blown before the wind.

They vanished as silently as they had assembled. There were no defiant calls, no abusive epithets, no parting shots of any kind. Billy was reminded again of the peculiar state of docile hostility in which these people lived. In which they chose to remain.

He watched the squad car pass slowly by, siren off but red, white, and blue lights coruscating off of trees and houses. It made a U-turn and came back to where Billy stood, suddenly alone, in front of Sister Mills's house.

"Just thought I'd check up on you," said Chief Harbart. He grinned knowingly. "This area's a little different from what you might have up in your county. Takes a little knowing."

"Yeah. I see," said Billy. He leaned heavily against the car seat. "Thanks."

"They do anything to you?"

"No," Billy said. "Just scared the shit out of me."

"Um. What I'm saying is, yeah, they can do that. You don't want to be alone with too many of them at once."

Was that all it was? Billy wondered. Being the only white face among so many black ones? Had anything else actually happened? Was it just paranoia and imagination?

"How do they do it?" Billy asked.

"What?"

"I don't know, walk in a white community, be the only black in a world full of whites, any of it. . . ."

"Mostly, they don't," said Harbart. "But anyway, that's different. It's not like *we're* going to hurt *them.*"

Some difference, Billy thought.

"So, what I'm saying, did you do what you went there for? Find out what you needed?"

"Some of it," Billy said.

"Did you send your message to Odette?"

"I did. I think he sent me one, too."

"I forget how you said you knew him," said Harbart.

"We played basketball against each other in the high school tournament."

"Oh, yeah? Who won?"

"I did," said Billy.

Harbart chuckled. "Those were the days."

Odette Collins walked heavily down the stairs to join his aunt. His knee worked well enough on the flat, but stairs still troubled him and always would. Since the age of twenty-five, he had possessed the legs of a septuagenarian, at least going up or down hills.

"You brought that man down on me," Sister Mills said angrily.

"I didn't know he would come here. I didn't think—"

"Been dealing with that man all my life. Thought I was shuck of him now, my age. Don't want him back here no more."

"Yes, ma'am."

"No more. You hear me?"

"He won't be back. He got what he come for." Collins slipped naturally into his aunt's accent and rhythms. Billy had been wrong in assuming that his accent was phony. He could speak with equal comfort in the flat, measured broadcaster's tones of Omaha or the patois of the rural ghetto. He could be either man because he was both.

"No more, don' want to see him no more," Sister Mills insisted. "See to it."

Collins nodded.

"Answer me, I be talkin' to you," she said sternly.

"Yes, Sismamma. I'll take care of it."

"How you take care of it?"

"I got to get the weapon."

"Never should have left it."

"I know that. I thought I'd pull them away from it," he said, his voice now crisp and precise. "It didn't work. I went back too soon. If he hasn't figure it out yet, he will."

"Forget him. Never should have count on him, first place."

"Yeah."

"Come at you with a club. What you spect?"

"Yeah."

Collins looked out the window. The crowd had dispersed and normal neighborhood activity had resumed. Like an insectivorous plant, it had returned to its placid, inviting appearance now that the prey had escaped.

"You be stupid to trust him," she said.

Insistent in her contempt, his aunt was of the "rub your nose in it" school of aversion therapy. She never let up until a lesson was learned and memorized.

"I didn't trust him," Collins said. He was speaking entirely in his Omaha voice now, deliberately distancing himself from her. Her ire could suffocate if he didn't fend it off in some fashion. "I wanted to enlist him."

"Enlis'," she said disdainfully. "Enlis' a white sheriff. He the *son* of one of them. What you be thinkin', boy?"

He turned from the widow to face her. With her weathered features, her wrinkled skin, her droopy eyelids and tired, rheumy eyes, she seemed the product of another century, not merely another generation. How to explain a hope that things had changed, at least a little, at least enough to try. Her life experience had taught her just the opposite. To his sorrow, he was not certain that his own had not done the same.

"I couldn't just walk in there and wave my arms and shout 'Justice.' They wouldn't treat me a whole lot better than Lawton."

"Don't do dat," she said darkly. "Don' talk 'bout Lawton dat way. So *eeeassy*."

"I just meant they'd lynch me, too. In their own way. They got new ways to do it now."

"Lawton *murdered*."

"I know."

"He *murdered*. And you know who done it and you know how."

Of course he knew. Took it in like mother's milk as he basked in the warmth of her smoldering rage, learned it like her catechism of sorrow and fury and vengeance.

"I know."

"Then what you standin' *here* for? Go fetch that weapon." She glared at him as if she hated *him* for it all.

"I will," said Collins. "As soon as it's safe."

"Ain't going be *safe*." She spat the word, taunting him. "Safe . . . This life, ain't no *safe* about it for a black boy."

He looked at her, nodding. She was a marvel. Enraged all her life, masking it with humility, the fierce inner fire visible in her working life only in glints of flame in her eyes. He wondered if anything was left within her, or if everything had been consumed in the blazing rage. By comparison, his own fire was but a flicker, yet it was strong enough to doom him, too.

"When I'm ready," he said.

"Ready? How many more years 'fore you ready? You gwin' do it while I still alive?"

"Yes."

"How 'bout when *they* still alive?"

"That part," he said, "isn't entirely up to me."

CHAPTER TWENTY-FIVE

H e's going nuts in here," said Gina Schul on the radio. Billy
had finally checked in after a day's silence. "He was about
to call in the state people. You know he'd hate to do that.
He was talking about dragging the river. . . . Can you drag the Missouri?"

"I doubt it," Billy said into the radio. "Not without state help,
maybe federal funds."

Gina spoke in the hushed tone she reserved for the times when
she had something particularly juicy to share. Billy doubted that Lapolla's distress was juicy enough to warrant the fierce stage whisper
Gina reserved for gossip.

"Tell him I'm fine. I'll be back sometime today," Billy said.

"Do you want to talk to him now? He's beside himself; he thinks they killed and ate you or something. You really should have checked in, Billy."

"Yes, Mother."

"He's not real good at dealing with anxiety, you know."

"Really? I hadn't noticed."

"You're bad, Billy. You are a ba-ad boy. I love that."

Billy laughed.

"Before I put him on—you remember you asked me to keep an eye out for your aunt's car?"

Ah, that's it, Billy realized. Gossip masquerading as police business, the kind of exchange that kept Gina Schul's day from being unspeakably boring.

"I remember. Did you see it?"

"A couple times in the past few days. I just made a quick survey when I got off work, nothing systematic. And I waited until I saw her in the same place twice, because once, you know, who knows?"

"Okay, Gina. I admire your methodology. Where did you see her car?"

"I ran the plates just to make sure it was her."

"Okay. Where?"

"I only know where the car was, Billy, now remember that. I didn't actually see her. She could have just parked and walked anywhere in town. I just saw her car."

"I'll take that into account. Where?"

She released her final information reluctantly, having caressed it as long as possible. "At Judge Sunder's. . . . You still there, Billy?"

"I'm here," he said, wishing he was not.

"I don't know what that means," she offered, although her tone indicated that she had a pretty good idea. Approaching fifty herself, Gina found the prospect of illicit sex between her elders not only quite possible but also encouraging. The only thing about Adley that surprised her was her choice of partners. Sunder had always struck Gina as being as appetizing as dried corn. Desiccated, mealy, and hard on the teeth. Probably good for you, though, if you could get it down.

The thought made her smile, but she was careful not to laugh into the radio.

"I don't know what it means, either," said Billy. "But thanks."

"Maybe she has some legal business."

"Maybe. Thanks, Gina." He didn't bother to ask her to keep the information to herself, because, in the first place, he didn't think it would do any good. If she were inclined to spread the word, she would do so. In the second place, if Adley's visits to Sunder's house had been going on for very long, it would already be well known in the community. Because he had heard nothing and because it took Gina several days to come up with the information, Billy assumed the visits were a recent phenomenon.

"Do you want to talk to the sheriff now?" Gina asked.

"I'll see him later. Just tell him I'm all right, that I'm on patrol and I'll give him a report later."

But not about his aunt. Not about his uncle Sean. Sean, the cuckold. Uncle to Billy, the cuckold. Billy wondered if there was anything good that ran in the family.

He pulled up the long driveway to Sunder's place and walked to the side of the house. The glass that had been shattered by gunfire had been replaced, but, surprisingly, the window was not locked, the blind not pulled down. Whatever precautions the judge thought he was taking, they did not include the most obvious. Billy was unable to keep himself from looking at the distant neighbors' homes with paranoid glances, like any other cautious burglar. Just in case they should wonder about the legality of a deputy sheriff climbing through someone's window, he thought wryly, might as well give them some typically shifty behavior to go with it. Don't want to confuse folks.

There was no need to rifle the drawers or look for secret compartments. The judge's life was on display, at least that part of it he was proud of, and the rest of it was not apt to be stored in a private cache, available to any cleaning woman, snoop, or random burglar.

Billy stood for a while, studying the walls of trophies, trying to make sense of a man's life, even though he knew little about the man who was living it. In Sean's case, he faced the opposite problem. He knew too much about his uncle, or thought he did. Just as he had thought erroneously that he knew about his uncle's wife.

He wandered through the house, not sure what he was looking for except some sign of Adley's adultery. He laughed at his naïveté even as he pursued it. What did he think he might discover? A lost slipper left behind when time ran out? That hoary device from bad fiction, the incriminating matchbook from some clandestine meeting in a bar? Adley had left her mark very simply: she had parked her car at the judge's house for everyone to see. DNA evidence from the bedsheets could indict her no more convincingly than that. Not that she would leave any incriminating evidence in any case. She was too clever for that. Her brazenness was probably smart, too. If she was doing anything wrong, would she do it so openly? Well, yes, of course she might, but she could argue pretty convincingly to the contrary. But argue with whom? Sean? How hard would it be to placate Sean? His temper was fiery enough, or used to be, as Billy remembered from childhood, but now it was nothing that another beer couldn't cool down. . . . Women were too clever about these things. Men left trails of their infidelity like elephants dropping spoor. It required willful disbelief on the part of their wives not to see it. But women were more accomplished than men when it came to the deceitful arts; Billy had no doubt of that. If it had ever been in question, Joan had shattered the illusion. He had known nothing about Collins, suspected nothing, been totally, blissfully, blindly secure in her love and devotion. If it had not been for a sleepless night, he still would be none the wiser. Some detective, he thought. Some brilliant observer.

It was a stupid, unfocused, dangerous errand. Bedroom, kitchen, closets, hall—he found nothing incriminating, as he had expected. What had possessed him? Sympathy for Sean? And if he'd found Adley's bra draped over the bedroom pillow, what good would that do for Sean? Would it help him to know it? Had it helped Billy to find out about Joan? Or was he simply empathizing with Sean to such an extent that he was confusing himself with his uncle? If he couldn't bring himself to investigate Joan's infidelity, was he using Sean and Adley's relationship as a surrogate?

He returned to the den and gave it another cursory glance. If Sunder was a womanizer, would he keep some record of that on his walls, too? If so, Billy could not decode the message. Everything in the room was about Sunder, no one else.

With one leg over the windowsill on his way out, he noticed that the one blind that seemed always to be up was never lowered for a reason. The operating cord had been cut, leaving only a few inches of thin nylon rope extending from the mechanism. Billy stepped back into the room. He fingered the frayed end of the fiber, then crossed the room and looked behind the door of the study. The citations from the Elks and the Odd Fellows still hung on the wall in their faux-gilt frames, but the noose was gone. After a brief search, Billy found the hole where the nail had been, reassuring himself that his memory was correct. The noose had been there, and it had been removed, purposefully. Billy studied the walls again to learn why. Surely it was a souvenir as important as a cheap clock won at a county fair. Sunder had been nearly killed as a consequence of receiving the noose, assuming the shots taken at him were connected. Surely that ought to merit a spot on the wall. What was the difference? Why had Sunder changed his mind? After a moment of study, Billy realized that the noose was ugly, the only ugly memory in the whole room. Why save it? Why be reminded of it if the purpose of the collection was to preserve good memories? Billy himself had kept the damned thing in his pocket, there for a touch, like a negative rabbit's foot, a tactile memorandum of the world's brutishness. And that's the difference between the judge and me, Billy thought. He's got that rosy outlook.

He pulled his own noose from his pants pocket and held it next to the pull cord of one of the other blinds. Unquestionably the same nylon material, twisted with several others to make a cable thick enough for the noose. He tried to piece together a scenario that made some sense. Billy's noose had arrived the same night that Sunder's study was broken into, and Sunder didn't notice his noose until the next day, after returning from a conference out of town. Did the burglar enter, take whatever he had taken, and then hit upon the idea of the nooses and cut a bit of whatever was available with which to weave them? Or had he entered with the idea of delivering nooses already in his mind. If that were so, why not bring some rope with him? The cord from the blinds was thin, slippery, difficult to manipulate. So if it was a spur-of-the-moment idea, what then? Did the burglar calmly sit down and construct the miniature cable and then the hangman's knot before slipping back out the window? It seemed that doing such would require considerable sangfroid, but then, that was a burglar's stock-in-trade. Or had the burglar come with something other than burglary on his mind? What if he had come to shoot Sunder, found him gone, and then cut the cord as a way of assuring that the blind would be up when he returned to finish the job? . . . But if that were the case, why leave the noose, since it could only serve to warn Sunder that something evil stirred, even if he would not know that it was a plot to take his life? And why had Odette Collins given one to Billy, as well? If you are stealthy enough to break into a house, demonstrative enough to strew symbols across town, were you also stupid enough to warn your intended victims ahead of time? . . . Billy realized that he no longer had the slightest doubt that the nooses had come from Collins. His visit to Sister Mills had made it clear enough that Odette was her instrument, delivering her message of unflagging remembrance. Further, he realized that he *wanted* it to be Odette who had shot at Sunder. Facts were becoming increasingly irrelevant. Billy had made up his mind as to the villain.

With a last glance at the severed cord, Billy made his exit through the window and returned to the car. He didn't bother to see if he had been observed. If his aunt could come and go as she pleased, why couldn't he? Let the neighbors ponder the relationship between Sunder and the family Tree. Billy was certainly in no position to enlighten them.

He found Adley in her driveway, carrying groceries from her car into the house. Billy took a bag in one hand and a six-pack of beer in the other. There was no question about alcoholic-enabling in the Tree household. That was a battle long since surrendered.

"The boys are over at Carl's, I think," said Adley. "Not that you need them to come visit me." She smiled broadly at him, and Billy saw again that flash of devilment in her eye that had first been visible only a few days ago. He started to wonder again how he could have been so blind, but he stopped himself when he realized that he had been blind, deaf, and generally impervious to a great many things.

He followed her into the house and watched her buttocks twitch under the tight denim, squirming like puppies in confinement. As he placed the groceries on the kitchen table, she gave him a particularly bright smile. Had she just come from a liaison with the judge? Was this a post-coital glow that made her appear younger and happier than usual? Or was it just his own post-enlightenment perspective? Or both?

"It's sweet of you to help your old aunt," she said, but the twinkle in her eye denied the "old." There did not seem to be anything particularly old about her, at least not that Billy could detect. Had her hair always been that color? Her cheeks that roseate? He did not know, and he cursed himself for being so unobservant.

Billy removed the last of the groceries from the trunk of the car and saw the rifle jammed back in the rear.

"I thought I'd keep it away from the boys for a while," she explained. "They were carrying it around, and Carl was sitting with it on the porch. . . . I thought it was all a little crazy, and I was afraid someone was going to get hurt."

"You were right there."

"Where did it used to be kept?"

"In the truck."

"How long have you been carrying it in your car?"

She shrugged dismissively, then put a hand on his cheek. "You look tired, Billy. Are you working too hard?"

"Not sleeping real well, I guess."

"Excesses of youth?"

"No, and I'm not that young, either."

"It's all relative, isn't it?," she asked. She fiddled with his hair briefly, rearranging wayward strands before letting her hand fall away. "You seem awfully young to me."

"So do you," he said honestly. "You seem to be getting younger. How do you manage that? Is it just clean living, or do you have a secret?"

She turned away from him. Billy thought he saw her blush.

"Charming Billy," she said.

She put away the groceries while Billy sat at the kitchen table. He waited a moment before asking, "The rifle. Is it Carl's or Sean's?"

"Who knows. Those two are like real brothers now; they share just about everything."

"I'll want to check it for ballistics."

She looked up from her groceries, alarmed.

"Why?"

"Somebody's been shooting at people with that caliber gun, Aunt Adley. It's just routine."

"You don't think Sean . . ."

"Probably not. It would just eliminate one rifle out of a few thousand that could have done it."

"You don't think he shot at Sunder, for heaven's sake. That's ridiculous."

"Is it?"

"Absolutely. Why on earth would he do that?"

Billy held her gaze for a moment before she broke away and returned to her groceries.

"I don't know. Could there be any reason?"

She spoke with her back to him. "No. Never. He'd be the last person on earth."

"Meaning Sean would be the last person on earth to shoot at the judge, or the judge would be the last person on earth Sean would shoot at?"

"What's the difference?"

"Are they great friends or something?"

"They are *old* friends. They were kids together."

"Would anyone have any reason to shoot at Sunder that you know of?"

"No. And why should I know anyway?"

"Would Sean shoot at *anybody*?"

She placed her hands on the table and leaned toward him. "No," she said firmly. "Your uncle would not shoot at anybody. And I remind you that he's your uncle . . . and I'm his wife." Anger flashed briefly in her eyes.

"Then why did you take his rifle away, if he wouldn't shoot at anybody. . . . Or were you worried that Carl might shoot somebody?"

"Carl's your uncle, too, don't forget. And no, I didn't think he'd shoot anybody, either."

"So . . ."

"So, I was afraid one of them might shoot himself."

She turned away again and busied herself in the cupboards. When she reached to a higher shelf, her breasts stood out against the fabric of her shirt. Billy wished he would stop noticing such things.

"Accidentally?"

She paused for a moment, considering. "Accidentally. Of course accidentally."

"Do you think Sean might have taken those shots at his truck himself? Under the influence, you understand."

She craned upward to reach the highest shelf with a box of cereal, standing on her toes and arching her back. Billy studied the table. When finished, she faced him again, her arms folded across her chest. The anger was gone from her face and she looked into the middle distance, speculating.

"It had occurred to me. He does a great many very stupid things when he drinks, and he doesn't remember half of them. . . . I really don't think so. He had cuts from the glass."

"He could have fallen. He could have inspected his work and slipped."

She shrugged but did not dismiss the possibility.

"I don't know," she said. "And I don't think he does, either. He would have been so drunk, he'd never remember."

"Well, a ballistics test will tell us."

"It will tell you that he didn't shoot at Sunder, too."

"Maybe. I hope so."

"He didn't shoot at the judge, Billy. Believe me."

"I'd like to. You said yourself that he does stupid things. He and Carl were out on the prowl that night; they admit it. . . ."

"I had the gun already."

"You had the gun the night Sunder was shot at?"

"Yes. It was in the back of my car."

"You didn't remember that a minute ago when I asked how long you've had it."

"I remember it now."

Billy studied her. If she was lying to him, he could not see it, but he knew enough not to rely on his powers of observation.

"What's the deal with Sunder anyway?" he asked finally.

"What do you mean?"

"Are you seeing him for something to do with legal reasons, or what, exactly?"

This time, he could see her considering a lie, the prospect passing over her face like a descending veil, then vanishing just as quickly.

"You don't go to a judge for legal matters, do you?" she asked. "I would think you'd see an attorney for that."

Billy waited.

"It was financial," she said finally. "I saw him on a financial matter."

"Financial."

"He's sort of a financial adviser to Sean and me. Sometimes. Sort of. He knows more about money than we do. He's done very well for himself; he understands investments, that sort of thing. I'm hopeless about money, and Sean . . . well, you can imagine. So that's what I was seeing him about."

Far too much of an answer, Billy thought. The babble of guilt.

"Is it possible that Sean . . . misinterpreted your visits to Sunder? Is it possible he got jealous?"

The thought amused her. "Sean? Billy, how would he even know?"

"Someone might tell him. Just like someone told me."

"And you thought maybe I was . . . Me and Lyle Sunder? Lyle Sunder? . . . I don't know whether to be insulted or flattered that you think I'm . . . I think I'm hurt that you think I couldn't do better than Lyle Sunder. Give me some credit."

"I'm sorry. I guess I really don't know that much about you at all, do I?"

She thought a moment, then said, "Probably not. No reason you should, I suppose. Not really. Just one of the older generation, aren't I?"

"I'm beginning to look past that, I think," said Billy. "The fog is lifting a little."

"Because you're getting along yourself," she said, smiling thinly. "But no matter what you know about me, you can't think Sean would be so consumed with jealousy that he'd take a shot at Lyle Sunder because of me."

"I'd say you were well worth taking a shot at someone for."

"You always know what to say, don't you? Joan is a very lucky woman."

"Indeed. I envy her . . . although not quite as much as I envy Uncle Sean."

"But all of your baloney aside, you're not really thinking Sean took a shot at Sunder, are you? In a jealous rage or for any other reason."

"What I have to consider as a sheriff and what I think as a nephew are not necessarily the same."

"Poor Billy."

"My own thoughts entirely."

She touched his cheek again, a gesture that no longer seemed so maternal to him.

"It can't be easy for you, putting up with us. But no one in this family shot at the judge, or ever would," she said. "Just dismiss that thought entirely. It's not possible; it's not even worth considering."

He wanted to believe her, but then he wanted to believe in lots of things that weren't true. Undying love, for one. Justice, for another. But love had been proven as false as any bathetic country song could have warned him, and justice seemed entirely outside the reach of the law, certainly his own arm of the law. Adley had been feeling guilty when talking about having a financial relationship with Sunder, of that much he was certain. A sense of guilt was not always an indication of legal culpability, of course. Just another complication of human nature that made his job difficult.

She sat on the porch and watched him drag two ancient bales of hay from the barn into the feedlot and set them on end vertically. He fired the rifle down through the bales and dug the shell from the ground without difficulty.

"I guess that means you don't believe me," she said.

"It's not you I need to eliminate. It's the gun."

From the chill of her smile, he knew she did not believe him, and that, he reflected, was fair enough.

CHAPTER TWENTY-SIX

ina Schul's playful voice sought him out a few times as he drove, and once Lapolla himself came on the radio, half-pleading with Billy to check in, but Billy ignored all the calls and eventually turned off the radio. He was, he reminded himself, a sort of volunteer, a temporary fill-in and adviser, not a regular deputy who had to respond to every call. Further, he could quit at any time. He didn't need the job, didn't like the work, hated the growing responsibility of being both brains and muscle of the Sheriff's Department. It was only a whim that had gotten him into the job in the first place—or perhaps an inability to resist Lapolla's lost-child neediness—and a whim could take him out of it just as easily. He had not sought the position, he did not want the position, and, increasingly, he did not *like* the position. Except for the fact that the car belonged to the county, he could think of no good reason not to point it east and drive straight to New England and abandon the ruins of his love life, the embarrassment of his family, and whatever mess in their past Odette Collins wanted to immerse him in. Leave Joan and his dysfunctional family where he'd found them and let the law take care of itself.

He could think of no good reason not to drive away from the chaos of his life, and yet he found himself at Carl Wittrock's farm, seeking his uncles. The "boys" were not there, nor was Alma Wittrock, Carl's wife. Given the way women in his family seemed to be shedding years and decades of propriety like an ill-fitting cloak, Billy was relieved not to find his aunt skipping through the clover of the back pasture in a bikini.

Halfway back to his car, he realized that the heat had returned with the sudden impact of a hammer blow. As if it had gathered strength in its absence, it pressed down upon him like a wrestler determined to extract submission. He cranked up the air conditioning in the car and drove to town, passing cattle that stood by the fences, looking stunned by the sudden oppression of the weather. Fields of wheat, approaching harvest, seemed bent by the temperature. Only the corn basked in the sun's suddenly renewed assault, stretching out its broad leaves like acres of Scandinavians on a southern beach.

What a place to live, Billy muttered to himself. The weather is always lurking like Iago, awaiting a chance to betray or slip in the knife. No place to hide, no more shelter than the desert, and so much creeping, expanding, straining plant life, it was frightening. On days such as this, he did not believe the science that told him that plants produced oxygen. They sucked it up, leaving too little for the humans. Just one more reason to head to New England, he thought.

The Richardson County Courthouse squatted upon the town square like the top layer of a wedding cake, rectilinear, stone-faced, the Great Depression's notion of Greek-inspired Federal architecture. There was something comforting about its stolidity and lack of imagination, something disquieting about its visual departure from the Golden Mean, although only the more discerning noticed, and then only from the right perspective. To come upon it suddenly, traveling north on Harlan, seeing it a full two stories above the elevated mound of the town square, was, to the whimsically minded, like encountering the base of a much grander design on which someone had neglected, from carelessness or lack of funds, to place the dome and portico.

There was definitely something magisterial about the interior of the courthouse, however. Or at least bureaucratic, with airs. With the only marble floors in town, the only stone staircase leading up (plain wrought-iron railings and wooden steps descended to the basement), and the only sculpted busts on public display in the entire county, the courthouse was capable of at least hinting at grandeur to the uninitiated. There were two manly heads and chests standing on sternum-high marble columns, facing each other across the central hall. One was thought to be of Seneca (the Roman philosopher, not the Iroquoian, even though the latter might have been more apt), although no one was sure (Cicero received a few votes, as well), and the other seemed to resemble no one so much as William Jennings Bryan, a famous son of Nebraska, naked shoulder, classical senatorial toga, and all. He bore a laurel wreath on his noble brow, but for what particular triumph, it was difficult to say, since he was remembered at the end of the twentieth century only for his shamefully close-minded, Bible-thumping appearance in the Scopes trial and no longer for his "Cross of Gold" speech, his skills as an orator in unamplified times, or his failed presidential bids. Not that anyone really cared who was truly represented by either sculpture. Both were seen now as ancient, irrelevant, and somehow entirely appropriate in a court of law. There was something to be said—although few in Falls City could articulate it—for clinging to the past, even if the past itself was misty and obscure, not to mention possibly improperly designated.

Billy passed the statues, resisted the local lawyerly tradition of stroking Seneca's pronounced Roman nose for luck, and climbed the curving staircase to the second floor. The county clerk, an imperious-looking woman with a long jaw and pronounced nose herself, bore a closer resemblance to the statues than any of the lawyers in the building. She had held her position so long that she was known to all as simply Ms. Kavanah, her married status, whatever it was, being wholly lost in the past. The "Ms." was not a feminist gesture but a simple slurring that covered all the bases. The occasional appearance in the newspaper of her given name, Jacqueline, without the honorific, only served to confuse people.

She regarded Billy with her usual steely gaze and led him to the record room, where bound volumes of deeds and tax assessments and surveys lined the walls from floor to ceiling. Placing the relevant journal in front of him, she regarded Billy with a suspicious air, as if she thought him capable of defacing documents.

"Sheriff's looking for you," she said sternly.

Billy smiled at her.

"Oh, yes?"

"That's what I said," she said.

Billy waited for her to leave, still smiling. She hovered over him like a schoolmistress.

"You're looking very lovely today, Ms. Kavanah," he said. "You have the look of a blushing maiden about you. What have you been up to?"

With a sound of disapproval, she turned and left Billy alone in the records room, even forgoing the usual reminder to leave the books on the table when he was finished. Flattery has its uses, he observed to himself.

He first studied the large map of the county that hung on the wall and located the plot number of the property adjoining Indian Cave Park to the north and the Missouri River to the east. Dragging the heavy volume of deeds to him, he carefully turned the double-sided pages until he found the listing for the land that held the derelict house where Collins and Joan had their love nest. Following a history of purchases and transfers, he came at last to the present owner of the property: Carl Wittrock.

Billy was stunned. He double-checked, making certain that he had read the right line on the right page. The name would not change, nor would it go away. Carl Wittrock, uncle by marriage to his aunt Alma, brother-in-law to Sean, owned the land and buildings and improvements thereon.

Billy was still seated in the records room, trying to puzzle through connections as entwined as a bird's nest, when Lapolla found him.

"Geez, Bill," he said. "Were you ever going to talk to me again? If Ms. Kavanah hadn't called, I don't know . . ."

Billy deliberately closed the book of deeds.

"I've been trying to work a few things out."

"Aren't we supposed to do that together?"

"I don't know, Bert. A lot of it seems to be family business."

"You've been out of touch for a whole day, Billy. You talk to Gina, but you won't talk to me. . . ."

"I think I'm going to resign, Bert."

"What? Why? No. Don't do that. Why?"

Billy leaned back in his chair, feeling relaxed for the first time in days. "I don't think I'm any good at the job. In fact, I think I'm lousy at it. I abuse the position, I bullied an old woman, I tried to brain a suspect with a tree branch instead of arresting him, I acted like a coward when we were shot at, and—"

"You went back there. That was brave."

"And I've been withholding information from you."

"You've got your own ways, Billy. I don't mind; you don't have to tell me everything. You get the job done; that's what's important."

"And I think I plan to frame somebody for a crime he might not have committed. Or he might have committed, I don't know. I can't figure it out. But it would solve so many problems if I just went ahead and framed him."

"Shhh! Shhh! Shhh! Don't say this to me. . . ."

"Or I might kill him instead," Billy said.

"Shhh! Billy, stop. Stop talking. You're tired, overworked. . . ." Lapolla lowered his tone to a frantic hiss. "What if Ms. Kavanah hears this?"

Billy stood and stretched his back. "So I think I'll just quit."

"You need a rest, Bill. You need time for yourself; we can talk all this over later."

"I think I may just go out and break the law in an interesting number of ways. But you're right, I shouldn't burden you with them, so consider me resigned."

"I don't accept it."

"Doesn't matter, Bert. I quit."

He walked past Ms. Kavanah and gave her a grin and a wink. She was unfazed by either.

The interior of the courthouse was protected by the stone and marble that encased it, and it stored the cool air like a larder, offering the somewhat clammy comforts of a mausoleum on even the worst of days, but the heat was waiting outside the building, and it pounced on Billy's shoulders with his first steps through the door. By the time he reached the car, he felt he was staggering with the burden.

His telephone was ringing as he walked into the house, but he let the answering machine take it. There was no one he wished to talk to except Joan, and he didn't trust himself to do that. The last time he had tried, he had manhandled her, then fought with her son in that stupid fiasco of dueling egos. Until he could control himself around her, until his pain and anger had become manageable, he would do himself more harm than good by speaking to her.

He was startled to hear Odette Collins's voice on the answering machine, but he recognized it even before he understood the words.

"Picking on an old woman now? Ain't it bad enough to come after me with a club?"

Billy sprinted for the phone.

"I'm not your enemy, man," Collins said into the machine.

Billy lifted the receiver.

"Where are you now?" Billy said.

"So is this the real Billy Tree now? The one who bullies old ladies?"

"Where are you, Odette?"

"And what was with that club in the river? What do you mean, swinging a tree limb at me? Don't you know we're in this together? I'm not your enemy."

"You seem like one to me."

"What? That gunshot at the farm house? She didn't mean to do that. I told you, it was an accident. She saw cops, she grabbed it, and it went off. . . ."

"She didn't see cops. She saw *me*."

"Yeah? Well, sometimes you look an awful lot like a cop. Most of the time you act like one, too. You can see how she'd be confused."

"Well, that's over. I don't look like one anymore. I just resigned, thanks to you."

"What? You can't do that, Billy. I need you. I'm counting on you being in the system."

"What are you talking about? What do you want from me besides ruining my life?"

"Ruining your life? I'm not hurting you, just making you work some, but hell, you must be tired of just watching the corn grow, aren't you? You're not afraid of exercise, are you? It's good for you— you're an old jock—you know that. . . . You're putting it together, aren't you? You're figuring it out, what happened? You're a smart man; they all say that."

Billy wondered at the hope in the man's voice. Could he really believe they were not enemies? Could he really expect Billy to assist him with something? *Anything?*

"I don't know what you mean."

"You're figuring it out; I know you are. You found my aunt in Sabella. You can do that, you can do the rest."

"Just tell me."

"It can't come from me. Who would believe me in this society? I'm an ex-felon, I'm unemployed, I'm an alcoholic and a drug user, and I'm a black man. I'm not stupid; I know how that looks. I know nobody in a position of authority is going to listen to me for one minute. . . . They'll listen to you. If it comes from you, they'll listen."

"*I'll* listen to you. Tell me."

"No, you won't listen, either. You're still a white boy; you still believe it's a white world because it's supposed to be a white world. You got no problem with that. Why should you? You're white, after all. You're not going to believe there's anything wrong with it just because some black man tells you. The only way you people believe anything is if you think you discovered it yourself. You got to figure it out, make it your own. I've never been able to tell a white guy anything in my whole life and have him believe me just on my word. We been telling you for half a century that you're a bunch of racists, but you're still having trouble believing it."

"I'm having a little trouble hearing it from you, that's for sure.

Anybody who screams *racist* every other breath is bound to be one himself."

"No, no, you got that wrong. I can't be one. A black man can't be a racist in this country. Not possible. Racism is all about politics—did you forget that from college?

Billy recognized the pedagogical rant of the selectively self-taught, a jailhouse specialty.

"A white person sees a black man running down the street and assumes he's stolen something. That's prejudice," Collins continued. "A white *cop* sees a black guy running down the street and assumes he's stolen something, and he shoots him, that's racism. Prejudice and power together. Billy, you got to keep up on your sociology, man."

A pedant along with everything else. Billy realized he didn't know anything about the man at all except that he was not the mush-mouthed, foot-shuffling stereotype he had met in the alley behind Joan's house.

Collins started chuckling. "Now, a white sheriff sees a black guy getting into a brawl with four or five white guys and jumps into a swimming pool to break it up, that's not racist. That's not prejudiced. That's just strange." He laughed aloud into the phone. "Right then, I knew you were the man for me. You may be bent—all you whites are bent—but you can still stand up straight when you have to at least."

"You finished with your lecture? Or do you think we're a couple of cell mates . . . you can jaw at me all night long? If you've got a story to tell, go to a reporter, or hire a lawyer."

"Can't afford a lawyer. All I got is you, Billy. They tell me you're a decent guy. They tell me you're honest. They tell me you're a moral man. The last one left, maybe."

"Bullshit." And who were "they"? Joan, of course. It sounded like her words being quoted at him.

"Maybe so. You came at me with a club; you wanted to kill me. Maybe you're like everybody else after all and I'm just one more black man—you can bash his head in and not worry about it. Things don't change much, do they? Like father, like son."

Billy concentrated on controlling his tone of voice. Collins was so right, Billy *did* want to bash his head in. But admitting it on the phone would get him no closer to being able to do it.

When he spoke, his voice was calm. "What exactly can I do for you now, Odette?"

Collins laughed into the phone. "Listen to you. Butter wouldn't melt in your mouth. So pissed off—what are you so pissed off about anyway? . . . Anybody talks to me that smooth, he's probably a shrink telling me I'm just fine, and meanwhile the big boys with the strait-jacket are on their way."

Billy responded with silence. Again, probably what a perfidious shrink would do.

"I want the freedom to move," Collins said. "I want to be able to come back without a redneck waiting behind every bush with a great big stick."

"I wouldn't advise you to come back. Just keep going. Wherever you are, just keep going and stay away from my county."

"I can't do that. I'm not through."

The attempt at sweet reasonableness was dropped.

"You're through as far as I'm concerned. If I see you, I'm taking you down."

"For not paying my motel bill?"

"For attempted murder of Sean Tree and Judge Sunder."

"Are you crazy? I never—"

"And for resisting arrest."

"How do you know I'm going to resist arrest?"

"So that I can beat the hell out of you before I take you in."

"That would be interesting."

"It would be a pleasure."

"You sound an awful lot like a typical cop to me. Guess you didn't resign after all, did you?"

"You're warned. Go away and stay away."

"I'm *counting* on you, Billy!"

Billy hung up the phone. There was real distress in Collins's voice, as if Billy *had* let him down. Yet another mystery. He expected fairness from Billy? *Morality?* After Joan? Could the man believe that she meant so little to him? Had the notion of fidelity been so degraded in the rest of the world that even Joan herself seemed unperturbed by the consequences of her behavior, that she showed no guilt, only anger with Billy for bothering to care?

What had he meant when he said Billy was figuring it out?

Collins was the nephew of a man who had been lynched over fifty years ago. The lynching was witnessed by Billy's uncle and father, among several dozen others. That much, he *had* figured out, but having done so, so what? It did not explain what Collins was after; it did not explain the shots taken at Sean and Sunder; it did not explain why Collins was risking his neck to provoke the ire of the community.

It was all over so quickly. He squirmed onto her body, trying to pull her dress out of the way at the same time as he struggled to undo the buttons on his fly. She was telling him to stop, but he knew she didn't mean it, because she liked it, liked him. She wanted it to happen as much as he did; he was sure of that. She wouldn't act that way otherwise, wouldn't dress that way and flounce around in front of him and give him that teasing smile, and she was saying no, but she wasn't screaming, wasn't crying for help. He knew she wanted him to do it—but damn, he wished she would help some, because he didn't really know what he was doing. He'd never done it before, and it was confusing down there. Underpants! How the hell was he supposed to get them off? She started wriggling really hard when he tugged at them, and she put her hands down there to stop him, and touched him. Christ, what with the wriggling and the surprising touch of her fingers, he knew he was about to pop, and he thrust at her twice, three times, and he was pretty sure he got it in before he exploded.

All so fast. He had no idea it would be as quick as that. He felt stunned. He could no longer remember what he had expected, but he knew it wasn't that. If that's all there was to it, why did everyone make such a fuss about it? He felt disappointed and cheated, and he hastened to redo his fly, when he realized she was looking at him. He glanced down and saw small scratches where she had torn at him.

"Oooh," she said with disgust. "What did you do?"

"Nothing," he said stupidly.

He got to his feet, straightening his clothes.

"Oooh," she repeated. "You did so."

He could not tell if she was disgusted by the sight of him before he buttoned up or the traces of him he'd left behind. She turned her back to him and put a hand under her dress.

"I'm going to tell," she said.

"No. Don't."

"I am."

"Please don't."

"Look at my dress. How'm I doing to tell my momma what happened to my dress? She'll kill me."

"Don't tell her, please. Please. I'll buy you a new dress."

"How you gonna do that?" She scoffed at the idea. A boy walking into a store and buying a dress for a girl. It was crazy—but it was also a little appealing. Still, it was a crazy idea; he was a crazy boy.

"I can get some money. I can do it. My father keeps some in the pocket of an old coat he never wears. He thinks I don't know. . . ."

He wasn't even talking about now, for Pete's sake. What did she care about money in his father's pocket tomorrow, when her mother would kill her today. And if her mother didn't, her father surely would. She would also have to clean her underpants somehow; they were all sticky and it really was disgusting. She couldn't just throw them away. How would she ever explain that?

"I'm going to tell."

"No," he said. "My father will kill me."

"Well, I am," she said. "I don't care."

He had a club in his hand—she didn't know where it had come from. He looked even meaner than Darryl Woodard all of a sudden.

"You got to promise not to tell," he said, lifting the club.

"Don't you dare," she said.

"Promise."

"I won't."

She started to walk away from him, then heard a sound that made her turn. She saw him start to swing the club at her head.

CHAPTER TWENTY-SEVEN

A dley heard them talking, or at least Sean's end of the conversation, muttered protests, each another small concession, another retreat before the inevitable. Whether he bothered to resist at all because of some latent sense of decency, or simple self-serving fear, she could not say. After all these years with him, she still could not say for certain what his limits were. It was not the first such conversation on which she had eavesdropped. He was having them several times a day, and after each, she could tell that he had ceded more ground, compromised yet further. What frightened Adley was that for the most part, Sean was sober during the phone calls, or as close to it as he was likely to get. He was slowly bending backward without the lubrication of alcohol, giving over his moral fiber strand by strand, until sometime soon he must inevitably fall.

And then she heard it, the sound of his ultimate collapse—not a snap, but a sigh as the last of the air went out of him.

"All right," he said. "I'm your man."

Such a mundane phrase for the loss of a spirit, she thought.

Sean hung up the phone and left the living room. He felt a lightness in his being, as if he had surrendered a heavy burden after a long struggle. The struggle was over. There was no way out and thus no point in fighting. He would do what he must do, and, being Sean, he would do it with courage and dedication, because that was the kind of man he was. He was smiling until he saw her in the kitchen with the storm cloud upon her face. Her arms were crossed and she had that Valkyrie look about her—large, beautiful, and dangerous.

"You can't do it," Adley said. "It's insane."

"Ah, what choice do I have? The decision is made; it's all out of my hands."

"Don't be an idiot. You don't have to do anything."

"Would you rather starve?"

"Die of thirst, you mean? That's what you're afraid of, isn't it, Sean? Admit it. You'll lose your drinking money."

"I'll lose all me money. What do you think we're living off of now?"

"We can get by on Social Security," Adley said.

It was Sean's habit during a disagreeable discussion to move slowly out of the room. Adley had learned that the only solution was to pursue him from room to room, positioning herself in front of him and herding him like a sheep. He turned and retreated to the living room, and she pursued.

"Nobody gets by on that," he scoffed. "You're living in a fool's paradise."

"We can sell the house," she said.

"Sell the house? Who would buy it? Who would want it? It's only a house now, without the farm; we already sold the land. Who would want to live out here if they didn't have to? And where would we live then?"

"I don't know. We could move in with Carl and Alma."

"Live with Carl? I'm a forgiving man, but I have my limits."

"Don't start that again. You love Carl—you know it," she said.

"It's not *me* I'm worried about."

She had herded him back to the kitchen, where the argument had commenced. He found himself with his back to the sink, his wife in front of him, relentless. He turned and washed a dish.

"You can't do it, Sean. That's it. There's nothing more to say about it."

"That's a relief. Now if you'd just leave off talking about it."

"Tell me you won't."

He turned back to face her. Her jaw was set and her eyes ablaze, and for a moment he saw in her face the feisty countenance of the girl he had courted and won a million years ago. He was tempted to surprise her with a kiss, then give her a bigger surprise, show her Uncle Willie, whom she had not seen in a long time, proud and still capable of a good day's work, he had no doubt. Sure, if he had just another drink in him, there'd be no stopping him. . . .

"What are you thinking of?" she demanded as he caressed her shoulder. His face had gone all soft and sweet. She hadn't seen the look in years, and because it had been so long, she thought at first to resist it, and then she thought she must not lose it.

"You're still a beauty," he said.

She saw his eyes well up with tears, caught somewhere between desire and regret, and she pulled him against her.

"My beauty," he murmured into her hair.

What came over him? she wondered later as he lay beside her in her big bed. What had sparked him after all of this time, after all of her failed attempts at seduction, after all of the moments that had seemed so right, when she had been so ready and he hadn't been? Men were so peculiar, so frustratingly alien, so determined to do everything the wrong way.

He began to snore, and it occurred to her, most unpleasantly, that he might simply have been willing to do anything necessary to end the argument. It was a tactic that he had not thought of in years, but perhaps the stakes this time were so high that he made the ultimate sacrifice. Maybe he knew that she would not be mollified with his usual litany of lies and promises.

She waited until his snores fell into the gasping, half-drowning rhythm that would last for hours, then quietly slipped out of bed, threw a few clothes on, and left the house.

The nightmare was still on him when he was awakened by the insistent noise at the door. He lay still for a moment, blinking at the darkness, the demons retreating slowly from his imagination. The air conditioner groaned loudly, struggling to maintain its slight advantage over the heat, so it took Billy a moment to be sure that it was really someone at the door and not more torment from his nocturnal imagination.

He expected Lapolla, importuning him, yet again, to stay on the job, although three o'clock in the morning was egregious, even given Lapolla's anxieties.

Adley stepped into the house without ceremony, brushing against his naked chest as she squeezed past him like someone trying to avoid detection. She wore a man's raincoat, loosely closed at the waist, which meant, since it was not raining, that she was scantily clad underneath and had come out in a hurry. He became suddenly aware that he was dressed only in his underwear.

"You've got to find Sean," she said urgently.

"It's not that late for Sean, is it? He'll be home eventually."

"Of course he'll be home eventually. I know that. Where else would he go? Who would have him? Do you think I'd bother you if he was just out drinking?"

She glanced at his underpants and stifled a grin. He wished he were in pajamas.

"Better get some clothes on," she said, the anger draining from her voice.

No nonsense about how she'd seen him naked hundreds of times when he was a little boy, no pretense that it didn't matter to be standing there, neither one properly dressed, and Billy still in the partial grip of nocturnal arousal.

Well, we're all adults now, it looks like, Billy thought as he retreated to the bedroom. Adley followed and watched from the doorway as he covered himself.

"I think he's gone to kill him," she said. "You have to stop him."

"Who's going to kill who?"

"Sean, Sean's gone. He took the rifle. You have to stop him. He'll never be able to live with his conscience if he kills him." She seemed unaware of the skewed emphasis.

"Sean won't kill anybody," he said automatically, not believing it himself.

She dismissed his empty sentiment with a toss of the hand. "He thinks he has to. He may not succeed, but he'll try it."

"He's already tried it and botched it," Billy said, pulling on his shoes. "Sunder may be waiting for him this time."

"Sunder? He would never harm Sunder. I told you that. He's going to kill the black man."

"Collins? He's going to kill Collins?"

"Is that his name? I don't know who he is. The one who's been around town. The one who gave you and Sean a postcard."

"Sean got a postcard, too?"

She shrugged. "I got it. It was on the porch, addressed to Tree. When I saw what it was, I kept it. I never showed it to Sean."

"Why not?"

She stared at him for a moment, wondering why any explanation was necessary.

"I protect him when I can," she said. "I protect him from his mistakes. How do you think he's survived this long, the way he lives? I can't protect him this time. I tried to stop him, but he's *still* too strong. You have to do it. And you have to do it right now."

Her "*still* too strong" echoed in his mind and bespoke decades of struggle and devotion and impatience awaiting the time of final dominance. There was so much about his relatives' lives he didn't want to know but seemed destined to discover anyway.

"How's he going to find Collins?"

"There's an old farmhouse just south of Indian Cave Park where he's been going. . . ."

"Carl's place," he said brusquely, taking her by surprise.

"Yes."

"How do you know he goes there?"

Adley paused a moment, toying with the belt at her waist, making him uneasy.

"I told Joan about it. She asked me if there was a place he could go for . . . a safe place. . . . I knew the answer. It's very compelling when you know the answer—but I shouldn't have told her."

"Why did she ask you?"

"We've become close since you've been going out with her."

"Going out"—is that what his relationship had been? Was that all it ever amounted to in Joan's eyes?

"How did you know about the place?"

"It's where I go," she said reluctantly.

"What?"

"It's where I go."

"With Sunder?"

"Sunder? Never . . . It's where I go with Carl."

"Carl? . . . *Uncle* Carl?"

"He's my brother-in-law," she said, offering a well-polished rationalization. "He's not related to Sean. He's not related to me. . . . He's not even related by blood to you, if that's what troubles you."

"Well, that makes it all right, then," Billy muttered.

"Oh, what do you know about it? You're so damned young. The big trick to life, Billy, is to get through it, just get through it. I'm not about to apologize to you. You can't imagine life with Sean—but I'm still with him and I'm still trying to keep him alive. And right now, I need your help to do that. You can condemn me later; there will be plenty of time. *Plenty* of time."

"Does Sean know about Carl?"

She shrugged. "He thinks he does. He doesn't, not really. It amuses him to pretend he's jealous now and then; he thinks it annoys me, which delights him."

"Does Aunt Alma know? Apparently, Joan knew, so I suppose everyone else does, except me. Does that include Aunt Alma?"

She regarded him for a long moment, her features impassive. Only the slight flaring of her nostrils gave any hint of the fury she was suppressing.

"Are you going to help?" she asked at last. "Or just stand there and judge me while your uncle kills a man?"

* * *

There was something different about the air, it seemed to have texture, a crinkly, electrical quality, as if he were standing too close to a power generator. Billy studied the sky for signs of lightning as he drove, but he saw only a ceiling of clouds, huge black humps of roiling anger so low, they seemed to rush just above the trees. Once off the highway and away from the feeble ambient light of the town, he drove as if encased in a tunnel, the only illumination in all the world coming from his headlights. The beams occasionally reflected back from the pinpoint red eyes of raccoons feasting on the new corn, or of foxes in search of the rodents seeking the insects that infested the fields. Somewhere deeper in the fields, warier of the road and men, roamed rib-thin coyotes seeking any of them, voracious for anything that moved, from grasshopper to vole to pet dog.

There was no other traffic; all signs of life were cut off by the high stands of corn that towered well over his head. If he turned off the continuing roar of the air conditioner and stopped the car, he knew he would hear only the sounds of the hunt, the sudden frenzied rustle of movement among the stalks, the high, brief scream of captured prey. Many died silently, or with only a flapping of wings, but a few died in protest, their final brief keening alerting all within hearing that death was on the prowl, this night as all nights.

He moved his car from the asphalt of the Indian Cave parking lot and parked behind a stand of scrub brush that stood at the far end of the lot. Although not exactly hidden, it might not be seen by someone who drove in hurriedly and parked as close to the farmhouse as possible. If he left his car in plain sight, it might serve to deter either party from trouble. That was the goal of a peacekeeper, wasn't it? To prevent things from happening in the first place? But he was not here as a peacekeeper, and he had to admit that from the beginning. He had far darker plans.

He had hoped to make his way to the farmhouse without using the flashlight, but the night was much too dark for that, so he turned it on in brief bursts, flashing a distance in front of him, going as far as he could without vision, then illuminating another small path through the trees.

Already drenched in sweat, he paused at the last screen of trees before the clearing behind the house. Listening, he heard only the rush of the river in the distance and the faint, intermittent rustle of life resuming its activities after he had passed. Close to him, all creatures held their breath, so he walked in a cocoon of silence broken only by noises of his own making. Behind him, insects stirred again, disturbed by his passage, and their predators, waiting for movement, pounced. Waiting in its turn, an owl spied the larger movement, swept down on wings audible only after they passed, and closed its talons on a vole. It was one of the silent, acquiescent deaths, and Billy heard none of it.

He saw nothing, heard nothing from the house. If Sean were there, he would have given himself away. Billy could not imagine his uncle remaining still and silent for more than a minute at a time. If Collins was in the house, he was either asleep or waiting.

Billy's skin prickled at the prospect of crossing the open ground again, exposed and vulnerable to anyone with murderous intent—and whom did that category not include these days? There seemed to be as many would-be killers as adulterers, and the latter were turning out to be as thick on the ground as blades of grass.

Why would Collins be here? Why would he return? The farmhouse was no longer any good to him as a hiding place, now that it had been discovered. Anyone looking for him would look there first, and Collins must know that. So if he'd returned, it was because he'd had to. Because there was something there worth the risk. Joan? Would she come to the house again? Was she in there now, sleeping in his arms? Was another night with her worth the risk for Collins? Love made fools of men—Billy could testify to that—but it did not necessarily render them complete idiots. He did not doubt that lust would make a man climb mountains, cross continents, swim oceans just to take a woman to bed, but was not that irresistible force usually directed toward a woman who was as yet unbedded? Wasn't that sort of passion as much for the thrill of the hunt as it was for desire for the woman herself? Once the conquest was made, was the impetus ever as great again? Would a man walk through fire to sleep with a woman for the fourth time, or the fifth, with the same determined lunacy as that which had propelled him the first time? Billy was no expert, but he didn't think so. Novelty had an all but irresistible appeal to men, greater than lust. Greater than love, as well? . . . Billy was no longer sure he understood love. He had thought so, but now he saw it as nothing more than confusion, a convenient mask for any number of baser emotions. Lust, in the beginning. Then what? Possessiveness, dependence, convenience? How many ordinary sentiments could you cram under the noble title of love? As many as you needed to. Was he about to deal with Collins out of love for Joan? Surely love, true love, would mean that he would want only what was best for Joan, whatever made her happy, and if that meant being with another man, a black man, then Billy should want that for her because he loved her so much. . . . Well, that was bullshit as high as the house. He was motivated by jealousy, rage, humiliation, and he was not sure that Joan actually had much to do with it anymore. . . . They would say, Oh, he loved her so much. He was not himself. He was driven to it by love of Joan. But they would say that because it was so much prettier than thinking that he did it because he hated being cuckolded by a black man.

He crept forward, leaving the cover of the trees reluctantly, sending himself across the empty space like a spurred horse. Breathing heavily through his mouth, he waited again by the back door, giving any occupant time enough to reveal himself through movement. He knew that when he stepped onto the aged boards, there would be no way to do it in perfect silence; he would give himself away with every step if anyone was within, listening. Since there was no possibility of surprise anyway, there was no point in creeping around in the darkness. Billy turned on the flashlight and made a quick tour of the downstairs of the house, then went up the groaning stairs to the bedroom. The warped stairs creaked with every footfall. He could ask for no better alarm.

He moved rapidly through the bedroom, checking under the bed, opening the single closet. He started for a moment at something in a roughly human shape—a bathrobe, stirred by the breeze caused when he opened the closet door, swayed slightly in the flashlight beam. It was not one he recognized as belonging to Joan, but who knew if she had a separate wardrobe for her separate life? Or was it Adley's? Why would either of them display such modesty, when they came here for such immodest purposes? Billy touched the sleeve, brought it to his nose, and sniffed the faint but cloying scent of perfume. It was Adley's, he decided, but that didn't mean that Joan had not worn it. As he snapped off the flashlight, he laughed suddenly at himself, experiencing a release he had not felt for days. When did I become such a prude? he wondered. And when did I start smelling women's clothes? Billy Tree, the prurient prude. What had Joan called him? The most moral man she knew? Well, there was no reason she should know his true nature any better than he knew hers.

With the flashlight off, he looked out the back window, keeping to the side, and studied the approach anyone would have to take coming from the Indian Cave parking lot. From the front window, he looked toward the road and the path he and Lapolla had used the day they were shot at. The third alternative was from the river, and that was obscured from Billy's view by the bulk of the building, assuming someone would carefully use the house as a screen for his movements. But even then Billy would detect any approaching light, and there was no way to come at the house from any side without light. It was all Billy could do to find his way across the room from one window to the other; no human was going to walk through that blackness without visual assistance.

The first light came from the direction of the parking lot. He was coming as Billy had done, using the flashlight as sparingly as possible. From Billy's elevated point of view, the form looked like a giant firefly wending its way through the trees, advancing mostly in the dark, illuminating itself just long enough to get its bearings. The figure paused at the edge of the clearing, just as Billy had done, and Billy stepped completely out of the line of sight so he could not be seen through the window. Seconds later, the flashlight beam swept across the glass, then returned and held steady for a moment. Had Collins caught a glimpse of Billy's pale skin through the window? Or was he just cautious? Billy moved toward the closet while the light continued to probe the windows of the house. As he did so, he caught a glimpse of another light, coming from the front. It was farther away, probably on the gravel road, and moving in a straight line toward the house. There was no blinking of the light, no attempt to hide. Sean had arrived, as usual, without subtlety.

Collins and Sean would not be able to see each other's light as long as the house separated them, but if Sean proceeded as he had started, blustering his way forward, oblivious to discovery, Collins would have to be very preoccupied not to notice.

Collins snapped off his light and made the same dash over open ground as Billy had made. Billy stepped into the closet, positioning himself behind the robe, and froze. Unlike most, he knew how to play the waiting game. He would not move unless Collins was moving, using the other man's sounds to mask his own.

It did not take long before he heard the groan of the staircase. Collins was on his way. Billy kept his eye to the crack of the door. He would be able to tell where Collins was most of the time just by the noise, and if he was anywhere in the half of the room that held the bed, Billy could see him.

Collins came into the bedroom, moving quickly now and confidently. His flashlight was very large, almost a rectangular box, with a handle and multiple features. He switched off the beam and turned on a fluorescent tube that ran the length of the box. The room was suddenly suffused with a ghostly glow, and Billy could see the man pull something long and black from his belt. Whatever it was, it was without sheen and absorbed light like another shadow. Without so much as a glance out the front window, Collins put the flashlight on the floor and let its glow fill the room as he grasped the bedstead and pulled it toward him with a powerful jerk. The metal legs scraped and screeched against the floorboards.

Collins was standing with his back to the front window as he worked. The fluorescent light would illuminate him like a figure on a movie screen for anyone in front of the house.

So here it was. All Billy needed to do was watch, and Collins would be a dead man. He could imagine the scene from below, Collins's figure filling the window, head tilted backward, looking upward, momentarily still. All he lacked was a bull's-eye pinned to his back. Billy had but to wait and let matters take their course. He was as innocent as he was ever about to be with a heart so full of hatred and contempt, and no one could ever blame him for being a second too late in reacting.

A moral man, Joan had called him. She was wrong. Not too bent by prejudice to stand up straight, Collins had said of him. He was wrong. He was no one's hero, no one's saint. He would keep quiet and let the world have its way.

But he could not do it. "Down!" he yelled, bursting from the closet.

Collins turned with speed and lashed out with the black instrument he held in his hand. Billy blocked the blow with his forearm and his momentum carried him into Collins's body. The two of them tumbled to the floor as the window exploded in a shower of glass. A second bullet slammed into the wall opposite the window as Collins rolled to his knees.

"Stay down," Billy said.

Collins needed no explanation; he was already crawling toward the doorway, keeping below the window, leaving Billy flat on his back. Billy rolled to his stomach and squirmed toward the light. As he switched it off, he heard Collins clambering down the steps in the darkness.

He gave himself a moment for his arm, knowing already that it was broken and also that there was nothing he could do about it now. He unbuttoned his shirt and carefully lifted the injured arm into the makeshift sling. Wincing at the pain, he lay quietly a moment, waiting for the blinding surge to pass and listening to the pandemonium of Collins's departure from the house. He heard the man trip on his way out the door and fall to the ground with an explosive grunt.

"Sean!" Billy yelled. "Sean, it's Billy! Don't fire! Don't fire!"

Fearful of standing lest Sean take more shots in his excitement, Billy wriggled on his back toward the door of the bedroom. His hand touched the cool metal bar that had broken his arm, and he placed it on his stomach, along with the flashlight, then slithered to the door and felt his way toward the staircase with his good arm.

"Sean, answer me, goddamn it!" he yelled. If he turned on the light, he would become a target. If he started down the stairs and Sean burst into the house, eager to finish the job, he would be shot before he could identify himself.

"Sean, you son of a bitch, answer me!"

He was answered by another shot, this time from the back of the house, where Collins had gone.

"Sweet Jesus," said a voice unmistakably Sean's. "Now what?"

Billy got to his feet. Whatever was happening, it was no longer directed at the house. He stumbled down the staircase, still careful not to make himself an inviting target by turning on the light. He missed the last step and came down heavily, sending a shock wave of pain into his throbbing arm.

There were more sounds from outside, rustlings, scurryings, then running feet. When Billy stepped outside, he was greeted by Joan's anguished voice, wailing with grief. He reached her in a moment and turned on the beam of the light. It fell on Collins's chest. The man was lying with his head on her lap, his blood as black as the surrounding night. Billy knelt and pressed his hand to the wound, but he knew immediately that he was too late.

"Oh my God," wailed Margie Duerfeldt, Joan's sister. "Help him, Billy, help him."

Billy looked at her numbly. She was not Joan, but Joan's sister. Why was she here?

"I can't," he said.

"Please, please, help him."

"Margie?"

"Don't let him die, please don't let him die!"

"Margie . . . He's gone."

She surprised him not with a scream but with a sigh, as if she was immeasurably disappointed in him. Her head slumped forward, almost touching Collins, and when Billy touched her shoulder, she toppled to the ground in a faint.

She was unconscious for less than a minute, but when she came to, it was with wide-eyed wonder, as if still baffled by a strange dream of death.

"Margie, where's Joan?"

"Joan?" she asked, befuddled.

"Where's Joan? Where is she?"

"She's at my house, baby-sitting," she said, puzzled. She looked down at Collins with the same air of puzzlement, as if seeing him for the first time. It took a moment for reality to return to her. Billy let her weep.

"It's my fault," she said, sobbing. "It's all my fault."

"No," said Billy, "it's mine."

CHAPTER TWENTY-EIGHT

The ambulance met them on the gravel road in front of the farmhouse, where Billy had managed to carry the body while shepherding Margie. Seeing Collins's blood soaked into Billy's shirt, the EMS worker asked Billy if he needed treatment, too. Billy dismissed the offer. He would deal with the arm when he had time; there were more important things to deal with first. The blood was not his own; it would wash off . . . or not. He was not certain that he would ever be clean of Collins's blood, but there was no need to explain that to the medic.

With Margie and Collins gone in the ambulance, Billy drove to Sean's farm. He was half-surprised not to find Sean there, drinking a beer and regaling the air with a new tale of his courage and accomplishment. Billy searched the house, turning on every light in protest against the black night, looking for Sean in closets, under the bed, as if seeking a naughty child.

His adrenaline carried him through the house in a rage, oblivious to anything but his quest. Finally, convinced that there was not only no trace of Sean but also no sign of Adley, he felt the fury seep out of his system and he was left with a horrible throbbing in his arm. He grabbed a large bottle of aspirin from the medicine cabinet and swallowed several pills, slurping water from the tap with his good hand. The rest of the bottle went into his shirt pocket, and he swallowed two more pills on his way to Carl Wittrock's farm.

Carl woke to find Billy standing over him in his bedroom, soaked in blood and enraged.

"Where are they?" Billy demanded.

"Who?"

"Oh, Billy," said Alma, jerking upright, her face ashen. "What happened?"

"I'm all right," Billy said, avoiding the question. "Where's Sean?"

"Is Sean hurt?" Alma asked.

Billy kept his eyes on Carl.

"I don't know," Carl said.

"Nobody's hurt, Aunt Alma," Billy said. "I need to find Sean. Where is he, Carl?"

"I don't know. I have no idea."

"Where's Adley?"

There was an instantaneous shift in the landscape, a change in voltage between man and wife, a deeper look of caution in Carl's eyes, all of it covered and denied to the outsider.

"Why would I know that?"

"What's wrong with your arm, Billy?" his aunt asked. "Why are you keeping it in your shirt like that?"

"What's going on?" Carl demanded, "Do you need help? I'll get dressed."

"If Sean comes here, call me right away," Billy said, already leaving the room. "And call me first."

Billy returned to the deserted farmhouse before first light, driving along the gravel road this time and taking the car as close to the house as he could. He would call Lapolla when he was finished. The site would be duly scoured for clues. They would find the shell cartridges, or they might find them, but he had no doubt that the weapon from which they had been fired would be long gone. Even Sean was not stupid enough to keep a murder weapon in the trunk of his car. Billy would allow the forensics team—a pompous term for the combined efforts of Lapolla and Schatz—to do their work, but not until he had done his own. The state police would be called in on a homicide case, of course, but he had no confidence that they would answer the questions he needed to ask.

Billy gagged down two more aspirin, wondering why he had settled for the uncoated pills and what impulse of bravado had made him think he could swallow them without water. Popping aspirin like peanuts, he imagined his stomach wall oozing blood. If it helped with the pain in his arm, he certainly had not yet noticed.

The sun crept over the tops of the cornfields, smiling malignly with a promise of yet more heat. Stirred by the immediate rise in temperature, a breeze began to blow, offering the only relief the day was likely to have in store. The black ceiling of low-lying clouds hung in the sky, listless now, as torpid as the animal life below.

He stood near the bed, where Collins had stood, looking upward. At first, he did not know what he was searching for among the dull brown planks. No great expense had been incurred in building the house, and the bedroom was no exception. The walls had been covered with Sheetrock, but the efforts had stopped there, as if the builder had run out of materials or patience, and the ceiling remained as crudely finished as the floor. Billy wondered if the builder had not been Carl himself, if the construction on the house had not ceased at the point when commodity prices had plunged to the level that cultivating the land made no economic sense. It was a tiny holding, separated from his true farm, a holdover from a time when a man could still eke out a living on less than a thousand acres. What had he been thinking? What hopes had he ever held for such a minimal scrap of land? Or was it intended as a playhouse all along? Was it always to be a love nest for Adley? Would a man buy eighty acres of marginal land and build a house just to have a place to meet his lover? How long had they been lovers? Carl had to be sixty-five. Did men begin a life of duplicity at that age? Well, why not? Or had the two of them been lovers for years, decades? Again, why not?

As the light increased, Billy could differentiate one plank from the other, and then the individual nails that attached them to the studs. Two nails were slightly different from all the others, newer, the plating less worn by time and weather. It was not a brilliant hiding place, but it would have taken Billy, or anyone else, a long time to find it without knowing where to look.

He inserted the end of the crowbar with which Collins had broken his arm into the tiny gap between boards and worked it upward before levering down. The nails released their grip easily and the plank sagged open. Billy reached into the gap and his fingers closed around an object encased in bubble wrap.

Working clumsily with one hand but trying not to tear the wrap, he removed the tape that held the package together, revealing the object within. Billy looked down at a golf club. All of this for a golf club? Collins had lost his life because he returned for a golf club? And a very old one at that. Grip, shaft, and iron head were all markedly different from today's variety.

Collins had limped when Billy first encountered him in the alley behind Joan's house, limped on his way to the motel, and then to his room after the incident at the swimming pool. There had been no trace of it when he ran from the slaughterhouse or through the rainstorm. Had this golf club been hidden in his pants leg on that first night? They had found bubble wrap in his motel room. Had he carried it to the motel in his pants leg, wrapped it safely, then looked for a place to hide his peculiar treasure? And why? Why bother? It wasn't old enough to be a valuable antique; it was just plain old.

He replaced the wrapping on the club and tapped the plank back into place with the end of the crowbar. The state boys would go after the bullet slugs that had come through the window and buried themselves in the opposite wall, but they'd have no reason to examine the ceiling. They would be investigating a murder, not a mystery. Crimes had perpetrators, puzzles had solutions, and that was what the police would be after. The motives of the human heart were obscure and bewildering and seldom lent themselves to clear definition or solution. Billy decided not to confuse the state boys with the passions of love.

When he stepped off the bed, the shock traveled to his arm and brought him to his knees with pain. He tried to swallow two more aspirin while still on the floor, but they stuck in his throat and he spat them out, then spat again to rid his mouth of the bitter taste. Stoicism had its limits and he admitted that he had reached his. He got himself back to his car like an invalid, walking gingerly, almost limping, as if the broken bone in his arm had affected his legs. Driving himself to the hospital, he grunted rhythmically in an effort to keep himself from screaming.

Joan found him in the hospital waiting room, smiling at her goofily from a wheelchair. They had sedated him while fixing his arm, adding a bit more to the dose because of the bloodiness of his clothes, and when he refused to check in or take to bed, they had plunked him into the chair with a stern admonition to check with a doctor or nurse before leaving the building. No one much expected Billy to pay attention to their orders, but they all had other things to do.

Staying in the chair seemed to Billy an excellent way to pass the time. The drugs had him in a mood of passive serenity, and he watched the comings and goings of the hospital personnel with the detached air of someone observing the activities of an anthill. All that expended energy, and it had nothing whatever to do with him except as a source of entertainment.

When Joan arrived, that was nice, too.

"Margie's sleeping," said Joan. "It must have been terrible for her."

"Um."

"She's known him since high school. Do you know where they met?"

Billy arched his eyebrows, trying to simulate interest. Margie had sobbed out a garbled account of her affair with Collins during their wait for the ambulance, but he was perfectly contented to hear it again. He loved to watch Joan when she talked. Beautiful Joan. His Joan. Always his Joan. He would have to apologize to her for his horrible thoughts—or maybe she could tell what he meant just by the dreamy smile on his face.

"The state basketball tournament—all of us girls were up to Lincoln and stayed in the Hotel Cornhusker to cheer you on, remember? His team was there; they were roaming the halls same as we were. Except for you—you must have been keeping coach's curfew like the good boy you were."

"I'm a good boy," Billy agreed, grinning. His eyelids drooped, but his eyes never left her face.

"I know you are," she said with a trace of rue. "That's why I didn't tell you she's been seeing him for over a month. I knew you'd disapprove. I was afraid you'd give me a lecture about 'facilitating' their getting together or something. . . . Actually, I was afraid you'd huff off righteously and tell her husband."

"I am very glad to see you," he said loopily.

"I don't think you even know what you're looking at. Are you listening to me at all?"

"Um."

"I was letting her use my house on the nights Will was gone, while I baby-sat for her kids, but she got scared. She thought they'd been found out—that's why I found the farmhouse for them. . . . That was you, wasn't it? You caught them together at my house. That's when you started acting funny, and I knew you were mad at me for letting her . . . Billy, she's my sister. How could I not help her? . . . What are you looking at like that?"

"You are very beautiful," he said, hoping that she would understand all that he meant by the statement, but if she did not, it would have to wait. His tongue was incapable of wrapping itself around anything more complex.

"And you're doped to the gills, aren't you? How much did they give you?"

Billy's grin broadened. He didn't know how much it was, but it was the right amount. He had not felt so blissfully indifferent to the turmoil swarming around him in weeks.

A nurse herself, Joan hurried off indignantly to find out what dosage of what drug they had administered, leaving Billy to float happily in space. There were a number of things he should be doing. He was aware of that, but he simply didn't care. Getting out of the chair and onto his feet was at the top of the list, but he was far too comfortable for that. The cast on his broken arm was wrapped in blue gauze tape. He thought it a most serene color.

"Jeez, Bill," said Lapolla, interrupting Billy's reverie, but not his peace of mind.

Billy gazed up at the sheriff, letting his eyelids droop and rise, watching Lapolla swim in place. The man seemed, as usual, apologetic.

"How you feeling?"

"Good," said Billy, listening to the word extend itself to several extra syllables. "Joan's here."

"Oh yeah? Great. Listen, Billy . . ."

Billy lifted a finger, signaling a brief time-out. He dropped his head to his chest and said, "Go ahead, I'm still listening," or thought he said it, or thought he should have said it.

"Jeez, Billy."

He definitely heard Lapolla say that. Or very nearly definitely.

Awaking, he had no idea how long he had been asleep, but he could see Lapolla's shoes still planted in front of him.

"Sean," Billy said. "Find my uncle Sean. And Adley."

"We found Sean," Lapolla said.

"Oh, good." He started to lower his head again.

"They found him in the river. He drowned. I'm awful sorry."

Billy managed to lift his head and look Lapolla in the face. He knew he was supposed to have a concerned visage, show that drowning was not a good thing, but the smile of contentment spread over his features again and he fell back asleep. As he drifted off, he heard, or thought he heard, the voice of Lapolla saying that Adley was missing, and then another "Jeez" of exasperation.

CHAPTER TWENTY-NINE

B illy awoke to find himself still in the wheelchair and the town siren sounding the five o'clock tocsin. Located atop the fire station, only a few steps north of the library, the siren screamed its alert daily at noon and five o'clock, advising anyone interested, as well as those who were not, that it was time to lay down the tools. It was a factory town habit that had somehow established itself in an agricultural community and was now so ingrained in the public consciousness that no one questioned why they were treated to a time check twice a day. Clocks were glanced at to verify their accuracy, watches set to it. Billy looked from habit at his wristwatch, only to see the blue of the cast encasing his left arm. He had no immediate way of knowing that it was not five o'clock.

The siren squealed again, this time in a series of bursts, followed by a howl that seemed never to end. Activity in the hospital froze for a moment as everyone looked to others in consternation. "Tornado," someone said softly, and the word spread instantly, so that Billy could hear it echoed throughout the halls in ever-louder variations.

Billy rose and made his way to the exit as the intercom crackled to life and an electronic voice announced the tornado warning to the whole building, old news already. The sky was leaden, as it had been for days, but there was no visible sign of trouble. Tornado warnings were not unusual. It was the time of year when the sky retaliated against the torture that rose to it from the ground below. Glutted with heat, tormented with energy, the clouds would finally strike back, releasing spiraling winds that struck with the speed and fury of warplanes. Devastating when they touched ground, they were as impossible to predict as fish breaching the surface of a summer lake in pursuit of insects, popping up at random and vanishing again just as quickly beneath the placid water. Statistics seemed to provide the best defense. Their killing swath was small and extraordinarily brief, and their killing ground of Oklahoma, Kansas, Missouri, and Nebraska was very large. Like cancer and stroke, they would happen, but always to someone else. The siren meant that there was tornado activity within a fifty-mile radius. Given that this meant 78,000 square miles, the odds were much the same as hitting Falls City by throwing a dart at the map, and the residents knew it. Looking through the automatic glass doors that led onto the lobby, Billy saw people searching the skies as they walked to their cars, but no one was running for the storm cellars.

He made his way groggily to the basement of the hospital, where the morgue was housed. Sean's body lay on a gurney and an attendant was removing his shoes. Sean must have arrived at the same time Lapolla showed up with the news of his drowning, Billy thought. Fresh catch from the Missouri, still redolent of those murky waters.

The attendant was a black man, a member of one of Falls City's three resident black families. Billy knew him only as Stan and had never thought to inquire about the rest of his name, although the man had been a fixture in town and at the hospital for as long as Billy could remember.

"Awful sorry," Stan murmured, stepping away from his work in deference to Billy.

It took Billy a moment to know what to say in response. "Thank you" seemed a ludicrous reply in the presence of his dead uncle, but he could think of nothing better.

"Thanks," he said finally. "You can keep working."

"I'll give you a minute," Stan said.

"No, go on. I want to see him naked." And before the autopsy, he thought, before they reduce the man to a cadaver, before he becomes an empty husk, sans blood, sans organs, sliced open from gullet to pubes, splayed out like a spatchcock chicken. That was a spectacle he definitely did *not* want to see.

Reluctantly and with more reverence than customary, Stan proceeded to undress Sean Tree. Billy watched the process in detail, studying each new section as it was laid bare. No bruises, no signs of violence. Would bruises show up on a man if he died within a minute after he was struck? Billy didn't know, which was only the beginning of his ignorance. He might pretend to have an expert eye for Stan's benefit, but he certainly wasn't fooling himself. Barring a bullet hole, Billy would not know how Sean had come to be in the Missouri River within an hour or so of having shot and killed a man on dry land.

"Sweet Jesus. Now what?" Billy had heard Sean call out after shooting Collins. What had he meant by that? Now that I've killed a man, I'll go hurl myself into the river? Wash away my sins? Make retribution by drowning myself, one life for another? It was the kind of bombast he might mouth, but never act on. His uncle had been, above all, self-centered. If he had ever sacrificed anything in his life, Billy had never heard of it, and it was certainly not himself.

"Could you roll him over, Stan?"

The attendant's hands seemed startling black against the total pallor of Sean's flesh. Billy had never thought of Stan as being particularly dark—but then, he had never thought much about him at all. What kind of life must it be handling the dead in anonymity? Billy wondered briefly about Stan's condition, realizing that he was considering him as a human being for the first time. Odette Collins would already be in the giant refrigerator where Sean was headed, awaiting his autopsy when some doctor could find the time. This man would have put him there, one black man tending to the morbid flesh of another, along with his murderer's—an irony too obvious to ignore. Billy looked into Stan's bloodshot eyes for what was probably the first time since becoming aware of his existence. I let you down, he thought. I failed you. He could have been speaking as well to Sean, and to Collins.

There were no marks on Sean's back to indicate that he had been struck with anything. But why assume he would need to be over-powered? A simple push would do. Sean, drunk as usual, unsteady on his pins—put him in a skiff and into the current of the river and induce him to stand, or look over the edge . . . The pressure of a fin-gertip would do it. Or Sean could have done it himself easily enough. How hard was it to imagine Sean rising to his feet in the unsteady craft, declaiming his innocence to the air, yelling into the dark night that circumstances had forced murder upon him? A shift of weight, a sawing of the arm . . . or a sudden violent swing as he hurled the rifle as high and far as he could into the roiling waters. Why else would he have been there if not to dispose of the murder weapon? Was he stupid enough to stand and wave it over his head before he threw it, thus assuring that he would be off balance? Of course he was. Drunks died unwittingly at their own hands all the time, wavering into the path of trucks, falling asleep with their heads on a railroad track, mistaking the hard iron for a pillow.

He went through Sean's pockets, the jeans still sodden with river water. The wallet was gone, which he had expected. It had been used to identify him and now the law had it, or it was simply stolen by whatever luckless fisherman had come across his floating bulk. It seemed fair recompense for the shock and distaste of hauling the body to shore. The other pockets held the usual detritus—coins, a paper clip, a button he had probably found lying like a treasure on the sidewalk outside the Sportsman's, a round red toothpick with a min-iature parasol, undoubtedly from the bar . . . and a shell cartridge.

"Oh, Sean," Billy said.

"I'll leave you for a minute," Stan said, having heard something in Billy's voice that suggested he might cry. This time, Billy did not stop him.

Drowning was said to be a good way to die. One liquid breath and it was all over. The drowned died happy, they said, although Billy had no idea how they would know. Sean did not look happy. He did not look unhappy. He looked dead.

Billy studied his uncle's vacant face, waiting for something to come to him, some informative emotion that would overwhelm him. After several moments of waiting, he felt nothing more than silly. His relationship with Sean had been long and complex, and his reaction to the man's death would probably be the same, but whatever it would be, it had not begun yet and would not be jump-started by staring at his corpse.

"Well . . ." he began, feeling the need to say something significant. As with the emotion, nothing came. "Well . . ."

After the third false start, Billy left the morgue and made his way to his car. Isn't it strange that I felt more looking into the eyes of the black attendant than I did regarding my dead uncle? he thought. Or is it? Emotions are inspired by the living, or should be. There's nothing that can be done for the dead, which was what made Collins's obsession with the lynching of Lawton Mills so pathetic, so hard to understand, until Billy realized that it wasn't about the dead; it was the living whom Collins was after. Justice could be administered only to the living.

The siren continued to wail in coded bursts of alarm, but Billy saw nothing threatening in the sky. People walked with their eyes cast upward, like so many bird-watchers, and even drivers bent their heads to look up through their windshields. Billy wondered if it wouldn't be like this in a city long accustomed to air raids, people looking up to see the bombs fall, rather than taking to the shelters to survive them. The siren protests too much, they seemed to be saying. *We* will be the judge of danger.

Billy fingered the shell casing that he had transferred from Sean's pocket to his own. There was no question of preserving it as evidence, although it had been planted on Sean for that purpose, he had no doubt. It was the one significant detail too many. Overkill, if that wasn't too apposite a description given the circumstances. Sean would no more think to stop to find the casing of the murder bullet and stick it in his pocket after shooting Collins than he would be able to walk across the waters that drowned him. Billy would keep the casing as a talisman along with the noose. He fingered them both briefly before making a phone call and then heading for his car.

He heard a crack, and she fell straight down, no staggering, no stumbling, but straight to the ground. Her legs crumbled and she fell like a dropped rock. He had never seen anything like it and he knew immediately that she could not be pretending. He and his friends had "died" many a time, staggering about, clutching their hearts in emulation of all those moribund movie villains, milking it for all it was worth, making a feast of it. He could not have fallen the way she did if he'd tried.

She didn't move, just lay there like a doll tossed across the room, limbs every which way. He slapped her a few times, begged her to wake up, but he knew it was futile. He listened to her heart, stuck a wet finger under her nose to see if she was breathing. Just in case she was faking, *he squeezed her nose shut so she would have to open her mouth—but of course she didn't. She was stone-dead, and he had known it when he saw her fall.*

He got to his feet, still holding the club. There was blood on the head of it, and he was rubbing it off on the grass when the two brothers came around the shed.

"We need you," said the older brother.

"Some men want us to carry their bags."

"He's too small to carry two bags," said the older brother, gesturing at the younger with a twist of his head. "We need you."

The last sentence was said as the brothers took in the scene before them.

"Criminently," said the little one.

"She did it," the killer said absurdly.

The older brother walked next to Alice's body and stared down at her.

"Judas Priest. What'd you do?"

"Nothing. I found her like this."

The smaller brother began to cry, still staring at the dead girl.

"You're in awful trouble," said the older brother.

"No," said the killer desperately. "Listen, you can't tell anybody. Never. Never, never, no matter what."

The smaller boy continued to weep and sniffle.

"I'll give you things, all right?" The killer put his arm on the older brother's shoulder. "Aren't we friends? I'll give you things. You just have to keep quiet."

"What kind of things?"

"Whatever you want. What do you want?"

The brothers were silent for a moment as they exchanged a look between them. The little one shrugged.

"I don't know," said the older boy.

He had won them over; it was a moment of triumph. He produced a package of gum from his pocket and gave each of them a piece.

"You have to promise. Will you promise?"

"What kind is it?" asked the younger.

"Blackjack."

"I promise."

The boy turned to the older brother. "You have to promise, too."

The older brother unwrapped the gum and popped it into his mouth. He shrugged.

"I guess," he said.

The boy led them away from the body, back to where the golfers were waiting for them to carry their bags. He still had the club that had killed her in his hand.

"You going to take that?" the smaller boy asked. "Can I use it sometime?"

"Whatever you want," he said, but even then he knew he would never let anyone use the club; he would never let it out of his possession. He certainly would not leave it next to the body. Much of what had happened was already a blur, a few minutes of lunacy and lousy luck, and he wasn't sure how or why any of it had happened. But the club was evidence. That much he knew.

CHAPTER THIRTY

Sunder hurried into his house as if chased by the noise of the siren that was still screaming tirelessly from the center of town. The sound diminished when he closed the door, and he stood there for a moment as if puzzled by his surroundings, although he was in his own home.

"In here, Judge," came a voice from the den.

"How'd you get in here?"

Billy tilted his head toward the one window without a blind.

"You left it unlocked. Not real good security."

"A locked window isn't going to keep out somebody who's shooting through the glass."

"True. Still, a worried man would probably lock it."

"I'm not worried. I wanted the son of a bitch to come in again—at least I want him to try. . . . What was the urgent call about? What did I rush out of court for?"

Billy sat behind Sunder's desk, his broken arm lying uselessly in his lap below the level of the writing surface. He watched Sunder's eyes, waiting for him to notice a subtle change in the interior decoration.

"There's a tornado alert, you know," Sunder said.

"Shall we go huddle in the cellar? I find this room so much more interesting."

"Just a room. A few memories."

"It's not a memory room; it's a trophy room. Once I realized that, things started to make sense. Everything in here is a record of something you've won in some way or another. You didn't *win* the noose, so you didn't keep it, not after you had a day or two to think about it; it wasn't a happy reminder of a victory. Keeping the postcard wouldn't do, either. For one thing, someone might recognize you in it, lots of messy questions. . . . Still, you pulled a good one that day in Sabella; you got somebody else hanged for a murder you committed. You had to have a reminder of that."

Sunder's eyes glanced sideways and took in the golf club, hanging again on the two hooks above the shelf that held the golf ball and the clock won at a carnival.

"Oh, you can turn and take a good look," Billy said. "It's your house, your trophy. I brought it back for you. . . ."

"I know you've had a hard couple of days, Billy. Lapolla told me you're all drugged up, so I'll make allowances."

"Sheriff Lapolla keeps you pretty well posted, doesn't he?"

"He's the county sheriff; I'm the county judge. If we're going to run things, we have to communicate. He tells me you've resigned, by the way. So I take it this is not an official visit."

"This has nothing to do with the law. I'm here for justice."

"I assume you're wearing a wire, or otherwise recording this little bit of playacting," he said.

"I'm not actually, but my memory is pretty good, if you want to say something incriminating."

Sunder gave him a wan smile. "Well, let's just assume you are recording, shall we? Not that I don't trust you, but I'm not sure you're entirely responsible for your actions at the moment. In any event, for the record, I do not know what you're talking about and I deny, categorically, any suggestion that I had anything whatsoever to do with the death of anyone at all."

"Not even Sean?"

"Of course not. Sean Tree was a lifelong friend of mine. I was deeply distressed to learn he had drowned."

"Such a lifelong friend that you made monthly deposits in his back account for as long as you've both had bank accounts. In cash, of course, in a branch bank in Omaha or Lincoln, no record on your part. . . . Until Collins came along and you realized that money might not be enough if someone was threatening to expose Sean as an accomplice to a murder. I assume that's why you tried to shoot Sean in his truck."

A gust of wind hit the house, rattling the windowpanes in their frames.

"Collins shot at your uncle, just as he shot at me," Sunder said.

"When you didn't manage to kill Sean that time, you had to convince him that you weren't the one who shot at him, or he might turn on you right then and there. So you shot at yourself, too. Once up close, resting the rifle on the sill so you could put a hole in your bathrobe within an inch of your heart—except, of course, your heart wasn't in it. Then the shots from the lawn, the same distance as the ones you took at Sean, so the pattern would be the same."

Something hard hit the side of the house and Sunder jumped, startled.

"Once again, not only do I deny everything you've said; I caution you to stop making baseless accusations."

"DNA is a funny thing, isn't it, Judge? Very mysterious the way it seems to cling to things forever. You've washed that club now many times? And still you can't be sure, especially if the FBI goes after it with those electron microscopes . . . and the FBI would come into it, since there's a racial killing involved. Civil rights violation, all of that. And what if they decide to dig up the girl and find your DNA on her? DNA must have been haunting you ever since they started doing these amazing things with it. All this *science* in the last couple of decades. Must have been very troubling, especially since there's no statute of limitations on murder."

"Once again, I have murdered no one."

"Not even Lawton Mills?"

Sunder paused only a moment before asking, "Who?"

"You remember him. Black fella, worked on the golf course in Sabella where you and my uncle and my father used to caddy on the weekends? No? Too vague? He was the one you accused of raping and killing that girl? The guy who was lynched while you watched? Surely you remember that, Judge. It was your very first lynching; it must have made an impression."

Sunder wrinkled his brow, looking quizzically at Billy.

"Careful, Judge. I've got a picture. My father, Sean, a couple other boys—and you, with Lawton Mills in the background, hanging from a rope. Collins could never prove it was you from a fifty-year-old photograph alone, of course. But Sean could. And Collins could never get anyone in authority to make the right connections and dig up the girl's body and check out the club for trace evidence—but I could. . . . And you know what? Being a famously moral man, I think I will."

A volley of loose sticks and pebbles cascaded against the side of the house, hurled by the wind, which now seemed to blow without surcease.

"Sounds like someone is coming to shoot at you again, doesn't it?"

"We should maybe seek shelter," Sunder said.

"No place for you to hide now, Judge."

"You have a rather extensive delusion going here, Billy. Is all this in reaction to your uncle's death?"

"And Collins's. And guilt in general. Guilt that I didn't figure it all out in time to stop it from happening. Guilt that I did a lousy job as a lawman. Guilt that Collins was counting on me to do something about it. And guilt about my aunt Adley. Where is she, Judge?

"Why should I know?"

"Did she go into the river along with Sean? Or did you just walk off and leave her behind a bush the way you did with the girl in Sabella?"

It sounded like a train rushing at them, but it seemed to come from all directions at once. The south side of the house rattled and shook and sagged with the pressure, and all of the windows on the north side shattered at once. The men were shocked into momentary inaction; then Sunder grabbed the golf club from the wall and ran toward the door. Billy rose from behind the desk just as the tornado assaulted the house in earnest. This time, the entire south side caved inward and upward at once, rising in a swirl of timbers shredded like paper. The desk slammed backward into Billy, turning upside down and pinning him to the floor.

Stunned, struggling to breathe, Billy watched the ceiling lift off as easily as a kite and sail out of sight, revealing a sky filled with objects never intended to take flight. Billy could not see behind him, but the east wall was still intact, although all the memorabilia had been torn off, every trophy, medal, and souvenir lifting at once, as if responding to a giant vacuum cleaner. Some flew directly up, some to the side, where he heard them clatter against the west wall, and some swirled overhead in circles, defying gravity.

Lying flat on its top, the desk provided no surface for the wind to use as a sail, and its crushing weight kept Billy pinned to the floor. Even in his stunned state, he realized that it was only the desk that kept him from joining the kaleidoscopic chaos overhead. Permeating it all, so loud that he seemed to take it in through eyes and nose and mouth as well as his ears, was the noise, sounding more than ever like the world's largest train—and he was directly under its wheels.

Malignant, fickle, and blessedly brief, the tornado moved on in less than a minute. In its wake came the deluge from the skies as the flying objects, abruptly released from its grip, fell to earth. Tree limbs, timbers, rocks, and furniture cascaded into the shell of Sunder's house, and Billy was saved for the second time by the desk that held him down. The storm's debris thundered down, crashing against the desk, bouncing off the floor within inches of his head. A stone the size of his head smashed into the desk, but its momentum was slowed by the spacious walnut surface, diluting its effect. Without the desk, the stone would have killed him. As it was, Billy was knocked breathless again, and he could only watch helplessly as the hail of potentially lethal objects fell about him while he struggled with the most immediate problem—breathing.

And then, wondrously, it was over. The train had moved out of hearing, the rain of debris had ceased, and Billy's immediate world was suddenly encased in a silence so complete, he thought at first he had gone deaf. No bird, no animal, no insect made a sound. Like them, Billy closed his eyes and held his breath, marveling at being alive.

He was not sure if he had slept, but he came to himself abruptly with the sound of a door opening. A door? Could there still be such a thing as a door with the whole world blown away? Footsteps approached, and Billy saw Sunder looming above him, the golf club dangling in his hand.

"Still with us there, Billy?"

"Barely."

"You're lucky, I'd say. Not as lucky as I am, though. The whole west side of the house is untouched. I made it through the door, fell to the ground, and—*whoosh*—the whole thing missed me. Cut like a surgeon's knife. It didn't want me; it wanted you."

"Didn't get me," Billy said. He moved his shoulders, trying in vain to wriggle free.

"Looks to me like it got you." Sunder swung the golf club like a pendulum above Billy's face. "Well, with all of that falling debris, something was bound to hit you."

The sound of an ambulance rose somewhere in the distance behind Billy's head. Sunder looked up, appraisingly. The golf club continued to swing inches from Billy's head.

"It'll take them awhile to get here. Looks like the damned thing ripped hell out of most of Chase Street."

"How about getting this off me?"

"Is it uncomfortable? Don't worry, you won't feel it much longer. Such a pity. You could have been sheriff. We could have run things together."

Billy heard a car approach and then stop. There was no sound of a door opening or closing. Sunder did not bother to look. He lowered the head of the golf club to Billy's temple.

"Where's Adley?" Billy asked.

Sunder adjusted his feet in a golfer's stance. He held the club so that the leading edge of the iron would crash into Billy's temple.

"Don't talk while I'm swinging. You don't want me to miss and take your nose off."

He tapped the hard metal once against Billy's temple in a golfer's prefatory waggle.

"We'll all wonder what could possibly have caused such a wound," said Sunder.

He lifted his chin, turned his head slightly to the side in imitation of Jack Nicklaus, and began to draw the club back—then fell forward onto Billy. Sunder twitched once, then was still. Billy never heard the shot, having already squeezed his eyes shut in anticipation of the blow. He opened them and saw only a patch of flooring out of the corner of his eye. Sunder's legs covered his face.

After a moment, he heard more footsteps and Sunder's legs were dragged away.

Adley bent over him. "Are you all right?"

"Broken ribs, I think. I'll make it until they find me," Billy said. "Has anyone seen you?"

She looked quickly around. "No."

"Go away," he said. "Let someone else find me. And throw the rifle in the river." It was half-filled with them by now anyway.

She patted his cheek and smiled briefly before hurrying away. Billy closed his eyes and rehearsed his story so that he would be as baffled as everyone else about who on earth would have wanted to kill Judge Lyle Sunder.

The doctor whistled tunelessly as he worked on the young girl's body, covering his distaste for his work with the noise. Because of the whistle, others who watched him during an autopsy thought of him as being professionally detached, even insouciant, but he had hated working on cadavers in medical school and hated it even more when it was someone from Sabella, someone who had lived and worked in the same community the day before.

He stopped whistling abruptly and the sheriff looked up.

"What?"

"Thought you said she was raped," the doctor said annoyed.

"She was."

"She's a virgin."

"Can't be."

"Somebody tried to poke her all right, but looks like he didn't get any farther than her thigh."

He waggled his finger as if tapping an ash from a cigarette. "Have a look-see," he said.

The sheriff glanced at the crusted splotch on the girl's skin.

"Christ," said the sheriff. "Don't tell anybody."

"There's some blood under her fingernails," the doctor said. "What me to test it for blood type?"

"Why?"

"Make sure it matches the type of the boy they hanged."

"What good will that do?"

The doctor shrugged. "Make sure they got the right man."

"Don't even think that," the sheriff said. "They got the right man."

"You sure?"

"Yes."

"You were sure she was raped, too."

"They got the right man. Christ, Doc. I mean, hell, don't think like that. No one's going to be better off knowing that."

"What, the truth?"

"Don't confuse the issue. There's just a whole lot of things people don't want to know about," said the sheriff.

The doctor did not argue with the obvious.